Love & Struggle
beyond the Rubber Estates

A Historical Novel

Dave Anthony

Gerakbudaya Enterprise
Petaling Jaya

Published in 2012 by
   Gerakbudaya Enterprise
   No 11, Lorong 11/4E, 46200 Petaling Jaya, Selangor, Malaysia.
   Email: sird@streamyx.com
   Website: www.gerakbudaya.com

First impression, September 2012
Second impression, April 2013

Perpustakaan Negara Malaysia Cataloguing-in-Publication Data

Anthony, Dave
   Love & Struggle Beyond the Rubber Estates : a historical novel /
   Dave Anthony.
   ISBN 978-983-2344-06-3
   1. Historical fiction, English.
   2. Love stories, English.
   I. Title.
   823

Cover design by Daniel Anthony
Layout design by Janice Cheong

Printed by Vinlin Press Sdn Bhd
2, Jalan Meranti Permai 1,
Meranti Permai Industrial Park,
Batu 15, Jalan Puchong,
47100 Puchong, Selangor, Malaysia.

To the memory of all the plantation workers in Malaysia past and present and to the thousands of faceless, nameless, forgotten Indians who laboured and perished in the Burma Death Railway.

Contents

Praise for
Love & Struggle
beyond the Rubber Estates

Brilliantly written and interwoven the people's struggle for freedom and rights with the search for love and unity. If you love romance, you will discover history especially workers struggle for dignity and if you love history, you will realize the meaning of love and struggle. It's a book worth for all generations.

Dr. Irene Fernandez
Executive Director, Tenaganita

In the shadows of colonial Malaya, Dave Anthony weaves together a tale of love and activism. He brings to light the everyday hero so relevant to the current political awakening of post-colonial Malaysia. The reader is left with a much longer view of Malaya's history, a rich landscape to provide perspective and context for today's struggle. He originally envisioned it as a screenplay. For the sake of the social media generation, this is one love story that we hope will make it to today's digital screens.

Premesh Chandran
CEO, Malaysiakini.com

History comes alive in this moving fictionalised account of the struggle of plantation workers in Malaya. For far too long, rubber tappers and weeders have been widely seen as silent figures flitting about in the dark shadows of rows of carefully cultivated trees. No more. Dave Anthony's immense contribution is in brilliantly articulating their decades-long ordeal through the voices of the protagonists, a group of heartlessly exploited migrant workers who toil while plantation bosses reap extraordinary profits in London. But this book is no ordinary tale of passive suffering endured under corporate domination. Rather, the characters leap out from the pages through their inspiring determination to change their fate and champion the struggle of their fellow workers while all around them the world they are familiar with crumbles. It's a timeless battle against the odds set in an era of tumultuous imperialism, war and the quest for independence.

Anil Netto
Freelance writer-blogger and Treasurer of social reform group Aliran

This is a fascinating novel - history as voiced by the oppressed working class plantation labour, an important marginalised group in British Colonial Malaya. It is an excellent way to learn the social history of South Indian plantation labour. It is indeed a forgotten part of the people's history of Malaya and every Malaysian should read this novel to understand the suffering of the working class in Colonial Malaya.

Dr. Subramaniam Pillay
Economist and Exco Member of Aliran and Bersih 2.0

This is more than a story of oppressed migrants from India in colonial Malaya's plantations. Through the lives – and love and friendships – of the protagonists, Love & Struggle provides insights into how empires that were created (British) or were nearly created (Japanese) divided peoples and nations. It is a tale of injustices by powerful countries and people, the seduction of ethnic communities through false rhetoric and of enlightenment that comes from the struggle for justice, equity and peace. This historical novel brings out the dignity and humaneness of people and their capacity to transcend ethnicity, sub-ethnicity, class and gender cleavages created by empire makers. Love & Struggle shows us why the struggle for a just Malaysia must continue.

Edmund Terence Gomez
Professor of Political Economy, University of Malaya

Novels written by Malaysians in the English language are rare and rarer still are those that belong to the historical genre. Dave Anthony has successfully written an interesting and gripping historical novel based on the struggle and love of exploited Indian workers in rubber estates mainly during the Japanese occupation in the then Malaya. It clearly depicts the social and political life of Indian estate workers and their efforts to unionise in order to secure economic alleviation, against historical background that shows accurate details. I consider it to be a creative work of high quality. It certainly deserves a readership that is not confined only to Malaysian reading public.

Dr. Syed Husin Ali
Senator in the Upper House of the Parliament of Malaysia

Endorsement

Dave, a close friend of mine since the year 1967, is a person of many talents and excels in whatever he does, be it in designing and manufacturing home furniture, in the area of social communication, multimedia and the like .

I can relate with what is written with the historical part of it, for example, regarding the Death Railway.

I was born in 1932 and lived in a rubber plantation, Lubok Seginatah Estate, Kuala Ketil, Kedah until the end of 1946.

In the early part of the Japanese occupation, many young men were recruited and sent to Siam to work in the Burma Death Railway.

The coolie lines were behind my house which was by the side of the road. Adjacent to it was the estate dispensary and my father was the Dresser. I used to watch the people going eagerly to the estate office and very often some received bad news that so and so had died. Besides, that would be the last time they would receive any money. They came back groaning and beating their chests. For me, it had been a heart wrenching experience every time.

As the days passed by routinely, there were hardly any young men even to bury the dead. Many of the people were dying as a result of malaria and malnutrition. There wasn't enough quinine (mixture or capsules) to go by and even my father succumbed to cerebral malaria in 1946.

Dave has done a great service in writing this historical novel which I consider to be experiential, imaginative and romantic. I am sure many, I for one, who have lived in the rubber plantation within the context during the period (1936-1948) will be grateful to him while the younger generation will find excellent literature and perhaps vicariously experience those hard times.

Archbishop Emeritus Soter Fernandez

Foreword

Dave Anthony's historical novel offers the human dimension that a history book does not. The impact of historical events on the psyche and lives of ordinary men and women caught in the ruthless maneuvers of imperialist aggressors is well captured in *Love and Struggle, Beyond the Rubber Estates.* The brutal gunning down of rubber tappers on strike and the agony of the bereaved families, workers exploited by British planters and swindled by *kanganies,* returning home empty-handed to expectant families in India, men dying in tens of thousands in the infamous Bangkok-Rangoon railway project – these are more than mere historical facts. The novel tells of how humanity was denied to the hundreds of thousands of nameless men and women in the unfolding of Malayan history.

The writer's involvement with estate workers in plantations throughout Peninsular Malaysia between 1970 and 1986 is reflected in his total familiarity with their lives and cultural practices, and his intimate knowledge of the estate environment as seen in the novel. But then again, he seems equally at home in a dozen other settings – the graphic caning scene in Taiping Prison, an MPAJA operations centre in the jungle, the numerous villages and camps along the Death Railway stretch that Janeki picks her way through in her search for Desa, the privations and peculiarities of life under the Japanese occupation etc. The writer has a gift for reconstructing historical events as if he were himself a part of them.

The 12-year period chosen by Dave Anthony from 1936 to 1948 was a turbulent time in Malayan history. On the plantations, it was a time of intensive labour struggles for decent wages and dignity. There were a number of other significant events during this period - the rise of reform organisations such as the Indian National

Congress-inspired CIAM, the ban on assisted labour migration, the Japanese occupation and the Death Railway, the armed struggle of the MPAJA for liberation, the mass recruitment of Indian men and women into the INA, the *Thondar Padai* campaign for social reforms, the struggles of the Putera/A.M.C.J.A. for independence, and finally, the proclamation of emergency in July 1948.

For the once docile Indian workforce in the estates, this was a period of political awakening, class consciousness and labour militancy.

The love story of Desa and Janeki is set against this suspenseful backdrop. Can there be a better way to recount history? I think it is a challenge weaving the love story into the events of the history of the period. The novel succeeds and this is doubtless due to Dave Anthony's skill, commitment and discipline as a writer.

Dave Anthony writes not about great heroes but about the heroic actions of ordinary men and women who choose not to accept injustice and oppression quietly. His faith in people's power in the fight against oppression is seen through the characters of Desa and Janeki. They organize and empower estate workers under very difficult circumstances to confront plantation owners for a better deal, and despite failing initially, they go back to the grassroots. In the novel we get to see how the collective action of ordinary men and women, united by a common purpose and activism can decide the course of history - as in the concerted labour struggles that resulted in the historic ban on assisted labour migration.

It is truly a privilege to write the foreword for a book which contains analyses, views and messages that social activists share and would like to communicate to others.

Rani Rasiah
Parti Sosialis Malaysia
December 2011

Preface

I have written a historical novel, not a history book. Many of the events and movements described have historical basis but I have reconstructed the scenarios with fictitious names and places. Some of the more famous people are named.

I began writing this story as a film script on the wage struggle of the plantation workers which began with the planting of the first sapling in Malaya until today where the issue of a minimum wage remains unresolved. The story of the plantation worker is a never-ending saga. The script spanned over many generations when I decided to cut the fabric of that script and stitch it into a novel for easy reading. I have peppered the dialogue with everyday usage of Tamil colloquialisms. The Tamil language is specific in addressing elders and equals and inferiors with suffixes to verbs. When addressing elders and with respect or in the plural form the suffix is *ngal* or colloquially *nga* is used.

Addressing inferiors or with disrespect and sometimes with familiarity among equals the suffix *da* for male and *di* for female is used.

The main sources of my research are Michael Stenson, *Class, Race and Colonialism in West Malaysia – An Indian Case*; Selvakumaran Ramachandran, *Indian Plantation Labour in Malaya*; Chin Peng, *My Side of History* and Rasammah Bhupalan, *Footprints on the Sands of Time*.

Mr. S. Marimuthu, 86, has provided invaluable first-hand testimony of the harsh conditions at the Burma Death Railway. He is a living survivor of that ordeal.

Thanks to my editor Juliet Chin for her untiring effort to improve the manuscript and for the back cover review.

My appreciation goes to those who have read and endorsed the book and provided me with invaluable suggestions on how to improve it. They are:

Dr. Syed Husin Ali, former Professor of Anthropology and Sociology, University of Malaya, resigned his post to engage in active politics. He was detained under the ISA for six years for supporting the peasants in protest against poverty and price rises. The staunch defender of the poor and marginalised is a senator representing Selangor.

Archbishop Soter Fernandez, former bishop of Penang and Archbishop of Kuala Lumpur.

Terence Gomez, an academic with a social conscience, Irene Fernandez, champion of migrant workers, Premesh Chandran of *Malaysiakini*, an award winning Malaysian independent news provider offering news and views that matter, Anil Netto, well known blogger from Aliran an organization for social and democratic reform advocating justice, freedom and solidarity, Subramaniam Pillay also from Aliran and from Bersih, which in Malay means 'clean'.

Bersih is a Coalition for Clean and Fair Elections in Malaysia. Its Walk for Democracy created a grounds well of people crying out for free and fair elections that was echoed around the world becoming Global Bersih dubed "the mother of all battles in Malaysia for democracy, freedom and justice".

These people represent aspirations that can be traced back to the early struggles for justice and freedom in Malaysia.

Thanks to Dominic Zeevandra Amalraj and Charmaine Reenita Raj for kindly consenting to feature on the cover as the protagonists in the novel.

Thanks to my son Daniel for the creation of the cover.

Finally thanks to Ms. Rani Rasiah of PSM for writing the foreword.

I hope you will enjoy reading the novel as much as I have enjoyed writing it.

Dave Anthony

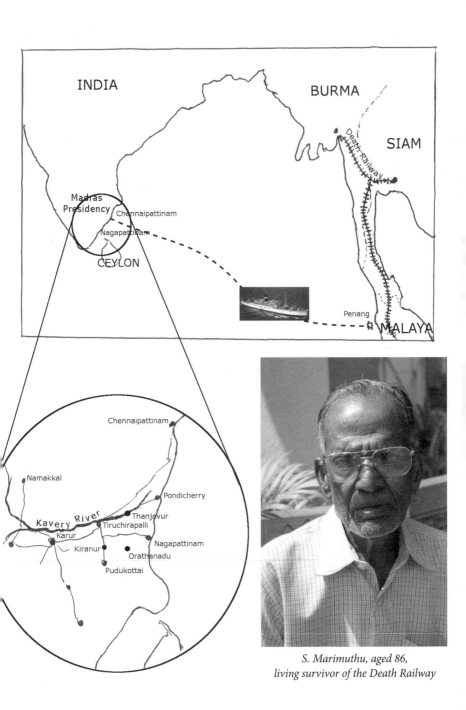

INDIA

BURMA

SIAM

Death Railway

Madras Presidency

Chennaipattinam

Nagapattinam

CEYLON

Penang

MALAYA

Chennaipattinam

Namakkal

Pondicherry

Kavery River

Thanjavur

Tiruchirapalli

Karur

Kiranur

Nagapattinam

Orathanadu

Pudukottai

*S. Marimuthu, aged 86,
living survivor of the Death Railway*

Chapter 1

Strike Action

"Fire! ... Fire!" shouted Roberts the young British police officer. Only a couple of the Indian police barely lifted their rifles. There was a pause.

"I say fire! Shoot the bastards!" he commanded. Nothing happened.

1937. It was a cool April morning in Dolby Rubber Estate in the state of Perak in Peninsular Malaysia, then known as Malaya. The rubber trees' foliage, reluctant to release the rising mist, shrouded the morning sun. A group of plantation workers, all of whom were indentured from the Madras Presidency or the State of Madras in South India, about forty five of them, went on strike for an increase of their daily wages from forty cents (Malayan currency) to fifty cents. They were angry but neither violent nor armed with any offensive weapon. When ordered to disperse, they stood their ground waiting for the planter to appear.

"The manager is nowhere in sight. We will wait and not move from here until he comes. Our brothers in the police are with us, but be ready for something else to happen. Stand firm ngada. Do not be afraid ngada." These were the words of Desa the leader of the strike. Alongside him stood Antoine, Arokianathan and Kuppusamy his close friends who worked with him in organising the strike. Desa was a natural leader among them. He was named Nadesan, popularly called Nadesa and eventually nicknamed Desa, which means light or brilliance.

That a British officer's orders were disobeyed was not at all a trivial matter. Roberts was an ex-British Army Non-Commissioned

Officer transferred by special permission from the British Army in Malaya. He was quite inexperienced with the conditions of the plantation in Malaya. He was in charge of a troop of local police. On the planter's request he was sent to quell the strike. His men were Indians recruited for service by the British. Many of them came from the same villages in India as the plantation workers themselves. They refused to fire on their fellow countrymen.

The officer was furious. "You shall all be court martialled!" he bellowed at them and immediately called for back-up. The strikers refused to budge until their request was granted.

The strikers stood their ground in the noonday sun when reinforcement arrived. These special police were the Sikhs seconded from the North Indian Punjabi Regiment, recruited for a paramilitary police service and known for their unquestioning loyalty to the British command. They had little contact with other Indian groups and were chiefly employed to control the unruly Chinese.

Immediately sensing danger, Desa told his men, "These northerners cannot be trusted. If they raise their rifles run gnada for cover; run ngada into the timber."

The Sikhs dutifully took their positions and when ordered to shoot they opened fire. The strikers dashed for cover and scattered. Six of them were killed and eleven lay wounded and bleeding. Others ran into the woods in different directions, each man for himself. The soldiers gave chase and rounded up most of the surviving strikers.

Desa, doubled up his *veshti,* a long unstitched cloth wound about the waist and reaching below the ankles, above his knees and ran down the valley cutting diagonally across the rows upon rows of rubber trees not even thinking of the wound in his arm until he reached a stream. He stopped to examine his wound. The bullet had torn the muscle of his left biceps. He was unable to flex his arm, it was limp. Cupping his right palm he scooped some water and washed the bleeding wound. He had lost quite a lot of blood. Tearing a piece off his head cloth he managed to tie a rough tourniquet using his good arm and teeth. He felt weak but he told himself that he had to get as far away as quickly as possible. He waded across the muddy stream into the thorn ridden bushes of the swamp. The bank was covered with undergrowth and he was knee deep in mud when he confronted a wall of *nipah* palms. Unlike coconut palms where the palm leaves crown the top of a high trunk, the leafy branches of the *nipah* sprout from the ground with tough, sharp spiky thorns. Desa was scratched all over as he penetrated this hostile barrier and came out a bleeding mess with his *banian,* a cotton vest, torn to shreds.

He ascended the next hill. He left the plantation proper and ventured into secondary jungle. The wounded arm, the cuts, the steep slope and the thick undergrowth all slowed him down. Feeling faint and unable to focus he fell to the ground half buried in the shrubs, bushes and *lalang*, the tall grass.

***

The estate compound was like a war zone. The womenfolk emerged from their *coolie* lines, labour barracks, and went searching for their men. The sound of the gunshots had barely echoed from the woods when the air was filled with the high pitched wailing of the women. They beat their breasts, threw up their arms in the air and cursed the white planter.

"You have put sand in my rice bowl da, you heinous sinner!" shouted one woman letting fly a fistful of sand. Children followed their mothers crying aloud, not quite understanding the situation. The *kirany* (estate clerk) had summoned dresser Devasagayam Pillay, the estate orderly, to attend to the wounded.

Roberts, discovering that not all the strikers had been accounted for, formed a posse with some of the British soldiers and Sikh policemen, and led them in hot pursuit of those who had escaped. First they entered the *coolie* lines and dragged some of the men and women out at rifle point. Neither Roberts nor the Sikhs were familiar with plantation environment. They were going round in circles lost in the maze of rubber trees all standing in identical rows as far as the eye could see. They managed to apprehend some of the workers but Desa and his close friends were nowhere to be found. They came to the stream and looking at the hill and the jungle, the wild undergrowth and the formidable barrier of the *nipah* palms, Roberts decided, "We need some native help to penetrate that jungle. Those buggers cannot get very far. We shall come back for them." He ordered a retreat.

*＊＊

Desa had a dream that he was shot and fell into the stream and was drowning. He suddenly woke up with the heavy splatter of raindrops on his face. An equatorial cloud burst brought down, in a flash, buckets full of rain. Just as his clothes were beginning to dry he was again thoroughly drenched. Daylight was fast fading and in a matter of minutes it would be night for there was no drawn out twilight in this part of the world. Desa struggled up feeling the intense pain in his arm. The bleeding had stopped but his whole arm was caked in blood. He found shelter under a big Kapok tree. The base of the tree dug into the earth with giant buttress roots rising like the sails of a yacht. Between these huge buttress blades Desa found a protective niche. The scent of his blood would surely attract wild animals, the wild boar or the tiger. Wild boars were frequently sighted but the tiger rarely. He looked at some of the trees with low branches. He made a feeble attempt but gave up the idea of climbing with one arm, besides tigers did climb trees. Venomous cobras were often seen slithering beneath the carpet of dry leaves. His best chance was to light a fire.

The two indispensable items of apparel for the male estate workers were the loin cloth and the *thalaipa* (the turban) which was an all-purpose thing. It was a long seamless piece of cloth roughly wound around the head unlike the neatly spun turban of the Sikhs. The headgear also served as a bed sheet, blanket, towel, rope and a sarong when other garments were being washed, and a pocket for essential items. It was even a first-aid kit when he earlier tore a piece of it to tie a tourniquet. Although he was wet with the rain, the inner folds of the *thalaipa* were still dry where he kept some tobacco, wrapped in newspaper, a box of matches and the dried leaves of the *nipah* palm all cut to the size of a cheroot. These *nipah* leaves, the same that tore at his body earlier, when tender and dry, naturally curled up and rolled themselves. He picked one of them, slightly unrolled it, spread a little tobacco and it rolled itself back. He lit it and deeply inhaled the smoke.

It was too dangerous to fall asleep again. Looking around he found several dried branches. Resting the long pieces on a rock and stamping them with his foot he broke them into four- foot length sticks. He stuck them into the soft ground about a foot apart in a semicircle between the buttressed fins of the tree roots. He then gathered twigs, small sticks and wood and set about lighting a fire. The first match he struck went out before he could put the flame to the dry leaf. He tried a couple more sticks without success. The sticks were damp and a slight wind was in the air. To save the sticks he put the fire at the tip of his *nipah* palm cheroot to the leaf and began to blow. It caught and soon he had a fire going. Holding one stout stick as a defence weapon he sat and waited. Except for the fire, it was too dark to see anything. There was no moon in the sky. He moved closer to the fire because he was being punctured by mosquitoes. In the invisible night, an orchestra of sounds began to amplify from the high pitched whine of the mosquitoes to small creatures to large animals. He sat listening and estimating the distance of the sounds. He was wondering what could have happened to the others who had escaped especially his close friends, Kuppusamy, Arokianathan and Antoine. Did they manage to escape or were they among the dead. He knew some of the workers would have died and wondered if he was responsible. *Do we have to pay with lives for the struggle to survive?* He mulled over the guilt feeling for a while and dismissed it. *This is a struggle also for justice and it must go on and we cannot give in.* His thought was interrupted by a scuffle in the grass. They were only rats; then he heard the growl of a tiger.

***

An eerie gloom settled in the *coolie* lines. The loud heartrending wails had softened down to helpless grief. The dead bodies were taken home, bathed and laid out in white linen. Pictures and icons were turned to the wall. Children fell asleep without their meal. The men went about collecting wood for the funeral pyres. The estate *kirany* had sent word that there would be no muster the next day. No work meant no pay.

***

Up on the hill, in the planter's bungalow all the lights were on with electricity supplied from a diesel generator and visitors were arriving for an important get together. The resident planter in a rubber estate usually acted as the estate manager too. His assistant was also usually a European but sometimes an Indian. In Dolby, the manager Mr Alan Humphreys was an Englishman and the assistant manager, Mr. Angus Erskine, was a Scotsman. The invited guests were Brian Greenfield, a member of the United Planters' Association of Malaya (UPAM); Dr. David Thomson, the son of a Scottish clergyman who operated a small wooden clinic in the nearest town of Sungei Siput and concentrated his work on the menacing disease of malaria and Mr. Roberts, the young police officer, whose first name was William.

Rattan chairs were arranged in a circle in the wide veranda under a ceiling fan. This portion of the veranda was screened by mosquito netting that was unfurled like a chic.

"Welcome gentlemen, make yourselves comfortable," said Humphreys.

"Splendid idea, this mosquito netting," observed Dr. Thomson.

"Thank you, gentlemen for coming at such short notice, I'm sure you've all heard of what happened here today," began Humphreys.

"Yes, yes. Oh yes," came a chorus of voices.

"What a shocking disaster," said Thomson.

"I'm sure this is the first time such a thing has happened in a British Malayan plantation," joined Greenfield.

"I have heard that there have been strikes also in Klang and in some estates around Kuala Lumpur," added Roberts.

"The natives are becoming rather bold, to say the least," commented Humphreys. Then he tilted his head and said, "Boy, *se stengah* all around. The term derives from the Malay word for "a half", a whisky and soda, served over ice.

Ahmad the Malay house boy who was standing alert at the door immediately responded, "Yes, *Tuan*." Tuan means boss in Malay.

Having everything on standby Ahmad brought a crystal ice bucket, filled with ice cubes and a pair of stainless steel ice tongs, placing them gently over an embroidered coaster on the glass tabletop in the centre of the seated men. He disappeared while the conversation was going on. He opened a bottle of Johnnie Walker, lined up five whisky glasses and measured the whisky to a depth of two fingers – the *se stengah*. He reappeared with the glasses on a silver tray together with a glass soda siphon wrapped in a towel. Placing the siphon on the table he did the rounds offering a glass to each one.

"Anyone for club soda?" asked Humphreys. To those who held up their glasses Ahmad, very carefully squeezed the trigger and dispensed a jet of carbonated water into the glass without spilling a drop.

Dr. Thomson declined and instead asked for ice cubes.

"All things considered," said Thomson, "these people do have a legitimate request for better pay, don't you think?"

"Utter nonsense, David. It is preposterous how these *coolies* have dared so much as to question the British system of wages. They would be starving to death if they were back home in their native India, for sure. Besides, we are being pressurised by the RGA (Rubber Growers Association) in London that the turnover is not conducive to the shareholders. We have received instructions to depress wages to a minimum. The *coolies* here are better paid than in the other colonies like in Africa, Ceylon and Fiji. They ought to be counting their blessings, I say," said the UPAM representative Greenfield.

"Hear, hear," supported Humphreys.

"But how can you justify the killing?" asked Thomson.

"Beg your pardon, Sir," said Roberts, "we were told that insubordination is like a cancer that will eventually destroy the British Empire. It is to be nipped in the bud wherever it appears. Not only were the *coolies* stubborn, the local police refused to obey an order. This is absolutely intolerable."

Erskine had this to add, "If my memory serves me correctly, it was captain Speedy, Tristram Charles Sawyer Speedy, the British resident of Larut who used the Sikh police officers after the Pangkor Engagement in 1873. They were sterling men, the Punjabis, who never questioned the British command. It was Lieutenant Swinburn who took over from him and recruited the local riff raff into the police force, a serious mistake. We have ended up with the policemen who have come from the same districts as the *coolies* themselves. What do you expect?"

"Gentlemen top your glasses or if you would prefer some brandy. Boy, cognac."

"Yes, *Tuan.*" Ahmad galvanised into action. He brought a tray of brandy glasses and a crystal decanter of Hennessy. Some had a refill of whisky while others cognac.

"While we are at it," said Humphreys and with a raised voice, "Boy, cheroot."

Ahmad immediately reappeared with a wooden box of cigars.

"You must try these Sumatras, they are excellent," invited Humphreys. "You know, the Dutch have left their mark in Indonesia by teaching them the art of rolling cigars."

Erskine added, "And the Spaniards left their cigar tradition in the Philippines, but unfortunately, even though we rule the waves, the British cannot boast of a good cigar tradition."

Thomson declined saying, "Thank you, no. I prefer my pipe." He proceeded to open a small yellow tin, took a pinch of tobacco, rubbed it in the palm of his hand and filled the bowl. After lighting it he exhaled a rich aroma of Erinmore from Ireland.

"As I was saying, we have to thank young Roberts for bringing the situation under control here today," said Humphreys.

"Aye, aye!" from the others.

"But we are not done yet, sir," said Roberts.

"Quite, quite," responded Humphreys.

"Some of the ring leaders are still at large and I intend to round them up tomorrow with the help of the *orang asli,* aboriginal trackers. I assure you I will get them."

"Splendid! This young upstart of a *coolie,* what's his name?" began Humphreys.

"Nadesan," prompted Erskine.

"Ah yes, Nedasan. He is a dangerous one, a real rascal of an instigator. Now, Brian, I would like to put in a formal request that these instigators be severely punished and promptly deported," asserted Humphreys.

"That should not be a problem, Humph. Right now the London rubber price is low and there is a world surplus, supply exceeding demand and repatriation is already in the books. I shall see to it that Nadesan and company are swiftly dispatched," concluded Greenfield.

They were still drinking and talking up the hill while a deathly silence had descended on the *coolie* lines below. Meanwhile Desa listened intently estimating the tiger to be at a distance of a hundred yards or more. The second growl was much louder. Desa slowly stood up and leaned against the tree with his stick poised, listening. The third growl was softer. He breathed easy. The tiger had evidently taken another path.

***

By six in the morning three aboriginal trackers from the *Semai* tribe, clad only in their loin cloths, were squatting clutching their blow pipes at the entrance of the estate office waiting for instruction. These bare footed *orang asli* tribesmen had often been used as trackers by the British army. The jungle was their home and hunting their everyday occupation. Roberts with six armed Sikhs began to explain the task to them through Ahmad as interpreter,

"There are at least five *coolies* out in the jungle and we have to find them."

They understood and one of them, pointing to the Sikhs, shook his head, lifting two fingers. Ahmad explained that there were too many men with boots and needed only two of them. So Roberts with two armed Sikhs and three trackers set out to find Desa and his friends. As they walked past the *coolie* lines a couple of women came out and spat at them.

***

The dead workers - among whom were two of Desa's cubicle mates

Lourdusamy and Govindaraj - were four Hindus and two Christians. Soon two Hindu priests arrived and went about preparing the funeral rites. The preliminary preparation was already done the night before by the women who applied gingelly oil to the heads, washed the bodies and shrouded them with white cloth. In the presence of the priest now the chief mourner in each family - the eldest son of one, father of the other and the closest male relative of the third - offered the *Arathi*, a worshipful rite passing an oil lamp in circular motions, over the remains and offering flowers. The fourth was married and the wife placed her *thali,* wedding pendant, around her husband's neck signifying her enduring tie to him. Abandoning the more elaborate ones they kept the rituals very simple. The priest threw some flower petals over the bodies and recited verses from the Bhagavad Gita. There were no coffins. The shrouded bodies were laid on planks and carried in procession to the *sudukadu,* the burning field, for cremation. The women let out a final heartrending wail that pierced the air. This was their goodbye because women did not go to the pyre.

At the funeral pyres the bodies were carried three times counter-clockwise around the pyres, then placed upon them, covered with wood and incense was burnt.

The chief mourners of the three deceased and a close male relative of the fourth circumambulated the pyres counter-clockwise. On their bare chests, the *poonool,* the sacred thread, which usually hung from the left shoulder had been reversed to hang from the right shoulder. The *arathi* was again offered with the circular motion also counter-clockwise. Everything was symbolically reversed at death. The chief mourner also carried a clay pot on his left shoulder while holding a firebrand behind his back.

At each turn around the pyre, a relative knocked a hole in the pot with a knife, letting water out, signifying life leaving its vessel. At the end of three turns, the chief mourner dropped the pot shattering it. Then, without turning to face the body, he lit the pyre and left the cremation grounds. The others did the same. While some of the men stayed to tend to the fire the rest went home for the ritual cleansing of impurity. They bathed and cleansed the house. A lamp and a water pot were placed where the bodies had lain in state.

In the meantime the Christian priest arrived to perform the funeral rite for Lourdusamy and another Christian woman. They were buried next to the *sudukadu.*

✶✶✶

With daylight Desa used the stick to kill the remaining ambers and covered the ashes with sand. With the stick in hand he set out climbing the hill away from the estate.

Meanwhile Roberts and his posse arrived at the stream. The *orang asli* trackers split in opposite directions along the stream while the others stood still. When they returned they decided to go downstream. Twenty yards on they stopped and one of them pointed to the *nipah* palms. The other one pointed downstream.

"I gather that one of the escapees had gone through the *nipah* while another had gone on downstream," surmised Roberts. The *Semai* held up two index fingers together and separated them implying that they split.

"No," decided Roberts, "we will not split but go downstream first after one of them and backtrack for the other," mixing his words with gestures. They understood.

Kuppusamy was wounded in the leg and he had gone downstream. He was lying on the ground hidden by the tall grass when the trackers found him. He was immediately apprehended by the Sikhs.

Roberts ordered one of the Sikhs who was about to handcuff Kuppusamy, "There is no need for that, he can't run anyway." He slapped Kuppusamy across the face. "You walk him back to the estate," he ordered the Sikh.

The rest backtracked until the *Semai* pointed to a gap in the *nipah.* They forded the stream, slashed through the *nipah* with *parangs,* heavy sheath-knives, and mounted the hill.

Desa had already descended the hill into the next valley. He was sliding down between the trees clearly marking his way. He was more interested in getting away than to conceal his tracks. The *Semai* had no trouble finding him. He too was apprehended, handcuffed and marched back to the estate after he was slapped across the face by Roberts.

***

Roberts walked triumphantly along the *coolie* lines leading to the estate office while the women and children and some of the older men came out to look. Some of them cursed with undertones. They expressed their disappointment with a murmuring buzz. Roberts looked at them and grinned. Fourteen of the escapees were made to squat outside the office with hands cuffed, Kuppusamy among them. There was no sign of Antoine or any of his close group.

"We've fifteen more of the bastards apprehended and I doubt there would be many others," Roberts proudly reported to Humphreys.

"You have done a splendid job, William. I will put in a recommendation to your officer."

"Thank you, sir."

***

Dresser Devasagayam was again summoned to attend to the wounds of the escapees.

"Devasagayam *Aiyiah* (sir), what happened to the other strikers?" enquired Desa.

"Many of them were rounded up within the estate itself, in the lines and in the timber. Six were dead and many wounded. They were all sent to the lockup in two lorry loads. You all too will be sent there. The severely wounded are in hospital. Your two friends Lourdusamy and Govindaraj are dead, I am sorry. Your other friends Ravichandran and Arokianathan were taken in the first batch. You take care da, *thamby*." *Thamby* is younger brother or lad."

Devasagayam attended to Kuppu's leg and Desa's arm. He cleaned and bandaged them.

"*Aiyiah*, what happened to Antoine and Sokalingam?"

"They were not caught and they are still looking for them."

They were all loaded onto an open truck and taken to the police station in Sungai Siput and locked up in a tiny cell. After three nights Desa and Kuppusamy, considered to be ring leaders, were taken to the prison in Taiping, the capital of the state of Perak, the name meaning "Heavenly Peace."

Under normal circumstances concerning prisoners the criminal law of England would have applied. The reception of English law, separated by half the world, was only slowly evolving during British colonialization. Very soon after what had happened to Desa, Kuppusamy and others, the Civil Law Enactment was promulgated. So at that time it had not yet become statutory.

Chapter 2

Punishment

With neither trial nor charge in a court of law they were, nevertheless, taken to Taiping prison for the purpose of detention and interrogation by the Malayan Security Services later known as the Special Branch.

The Taiping prison or gaol was originally called the Perak Prison. Established in 1879 it was a formidable building in stone with high walls. Not only was it then the largest prison complex in Malaya it remains also the first and oldest.

The two of them were taken through narrow corridors and locked up in a single cell. Kuppusamy, who was limping badly, sat down on the cement floor, stretching his legs. There was neither chair nor bed.

"How did they find you da, Kuppu?" asked Desa.

"I couldn't get far with the wound. I just kept going along the stream. I heard them coming and I threw myself into the *lallang* and crawled away from the stream. If not for the *orang asli* they would not have found me."

"Did you hear the tiger that night?"

"Yes, but I just sat there and surrendered myself to fate. Whatever comes, let it come, I said to myself. Why da do you think only we are here?"

"Since only the two of us have been brought here, I think they are going to question us about the strike. Let us not say anything of what we know of the other strikes. Only we decided on our action. OK da?"

The Malayan Security Service (MSS) was the main intelligence agency of the British with the responsibility of obtaining and collating information on subversive organisations and personalities particularly the Communist Party of Malaya. The Assistant Superintendent was one Charles Neagle. Some of the other strikes that took place were by the Chinese workers and the Chinese were closely linked to the Communist Party. Desa and Kuppusamy were summoned separately for interrogation.

Desa was led by a Sikh warder into the interrogation room and motioned to sit opposite an Indian police officer. Desa hesitated because as subordinates they were never allowed to sit, only stand. The officer was not a Tamil but a Malayalee from Kerala on the western side of southern India while the Tamils were on the eastern side. They never saw eye to eye. His name was Thomas Kochery. He made Desa sit because he did not want to look up to him. He began.

"Are you Nadesan Pillay from Tiruchirapalli?"

"Yes."

"Yes, *Aiyiah!*"

"Yes, *Aiyiah.*"

"You went to school up to the tenth standard?"

"Yes, *Aiyiah.*"

"Because you have some education, you think you know too much, do you?"

"No, *Aiyiah.*"

"You are a trouble maker. Everybody in your estate was happy and peaceful until you came along. You stirred them up to make demands. Do you think your people in Tiruchy are better fed?"

Desa remained silent

"Answer me!"

"Yes, *Aiyiah.*"

Thomas thumped the table with a loud bang and stood up.

"What did you say?"

"Yes, *Aiyiah*, they have more rice to eat, *Aiyiah.*"

Thomas came up to him and slapped him across the face.

"If they are better off there, why did you come here to work?"

"I was promised a better deal, *Aiyiah.*"

"You are ungrateful and you bring a bad name to all Indians by challenging the British authority. You put all of us in danger. There is no place for people like you here. Dismissed! Warder!" he yelled. This was the first of a series of abusive interrogations.

Desa was returned to his cell and Kuppusamy was led out. Kuppusamy never returned. They were separated.

Before long, Desa was again led out to the interrogation room.

"Nadesan, please sit down." The polite voice belonged to Charles Neagle.

"I believe you are the leader of the strike action."

"We all decided to strike."

"But you led them by instigating them, by holding secret meetings and planning the action."

Desa remained silent.

"Did you know about the strikes by the Chinese workers?"

"We heard."

"Did they instruct you to go on strike?"

"No, *sar*."

"Did you communicate with them?"

"No, *sar*, we don't speak their language."

"How is it that you all went on strike about the same time?"

"I don't know, *sar*."

"Do you know that the Chinese workers are also secret members of the Communist Party? The communists are enemies of the country and if you are in any way linked to them you will be punished by caning, imprisoned for life, banished or shot dead. Do you understand that?"

"Yes, *sar*."

For five days both Desa and Kuppu were repeatedly interrogated with the same and similar questions with both Thomas and Neagle taking turns. The primary purpose was to find a link between the plantation workers and the communist party. They were in solitary confinement without any remand order, or trial by judge or jury.

Neagle and Thomas talked about the next course of action.

"There seems to be no connection with the Chinese communists," said Neagle.

"It could be an isolated case, sir," completed Thomas.

"Nevertheless, they have set a precedent that cannot go unpunished."

"But there is a penal code that requires a court sentence, sir."

"We are not bound by any judicial penalty, there is no statutory provision, not yet anyway and besides these people are not citizens of the country."

It suddenly hit Thomas between the eyes that he belonged to the same category.

***

Without being charged in court, punishment was meted out. Charles Neagle ordered that they be caned with nine strokes each of the *rotan,* a junggle vine. That was that.

Two Sikh prison warders led Desa and Kuppusamy through a narrow strip of grass surrounded by high walls with no windows. Desa felt the crunch of the newly cut lawn, the only sound in the sinister cloistered seclusion and looked up at the only friendly sight of the open sky overhead. There were other prison officers and a dresser standing around an A-shaped wooden trestle. Desa was stripped naked and shackled upright to the trestle by strong leather straps and his legs were kicked apart. Kuppusamy was made to watch the procedure in the event he decided to make a confession. A tall heavily built Sikh warder stood wielding a four-foot long flexible *rotan* with a specified width of half an inch. The striking half of the *rotan* had been soaked in water to make it supple. The hefty Sikh took his position standing five feet away testing his swing as a golfer would but with an elevated angle.

The prison officer who happened to be Mr. Thomas Kochery sat on a chair behind a small table with some procedure papers. The prison dresser placed his stethoscope on Desa's chest and listened. Then he nodded to Thomas implying that the prisoner was in a fit state of health to undergo the punishment. Thomas looked over his shoulder and saw Neagle standing at a distance.

"Remember that these men are criminals and it is the intention of the authorities that the caning be as painful as possible and as humiliating as possible." He was looking at the caner then nodded to Thomas.

Seeing that all was in position Thomas gave the order, "*Satu!*"

The Sikh held the cane rigidly at arm's length, pivoted on his feet and delivered the stroke using not just the strength of his arms but the whole of his body weight. The cane, whistling through the air, hit the soft flesh of both the cheeks of Desa's buttocks at the speed of 160kph producing a force upon impact of 90kg.

Desa howled in pain as his soft flesh trembled. At the point of contact his skin was split open. The white line turned crimson and blood began to flow.

"*Dua!*" shouted Thomas.

Desa's body arched backwards but his arms held him bound to the trestle. He was shivering with excruciating pain. Every nerve in his body was reacting to the sting.

"*Tiga! ... Empat!*" Desa could feel the flow of blood streaming down his legs. Too weak to struggle, he slumped. The medic checked him, saw the open raw meat in the buttocks and yet gave the green light to go ahead with the caning. By the ninth stroke Desa was already too weak to react. The dresser swabbed a dark violet blue lotion, the antiseptic gentian violet, on the raw backside.

Two men dragged him to his cell where he flopped face down and remained in that position for two days with his whole backside totally swollen to twice the normal size.

Kuppusamy was on the verge of making a confession.

***

On the fourth day Desa tried to get up to go to the toilet. He could neither walk nor squat down so standing he urinated in the cell and went back to sleeping on his belly with no interest in food losing count of time or day.

He was forced to eat and a week later he was able to wear his *veshti* loosely around his body. He was brought out together with Kuppusamy who looked no better.

"They asked me if I had anything to say. After I saw what they did to you I almost gave up and wanted to tell them anything they wanted to hear. I couldn't," said Kuppusamy.

"You did the right thing da, Kuppu. We mustn't give up now. If we do our people will forever remain slaves," encouraged Desa.

They were put on the back of a lorry, still standing for they could not do otherwise. They were taken back to Sungai Siput and locked up with the others, but only half of the original number. They had no idea what happened to the rest and wondered how long they were to be held there.

Chapter 3

Deportation

Early the very next day, the twenty- second day after the strike, they were brought out of the lock-up and transported back to the estate with orders to collect their belongings. This was when Desa and Kuppu met Ravichandran and Arokianathan. They were black-listed and banished to be sent back to India. They only began to talk freely once they were on their way to Penang to be shipped back to India with no remuneration whatever for the work they had done.

"What happened to the two of you?" asked Ravi.

"It's a long story. We have plenty of time to talk about it. What did they do to you?" asked Desa.

"Nothing da. They just locked us up and left us there," responded Arokia.

"You know we lost Lourdu and Govind?"

"Yes," sighed Desa, "I am so sorry things turned out like this."

***

They drove north again some sitting and others standing on the back of the lorry. Desa and Kuppusamy preferred to stand. Desa was staring at the mesmerising swift sliding rows upon rows of rubber trees until they stopped at a junction where a large signboard read TAIPING with an arrow pointing right. Desa and Kuppu looked at each other and said nothing but were happy that they were not turning right. At Prai Junction Railway Station the lorry was loaded onto a ferry and they crossed over to the island of Penang. Watching a piece of wood floating on the undulating surface of the sea Desa wondered if life was just like that piece of wood drifting aimlessly. He admitted to himself that he had failed, failed the people who believed in him and failed also his parents and family. On disembarking they were ordered to sit on the wharf. The ship was already in port.

Desa knew that all eyes were on him. He was trying to fight the guilt feelings within himself. Most of them blamed him for their misfortune. After years of hard labour now they had lost everything all because of the strike. One of the men walked up to Desa, kicked him on the shin and spat at him. Others too stood up and a fight began. Punching and kicking. Desa and Kuppusamy were the main targets. They fought back while Ravi and Arokia tried to separate them. The guards arrived and hit them all with the lathi.

Desa spoke, "I ask you all to forgive me. I believed strongly that our lives would change for the better and that we would not die as slaves. We were not alone; others in other estates were also fighting for better pay. I have failed ... for now ... but this a lesson from which we can learn."

"Learn what da?" interjected an older one of them, "and learn for what da? We are finished here da. The sweat and blood of months and years have been swallowed up by this cursed land. Even if I go home empty handed I will die in peace in my village."

"I ask you, please don't give up. Think of all our brothers and sisters still being bullied, slaving away in the plantations. We have the numbers but we need good leadership and organization," said Desa.

"What da can you do now? You are a marked man, da. Do you want to come back da and help them?"

After a pause Desa looked up and said, "Yes."

They spent the night on the wharf. Among his belongings Desa kept his journal. He sat down and wrote all that had happened in the last few days.

***

In Dolby estate, at the muster the following day, the *Peria Dorai*, big boss, addressed the workers in broken Tamil. The *Peria Dorai* is usually the planter or manager.

"We have put behind us the problem created by some of you. The trouble makers have been punished and sent back to India. Those men have been black-listed, that means, that if they are ever seen again in this country they will be arrested and punished, especially the leaders among them. Let this be a lesson to all of you and if anyone at any time tries to stir up trouble the same thing will happen to you. They are now going back with nothing."

***

Late afternoon the following day they boarded the ship, the SS Rajula. They were each given immigration papers and a paltry sum of ten rupees. On the way to the steamer, noticing a newspaper lying on a crate, Desa quickly grabbed it and shoved it inside his *banian*. The Rajula was the same steamer in which they had all come to Malaya. It plied regularly between Madras and Penang with indentured labour as its main cargo. They were deck passengers. The cabins were reserved for paying passengers. Their places on the wide deck were chalk-marked and numbered just as they were. Each man's small bundle of belongings was the pillow and the *thalaipa* served other needs. The four companions, Desa, Kuppu, Arkoia and Ravi clustered together.

The Rajula pulled out just before sunset. Desa and Kuppu stood leaning on the rail looking at the land of promise slip away. They were given a meal of rice and dried fish with half a piece of ladies finger. Desa and companions began to reminisce.

"They promised us da, they promised so much, building up a false hope. We have been cheated and used so that they can make huge profits," began Kuppu.

"Even our *kangany*, an overseer of the workers who also acts as a recruiter of workers for the plantations, cheated us. I found out that he had billed us as third class cabin passengers while we travelled as deck passengers, no better than livestock da," said Ravi. A *kangany* is an overseer of the workers who also acts as a recruiter of workers for the plantations.

"There must be some way of breaking out of this slavery," said Desa.

"Strike action didn't work. They have all the power and we don't have any," added Arokia.

"Don't underestimate *makal sakthi*" (power of the people). They need us and the rubber industry will come to a standstill without our work. Yes or no, da?"

"Yes, they want us only in so far as they need us. When the demand for rubber is down, they throw us out or send us back like sucked oranges."

"To realise *makal sakthi*, the people have to be better organised."

They suddenly realised that the coastline with the dotted lights had disappeared and the darkness was total except for the waves, reflecting the ship's light, breaking in the path of the steamer which had veered northwest cutting across the Bay of Bengal.

"I'm tired da. I want to sleep." Unfurling a spare *veshti* and with the *thalaipa* as a pillow, Kuppu stretched out on the hard deck and so did the others. Desa did not move from the railing, he stood smoking his *nipah* cheroot and looked into pitch darkness wondering if he would find a light showing him a way to finish an unfinished task. What was he going to tell his father and mother? What happened to the hope of educating his brother and sister? Should he just forget about the whole thing as a bad dream? He had fallen from the frying pan into the fire and still lived.

There were some dim lights on the deck, so Desa wrote his journal before sleeping.

The sun was rising over the horizon casting pale light that quickly poured out an orange and red splash over the waters - the skyline a shimmer of brilliance. The dawn was like the beginning of new life.

When Kuppu woke up he found Desa reading the newspaper.

"What are you reading? And where, da, did you get that from?"

"Oh, I picked it up from the top of a box before we embarked. This is the *Tamil Murasu* published by the Tamil Reform Association. Kuppu, you know Sastri, V.S. Srinivasa Sastri, who has been talking a lot about the rights of the Indians working outside India? He has been in Malaynadu, da, for the last six months." Malaya was called Malaynadu by the Indians. It meant hill country.

Malay means hill and *nadu* means country.

"And we knew nothing about it. Desa, I think our isolation in the estate is for the purpose of keeping us ignorant."

"Yes, look, all the English educated Tamils are giving him a grand send off with a huge garland around his neck. He left last week. He came representing the Indian National Congress to study our situation. He has made two recommendations. One, he recommended that wage rates be restored to their 1927 levels and failing this, that a ban be imposed upon all assisted emigration to Malaya."

"Bloody hell! This is exactly what we have been striking about. No, da?"

"There is no mention at all about the strikes in the estates. The second recommendation is that the *kangany* system of recruitment be ended as soon as possible."

"If you are thinking of going back to Malaynadu, it is not going to be easy, remember we are black-listed."

"I think the *kangany* system of recruitment should be stopped anyway. By the way, how da did you get recruited, Kuppu?"

There was a wail of the siren. It was not an emergency alarm, as they feared. It was breakfast time. At the stern of the deck on both the starboard and portside, breakfast was served at two points. The deck passengers were to line up. On tin plates, each one was given two *itlies* (steamed rice buns) with a ladle full of *sambar* (dhal curry) and a tin mug of black coffee. They were not prisoners but passengers. Having collected their breakfast, Desa and Kuppu returned to their spot resuming their conversation.

Arokia began, "There was an old couple who went to a restaurant to have breakfast. They ordered one *itli* and one coffee. The man broke the *itli* into half and began to sip the single cup of coffee. The old girl dipped her finger into the *sambar* and licked it. A man seeing the poor couple came forward and offered to buy them a proper breakfast. The man said, 'No thank you, we share everything.' The man began to eat his half of the *itli* while she had another sip of the coffee. The man came again and offered to buy at least another *itli* for them. Again they politely thanked the man and said, 'We share everything.'

"The wife sipped the coffee but did not touch the half *itly* at all. The man could not stand it watching them. He went over and said to the woman, 'Why, ngah, aren't you eating, what are you waiting for?'

"She said, 'Teeth.'"

Arokia was ever ready to lighten the moment.

Having deposited their plates and mugs in a big tub they went downstairs to the lower deck to use the toilet and washroom. The smell of tobacco mingled with that of onions and urine came wafting across the deck in waves as the steamer began to sway on the rough sea. It was so nauseating that they rushed back to the top deck. All the deck passengers were sitting or squatting on the deck chewing betel leaves or smoking. Desa repeated the question of recruitment.

"I was recruited by the *kangany* who came to my house in Keeranur," said Kuppu.

"Was it our Perumal?" asked Ravi.

"Yes, the very same idiot."

"What do you know, da? The same fellow came to Thanjavur to recruit me," said Ravi.

"And me too," said Arokia who was from Orattanadu.

"And then he must have come for me in Thiruchirapalli," added Desa.

"And here we are victims of that cunning bastard," said Kuppu.

Most of them now being expelled were from villages while Desa and his companions were from the towns. Tiruchirapalli was a big town with schools and colleges. Desa was fortunate to have had some education while the others had very basic education or none at all. Kuppu, Ravi and Arokia dropped out of school before reaching the secondary level mainly because of poverty and they had been doing odd jobs.

Chapter 4

Beginning

Desa was saying, "I was doing my homework by candle light even though it was daylight outside when the *kangany* came to visit us. My father greeted him, 'Come nga, come nga, Perumal, *Kangany*, *aiyiah*, please sit down, nga.' Perumal, the *kangany*, got off his shining new bicycle. It was a Raleigh high cycle with a straight handle bar and a metal carrier frame attached to the rear behind the seat. All the children around came running after him and were admiring his pride and joy. From inside the house I could see the sunlight reflect off the rim of the bike's wheel casting a silver arc on the wall inside the house. The bicycle was a rare sight and very few people could afford to own one.

With the sharp ends of his twisted moustache, resembling the handlebar of his bicycle, a lased turban on his head and costly jewels in his ears and fingers, Perumal dispensed sweets to all the children."

When the indenture system of labour acquisition declined, the *kangany* became almost indispensable as a labour recruiter. Thus he gained power over the labour force and importance among the planters. There were several *kanganies* operating in the state of Madras and through this *kangany* system about one thousand recruits were brought to Malaya annually. While some of the *kanganies* commanded respect from the village communities displaying generosity like giving out money and being invited to all social and public functions, becoming popular figures, others were unscrupulous and corrupt. Through fraudulent methods, these *kanganies* indulged in coercion, malpractice and abuse inducing the village officials, brokers and hotel-keepers with commission for recruitment often by-passing the village heads. Ignorance being a factor, young men were enticed away from their homes, husbands separated from wives and even young girls were kidnapped. They matched strangers as brothers, father and son, brother and sister and husband and wife, forging signatures on licenses to avoid legal hurdles.

There were three steps leading to the front entrance to Desa's house. On either side of the steps were raised cement platforms, the front corners of which held wooden beams that supported a leaning thatched roof. Guests were often welcomed to sit on these platforms outside the house because the inside of the house was often dark and stuffy.

Desa continued, "Perumal, doubled up his *veshti*, folded and tucked it below his waist. Climbed on top of the platform, crossed his legs and sat down beside my father who gently nudged the ever-silver tray toward Perumal. The tray contained betel leaves, shaved areca nuts and a selection of ingredients. Perumal prepared a helping. Having skilfully folded a mouthful he neatly inserted it into his mouth and started chewing on it.

"Even with his mouth full he began to talk. My father's name is Mahalingam. 'You see here, nga, Lingam *aiyiah*, Malaynadu is the land of opportunity. Rubber is in great demand. The British there are opening up new plantations all the time. Our young men will work in rubber plantations now and no longer in the old sugar cane and coffee plantations. The work is much easier. Under this new scheme of free labour recruitment a house and everything will be provided. Your travel and all your expenses will be taken care of. You have nothing to worry about and, above all, you are not bound by contract to serve for any fixed number of years like before. You will be free to change jobs or leave whenever you want. These are the new regulations. But how long this system will last is anybody's guess. I may well find myself without a job. You see, the opportunity is now. You can save money and return home a rich man. You cannot earn that kind of money here and besides there is no future for our young men here.'

"As he kept on talking, I could no longer concentrate on my homework. Wow, what a great opportunity, I thought, making my way to the door where they were seated. '*Anghi*,' (an endearing form for dad) I said, 'I would like to go and work there. We can get things there that we cannot even dream of here and I will bring home money.'

"My mother, who had also been listening, walked in with tumblers of water. She silently placed them in front of the two men while all the time, I knew, her attention was on me. She left the scene without saying a word.

"'*Thamby*,' (younger brother; but it is also an endearing way of calling one's first born son) said my father, 'Perumal here is an old friend and I would like to believe him. Yet, I know that many of those who have returned from Malaynadu have different stories to tell. They had very difficult times and were badly treated.'

"Perumal butted in, 'But now, Lingam *aiyiah*, things are different. A Labour Commission has been appointed to investigate labour conditions and to recommend improvements. And...Hmmm...'

"He paused, placed two fingers over his lips and spat out a jet of red bespitalled betel juice.

"'You know, our Panditji Jawaharlal Nehru himself visited Malaynadu. Yes, nga, an Ordinance or an Act has been passed to safeguard the rights of Indian labour. There has been an increase in the minimum wage of indentured labour. Actually, it is no longer called indentured labour but free labour. It is now the responsibility of the employers to provide housing, medical facilities and sanitary arrangements. I promise you, things are now different and better.'

"Father turned to me, '*Thamby*, here you have the opportunity to pursue your education even though I haven't the money for it, I shall find a way to acquire some. Even though we are poor we are still free here.'

"And I said, 'How free can we be without money?' Father said nothing for a long time and then, 'If you really want to go, son, I don't think I would want to stop you.' The *kangany* immediately picked up the cue.

"'*Thamby*,' said that Perumal, addressing me with the same noun, 'You are young and strong. You have a bright future. I will personally look after you. You stay close to me. I will be like a father to you.'

"That was it; I was happy and sad at the same time. Opportunity was knocking on my door but it also meant I had to leave my family and stop my education. I thought that after a few years I will go back with enough money for the family and also to make sure of education for my brother and sister and also continue my own education."

Chapter 5

Land of Opportunity

"Within two weeks the papers were prepared and my thumb prints taken. I was sent to a depot where I was vetted and passed as medically fit.

"In no time I was on board the ship. Can you imagine, this very same ship, the SS Rajula, on which we are homeward bound now. I left on the first of June last year, and it's 6th May today, almost a year later," sighed Desa.

"The same *kangany* came to our village and told the very same story. We all went through the same drill. A well-oiled machinery was in place. There were twenty of us from around our village, Keeranur on the road to Pudukkottai. This Perumal also said that he will take us to the estate in which he works as a foreman," said Kuppu.

"It didn't seem long before we were on this same ship on the way to the land of opportunity - Malaynadu," said Desa.

Desa was enthusiastic to see the new land of promise. After six days of sea voyage they arrived at the port of Penang. The passengers were all immediately put into the quarantine station. The new recruits were lined up and shunted into a corral and asked to remove their clothes and leave all their belongings and have a bath. They were vaccinated by a hospital assistant. Then they were given fresh clothes to wear and a meal. Their clothes, marked with indelible ink with dots and dashes like some Morse code, were boiled in a big pot and disinfected. They were kept there for seven days. Meanwhile Perumal, the *kangany*, reported to the immigration officer.

***

The immigration officer listening to the *kangany* wrote some notes in the log book. "In my batch," (there were other batches led by other *kanganies*,) said Perumal, "there were 67 recruits. Six died on board and their bodies were disposed off into the ocean. The total amount I spent on each person is M$ 29.39. For the six who died you must include M$ 16.00 per head for the passage by the steamer. Since nine of them are being held back in quarantine I will come back to collect them. Now I request the recruitment documents for all the 61 of them. I have two lorries ready to take them."

***

Together with their new outfits each worker was given a tin ticket with a number punched into it referring to the particular plantation he was assigned.

They were loaded on open lorries and transported like indentured goods for delivery. They were ferried across from the island of Penang to the main land and they proceeded on road to their estate. The word "estate," an English term, sounds grand and classy but it refers to the rubber plantation.

Their lorry was an old Bedford with a wooden platform mounted on the chassis and the sides and the back were boarded with planks. The men simply stood on the platform holding on to the boards or squatted down. It was a long and winding road. Soon it began to drizzle. The drops became heavy. The driver immediately knew that there would soon be a cloud burst. He pulled up on the side of the road and told the men who were sitting on a folded tarpaulin to get up and spread the tarpaulin. He got all the men to squat down and unfolded the tarpaulin over their heads. He got behind the wheel and drove on. The driver knew well the nature of a tropical shower. It soon came down in buckets full. It was dark and musty under the tarpaulin. Their heads were bobbing out like eggs covered by a piece of cloth. The rain water soon collected in puddles on the tarpaulin. It was beginning to get heavy. A group of men would push their hands up and heave and the water would shift to another spot on the tarpaulin until it was thrown out of the moving lorry. It was a new experience for the men and they were actually having fun. It did not last long. Tropical showers were heavy but they were localized. Once the lorry moved out of the area, the rain stopped. They removed the tarpaulin and breathed the fresh air.

The road cut through some rubber plantations. For the first time they saw what a rubber tree looked like and marvelled at how the trees were planted in neat straight rows.

They passed through small villages or kampongs and saw Malays, not quite as dark in complexion as they were and looking different. Now driving through the streets of Kuala Kangsar they saw many Chinese people on the streets. Most of them had never seen a Chinese before. The complexion of others on the street appeared to be some kind of mix between the Indians and the Chinese. These were the Malays. They saw more Chinese and a few Indians in Sungei Siput where they had a simple meal of curry and rice on banana leaves at an Indian restaurant.

It was beginning to get dark when they turned off the tar road into a narrow cart track that wound its way between the trees and eventually brought them to the estate's settlement area.

Their belongings were either wrapped up in bundles or tied up in gunny sacks. The living quarters of the workers were single-room wooden cubicles all attached in a row. They stood on high stilts with stepladders into each cubicle. They were called *coolie* lines or labour lines. Eight of them shared one cubicle like a little dormitory. They spread out their mats and used their luggage as pillows. Since they had just arrived a meal was cooked for them by the resident workers. It was a simple meal of rice and dhal curry.

Introductions were quick to identify the villages and towns they came from. The same *kangany* had been recruiting men from the same areas. The resident workers were eager to find out how things were in their villages and enquired about their families. The *kangany* delivered letters to some of them from their families.

Even though it was late they continued to talk into the night. The new comers were bombarded with questions on the situation in India. Did they have a good crop of rice this season, was it dry or did they have floods. Did they have the same village headman? Who got married and who were dead. Has anything changed in their village, etc…etc…? Desa was the last to sleep for he always tried to jot a few lines in his journal before retiring.

***

Another day dawned on board the Rajula and they continued with their reminiscence. At four in the cool starry morning of 14 June 1936 the factory siren sounded four times. The watchman shouted the wake-up call from a distance. The settlement began to stir. The first sounds came from the lines occupied by families. The watchman moved closer to the lines shouting, holding a kerosene lamp to find his way. People began descending the stepladders. Here and there kerosene lamps were being lit in the houses. Some started wood fires within the space of four bricks placed at ninety degrees apart that acted as the stove.

The roosters began their crowing one after another. There were sounds of tin buckets being washed, the chopping of wood, the cackling of geese mingled with the occasional cry of children and dogs barking. The women ground chillies and turmeric on granite stone mortars to prepare paste for the day's curry. The pungent smell of freshly ground chilly tingled in the nostrils. Other women prepared tea and poured it into bottles to be taken along to the tapping task areas.

5.00 a.m. The second signal sounded from the factory. The *kangany* got up. Covering his head with the *kangany's* head cloth he set out to wake up the members of his gang, shouting high-pitched abuses at the top of his voice. Perumal, the *kangany* of the new recruits, told the new arrivals that they need not show up at the muster together with the others that morning.

Some of the women were brushing their teeth with their forefinger using charcoal powder and salt kept in a paper bag. The men brushed their teeth with the frayed piece of the coconut tree root or the frond that attached to the coconut. They chewed its fibrous end turning it into a toothbrush dipped in salt.

At the sound of the third siren at 5.30 a.m., the workers ambled towards the muster ground. Perumal, who had been the foreman, resumed his role. After seeing to it that his gang of workers had been assigned to their tasks, he returned to the lines and instructed his new recruits to hurry up and assemble at the office area in half an hour.

They were made to line up for inspection. The *kirani*, a Malayalee clerk, came out of the office to take a look at them. He counted them with disinterest, returned to the office and ordered the office staff to bring out their rations. Four gunny sacks were brought out containing the rations. Each gunny sack contained the amount for eight men assigned to one cubicle of the barracks. They were asked to wait. They waited standing or squatting for half an hour. Then it was announced that they were to stand up and look smart. Two white men appeared like gods before them dressed in khaki shirts, short pants and stockings. They were the *Periya Durai*, the big boss who was lord and master of the estate and the *Sinna Durai*, the small boss. They were the planters - the manager and the assistant manager, Humphreys and Erskine.

The manager looked each one up and down as a farmer would inspect healthy livestock. Then in reasonably good Tamil but with a heavy English accent he told them that they should start work the next day. He turned to his assistant and said, "Carry on," and walked away.

The assistant manager ordered the rations to be distributed and told the *kangany* to initiate the men into their tasks.

Perumal rounded them all into a group and briefed them on the timetable and together with Siva, an experienced tapper, he took them to a nearby tree to demonstrate the art of tapping a rubber tree.

"This tree is called the Para rubber tree. It takes seven years to grow before it can be tapped. Very good care has to be taken of the trees."

Siva first explained the knife, holding it and twisting it. The knife was a curved metal piece with a wooden handle. The curved metal ended up in a folded V-shaped blade. One side of the V was the cutting edge. Siva gently touched the sharp edge with his thumb saying, "The knife should be sharpened everyday and the cutting edge must not be dented. If it is dented you will not get a clean cut and you will damage the tree."

He rested the knife against the bark of the tree and made the cut by a pulling motion with both hands removing a thin sliver of bark along a downward half spiral on the tree trunk. Immediately the white latex emerged from the cutting and began to run down the spiral slope and then vertically down some inches into a V-shaped piece of tin acting as a drainage gutter and into a small clay cup tied around the tree with wire.

Perumal said, "When the cutting line reaches the level of the cup tapping will commence on the opposite side in the same fashion allowing this side to heal over. If done carefully and with skill, this tapping panel will yield latex for up to five years. Learn the skill, ngada, and work carefully." And he warned them, "If the tree is injured, na, the penalty is pay deduction."

Each of them was issued with a tapping knife and a honing stone. They were also given a small tin can with a wick protruding from a nozzle. It was a kerosene lamp meant to be tied to the forehead and wicker baskets. Four tin buckets for the whole team for transporting latex.

It was midday when they got back to their line. Desa and his seven cubicle mates unpacked the gunnysack and examined its contents. There was rice, a bottle of coconut oil, a can of kerosene oil and cooking ingredients and condiments in small packets. All eight of them were to share the contents which were meant to last for one month. Desa was particularly curious about the selection of goods and their quantity.

They had already been issued with mats and cotton sheets called *cumblies* for use as blankets. A cumbly is usually a sheet of woollen cloth but because of the hot weather they were given cotton sheets. They were also given three *veshties* and three pairs of *banians*.

Doraisamy, one of the veteran workers in the estate told them, "All these supplies are not free, you know. The cost of all supplies will be deducted from your wages."

5.00 a.m. the next day while it was still dark the daily routine began. At the sound of the third signal they marched to the muster ground with their tapping knives and small wicker baskets strapped around their waists and the kerosene lamps secured to their foreheads but not yet lit. Some of the workers were carrying cylindrical tin buckets suspended from the two ends of a pole resting across the shoulder. These were for collecting the liquid latex. They stood facing their *kangany*. The senior conductor, Vergese, inspected the gangs while the *kangany* reported the absentees. Replacements were ordered by the conductor from the relief tappers. The muster was called and the details recorded in the check roll. Each worker was given a dose of quinine and they were marched off to their tasks. Each one had to tap 350 trees that morning.

Desa's cubical mates were Kuppusamy, Ravichandran, Lourdusamy, Govindaraj, Antoine, Arokianathan and Sokalingam. Lourdusamy, Antoine and Arokianathan were Christians. The other five, including Desa, were Hindus. They had already got to know each other quite well. Even though there was caste disparity among them it was not a major factor in this foreign land. They were all in the same gang.

"What's your *vur* (village, also referred to towns)?" Desa asked Kuppusamy. "I'm from Kiranur on the road to Pudukattai," said Kuppusamy.

"I'm from Pudukottai," said Lourdusamy, "and we are from the same district."

"I am from Tiruchirapalli," said Desa.

"We are not far, I'm from Karur, where the Kaveri river branches off," said Sokalingam.

"You, Ravichandran?" asked Kuppusamy. "Thanjavur," said Ravichandran.

"Hay, we are from the same district. My *vur* is Orattanadu," said Arokianathan.

"Govindaraj, your *vur*?" "I'm from Namakkal."

"Antoine, where are you from?" asked Desa.

"I'm a little further away, my hometown is Pondicherry."

They were all from neighbouring districts in the state of Madras. They threw themselves with enthusiasm into their task and learnt their new trade very fast bringing in a good supply of latex. They got into the routine. Up before the crack of dawn, to the muster and off to the task area to tap up to 350 or more trees. After a quick lunch from the lunch pack, collect the latex and bring it to the weighing centre, wash up the utensils, and go home to rest. Then its knife sharpening time after which some would go off to the toddy shop. At night if there was a film show, everybody would gather in the football field where it would be projected on a big screen.

A couple of weeks later in the timber they heard a shouting. It was Perumal.

"You idiot," he shouted at Sokalingam, "You have injured the tree, look at the hole you have made on the trunk. That will cost you one day's pay." He jotted that down in his notebook.

Chapter 6

Reality Dawns

One afternoon six months later Desa, Kuppu and Antoine sat on the cement floor next to the culvert sharpening their knives.

"We have worked now for six months and Perumal has been constantly finding fault with us. We have not been paid anything or told anything about our pay," said Desa.

"Now our food rations too have been reduced," noted Antoine.

"All the promises the *kangany* made were lies. What a disappointment! Why don't we confront Perumal and ask him?" added Kuppu.

"But who, da, will dare to ask him the question?" said Antoine.

"We will never know unless someone asks him," said Desa.

"Then you ask him, da," Antoine addressed Desa.

"Let us find a suitable time and sound out the others too," said Desa.

"We must do it quickly before the word gets to him," warned Kuppu.

On another day, Desa's gang was regrouping at the completion of the task and having a chat discussing the confrontation when Perumal himself approached them.

"Hey, what da you fellows, what are you doing grouping and talking instead of working at your tasks?"

Everyone folded their arms and bowed their heads while Desa looked the *kangany* in the eye. Perumal cracked the whip and it caught Desa on the cheek. He wiped the blood with a rag. They all dispersed.

That same afternoon at 3 o'clock they were summoned to the office. Desa, Kuppu, Antoine, Ravichandren and Lourdusamy, the five who were caught chatting, approached the office. Perumal was with the estate conductor.

"What audacity is this, da? How dare you come in here with your slippers on? Take them off, ngada, and fold your arms." Perumal turned to the conductor, "These *coolies* were talking in a group when they should have been working. That fellow Desa talked back to me and challenged me showing me no respect," said Perumal.

"You all were with him. Is it true that Desa was insubordinate?" asked the conductor Vergese.

No one spoke. Desa began, "We had finished...."

"I did not ask you, so you shut your mouth da. Desa, you are struck off the check roll for three days," decided Verges. They were dismissed.

Back in their cubicle Desa, ignoring their lack of support because that was the way they were, said, "I still want to know about our wages. I promised my father that I will save money and take it back home."

The others were afraid of broaching this subject.

Desa continued, "What, ngada, don't you all want to know? We have the right to know."

"What do you mean by right to know?" asked Ravichandran.

"We are not slaves but employed workers. We were told that we would be paid 40 cents per working day. We do not know how many non-working days there were over the last six months and today I just lost three days. We must keep track or else we will never know how much we have earned. The money is ours and to know how much we have is our right. We have to meet Perumal on his own because he it was who made all those promises."

Finding strength in numbers all eight of them went to see Perumal one week later. They found him alone.

"Perumal, *aiyiah*," began Desa, "We have been working for six months and we would like to know how much each of us has earned."

"You must be patient," said Perumal, "There has been a

worldwide depression and thousands of workers have been dismissed. You must consider yourselves very lucky ngada, to find yourselves still employed."

Kuppusamy plucked enough courage to ask, "We have not been paid proper wages for six months except for some pocket money now and then. What happened to our wages?"

Perumal, surprised at their audacity, "Why, ngada, do you ask, have you no faith in me? You see I have got all your wages in my account book here," tapping a thick ledger.

"Can you tell us what's in the book, we cannot read?" asked Antoine.

Perumal cleared his throat and spat out the betel leaf he was chewing, "What da is this! You see, I paid for your passage and your food and all expenses from the day you left your home in India until you started work here. Your train fare to Nagapatinam, your food and medicine while you were at the camp waiting for the boat; then the steamship passage to Malaynadu, quarantine fees and then from Penang to here, your clothes and rations and so on, who da do you think paid for all that? All that will have to be deducted from your wages first. You owe me that money and only when all expenses have been deducted you will receive your wages."

"You never told us that before, but since you gave us the jobs you tell us how long we have to keep working before it is settled," said Kuppu.

"Normally, you should be getting forty cents per day but now wages are low because of the recession. Things will soon change. I have all your records in my book. You do your work properly and do what I tell you and you have nothing to fear. One more thing, don't try to be clever. Don't even try to leave the estate. If you do the police will be after you and they will bring you back here and you will be severely punished. Do you understand?"

Most of them said yes.

Desa spoke up, "Can we look at your book?"

"What da is this! Do you think you are some kind of inspector? The book belongs to the estate and all in good time we will let you know. You can go now," concluded Perumal.

They left feeling quite helpless. Desa was determined to do something about it.

Weeks went by and they worked for ten hours a day putting up with the abusive language of the *kangany*.

"Although we are out at sea now, this is what is happening all the time in the estates. Our people are being treated like slaves," Desa said to Kuppu on the deck of the Rajula.

"That is our karma. I've had enough of it and I'm never going back to Malaynadu" said Kuppu.

Arokia began, "Hitler and the Japanese Emperor are sitting together under a tree talking seriously. A Chinaman walks up to them, and says, 'Hello, what are you guys doing?' The Emperor says, 'We are planning a world war.' The Chinaman says, 'Really, What's going to happen?' Hitler says, 'Well, we're going to kill 15 million Indians and one Malay policeman.' The Chinaman exclaims, 'A Malay policeman?'

"The Japanese Emperor turns to Hitler and says, 'See, I told you no one would worry about the 15 million Indians!'"

Suddenly there was a commotion on the deck of the steamer. There was an argument over the sleeping space allotted to each one. The chalk marks had partly disappeared. The argument developed into a fist fight. All the men converged to the spot and some were attempting to separate the two individuals. The ship's bursar appeared and ordered them to stop. The chalk markings were reconfirmed and there was calm.

"Do you remember the *bhai* (a friendly way of addressing a Sikh) who used to come to the estate on his bicycle with a huge bundle of cloth to sell?"

"Yes, he was a nice fellow and not like the bloody Sikhs who shot us and whipped us," said Kuppu.

"It was through him that I gathered what was happening outside our secluded estate."

***

Desa made friends with the *bhai* and got him to deliver newspapers whenever he visited. They were days old but still news. The editor, R.

H. Nathan of the Tamil Weekly, the *Tamilaham*, a reformist paper, wrote about the sad conditions of Indian workers in many of the estates. Desa found out that some significant events were taking place. In May Jawaharlal Nehru had visited Malaya and the estate people knew nothing about it. The paper mentioned that Nehru merely made a tour of Malaya with his daughter Indira and did not address the issue of Indian workers at all.

Desa discovered that there were two trends among the Indians and the different Tamil papers were fostering one or the other. One trend advocated the Indian identity and Indian nationalism with eyes set on India while the other called for unity among the Indians in Malaya be they Bengalis, Bombayites, Punjabis, Tamils, Malayalees and so on. He read the words of A. K. Surrattee, chairman of the Singapore Indian Association in his 1936 annual address published in *The Indian*, a weekly newspaper, saying, "Unless we sink all personal, communal and provincial differences, consolidate our position and stand as one body, one indivisible whole, to establish our rights now, our succeeding generations will be pushed to the background and counted for nothing." Desa found this rather idealistic when there was, apart from caste differences, a deep disparity between the Indian Associations and the Tamil majority, the plantation workers, predominantly Dravidians. The association members were mainly Indian merchants, forming the Indian Chambers of Commerce, prominent among them being the Chettiar Chamber of Commerce. They were politically aware professional men mainly English-educated Malayalee and Ceylonese. Among them they managed some form of unity when they inaugurated the Central Indian Association of Malaya (CIAM). It became the interlocutor between the colonial government and the Indian Congress. It was a top heavy organisation whose members were more interested in acquiring nomination to government councils and boards with little concern for the living conditions of the isolated plantation workers.

Desa began to realize that no outsiders would throw their weight behind the plantation workers to help them. That was when he decided to start organising his fellow workers.

***

"Do you remember our first meeting at the back of the temple?" said Desa, on board the Rajula. "There were eight of us with Lourdusamy, Govindaraj, Sokalingam and Antoine. Poor Lourdu and Govind. I hope they have found their peace. But they and the others should not have died in vain. They will not be forgotten."

"Wonder what happened to Soka and Antoine?" said Ravi.

***

The core five members who had talked about doing something about their wages felt that it was rather risky to talk openly even among their cubicle mates. On the pretext of going to the temple which was the major structure in the estate, after the *pooja* (Hindu religious rites) they went to the back of the temple, sat across the cement culvert and started to plan what to do. The three others joined them. It was evening and they were all alone except for a couple of men who came to pee.

"Perumal doesn't want to reveal to us what is in the ledger. We have no idea of what we owe or what is due to us," said Desa.

"All we know is that after six months of no proper wages we are only getting two or three dollars and that too not regularly plus the rations," said Lourdu.

"The rations too have diminished in size, we are running out of rice even before the next supply," added Kuppu.

"The next time we get our rations could you, Lourdu, weigh each item of provision we receive? Can you borrow weighing scales from the shopkeeper and weigh each of these items?" asked Desa.

"Lourdu and Antoine, can the two of you find out first from the sundry shop the prices of the provision we receive each month. Kuppu, try and list down all the complaints from the workers. From this we can calculate the monthly budget of every worker. When we have some solid facts and figures we can call for a bigger group meeting and let the workers know what kind of a deal we are getting," said Desa.

"But we don't know of the expenses incurred by the *kangany* on our behalf," said Kuppu.

"I will see what I can gather from the newspapers and, perhaps, if we could somehow get our hands on that ledger..." schemed Desa.

This was their first task, to collect data. Kuppu and Lourdu got busy each day after work to go to the sundry shop and list down the price of commodities. At night they were juggling away with figures and when others walked in asking what they were doing, they said, "Oh, we are just gathering information to see how much our money can buy," said Lourdu.

Each night Kuppu and Lourdu were chalking up figures and matching them with food items. Meanwhile Desa searching through the papers found out that the pre Depression wages were 50 cents, that is for the men and 40 cents for the women. Now they are supposed to be getting 40 cents for males and 32 cents for females. They calculated the amount in weight of the provisions received and costed them against the sundry shop prices. If that was deducted from the pay and whatever still owing the *kangany*, they should be receiving the balance. The latter remained the unknown quantity.

Chapter 7

Strike Action Plan

After spending six days collecting data Lourdu offered a plan.

"I think I know a way of breaking into the office. There is a weak spot in the back window and it is often unlocked. I know that Perumal keeps the ledger in the bottom drawer but that is locked. If we can get that key we can get hold of the ledger."

"And I know how," said Antoine, "I know where Perumal keeps all his keys in his sleeping quarters. I can sneak in and get it."

"We must do it in the night and leave everything as it was without any evidence before the morning. Alright when can we do it?" asked Desa.

"On Tuesdays Perumal goes to the toddy shop and is often a little under the weather when he gets back. Those nights, I know, he will sleep well," said Antoine.

"How come you know so much about Perumal?" asked Kuppu.

Antoine did not respond.

"Next Tuesday, then. Will he be asleep by 9 o'clock?" asked Desa.

"Yes," said Antoine.

"O.K. ngada, you get the keys. Lourdu and I will be waiting behind the office. Kuppu, you will hide near the tool shed at the muster area keeping watch that no one comes near," directed Desa.

Antoine met Perumal on his way back from the toddy shop and walked with him to his quarters.

"That fire in the second task area today was almost reaching the trees," said Antoine watching Perumal to see where he would place the keys.

"I have repeatedly told the weeders that when they burn rubbish they have to watch the fire."

"I was there and snapped off a branch and beat the fire to death. It almost got out of hand."

"Well done. It's a good thing the senior conductor does not know about it. Surely, he would have told the manager. Don't talk about the fire with the others."

"You look tired, you need a good sleep," said Antoine closing the door behind him but leaving it a little ajar. He did get along well with Perumal.

Outside Antoine waited half an hour after Perumal turned off his lantern and slowly eased the door. It was not locked. He groped his way in the dark towards the nail on the wall on which hung the keys. His knees knocked the lantern and tipped it over. Luckily it was not lit or he would have had to douse another fire.

"Hay! What, Who da is there?" exclaimed Perumal.

"It's me, Antoine; I left my *thundu* (a small piece of towel) behind and came to collect it."

"O.K., da. O.K. da, go away." responded Perumal and turned over. Antoine lifted the keys and left. He nodded to Kuppu as he passed him.

Lourdu had already got the window opened. He took the keys and entered the office. He passed the ledger through the window to Desa and climbed out. After closing the window they made their way into the timber deep enough to light a lantern. Desa poured over the figures. He took copious notes. They had gathered enough information from the ledger. They retraced their steps and while Kuppu stood guard Desa told Lourdu to put the ledger back exactly as he found it and lock the drawer. Antoine stealthily went back to replace the keys. They all retired to the cubicle and slept.

Desa and Kuppu visited the families and talked to the women working as tappers, weeders or rubber processing workers in the estate factory along with other men.

Kanniammah told them, "The working hours are very long even though my fourteen year old son, Rajan, helps me, there is so little time to cook when I get home."

Her husband, Ragu told Desa and Kuppu, "Why nga are you wanting to know all this, as though you don't already know? You can't do anything to change things. And, adiyeyi, Kanniammah, you just keep quiet and do your work and stop inviting trouble."

Another woman complained, "I have just given birth and I have to go on working and carry my baby. I cannot leave her in the creche because I breast feed her. Besides, there is only one old lady looking after the creche and it is dirty, babies not washed and full of flies and rats. The first two days I didn't go to muster and there goes my two days' pay. My houseman insists that I go to work."

Another family's complaint was education.

"There is one school building in bad repair and only two teachers and 23 primary students between six and 12. They have no proper books and the teacher lumps them together teaching the same lesson to the six-year-olds and the 12-year-olds. What nga is this?

Another woman said,

"I went to the dispensary and the dresser gave me some pills and said you need better medicine but I do not have them. You have to go outside the estate to the town dispensary to get them."

"My teenaged daughter was disturbed by the *kirany*, the junior conductor, when he found her alone in the timber," complained a mother.

They listed down all the complaints. And at night they arranged them in some order.

During the night Desa worked out the details. Perumal had made his passage claims to and from Madras, his internal travel claims and his stay in India for a month from the estate management. On the recruits he had itemised each individual by name and had converted Indian Rupees into Malayan dollars. For each individual he made the following claims:

In India

Transport to the depot	3.00
Vaccination, inoculation	2.00
Medical report	1.00

Travel Documents	1.00
Camp fee and food for 3 days --	3.00
Passage plus meals	20.00
	30.00

In Malaya

Disinfection of clothes	1.00	
Quarantine fees	2.00	
Fresh clothes	7.50	
Meals 2.5 days	1.50	
Lorry fare	4.00	
Lunch	0.50	
First meal on arrival	0.50	
	17.00	47.00 Malayan Dollars

"Now let us look at the rations," said Desa.

"The main item is rice and we get half a sack of rice in two installments on the first and fifteenth of the month. They are afraid that if they supplied the whole amount we will eat it all up too quickly. One full sack is about 48 *gantang*, which works out to be six *gantang* each for a month. One *gantang* at 55 cents would be 3.30 for six. Antoine and I have worked out how much one person would need to spend on the basic provisions for one month. You read out the other list," said Lourdu to Antoine.

Antoine began:

Salt – one and half *chupak*	11 cents
Chilly – ½ *katty*	17 cents
Coriander – ¾ *chupak*	10 cents
Tamarind - one and half *katties*	22 cents
Dhal - 1 *chupak*	16 cents
Green peas – 1 *chupak*	14 cents
White beans – ½ *chupak*	10 cents
Onions – 1 *katty*	14 cents

Garlic – ½ *chupak*	6 cents
Cumin seed ½ *chupak*	6 cents
Mustard ½ *chupak*	7 cents
Pepper ½ *chupak*	10 cents
Tumeric ½ *chupak*	6 cents
Curry stuff – ½ *chupak*	12 cents
Coconut oil – 1 bottle	36 cents
Kerosene oil & matches	17 cents
Mutton, salt fish, vegetables	72 cents
Bar soap	12 cents
Dhobi	12 cents
Barber	12 cents
Temple deductions	36 cents
Betel nut, tobacco	17 cents
	3.75

Other one-time expenses

Veshties – 3	9.00
Banyans – 3	9.00
Upper clothes -3	9.00
Cotton *cumbly*	11.00
Pots and pans	1.45
Mat and pillow	3.00
Knife & sharpening stone	2.00
Wicker basket	0.50
Tin bucket 4.00/2	2.00
Head lamp	1.20
	48.15

One gantang is approximately 2.5 kg or 4 cups.
One chupak is one quarter gantang or 1 cup.
One katty is one and a third pound.

This is the full estimate we have come up with.

Desa totalled the package.

"Our monthly wages are supposed to be based on 40 cents per day. Given rainy days and non-work days we could average 26 days per month and that would be 10.40, ten dollars and forty cents. And if we minus the cost of the rice supply at 3.30 we should get 7.10 – seven dollars and ten cents per month. For the first six months we were not paid wages at all and we should have received 7.10 x 6 = 42.60. That much he owes us. That is the money we should have received for the first six months. Passage and one-time expenses were 47.00 + 48.15 = 95.15. If we take away our six-month wages from that, that is, 95.15 – 42.60 = 52.55. This is the amount, fifty two dollars and fifty five cents that we still owe Perumal. And we are not sure exactly how much he is continuing to deduct from our pay. We can more or less work that out from what we get. We receive between two and three dollars a month depending on latex collection. If we take an average of 2.50 and deduct that from 7.10, he is withholding 4.60 or thereabouts each month. If he is not deducting this, then we are being paid even less than 40 cents a day. This is also the hold he has on us. This applies only to our batch."

"But the others too are not being paid in full. That means he also has a hold on them as well," said Kuppu.

"*Aiyo, Kadavule,* (Oh, God) We have been calculating all this based on the wages for men and forgot that women and weeders are paid even less. Let me work it out." Desa started writing figures on a piece of paper. Then he said, "Women are getting only eighty percent of what we get, so if we are supposed to be getting 7.10, the women get only 5.68."

"We need to let the women know that," said Kuppu.

***

Two weeks later the eight of them met; this time in the temple precinct together with a number of families discussing with them a proper list of complaints.

Desa addressed them,

"A few of us have been studying our life situation in the estate.

We are supposed to be paid ten dollars and forty cents a month. Take away the rice money of three dollars and thirty cents we should get seven dollars and ten cents a month. This is for the men, the women get even less, only five dollars and sixty eight cents. Some of us receive slightly more or less depending on the quantity of latex we bring in everyday. With the price of provisions today we have calculated that on essential provisions alone each one of us would need to spend three dollars and seventy five cents and that only leaves us three dollars and thirty five cents for other expenses or savings. And for the women and weeders only one dollar and ninety three cents."

Kuppu went through all the items of provisions one by one and quoted the cost of each. When it all added up to more than three dollars, they were quite surprised. They had never calculated things like this before.

"I owe the sundry shop money," said one woman and another said, "I owe *bhai* money for cloth."

A man at the back said, "I owe the toddy shop."

"Yes we are living in debt especially to Perumal," said Kuppu.

"We have also listed out what we need based on all the complaints from you all," said Desa, "Antoine will tell you."

"They are:

1. A reduction in working hours to 9 hours;

2. Increase in pay to 50 cents per day;

3. Equal pay for both men and women;

4. Maternity leave;

5. Better conditions at the crèche;

6. Better medication for health care;

7. Proper education with curriculum and books and school maintenance;

8. Stop molesting our women."

"We are planning to present these demands directly to the estate manager. It is no use going to the *kangany*. Perumal doesn't care for our welfare. We would like you all - and tell all the other families too - to come to the muster area tomorrow evening at 4 o'clock. In the morning we will inform the office that we would like to meet the manager."

"Please make sure that everybody makes it a point to come because this is very important for us. We have to present *makal sakthi* to them," urged Kuppu.

Friday 3.30 p.m. before their usual trip to the temple at 6.00 p.m. the estate employees began to gather.

Perumal came out with Vergese who asked, "Why, ngada, are you all gathering here? What, ngada, do you people want?"

Desa said, "We want to meet the *Peria Dorai* and we have already informed the office this morning."

Vergese: "*Peria Dorai* is busy and unable to meet you. You can tell me what you want."

Desa: "I am sorry, *aiyiah*. The people want to meet the *Peria Dorai* so that we can personally hand him a petition."

Vergese: "You can't do that! Let me have a look at the petition."

Desa: "The people want the *Peria Dorai* to look at it."

Vergese: "Give it to me and I will pass it on to him."

Silence. Desa looked at the people. Some were feeling uneasy, shifting from one foot to the other. Desa said in a loud voice, "We will not move from here until we see the *Peria Dorai*."

Vergese and Perumal were taken aback.

Perumal: "Who da do you think you are? Have you become the *kangany* of the people?"

He took a step towards Desa to strike him. His cubicle mates also moved up and the crowd began to stir. Perumal stepped back. His dignity and authority had been challenged.

"Come," said Vergese and they both went into the office. All waited. The first step was a victory. Nothing like this was ever done in the estate before. They waited until five o'clock. The children were running around playing catching. Some of the people were getting impatient to go to the temple.

5.30 p.m. The *Sinna Dorai* came out.

"What is your problem that you cannot settle with the *kirany*?"

Desa: "Sar, we would like to hand over a petition from all of us to the manager and ask him to please consider what we are asking."

"And what may you be asking?"

Desa getting the tacit approval from everyone that the *Sinna Dorai* is as good as the *Peria Dorai* to be given the petition, handed the neatly folded and hand-written petition to the assistant manager, Mr. Angus Erskine, with both hands. Erskine read it and although he was surprised he tried not to show it. He looked up and said, "Alright, the management will consider your demands and get back to you. You all can go now."

All the people clapped their hands and noisily made their way towards the temple.

***

The two *Dorais* met over tea in the manager's bungalow on top of the hill overlooking the estate settlement layout. Besides the *coolie* lines and staff quarters, the school, football field, temple and the main office were clearly visible like an island in a green sea of rubber trees. Humphreys must have been watching from his window what was going on in the muster area in front of the main office. He put on his glasses as Erskine handed him the petition. Erskine noticed a pair of binoculars on the window sill.

"Written in a good hand in reasonably good English too. Wonder who they got to write it for them?"

"It was by one of them, a leader in the group. His name is Nadesan Pillay and he has evidently had some education."

"And the audacity, may I add. They are not asking, mind you, they are demanding that working hours be reduced from almost 12 hours a day to 9 hours a day. Now, that depends on the market price of rubber and we can do naught about it without directions from London. It was a grave mistake on the part of the *kangany* to have recruited someone with an education. Now, this pair of glasses needs to be changed. You read out the petitions to me, one by one," handing it over to Erskine.

"They want an increase in wages to 50 cents per day and equal pay for both men and women."

"That, of course, is preposterous."

"They want maternity leave with pay."

"Unofficial labour unions in other estates have also made similar demands. We have no union here so we can skip it. You know these women are tough, they will drop their bundle like a cow and carry on with what they are doing. Why soften them up!"

"The crèche is unhygienic and needs trained staff."

"We have provided the space and they will have to maintain it. You don't need trained staff to babysit. Get the dresser to inspect it."

"The dispensary is ill-equipped without proper medicine. They want proper treatment of illness in the hospital and transport fares provided to go to the town hospital."

"Medicine is a government controlled item. We can only buy what we can get. We do not have the numbers to provide a hospital. We cannot provide transport to everyone who is sick. They'll use that as an excuse to go to town. We have the medicine for common illness. Anyway I will have a word with the dresser."

"They want the teachers in the school to provide proper books and proper division of classes. And repair the leaks."

"The school is bloody awful but then the teachers are the government's responsibility, not ours. Besides, these savages should not be educated too much. The next thing you know, they will all be writing petitions."

"A junior conductor has apparently molested one of the girls, and they want him removed."

"Well, no police report has been lodged; hence we cannot act on that. I don't think we need to grant a single one of those petitions. It will be interpreted as giving in to their demands. They just don't realize what a good wicket they are on here."

Erskine added, "Not only should we deny the petitions we should also issue a warning to them that their wages will be further decreased if they tried to push it."

"That may be rather awkward because there are already rumours of active labour struggles in some of the estates. The CIAM is also starting to voice support for the workers. The Malayan Communist

Party is another menace becoming more and more active among Chinese workers both in and outside the plantations. Although nearly all our workers are Indian they might just take the cue from the Chinese. We will deny the wage increase and just leave it as it is."

"Then we should threaten the leaders with arrest for insubordination."

"Anyway, I will draft a note making the denial official."

One week later Desa was summoned to the office.

He was made to stand outside the office for twenty minutes just to make him aware of his lower standing. The clerk ushered him in. The conductor's table was in the centre and the smaller *kangany's* table was by the window. Both were seated while Desa was made to stand barefooted.

"Dai! Fold your arms, da!" demanded Perumal.

Desa hesitated.

"Come on," prompted Perumal.

Slowly Desa folded his arms.

"You and your cubicle mates have been sneaking around doing a lot of dirty work behind our back, haven't you? asked Perumal.

Desa wondered if the break-in for the ledger had been discovered.

"How much schooling have you had, da?" asked Vergese. "I finished standard nine, going on to ten."

"Because you can read and write you make yourself a leader and try to champion the cause of the people," said Vergese.

"Can't you see, these are our own people being cheated and bullied so that the white people in England will get all the big profits from the rubber. How will they get the rubber without the labour, sweat and blood of the workers?" Desa spoke up.

"Dai! Shut your mouth, you cannot talk like that here. Without the plantations we will have no jobs," replied Perumal.

"You listen carefully, da, Nadesan, the manager is very unhappy with you and angry with you for instigating the people. He could have you arrested by the police for insubordination. So you are lucky no action is being taken against you and your friends now. Learn your lesson and stop all this nonsense at once," warned Vergese.

"What is the response to the petitions?" asked Desa.

"The *Peria Dorai* has given you a reply in writing. You go and explain it to your people. Dismissed," concluded Vergese handing him the envelope.

When Desa went back to the cubicle, it was knife sharpening time. He sat among his mates across the culvert drain, took out the letter and read it to them.

"To the employees of the Dolby Estate:

Your petition consisting eight demands have been received and duly considered by the management.

We believe that you are given more than a fair treatment in all respects, all things considered.

Your demands are considered impudent. All your demands are denied.

The leaders among you are warned against pursuing these petitions further with warrants of arrest and incarceration for insubordination with subsequent dismissal and deportation.

Mr. Alan Humphreys
Manager
Dolby Estate
Date: 29th March 1937"

Desa explained the difficult words of the letter and their implications. They were disappointed, sad and angry.

"How are we going to tell the people?" asked Antoine.

"There are three things we can do. Accept the letter as our karma and continue to slave in the estate. Leave the estate and find a job in another estate or fight back. We have to put these options to the people."

"Friday seems to be the best day to meet," said Kuppu.

This Friday then, at 4.00 p.m. Where?" asked Desa.

"In the temple?" offered Govind.

"No, that would be too public. One of the classrooms in the school might be better," said Soka.

"In that case, we should meet later, about 8 o'clock, after they have done the *poojas* in the temple. Some of them can slip away towards the school without attracting too much attention," said Ravi.

"Alright, then, pass the word around, discreetly. We have two days," instructed Desa.

By 8 o'clock on Friday there were only 12 men around. By 8.30 there were about 30 with some women, so they began.

Desa addressed the people, "The *Peria Dorai* has replied to our petition." He waved the letter, "and it is bad news. He has rejected all our petitions. He has also threatened some of us that we could be arrested, jailed, dismissed or sent back to India if we continued pushing our claims."

"*Aiyooo, Kadvule*," came from a number of them. "This is fate on our heads," said others.

"What, nga, can we do now?" asked Kaliammah.

"What can we do, we just have to accept our fate," said one man.

An older man said, "When I started work here the wages were even lower than what we are getting now. That is when many of the workers went back to India but I stayed behind and continued to work and wages got better."

"But the cost of everything has gone up so much now," rebutted another.

"We deserve better," said Desa. "Huge profits from the sale of rubber are collected by the estate and sent to the company in England. They are living luxuriously from our blood and sweat. We are human beings and we have rights. We really do not have to work ten to twelve hours. We do not have to work for the *kirany* in our spare time.

"The country is short of labour and there is very little immigration at present. We are in a position where we can ask what we need. We are not asking for luxuries but for basic necessities to live with health and comfort. So, we can either accept the fate of being slaves all our lives or fight for a better life. We can also leave the estate and look for work outside or in other estates. But the situation in other estates is no better. If we stay and fight there are risks. He has already warned us."

"If we fight we may lose everything," from one man.

"True, but if we fight and win we will have a better life. Remember when we were at the muster station to hand over the petition, Perumal came over to strike me, but when he saw the numbers he retreated. That was a sign of *makal sakthi*. The strength is in us if we stand united against the few bullies. I think that our petition has really shocked the manager. We are always considered to be docile, subservient and law-abiding, that is how the British Raj has kept us in India. Now there is a growing *Swaraj*, a nationalism for independence in India. The Indians are rising up."

"How, nga, can we fight?" asked a young woman.

"We don't have to take axes and *parangs* or shed blood. We just say we will refuse to work."

"Then we will not get our money."

"True, but they will also lose. If all of us stop work for one hour they will lose more. The Chinese workers are better paid than the Indian workers. They have their own associations that support them. We also have our newly formed CIAM. Unfortunately we do not get much support from them. They are more like the *kiranies*. They are the educated Brahmins who have their own business and political interests. They want to play politics with the British government and they will not risk their interests to help us. We are on our own but we are not alone even though we are isolated from the other estates. We are big in numbers but not united whereas the Chinese, although smaller in numbers are well united and we can learn from them. I suggest we call for stoppage of work until the demands in our petition are met. Are we ready to stand together?"

There was a murmur and a buzz and they began to talk among themselves. Desa realized that they were afraid. He waited.

Suddenly one loud voice rang out, "We are ready to stand." It was Govind.

"Yes we are ready!" It was Lourdu.

"Yes, we should stand," from the audience joined by a few more, but by no means too many.

"We have too much to lose," said one voice.

Another, "We do not have too much to start with anyway."

"I think we are not ready to decide tonight. You talk it over quietly among yourselves. Perumal or the *kiranies* must never know. If they do we are dead even before we start.

Can we meet again on Sunday night?" asked Desa.

"We need more time," said one voice.

"No. We must treat this as urgent. Any delay would be dangerous for all of us."

They dispersed in twos and threes talking about the denial of the petition and the meeting. The next day, (Saturday) 8 April, Desa met *bhai* who had the usual bundle of newspapers for him.

"*Thamby*, here, I have been asked to distribute these pamphlets quietly to some of the estate workers. I am sure it will interest you."

"Thanks, *bhai*." Desa took the newspapers and the pamphlet to his cubicle to read.

He called his mates and shared the contents of the pamphlet. They were all very excited. Let's keep this quiet until tomorrow. If we let it out now the management will get to know and do all they can to prevent something like that happening here."

The next evening 9 April at the school room there were almost 40 workers gathered. That was a good sign because if they were not interested they would not have turned up.

Desa spoke, "Thank you all for coming and I hope you have seriously thought about what we should do. I have some news for you.

In the state of Selangor there are a number of rubber estates with Chinese workers. In the district of Ulu Langat a number of Chinese rubber tappers have gone on strike for better wages and living conditions. They have been on strike for 20 days now. They have been joined by other estate workers not only in Selangor but also in Negeri Sembilan, Malacca and Pahang, altogether about 25,000 workers. Another five thousand workers both Chinese and Indians from factories and tin mines have also gone on strike in sympathy. The Chinese are demanding 75 cents per day and we are only asking for 50 cents. They are not going to give up. They are going to prolong the strike as long as it takes until their demands are met. They are calling workers from all rubber estates to go on strike for the same purpose and also in sympathy with them. All together there are

30,000 workers on strike. This is strength in numbers. This is *makal sakthi*. Now is the time for us to go on strike too."

"Yes, we will stand together and demand our rights too," came one voice with others nodding their heads.

"There are many, especially families with small children who are scared as to what might happen and they don't want to take part in the strike."

"That's alright," said Desa, "we must respect their wishes although numbers would mean a lot to this action."

"There are also others who have not made up their mind. Perhaps when they see us standing they might join us."

"Let us hope so. Now, if we are all agreed, we will call for the same demands in our petition. We will refuse to work until our demands are met. Tomorrow let us go to the sundry shop and buy whatever we and the family need and carry on working as usual. Don't tell anybody outside, not even the sundry shop keeper. Perumal and the *kiranies* should not know. The management thinks that they have scared us off by refusing our demands and frightening us. Let us surprise them. Let us all turn up for muster on Tuesday morning. Bring bottles of water for we may have to stand there for a long time. Be strong nga, be brave nga, show no sign of weakness nga. *MAKAL SAKTHI VALGA!*" (LONG LIVE PEOPLE POWER)

They started to repeat, "Long live people's power." "Shhhhh..." said Desa, "not so loudly."

They went back quietly, nervous, scared but determined.

The next morning everything went on as usual. The 30 men and 15 women assembled at the muster station. They went through the normal procedure of registering into the check roll. After supervising the administering of quinine, the morning staff, Perumal and Vergese went back into the office. After a while Perumal noticed that the gangs had not moved on. Curious, he came out. "What are you waiting for, get moving to your tasks. Hurry up! *Jalthi!*"

Nobody moved. Vergese came out followed by the staff. They gathered something was up.

"We want what we asked for in our petition," said Desa.

"You have already got your answer from the *Peria Dorai* and there is nothing more to talk about," said Vergese.

"We are not working until our demands are met," said Desa.

"Do you want to be whipped, da?" shouted Perumal.

"You do what you want, we are not moving from here," said Kuppu.

The *kiranies* became frantic. A messenger was sent running to the manager's bungalow.

***

On board the Rajula, Desa said, "We really did not expect their reaction to be so drastic. That inexperienced ex-army fellow, Roberts was trying to demonstrate the supremacy of the colonialists."

"And those bloody Punjabis were no better than mindless and heartless machines," added Ravi.

"Our six brothers and sisters did not die in vain. They are the first heroes of the struggle. The struggle has only just begun," Desa was thinking aloud.

Desa, Kuppu, Arokia and Ravi did not realize that during their reminiscence they had almost lost count of the days on the sea. They could see land – their motherland. The ship had stopped and was dropping anchor.

Chapter 8

Home

They had reached the off-shore of Nagapattinam. There was no harbour in Nagapattinam. Small boats were heading toward them. This was where they had embarked the ship when they left for Malaynadu.

"I remember when we were getting on the ship they were loading bails and bails of onions," said Ravi.

"There, you can see the lighters coming loaded with onions. What export material have we brought from Malaynadu?" wondered Kuppu.

"Malaynadu has just exported undesirable, rebellious Indian workers," said Arokia who could insert humour in almost any situation.

"I heard from one of the passengers that the ship carried rice, sugar, coffee, rubber, shoes and slippers," informed Ravi.

Even before the light vessels arrived, small boys between nine and 10 years old were already there. On a couple of logs tied together they rowed out to the deep sea.

"You know, when they lash two tree trunks together they call it *katumaram*, (trees tied together). The *velekaran* (white man, used collectively) has built a boat calling it by a similar sounding name of katamaran," said Arokia.

Some of the passengers threw coins at them. Clad only in loin cloths the small boys would dive into the water and grab the sinking coins.

"Wow, they swim like fish," admired Kuppu.

"I believe we cannot disembark until the lighters have unloaded and loaded the cargo because we are going ashore on them. We reached here about seven in the morning after six days at sea and now it is midday. Let's go back and lie down," said Desa.

It was well into the afternoon before the first of the cargo boats was ready to leave.

"Now they are lowering the accommodation ladder," observed Arokia.

The deck passengers began to rush. Hardly any of the cabin passengers were disembarking. They were bound for Madras.

"What's the point of rushing? What are we going back to? Our families don't even know we are coming back. I don't know how I am going to face my father. He will be even more disappointed than me," said Desa.

"Hey, let's not just go our separate ways. Let us meet again da, say, in one month's time?" suggested Kuppu.

"That's a good idea, *machanh*," said Desa. "You could come to Trichy and see what path karma is taking each of us," said Desa. *Machanh* is literally brother-in-law, but also used to address a close friend, among men.

"O.K. da, let's write down all our addresses," said Ravi.

They managed to find some brown packing paper and a pencil and got to work. It was already six in the evening when they touched land in Nagapattinam. Having handed over the immigration papers they were given, they studied their resources of whatever meagre savings they had plus the plantation's generous ten rupees.

"We do not have enough to waste it on a hotel or a lodge. I suggest we have a simple meal and sleep in the temple tonight," said Kuppu.

All agreed.

"How da can we go home empty handed? I would like to buy some little things for the children, my younger brothers and sisters if not for my parents with whatever is left over after the bus fare," said Arokia.

"We have brought nothing to show from the great land of fortune. All we can do is visit the *mithai* (sweet) shop and buy some sweetmeats," suggested Ravi.

The four of them went looking for an eating shop. They ate rice and mutton curry with *rasam* and *moru*. *Rasam* is a soup made from tamarind and pepper and anglicized as "molugu tawny" literally meaning pepper water in Tamil. *Moru* is buttermilk, a diluted form of yogurt. They could help themselves with as much rice as they wanted. They were indeed hungry. The genuine Indian curry was superb. After the meal they all took a helping of betel leaf and areca nuts to clinch the meal. Talking with mouths full they went looking for the temple. They said their own prayers and stretched out in the precinct with their meagre belongings.

Before they slept Desa said, "There are two important things we have to do. We have to meet the families of Lourdu and Govind. If all the four of us can do it together, that will be good, if not, I will make the effort to go and see them as soon as I can. I am responsible for their deaths."

"You don't have to bear the responsibility alone. We all knew what we were doing and the risks involved," said Kuppu.

The next morning at the bus station they bought different kinds of sweetmeat, *ladu*, *muruku*, *Mysore pak* and *halva*; embraced each other and boarded the different buses or the same bus if it was heading in the same direction.

From the bus station Desa walked home, slowing as he entered his street. Desa's father was sitting on the cement platform outside the house. Catching sight of Desa, he looked hard to ensure it was his son. He got up and walked down to meet him limping as he came along.

"Nadesa, *thamby*, what is this da? You, coming all of a sudden? No letter, no news! Are you alright da, *thamby*?"

Desa embraced his father, "Yes, *anghi*, I am alright. Things didn't turn out as I expected." Tears broke loose from his tear-filled eyes and streamed down his cheeks. They walked home - father's arm over son's shoulder and son's arm around father's back. Before they reached the entrance the mother came running out crying, "Nadesa! What da, Why da have you returned without telling us a word? Come da, come da," touching both his cheeks with the palms of her hand, then drawing them back and placing her knuckles on her temples, bent her palms down cracking her knuckles and kissing her hands. Desa embraced his mother. Both parents ushered Desa through the entrance into the house.

"Let me go and mix some coffee," said his mother rushing off into the kitchen wiping her eyes with the end of the sari that was thrown over the shoulder which she grabbed under her arm. She was too embarrassed to cry in front of the father and son.

"Where did you buy the sweetmeat?" asked the father.

"Oh, something for Kamala and Krish, I bought them in Nagapattinam. Are they in school?"

"Yes, they will be home in an hour. They're going to be surprised to see you."

"How are you managing with their school fees and books?"

"My pension is not enough and your mother makes *vadai* and I sell them at the morning market." *Vadai* is a fried cake made of black gram flour.

Desa said nothing but was feeling bad inside.

"After the first two letters you did not write for so long. You did not send us any money, was something wrong there?"

"Perumal, the *kangany*, cheated us all by withholding our wages and that is why I left. I will look for a job and earn money here. I am very sorry, *anghi*."

"It is all so disappointing, but I am happy you are safe and well."

Mother has been listening from the kitchen. She brought the coffee and some *vadai*. "I never liked that Perumal. He is clever to talk. He was too nice and his words empty. Never mind, *kanna*, you are home safe and that is all I want." *Kanna* literally it means eye, like the apple of my eye.

"During *Thivali* (festival of lights) and *Sivarathri* (the night of Lord Siva, another Hindu festival) he used to come around and distribute sweets to the children, that's how I came to know him, and he would always ask, 'How are the children, Lingam?'" said Desa's father.

"And all the time he has been eyeing the boys and taking note, the cunning rascal," added the mother.

Desa was lost for words. He could not bring himself to tell them the truth. *Maybe, in time I could tell them what happened; for the moment enough said*, he thought.

Kamala and Krish came home.

"*Anna!*" (elder brother), they both acclaimed together rushing to embrace him. He held them both very tightly for a long time and then kissed them both.

"Kamala, you have grown so much into a beautiful girl; and you, Krish, into a handsome young man," said Desa holding them at arms' length. Kamala was sixteen going on to seventeen. Krish was thirteen going on to fourteen. Desa's father, Mahalingam was a railway worker who had to retire early because he had injured his leg. The mother, Jeyaletchumi, was shouldering the burden of the family.

He offered them the sweetmeats he had bought in India. He sensed a slight bit of disappointment in their faces because they would have expected something different from a foreign land.

Suddenly Desa felt a new responsibility to his family forgetting for the time the responsibility that he left behind in the Malayan plantation. He had to make new plans and work out his priorities.

He slept up on the roof. Actually his house had no tiled roof. The roof was a flat cemented top with a low wall surrounding it accessible by a stepladder from inside the house. It served as a common area for hanging clothes to dry and recreation when the weather was pleasant especially in the evenings. Desa used to fly his kite from up here. There were earthen jars to collect rain water when it rained and in the dry season the family members would sleep there.

Gazing up at the stars Desa was wondering what to do with his life. His priority was to get a job and help the family and make up for the lost time and unproductive effort. He had been away for more than a year. He left in January 1936 and now it was May 1937. He was already going to be twenty years old.

Was it a mistake to have opted to go to Malaynadu? Was it entirely wasted? No, it was a learning experience. This defeat will not make me give up. I started something and it remains unfinished. Friends and fellow workers have died because of me. Their families who depended on them are now suffering also because of me. I have to make it up to them just as I have to make it up to my family. Right now my family

comes first. If I found my way back to Malaynadu what could I do?
The planters are big and powerful and now, after years of slavery the
workers are waking up to the reality, becoming conscious and aware of
their rights. How quickly have the events changed my life?

He fell asleep dreaming of rubber tapping. His dream was
wandering in all directions when he suddenly sat up wide awake. He
dreamed that he had been shot but he was dying in his house with
his family members watching him.

In the morning he ate breakfast with the family and saw Kamala
and Krish off to school with their tiffin carriers. Soon after, he left to
look for a job. He went to the railway station hoping for a vacancy.
He was sent to the Railway Department where some of the men
knew his father. They considered his qualification.

"Nadesan Pillay, there are so many young men more qualified
than you, and they too cannot get jobs. Times are bad," said a clerk.

He tried the Public Works Department, Telephone Company,
Municipality, Hospital and even a restaurant for any kind of job
without luck. Two weeks had gone past and he was still unemployed.

On the third week, however, he got lucky. There was just one
vacancy that had to be filled immediately in a bus company and
somehow he had beaten the queue. He just happened to be in
the right place at the right time. Good *karma*, he thought. They
found he had sufficient education to be a bus conductor. His job
description was that he had to get on a bus at a given point on its
route and get off at another point and repeat that with another
bus of the same company and do the same on the return route of
other busses. He was to check the tickets of the passengers that had
numbers on the margins designating the bus-stop points on the
route. He had to familiarise himself with the points and the value
of the ticket. The point numbers determined the stops and the value
of the ticket. Thus, he would know if the passenger had travelled
beyond any point. The ticket vender would have already punched
the number where a passenger had got on the bus. After checking
he would counter punch the ticket for verification. If any passenger
had over travelled he had to order the person off the bus. He was to
report for work on the first of the month. If his work was satisfactory

he would be confirmed in three months.

Desa went home jubilant. The next day he went to the tailor and got fitted for a pair of pants because he had outgrown his school pants. The tailor measured him and then found another pair of pants slightly bigger.

"I will alter this pair of pants, if you will accept it," he said.

"How much nga?" asked Desa.

"Four rupees."

"Can I pay you two rupees now and two later in the month?"

"You are Mahalingam's son, aren't you? You are the one who went off to Malaynadu?"

"Yes, that's right."

"And your name is Nadesan, right?"

"How do you know?"

"It is my job to know everybody around here. Alright, *thamby*, I will have the pants ready in two days time by 3 o'clock in the afternoon."

"Thank you, *aiyiah*."

On the first of June 1937 Desa reported for work. He was initiated into the job by an experienced conductor and he quickly got the hang of it. Weeks went by quickly.

At the end of the month 30 June he got paid twenty five rupees. He settled the tailor, kept five rupees for his expenses and gave the rest, eighteen rupees to his mother.

Chapter 9

Condolences

The death of his friends was still troubling Desa. He was still apprehensive of meeting their families all by himself. He wrote letters to Kuppu, Ravi and Arokia that he planned to visit the family of Lourdu who lived in Pudukottai. Since Kuppu's home was on the way to Pudukottai from Trichy, he asked Ravi and Arokia if they would join him at Kuppu's house so that nobody had to travel too far. From there they could all go to Pudukottai. Desa suggested the Sunday after the next, 14 July. In a week he received replies from all of them. They could all make it and Kuppu welcomed them all to his house.

They were so happy to see each other again and they exchanged notes. Arokia and Kuppu were working on the family farms growing rice. Ravi was helping his father in the oil mill churning out gingelly oil. Desa explained his job as a bus conductor. Kuppu's mother had prepared a nice meal of chicken curry and rice. Desa had brought a tin of Marie biscuits for Lourdu's family; Ravi, a bottle of gingelly oil; Arokia, six home grown corn cobs; and Kuppu, a small bag of rice. They had spontaneously brought gifts because it was customary that you never visited empty-handed. They discussed how to explain what had happened because by now Lourdu's family would have already received news of his death. They insisted that Desa not take all the blame.

In the afternoon they took the bus to Pudukottai. They had no address, so they had to ask around. They went to the obvious place, the barber shop. They had to take another bus because it was on the outskirts of Puddukottai, a place called Kurinji Nagar.

They easily found the house. At the entrance they were met by a middle-aged man, Lourdu's father.

Desa brought the palms of both hands together, bowed his head, saying, "*Vanakam* (greetings), *Aiyiah*. We are friends of Lourdusamy."

"Is that so? Well?"

"We have come to pay our respects because we were all working with Lourdu in Malaynadu,"

"If that's the case, come nga in."

They all left the gifts on the floor near the entrance.

The mother appeared, "Who are these people?"

"They are Lourdu's friends who had worked with him in Malaynadu," the father told the mother.

"What do they want? They are alive and our son is no more. May God curse that Malaynadu."

The parents were talking to them by addressing each other.

Then Desa said, "Your son, Lourdu, was very brave. He gave his life to bring justice to our people there. He will always be remembered by the people suffering and working there."

"We are also suffering here. He was our only son." She began to cry.

"Alright, *ammah*, fate has struck our head. Let us hear what these men have to say," said the father.

She wiped the tears with her sari and sat down on the floor.

Desa began, "We all were recruited by Perumal, the *kangany*. He played us out, cheated us and did not give us proper wages. All the people there were and still are suffering at the hands of estate *kiranies* who take orders from the *velekaran*. This has been going on for a long time. We petitioned the manager and asked for higher wages and other things. He refused and we went on strike. The *velekaran* with Punjabi Police shot us. Six were dead including Lourdu and Govindaraj from Namakkal."

"We tried to escape but they hunted us down," said Arokia, "Kupu, here was shot in the leg and Desa was shot in the arm."

"They jailed us and punished us before sending us home with nothing," said Kuppu.

"The *velekaran* rules not only India but also Malaynadu. They have done similar things here too, killing thousands of Indians with their rifles and machine guns. How long are we fated to be under their rule? Ghandiji has been travelling up and down the country, but the brutality of colonial rule has not ceased," said Lourdu's father.

"*Aiyiah,* can we ask you your name?" asked Desa.

"My name is Anthonisamy. Your names?"

They each introduced themselves and the *vur* they came from.

"How did you receive news about Lourdu?" asked Ravi.

"One of his close friends from our same street went with him. He wrote back. He said that they should never have gone on strike. They failed and are worse off than before. He also said that *kangany* Perumal is taking revenge on them," said the mother.

The four of them looked at each other, but said nothing.

"We are terribly sorry for what had happened. Lourdu was a very good friend. He stood bravely against the oppressor of our people. We know he is a great loss to you but you can be proud of him as we are proud of him," spoken by Kuppu.

They took leave of Lourdu's parents who thanked them for the gifts.

"Well, that went alright," said Desa, on the way to the bus station.

"We have to visit the family of Govind next," said Kuppu.

"Since Govind's family lives in Namakkal, just north of Trichy, you could all come to my place and we could go from there," invited Desa.

They all agreed on next Sunday. At Kiranur, Kuppu invited everyone to spend the night at his place. Desa said he was working the next day. Ravi had to start early too the next day because a new shipment of sesame seed would be arriving. Arokia, however, agreed to stay the night.

***

On the way back Desa was reading the local newspaper in the bus. The bold headline on the front page caught his attention. "**Massive strikes in Calcutta, Madras, Bombay and Kanpur.**" Desa read on: It began with the textile mill workers in Bombay where the proletariat staged a general strike. Police shot down workers in

Bombay, Kanpur and Madras. Congress ministries, instead of supporting the workers intervened against the strikers defending the *zamindari*, the landlords. Peasant leader Swami Sahajanand, a Congress Socialist, denounced Congress as a tool of the landlords, and quit.

The same thing is happening here as in Malaynadu, reflected Desa. Malaynadu is only an extension of the British rule in India. The saddest thing is that the front-liners of oppression are our very own people. I must find out more of what is happening here in India.

After work the next day Desa went to the bookshop and the library to browse through old newspapers and magazine articles. He discovered a number of movements gaining momentum in the form of non-cooperation, civil disobedience, peasant and working class movements and revolutionary movements. The Communist Party of India and the Socialist groups within Congress were talking about the economic emancipation of the masses along with the importance of the struggle for independence. All these struggles were not new and yet through his school years he had no political awareness at all. He read about the Rowlatt Act, known as the Black Act, which authorised the government to imprison any person without trial. The people rose up in protest against the Act in the notorious incident known as the *Jallianwala Bagh*. It took place in Amritsar on 13 April 1919. He realised that he was only one year old then. A peaceful crowd of protesters was cordoned off by a unit of the British army that opened fire on them. Literally thousands were killed and wounded. Now he remembered that this was the incident that Lourdu's father was referring to. He was able to accept it with more resignation than the mother.

What we experienced in Malaynadu was just a repetition of this on a smaller scale, reflected Desa. He borrowed some books to go home and read.

***

"*Ammah*," said Desa, "on Sunday some of my friends who went to Malaynadu with me are coming to the house. Then we are going to Namakkal to visit the family of another friend who died in Malaynadu."

"Oh, how did he die? Was he sick?"

"No, it was a very bad accident. There will be three of them coming. Can you prepare a meal for us? Can, ma?"

"Ah," she hesitated and then said, "Yes."

"Tomorrow morning I will go to the market and buy some mutton for the curry."

She smiled, "What time are they coming nga?"

"They should be here by noon time."

"Have you told your father, *appa*?" *Appa* means father, but also used to address the son.

"I will tell *anghi* tonight, *ammah*."

That was settled. They would have to go through the same routine as in Lourdu's house. They arrived with their usual gifts and also a little extra for Desa's family. They were introduced to Desa's parents.

Desa called Kamala and Krish, "This is my sister Kamala doing her standard eight now." They couldn't take their eyes off the budding beauty dressed in a half-sari over a baggy skirt.

"Krish is cricketer in school. He is in standard six." They exchanged small talk.

Lingam asked them the circumstance of Govindaraj's death.

Desa quickly responded, "It was a bad accident. He was doing upper tapping on top of a ladder. He fell down and hit his head, bleeding badly. By the time we brought him back to the estate office, he was gone."

The others immediately picked up the cue.

After a sumptuous meal of mutton curry and rice they left for Namakkal. Desa had already purchased the bus tickets, so they caught the bus on its way to Namakkal instead of going to the bus station. Govind's place was in Singilipatti, south of Namakkal so they had to take another bus and backtrack.

The reception by Govind's parents was somewhat different. They were sad, angry and bitter at what had happened. When they heard who these men were they were ready to chase them all out of the house. They had been informed of Govind's death by letter from Perumal. He blamed the leaders of the strike especially

Desa for disobeying his orders. Govind, a good worker, had been brainwashed by Desa to stand in front and face the fire while he and the others stood back and escaped.

Kuppu said, "Would you like to hear our side of the story?"

"I am not interested to hear what you have to say. We have lost Govinda, all because of you. And now you dare come to the house," said Maniam, Govind's father.

"Govind was our friend and we were like brothers; we are sad that we lost him," said Ravi.

"Govind was brave; he was a hero of the people there," added Arokia.

"What you heard from Perumal is not true. He is a liar. It is because of him that we had to come back. It is also because of him that Govind is dead. He's working with the *velekaran* against us. Govind did not send you money because Perumal had cheated all of us. He held back our wages which were very low. It was not enough for our own food. All the workers there, and all of them from our districts here, are suffering like slaves," said Desa.

"We petitioned for better wages and better living conditions. They refused and we all agreed to go on strike. They shot us and six were killed, Govind among them," said Kuppu.

"We came to pay our respects and say sorry for what had happened."

"If Perumal ever showed up here again I will hit him with the slipper," said Maniam. With those words they knew that Govind's family had accepted their version of what had happened. The family had also known of Sokalingam whose family lived not far away.

"We also heard that Sokalingam ... was he also with you all?"

"Yes."

"He too had died. They found his torn clothes in the jungle. They say he was eaten by a tiger," said Maniam.

"*Aioo, Kadavule!*" said Akokia, "He was one of those who ran away and they never found him."

Desa and Kuppu looked at each other. It could easily have been one of them.

"Maybe we could go and visit his family also," said Desa. "We still have time. How far is it?" asked Desa.

"It is within an hour if you take the bus," said Maniam. "Shall we go?" said Desa looking at the others.

With unanimous agreement, they said farewell to Govind's parents.

In Sokalingam's house they extended their sympathy and did not elaborate on the strike action about which they were rather vague. They had accepted his death as the hazardous circumstance of his work and it was fated. They paid their respects and left.

They went back to Trichy and dispersed from there.

Chapter 10

Romance

Desa got into the routine of work and reading material on Indian immigration. In the library he picked up Dostoevsky's *Poor Folk and the Gambler* translated in Tamil and some literature on socialism. In three months his job was confirmed. He was put on a different route on buses that plied between Palakarai and Trichy Junction. It suited him fine because he lived in Palakarai.

He noticed a particular passenger who regularly got on the bus in the morning going south towards Trichy Junction and back again in the evening. She was an attractive young girl who seemed to deliberately avoid looking at him. He did his job punching her ticket which she kept tied inside a knot at her sari's end.

One morning while he waited, she undid the knot at her sari's end, took out her ticket to hand it to him when it fell to the floor. They both bent down to pick it up when their heads touched. Both apologised. He punched the ticket and handed it to her. She bowed her head and turned to look out of the window. Desa noticed that she was on the same bus every morning, seated most often on the same window seat. On the return bus each evening she would be there again. When he looked at her she would quickly turn and look out of the window. She tried not to meet his eyes when she passed the ticket. On days when she did not show up he found himself looking out of the bus' window for her at the bus stop. He began thinking about her more often. She looked nice, intelligent, long black hair combed back parted in the middle, a tinge of homemade *kajal* (a form of homemade eye makeup) on her eyes and light powder on the face and apart from the black *pottu* (a dot in the centre of the forehead), no other make-up.

His interest in her was building up and he made up his mind to break the silence and talk to her. He couldn't just do that on the bus so he found a way. He knew at which bus stop she waited. He had the choice of where he could get on and off the bus. He timed it such that he was at the bus stop before her. He thought he noticed a blush on her dark complexion when she saw him.

"Hello, I'm Nadesan. We see each other every day, twice a day in fact, and I never get a chance to talk to you. Where do you travel to?" asked Desa.

She hesitated and said, "I work at the hospital."

"Are you a nurse?"

"Not yet, I'm a trainee nurse."

"May I know your name?"

"My name is Janeki."

"Where do you live?"

Before she could answer the bus pulled up. Desa got in after all the passengers.

At home that night he tried to read, "The national movement is now on a firm footing with all sections of the masses participating in the struggle," but his thoughts kept going back to Janeki.

Desa's mother approached her husband, offered him a tumbler of tea and sat beside him on the platform.

"Here nga, our son is already twenty and we should be looking for a bride for him. What do you think?" she began.

"Jeya, what's the hurry di? He has just started work and has just been confirmed. Let him become more stable. If he has a wife we will have another mouth to feed. Kamala and Krish have not finished school yet. Soon you will be looking for a husband for Kamala."

"There is already talk of Kamala coming of age but there is more interest in Desa. Just the other day I was approached by the uncle of the girl who lives on the third street. He was enquiring about Desa's age and job and salary. She is the daughter of Perianayagam of our caste. She has only studied up to standard three but a homely girl good in housekeeping. I told him I will talk with you first."

"No, Jeya, leave it for the time being. Just tell him Desa is not ready yet."

"As you say nga."

They had no inclination at all that their son was developing an interest in a girl all on his own initiative.

***

Janaki lived with her family near the Catholic bishop's house from where she walked a short distance to Our Lady's Cathedral to catch the bus. Desa was always anxious as his bus approached the bus stop. That day she was wearing a green sari exposing her midriff. He waited until she had bought her ticket before he started the rounds of checking tickets starting from the back. When he came to her they both smiled and said nothing. That made Desa's day.

After work Desa went past Trichy Junction to the District Central Library to look for more reading material. Mahatma Ghandi was already commanding a huge following from all over the country. The second most prominent figure was Jawaharlal Nehru who for the third time was elected president of the Congress. He too toured the length and breadth of the country. In his speeches he propagated the ideas of socialism and declared that political freedom would become meaningful only if it led to the economic emancipation of the masses and would therefore be followed by the establishment of a socialist society. Desa committed to memory the words of Nehru:

> "I am a socialist and a republican. I am convinced that the only key to the solution of the world's problems and of India's problems lies in socialism ... That means the ending of private property and the replacement of the present profit system by a higher ideal of cooperative service ... I see no way of ending the poverty, the vast unemployment, the degradation, and the subjection of the Indian people except through socialism."

Desa was inspired by these words.

Mahatma Gandhi's - his real name, Mohandas Karamchand Gandhi - form of struggle was non-cooperation and *satyagraha*, a technique of resistance to tyranny through mass civil disobedience whose methodology was founded upon *ahimsa* or total non-violence. This struggle had claimed many Indian lives. Gandhi actually started off fighting for the rights of immigrant Indians in South Africa. Desa read up all he could of Gandhi's activities in South Africa and drew parallelisms to what he had started in Malaya. Gandhi, with a stubborn streak, began to challenge the system and rock the boat. From both Gandhi and Nehru, Desa drew great inspiration. He was torn between staying in India, joining the national movements to struggle for *Swaraj* and going back to struggle with his people in the Malayan plantations. He was beginning to feel a pull towards the former because of his feelings for Janeki. If he were to put his roots here then he would join the fight for India's independence. If it did not work out with Janaki, which was only in its embryonic stage now and it might or might not work out, then he would go back to Malaya.

Before he went to sleep Desa wrote a note, actually he rewrote it four times till it was finalized:

Dear Janeki,

I would like to meet you and spend some time with you. On Sunday could you come to the same bus stop at the same time as usual and wait on the other side of the road and we can take the bus and go in the direction towards Teppakulam? If yes, can you give me an indication?

Desa

He folded the piece of paper to the size of a bus ticket.

The next day as he returned her ticket after punching it he slipped her the note together with the ticket.

The next two days she kept looking out the window and there was no indication at all that she had even looked at the note. He concluded that she was not in the least bit interested. The third day it was still the same.

✳✳✳

After she received the note Janeki told her mother about it and she wanted to know all the details of how this happened. Who is he?

What's his caste? What's his name? Where does he live? How does he look? How does he dress? What work does he do? Why does he travel with you in same the bus? Did he speak to you? Did you speak to him? She went on and on. Secretly she was rather happy.

"*Ammah*, his name is Nadesan and he is the bus conductor. I don't know anything else about him. I noticed that he has been looking at me but I did not encourage him. He is interested in me. We just said hello at the bus stop."

"You don't know anything about him di, and you want to go out with him?"

"How else can I get to know him, if I don't have the opportunity to talk to him?"

"I have to discuss this with your father."

That very night there was a family discussion. Her elder sister was also there. The father was non-committal.

The mother, whose name is Dhanam, said, "We have to make enquiries, nga, about him. I will get my brother to find out. We know his name and the bus company he works for. And we will talk again.

"*Ammahdi*, how do you feel about him?" asked her father, Kaliaperumal. Ammahdi is same as *ammah*, but a more loving way of addressing, especially, a girl who is not yet a mother.

"He seems a nice man and he likes me. I am not sure how I feel about him yet."

"Alright, we must know more about his character."

It took two days before her uncle, Gopal, came with some news.

"Nadesan has been working with the bus company for only three month. He is from Palakarai, the son of Mahalingam Pillay who used to work in the railways. They are Pillayars, a respected family in Palakarai. He finished his standard nine when he went to Malaynadu to work. Very suddenly he came back within two years. There is no criminal record on him that we know of here."

"I think Janeki should go, she can take care of herself," said her sister Susila.

"Where do you plan to go on Sunday?" asked Kaliaperumal.

"He mentioned Teppakulam."

"Alright, as long as you remain in the public place."

Janeki was excited and the two sisters retired to talk at great length about this new venture.

It was Friday and Desa gave up hope that she will ever respond. He casually collected her ticket but felt there was a note with it. Desa pocketed it and looked at it only after he had alighted from the bus. The note simply said, *I will be waiting.*

Desa was elated. Instead of going home he went straight to the barbers and had his hair cut with a clean shave. At home he set aside a clean *veshti* and *juppa,* the upper garment. He was excited to be taking a girl out. He had already planned his day, his first date.

On Sunday Desa bought a large packet of *mixture,* an assortment of nuts and muruku prepared with spice; often pronounced as "micher", and went early to the bus stop and waited for only ten minutes which appeared like ten hours to him. He spotted her. She crossed the road and came towards him somewhat shy and nervous. Over a gripping white bodice with laced sleeves she wore a purple sari. Grabbing the end of her sari at her back she brought it forward and wrapped it around her outlining the curves of her body. She wore a string of jasmine flowers in her plaited hair.

"Morning *vanakam,* are you well?" Asked Desa

"I am well, you?" she tilted her head with a tiny black *pottu* on her forehead.

"I am very well and so happy to see you. This is what I have planned to do. We will go to Teppakulam, have lunch, climb the Fort Rock and visit the Thayumanavar temple. Does that sound alright to you?"

"That will be very nice."

A bus arrived.

"Not that bus; it goes in a different direction. We will take the one to Teppakulam," pointed out Desa.

On the bus they sat on different seats across the aisle because of sex segregation. They didn't mind; it was the accepted thing. At Teppakulam they strolled along the rectangle shaded by big leafy trees. Vendors were selling mangos, peanuts, soda water and aerated drinks or coloured water. The vendor, a young boy was shouting, "Kalar, Kalar." Desa opened his newspaper packet of mixture and offered her some.

"How long is your nurse's training course?" asked Desa.

"Three years and I'm doing second year."

"What do you plan to do after that?"

"Carry on working at the hospital."

"Do you like nursing? People think it is a dirty job handling sick people and not very prospective when it comes to match making."

"Do you think it is a dirty job?"

"Not at all. I think it is a very noble job caring for sick people and being prepared to get your hands dirty for them."

"Do you think your parents will object to you seeing me?"

"They don't know that I am seeing you. I have a feeling that they might have other plans for me."

"Can we sit down for a while," she said spotting a bench.

They sat not too close to each other but close enough. They talked about their families. She had one brother and three sisters. The brother who is older than her was working out of town and her sisters, the one older than her stayed at home while the two younger ones were schooling. Her father was working as a sorting clerk at the post office.

He told her of Malaya without mentioning anything about the strike action and its consequences.

After completing the circuit around the tank they sat at a restaurant looking across the lake or tank in view of the island shrine in the middle of it with the rising Rockfort behind it. They ate *puri* with potatoes. *Puri* is a dough of flour flattened and deep fried in ghee. Then they took a walk across the road, about 200 meters to the Rockfort. The rock itself, one of the oldest in the world is about 3 billion years old and on top of the rock, 83 meters high is a temple dedicated to Lord Ganesh, built in the 7th century. At the bottom of the rock is the Thayumanavar temple where Shiva came in the guise of a mother. Shiva was worshipped by the demon ruler Tirisiran from whom Triruchirappalli gets its name.

They started ascending the steep steps carved on the rock. The fort itself with solid walls sat on the rock. On reaching the top they were greeted with a stunning view of Trichy.

"Over there is Srirangam, and the river branching out must be the Kollidam," said Desa.

"Kaveri river looks so beautiful from here," said Janeki.

They sat down with a strong breeze blowing and just enjoyed the view.

As they climbed down Desa held her hand in support. The first time they touched and Desa felt an electric current go through his arm and into his body to his heart, a feeling he had never before experienced. In the centre of the Thayumanavar temple was a massive *Sivalingam*, symbol of the male creative energy associated with Siva, situated on the *Yoni*, symbol of the female creative energy associated with the goddess of Shakti. The coupling agents graphically symbolize the source of life, at the threshold of which, Desa and Janeki stood holding hands. As they went down, Janeki, almost missing a step, reached out and put her hand on Desa's upper arm. He flinched and pulled away.

"What's wrong?" asked Janeki.

"Oh, nothing; I also almost lost my balance too," lied Desa. The bullet wound in his arm was still hurting. He always wore a long sleeved shirt.

They took the bus back. He went all the way to her bus stop and saw her off there not attempting to walk her to her house. That might come later. He took the bus back to Palakarai.

His mother was cooking in the kitchen. "Where did you go today? It is not your working day."

"I met a girl, *ammah*."

"Oh, who is she?"

"Her name is Janeki. We went on a little trip to Teppakulam, Fort Rock and to the Thayumanavar temple.

"You know *appa*, there are already people enquiring about you and there you go looking for one of your own. Well, we have to know more about her and the family background. Your father thinks you are not ready yet for marriage."

"I don't know if I am either. I've only just met this girl and I like her very much." He was glad that it was no longer a secret.

Desa continued to read. After reading about Gandhi's exploits in

South Africa, he looked into the situation of colonial Malaya. He was able to gather some documentation from the immigration archives in the library. He found that all real legislative, executive and even judicial powers lay in the hands of a Resident appointed by the British. Through the gullible Malay rulers they were able to acquire huge amounts of land either on long term lease or cash purchase. About two million acres of land were under rubber plantations. The government offered loans on very easy terms to British buyers. British capitalists were making fortunes with companies paying dividends of over 200 per cent. The huge profits were made possible through depressed wages paid to the plantation workers most of whom were from the Madras Presidency which was a fertile recruiting ground. Here at that time there was frequent drought and famine. The British Raj imposed huge taxes resulting in poverty and indebtedness. Recruitment was an alternative to starvation which was by and large still the case.

Until 1912 Indians were recruited under indenture. Recruiting firms, through agents, offered cash advances to those who put their thumbprints to an indenture agreement which bound the worker to a single employer for a fixed time with a fixed wage. The cash advance was a charge against money earned. So he had to work off his debt. The indenture system was replaced by free immigration through a *kangany*. The agent was replaced by the *kangany*, otherwise the system remained much the same. The Indian National Congress took an interest in the employment of Indians abroad and appointed an Agent of the Government of India to supervise wages. However, there was little or no change in the wages of the workers. During the Depression when the price of rubber fell, planters dismissed workers and hundreds were repatriated.

The Chinese were recruited on the "credit ticket" system which obliged them to work for the ticket purchaser - a labour contractor who would lodge them in *kongsi* houses. *Kongsi* is a clan-hall, a place where the Chinese lived together. The Chinese *coolies* would work under his supervision and he would pay them. The estate management would have no direct contact with them. The Chinese, under this contract system, made up one third of the plantation workforce. Also exploited by the contractors, they went on strike in 1937.

Desa thought back on how well the Chinese had organized themselves and could prolong a strike for a month while he could not hold his men for the duration of one morning.

My work there is not finished yet. I raised the hope of the people and let them down. They will never rise again without proper organization. Perhaps I should drop my dream of Janeki. She was rather aloof today and did not say very much about herself. Is she really interested in me? Or is she merely testing the waters. I have to know her feelings for me and the sooner the better. Should I discuss Malaynadu with her and let her know my desire to go back there. It is only fair that she knows.

His work was becoming a routine if not for seeing Janeki twice a day. On Sundays he would try to spend time with her. He could not bring himself to tell her that he planned to return to Malaya although he spoke about his sojourn in Malaya again leaving out the details of the strike action. They were growing fond of each other's company. Desa was being drawn into a more serious relationship. Having made a public demonstration of their friendship or courtship it would be very embarrassing and difficult to break it off especially for the girl because her public record would be tainted in relation to other future match-making efforts. Courtship, in general, was never encouraged. Most couples met only on engagement day. Desa and Janeki broke this primary ground rule even before their parents could object. The families had gathered sufficient background information about the two of them. It only remained to confirm each other's feelings.

One Sunday when they met to have a meal, Janeki asked,

"Desa, have you had any proposals before?"

"No, have you?"

"There were some enquiries and approaches but they got no further. Were you in love with any girls before?"

"No, you are my first girl friend."

"Are you prepared to get married?"

"I was going to ask you the same thing."

They both laughed. He held her hand and looked into her eyes.

"I love you. If I ask you to marry me will you agree?"

She squeezed his hand with her other hand and said, "Yes."

After a few weeks the parents on both sides came to know of their friendship and desires. Having gathered sufficient information from the two lovebirds the families dispensed with the usual procedure of first making third party enquiries. Before arranging a face to face meeting both families consulted their respective horoscope matching to ascertain compatibility. They both passed the tests with flying colours. For the face to face meeting, Desa's family members visited Janeki's family and were cordially greeted.

"Come nga, come nga, come inside and sit down nga," Janeki's mother welcomed the guests.

"Susila, come *ammah*, do the needful."

Janeki's sister, Susila, offered a tray of flowers, betel leaves, nuts, bananas, a coconut and a ring. Her brother, Subranamiam, who had come home for the occasion, applied *tilak* (a small circular mark on the forehead) with *santhanam* (sandalwood paste) and *kungkumum* (saffron powder or red turmeric powder) on Desa's forehead and put a garland around his neck and a ring on his finger. Susila performed the *arathi*. Desa's family also presented a tray with similar items together with a sari, a gold chain and glass bangles. A coconut was broken.

Janeki's uncle, Gopal, was the middleman who negotiated the agreement between the couple's parents. Desa's father formally asked Janeki's father for Janeki's hand in marriage to his son Desa. Kaliaperumal consented by saying, "The *mapillay* (bridegroom) is ours, nga." And Mahalingam responded, "The *ponn* (bride) is ours, nga," after the gift tray was offered and accepted by Janeki. This served as the engagement. An engagememt is usually a foregone conclusion that marriage will follow. The agreement was made and they went on to discuss the wedding date.

On a propitious day, 12 December 1937 Desa and Janeki were married. Kuppu, Arokia and Ravi came to grace the occasion. It all happened so quickly. She became part of the family; Kamala and Krish accepting her as *akka*, an older sister. In the mornings they both took the bus together with her.

Desa began to talk to her more and more about Malaya and the plight of the workers there. Although he was hesitant to reveal to her his desire to return to Malaya, she began to get the message.

The Indian newspapers carried news on Nehru's visit to Malaya. On his tour of Malaya, Nehru encouraged the CIAM to extend its political efforts to the labouring mass of Indians in Malaya. He argued that the Indian labourers needed trade unions and deserved better education and wages equal to those of the Chinese. He urged the Indians to become part of the Indian nationalist movement, saying, "On India's freedom depends your status and the protection of your interests and the place you occupy in the world." At the same time he was questioning why the Indians were not considered sons of the soil and not granted full citizenship rights in Malaya. Nehru's appearance heightened nationalist awareness but did little to provide any clout against the Malayan government or the planters to improve the living conditions of the workers.

***

Desa felt that if he seriously wanted to go back to Malaya and take up the cause of the plantation workers there, he had to know the whole historical background of the immigrant labour and the wage struggle in Malaya. He went to look for sixty year old Sivakumaran who lived on the back street to talk to him.

"Sivakuamaran, *aiyiah*, are you well? I am Nadesan, from the next street, son of Mahalingam," said Desa.

"Ah, yes, *thamby*, come, sit. I am alright, except for this bad cough. I heard you went to Malaynadu to work?"

"Yes, and that is what I came to talk to you about because you had also been there to work."

"That was years ago. I went to Malaynadu alone with other men and women but no family members. I worked in a sugarcane plantation in Province Wellesley. I was bonded to work for five years and was denied the right to change employment or employer, much as I would have liked to. We worked all day in the hot sun. It was very hard and like many others I went down with malaria. I spent several days in a quarantined area separated from the main *coolie* line with other malaria victims. The dresser came everyday and gave us medicine. Wages never increased and we were paid seven cents a day to buy rice. After that I could not work anymore. Many of the workers were being retrenched and I was told to pack up and go home. I was given six dollars to take the boat back. When I got home, there was no more money left. My father scolded me for coming home empty handed and accused me of squandering my earnings."

Desa found that familiar but his parents were more understanding. He gathered all the reading material he could and began to pour over them paying particular attention to wages. The worker, he gathered, was completely and utterly inarticulate in arriving at a suitable wage agreement through negotiation. Under the indenture system, wages were fixed by Indian law. In 1884 the Indian Immigration Ordinance drew up guidelines to safeguard some of the interests of indentured labour but the act was ill administered in spite of the fact that the Government of India had appointed, in the same year, the first Indian Immigration Agent. In the same year the first attempt to fix wages was made by the Straits Settlement Ordinance. It stipulated rates for three years contracts. Adult males were paid 12 cents a day for the first year, 14 cents for subsequent years; for females and under twelve years old, 8 cents per day for the first year and 10 cents for subsequent years. The work was for only six days per week and no more than nine hours a day and not more than six hours could be consecutive. If the labourer worked for six full days he was entitled to the seventh day's pay without working. Food was to be provided on working days by the employers free of charge.

"*Wow, half a century ago the workers were given such a good deal. The companies and employers must have become very greedy since then,*" thought Desa.

Even then in 1890 a commission was appointed to investigate labour conditions in order to recommend improvements. In 1892 an ordinance was passed to improve the working conditions. The planters, however, opposed this ordinance and it was never brought into operation.

In 1896 another Labour Commission was appointed which

endorsed the recommendations of the earlier commission. An act was passed in the Straits Settlement Legislature to safeguard the rights of Indian labour. This too was never brought into operation.

The thirst for profits was getting into the heads of the companies in London.

The Act of 1899 increased the minimum wage of indentured labour and made it the responsibility of employers to provide housing, medical facilities and sanitary arrangements. They must also allow the inspection of places of employment. This was made necessary because of the alarmingly high mortality rate in indentured labour.

The Act of 1904 further improved wages and conditions of indentured labour.

Desa began to read between the lines and concluded, *All this was brought about not by any struggle by the workforce. The workers remained docile and subservient. It was motivated more by a desire to ease the flow of labour than by a desire for justice. It was more important to have the Acts in the statute book for good relations with the Indian Government than to enforce them.*

In 1907 an Indian Immigration Committee was formed to look into wages and conditions. In 1911 a Labour Department was formed and enforcement measures were undertaken. The 1912 Labour Code brought together all labour laws. The planters criticised the penal sanctions.

In 1913 the Colonial Office took steps to abolish the indentured labour contracts. When free labour fully replaced indentured labour there was no statutory control of wages.

Although indentured labour was dehumanising, free labour opened the door for abuse. What appeared good on paper was not the case in reality.

In 1920 the Planters Association appointed a committee known as the General Labour Committee which recommended a minimum wage to be fixed, 50 cents per day for males and 40 cents for females.

After seventeen years this is what we have been asking for without taking inflation into account. We even calculated the price of every food item in 1937. Conditions fluctuated in the plantations for better or for worse depending on the fluctuations of the stock market in London.

In 1922 an Agent of the Government of India in Malaya was appointed to look after the welfare of the Indian immigrants. Stationed in Kuala Lumpur with the right to visit and inspect plantations, he sent annual reports on the conditions under which these people lived and worked. The Indian Government looked into the wages, cost of living, housing and health facilities of the Indians. A standard wage in place of the minimum wage was accepted by the Malayan Government and the Indian Immigration Committee was authorized to prescribe standard rates. It defined two different standard wage structures for two types of areas. Well located and healthy areas were considered key areas deserving lower rates and inaccessible interior areas considered non-key areas deserving higher rates. In 1924 in key areas males were given 35 cents and females 27 cents.

Standard wages under so-called free labour actually lowered the 1920 wages which was supposed to replace the minimum wage. Evidently politics were at play.

In 1925 they were raised to 40 and 30 cents; in 1927, 50 and 40 cents.

This came back to the 1920 rates.

The non-key areas in 1927 commanded 58 and 46 cents.

The Code of 1923 replaced the Code of 1912 by making provisions for repatriation of Indian labourers within one year of arrival for reasons of ill health or unjust treatment by employers. The labourer could not be held to make contracts of more than one month's duration. The minimum age of child labour was ten. The Controller of Labour's powers were now conferred on the Agent of the Government of India, who was to be Resident in Malaya. He could enter and inspect places, and order the establishment and maintenance of nurseries and schools for the children of labourers. The employers were required to provide maternity allowances for female employees.

In 1927 a further amendment was made to the Code whereby the employers had to set aside a minimum of 1/16 of an acre of estate land for the use of each labourer with dependents living on the estate for food crops and raising livestock. The land had to be cleared and prepared by the employer at his expense.

From information Desa was able to gather from some of the old-timers who had returned that the planters did not like these provisions and did not expect the Labour Department to apply them strictly. In most cases the estate management disregarded them and they remained dead letters. Of course, none of these provisions were ever explained to the illiterate workers.

Then came the Depression (1930 – 1934) when wages were reduced to below official subsistence levels. Employers forced proportionate wages not to fill nine working hours, so the rate dropped to 28 cents for males and 24 cents for females. Also during the Depression surplus labour, of up to 180,000 Indians were repatriated to India.

In 1936, of course, the Sastri Inquiry recommended the restoration of pre-Depression rates of 50 and 40 cents.

Under such pressure from the Government of India, the Planters Association agreed to increase the wages only up to 40 cent for males and 32 cents for females.

These were the wages we were supposed to have been receiving and not in fact receiving when we went on strike.

***

During a night of love making Janeki felt Desa's buttocks. She asked him to turn over and lit the lamp to examine it.

"Why nga have you got such bad scars on your buttocks? She asked.

"Oh it's a long story...," and he began to tell her the whole story in detail.

"So that explains the wound in your arm that you tried to hide at the temple."

Now she began to understand a little bit more on why he had hinted several times that he wanted to go back to Malaya although it sounded like a suicide attempt. Naturally, she did not want him to go.

"You had to go the first time because the family needed the

money and I understand that, *athanh*. Now you have got a good job and in less than one year I will have completed my training and start earning money too. We should have a comfortable life and, may be, children of our own," said Janeki. *Athanh* is son of father's sister, a cousin or brother-in-law, also used as a love expression for a husband.

"My *kannu*, I know," sighed Desa. "My work there is not finished yet." (*Kannu* or *kanna* is the eye like 'the apple of my eye.')

"Do you plan to leave me and go alone?"

"I have thought about both of us going, but it will be dangerous for you. I will have to be very careful how I move around."

"Please don't go."

"Let's leave it for now and give more thought to it," said Desa bringing this conversation to a close.

They seldom brought up this subject because it caused some tension in their relationship. Eventually Janeki spoke to Kamala about Desa's intention of returning to Malaya and it became an open family discussion. Everyone was against it. Desa dropped the subject for a while and in the New Year he spoke to Janeki again.

Chapter 11

Return to Malaya

They were on the "roof" of the house.

"I've been thinking. You have slightly less than a year to finish your training. You should finish your training. I would like to go to Malaynadu and make one more effort to improve the living conditions of the workers there and get them to negotiate for better wages. I will be back by the time you finish your training," said Desa.

She remained silent, she was angry.

"You have not been honest with me. All the time you had planned to go back even when you asked me to marry you. If you had told me of your plan I would not have married you," tears welling up in her eyes.

"It was my mistake not to have made known my intention. I am sorry."

"If you cannot be honest with me how can I trust you that you will ever come back?"

"I love you and I will come back."

"What if you get shot and killed? I will have to shave my head and remain a widow the rest of my life."

"Please don't say that, *kannu*."

"I might as well jump off this roof now."

She suddenly jumped up, made her way towards the wall when Desa grabbed hold of her. She struggled but he managed to make her sit down and he sat with her on the floor. She was crying.

"I don't know what makes me want to go. I failed the people once and don't want to fail them again."

"It is no longer your problem."

"I started the problem and six people, no seven people are dead including two women. I feel responsible."

"I'm sure there will be others who will stand up for them."

"Here too, the people are rising up against the *velekaran* and dying and giving their lives because they follow Ghandi. We have good leaders and mass support here in India. In Malaynadu there is no proper leadership among our people. The Chinese have good leadership while our people are isolated in small numbers mostly illiterate and unaware of their rights. They are bullied by the British system and the *kiranies*, the black *velekaran*. I can get them to fight for justice. They can earn good money if they learn how to make their demands. This time I promise you and our family that I will send home money, at least to keep Krish in school. Kamala will finish school this year."

Janeki felt that Desa had made up his mind. He was not putting her first in his life. For the first time she doubted his love for her. Is this her fate? Karma? She tried again to dissuade him, "There are prospects of promotion in your job in which you are doing well. The family is financially more stable. You are throwing everything away. What a fool you are!"

Desa broke the news to his family that he had decided to go to Malaya and would return within a year or two. He asked his company director if he could take two years no-pay leave and resume his work when he returned from Malaya. They said no as he had not been working long enough in the company to be eligible for such a privilege. He could re-apply but had to give one month's notice of resignation.

Desa wanted to meet up and discuss his plan with his friends. They did meet up in Kuppu's house. Desa outlined his plan of returning to Malaya and take up the cause where they left off and fight for justice for the rubber workers.

"You can't go back there; they will lock you up again. Knowing them they might even hang you and no one will know," said Kuppu.

"Why do you take the whole responsibility upon your shoulders? There will be other leaders there," said Ravi.

"Yes, those leaders are the Association members who live in

towns and do not really understand the sufferings of the estate people, while we worked and suffered with them," replied Desa.

"It is very noble of you to help them, but you will be risking your life and throwing away everything you have done to build yourself here," said Arokia.

"Desa, be reasonable, you just got married and should be starting a family. How can you leave Janeki behind?" reasoned Kuppu.

"There is something inside me that tells me I must go. Will any of you go with me?"

"My father needs me to take over the oil mill," said Ravi.

"I have to work on the land to make sure we have enough food," said Kuppu.

"You, Arokia?"

"I don't mind going with you but I need time to think about it and talk to my parents."

"I plan to go soon."

"Give me a week."

"Kuppu, I want to ask you a favour. You thought of Janeki, well, can I ask you to look after her? Visit our home when you can. Just make sure she is OK. I plan to be back within two years."

"Yes, but you must also inform Janeki otherwise she will be wondering why I am visiting. And tell her to write to me if she needs anything."

"Thank you very much. I will write to you all and tell you how things develop."

"We think you are making a big mistake da, but if you must go, then you must go."

Five days later Arokia wrote saying he is prepared to go with Desa.

Desa made arrangements for the immigration papers for both of them. He informed the immigration that he and Arokia had been back on leave for the last eight months and were now going back to Malaya to resume work. They were employed in an estate in Malaya.

They showed their previous immigration papers and their tin tickets and were issued new papers. Of course they had to grease the palm of the immigration officer. No cogs would move in India without greasing. They booked the passage on the same Rajula and left Nagapatinam on 20 January 1938.

***

In Penang Desa and Arokia showed their tin tickets, which they had kept, to the immigration as proof of employment and got through. They weren't game to barge into Dolby estate from which they were expelled, so they stopped in Sungei Siput, the nearest town. Desa made enquiries about the situation in the estate and learnt that it had deteriorated very badly. They had arrived at another crisis point. In the second half of last year there was another recession on the US rubber market and its impact was being felt only now in the plantations. The price of rubber had dropped by 30 per cent. Rubber export had been drastically reduced. Now, employers, including Dolby estate management, had arbitrarily cut wages and dismissed workers disregarding opposition from the Labour Department. More and more employers were following this pattern. Even Indian nationals in India were outraged by this.

The Sastri Report had recommended the imposition of a ban on all assisted emigration to Malaya. No action was taken on it. At this time the CIAM took the initiative and sent a telegram to the Indian Government asking for the Sastri ban to be implemented. This was in retaliation to the arbitrary wage cuts and dismissals. There was no immediate action.

Desa decided that now was the time to start mobilising the workers. But first he had to get a job and given this new crisis it was impossible to get a job in any estate. They looked elsewhere and within a month, as their reserve cash was running out, they both found jobs in a coal mine. They were working along with Chinese workers. They registered under different names. There was no need to prove identities. Desa was Subramaniam and Arokia was Ramasamy.

After work Desa tried contacting some workers secretly. On a Sunday, his off day, he slipped into the timber where the tappers were working. He caught sight of Doraisamy, the first estate worker whom Desa met on the first day, and who had explained that the provisions were not for free. He approached him and they renewed acquaintance.

"Doraisamy, *aiyiah*, how are things in the estate?"

"Oh, it's terrible. Wages have been cut to 30 cents and we don't have enough money to buy provisions. Those who are old and weak and partly disabled have been dismissed. Some of us have started planting vegetables while others have gone into town looking for odd jobs. You see we are not trained to do any other work than tap rubber. All we can do is dig the road."

"How is Perumal?"

"He is as arrogant as ever, pushing people around and whipping them."

"How are the families of the people who got shot during the strike?"

"They are managing like the rest of us who are fated to this kind of life; except for your friend Antoine."

"Oh, what happened to him, he is still around is he?"

"Yes, very much so; he is Perumal's second in command. Let me tell you."

Chapter 12

Antoine's Betrayal

Desa pieced together the episode.

On the day of the strike, after the shots were fired the strikers ran helter skelter in all directions into the *coolie* lines or away from the settlement area into the timber. Most were rounded up while a few fled the estate into neighbouring estates. Antoine, as he ran past Perumal's cabin had a second thought. He stopped in his tracks and hid behind the cabin and then eased himself into the cabin. Perumal hardly ever locked his door. Once inside he closed the door latching it from the inside and sat quietly on the floor in a corner. He was right in thinking that nobody would consider searching the *kangany*'s cabin. From the wailing and cursing outside he knew some had been killed. Roberts was issuing commands to his Punjabi troops. The dust settled a little when night fell and the search was called off. Antoine slipped out of the cabin and hid in a dark corner behind the cabin. He heard Perumal return but remained where he was. Perumal fetched some water from the well and bathed himself in an enclosed out-house. Back in his cabin he dried himself, lit some incense, heated up some food, ate it and went to sleep. Antoine also curled himself in the corner outside and went to sleep.

The next day Perumal did not wake up before the crack of dawn since there was no muster and no work. He prepared breakfast for himself. He had his own little kitchen, made himself some coffee and ate some biscuits from a tin and left. Antoine was familiar with Perumal's routine. After waiting a little while longer and before it got too bright Antoine slipped back into the cabin and latched the door. There was some hot water left, though not too hot. He made some coffee, found some remnants of rice in the pot and taking the biscuit tin and the rest he placed them on the floor and sat down so as not to attract any attention from the outside. Scraping what he could from the pot he ate the rice and just a couple of biscuits so they won't be missed. After drinking the coffee he replaced everything as it was and went back to his corner to wait. There were movements outside but not much activity. He knew funeral preparations were underway.

That night Antoine left a note for Perumal saying that if the latter did not report him to the authorities Antoine would do whatever Perumal asked. Furthermore, he had information for Perumal. If it was agreeable, Perumal was to go out and hang his towel on the clothes line. Antoine stood at a safe distance and watched. If Perumal were to go out and call for help he would bolt, and if Perumal did as instructed he would approach Perumal.

Perumal pondered the note for a long time. He went and did his routine chores; had his meal and taking his sweet time went out and hung his towel and returned.

Antoine waited and watched a while longer before approaching the cabin door. He knocked gently.

"Who da is there," said Perumal. "It is Antoine."

"Come da."

They had a long conversation. Antoine told Perumal all the planning done by Desa and Kuppu and others without mentioning the break into his office.

Perumal said, "You go away from the estate, stay away for about two weeks and then come back quietly in the night. We shall see what we can do then."

∗∗∗

Antoine had betrayed the group and can be dangerous now.

"The people still remember what happened and are afraid to do anything, even talk about it. Some of them blame you and others praise you. Now, once again, they wish somebody will come to their assistance, not in the form of resistance but in the form of hand outs," said Doraisamy.

"All our people know is weakness. Do they want to be beggars all their lives? Look, Doraisamy, I came back to help our people to rise up and be human beings with dignity. If you know of some men or women who would be willing to do something to bring a change for a better life, can you gather them somewhere secretly? I would like to meet them. Make sure Antoine does not get to know. When can I meet you again?"

"Next Sunday, same place same time."

"Good, we must keep it a secret."

Desa and Arokia worked with the Chinese in the mine but were free to move about. They met up with Doraisamy again.

"I have got eight people who are not against you and are willing to hear what you have to say," said Doraisamy.

"Where?"

"The school is now practically abandoned. The children, even the young ones, are out working in the timber helping their parents. We can meet at the school."

"When?"

"On Friday. It will have to be late at night, at 10 o'clock."

"I will be there. Thank you and you be careful."

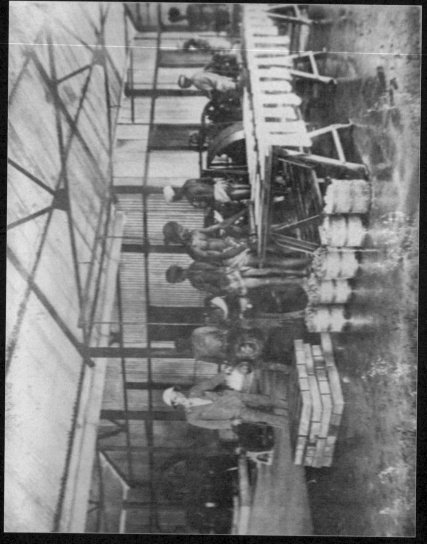

Interior of factory, Midlands Estate, Klang

Chapter 13

Organising Workers

Desa and Arokia met eight men and four women. There were greetings and questions about India. They complained of how bad the situation had become in the estate.

Desa spoke.

"Nobody should know we are back. You have to call me Subramaniam and Arokia is Ramasamy. These are common Indian names. We are like frogs in a well, kept isolated from the outside world. In India there is a ground swell. Ghandi and Nehru are giving the people hope of independence from the *velekaran* raj. They are calling it *Swaraj*. People are openly disobeying the authorities and, of course, they are being punished, but they carry on nevertheless. India wants to be an independent nation. They don't have the armed power of the *velekaran* but they have the power in numbers. They have *makal sakthi*. In the plantations of Malaynadu too we have the numbers but we are kept separated in the woods. We need to communicate with the workers in the other estates.

"Nehru, our leader, was in Malaynadu last year and most of us did not even know about it. He went around the towns and was greeted by huge crowds. He was saying that Indians needed trade unions and equal pay on the same scale as the Chinese. They also needed better education and should stop drinking toddy. He further advised the Indians to be self-reliant, to seek self improvement and not be dependent on others.

"We went on strike last year and failed because we were not united. The Chinese went on strike even before us and did not give up and they got a pay increase and we didn't.

"In December of 1936 Srinivasa Sastri from the Indian National Congress (INC) came here to study our situation and again we knew nothing about it. He recommended that we should get the pre-depression wages of 50 cents and 40 cents. We went on strike not even knowing about this recommendation and yet we did not get it. He also made a second recommendation - a ban on the *kangany* system of assisted emigration. Both the government and the planters have treated these recommendations with total disregard. Now I just hear that the CIAM, whose members are mainly from the Indian Associations in towns and whose business and political interests are more important to them, had sent a telegram to the Indian government. They are asking the Indian Government to implement Sastri's emigration ban. What response the Indian government will give to this request remains to be seen.

"If they impose it then there will be fewer workers and then we may be in a better position to bargain for higher wages. In the meantime we have to start organising our strength not only in Dolby but also in the other estates. Arokia, I mean Ramasamy, and I are now outside the estate and we will get information from the other estates.

"I am sure there is hope. Pass the word around quietly, don't mention our real names. Continue to grow vegetables and rear chicken and goats. Become self-sufficient. We will arrange for another meeting through Doraisamy. Thank you for coming."

The work of Desa and Arokia at the coal mine was purely manual loading of coal onto the open freight wagons of the goods train that ferried coal to the main line. It was hard work but the pay was better than that of the plantation workers. The workforce was predominantly Chinese who were quartered in *kongsis*. The Indian workers were allotted a separate *kongsi*.

Desa was opening his heart out to Arokia and a dozen other Indian workers in the *kongsi* on the pathetic situation of the Indian workers in the plantations. Many of them had opted out of plantations to work at the coal mine.

"The Indian worker in the rubber plantations is the most miserable of all workers in this country. For years and years the

Indians in India have been kept subservient by the *velekaran* to such an extent that we are no longer persons but working tools in the hands of the *velekaran* and the *jamindar*. We bow to their wishes and crawl at their commands. With the shovel of deception they scooped the dregs of Indians and brought them here to work. Here we are faithful and docile taking all the whipping and cursing by both the white and black Europeans without a murmur of protest. As a result we remain miserable.

"Who can we look to, to lift us out of this lowly situation to better our conditions? The CIAM members from the Indian Associations made up of middle class English-speaking Indians, Brahmins, Chettiars, North Indians and Malayalees, and others who draw up nice laws and codes? They stated their aims and objectives as to protect the interest of the Indian community as a whole. What a general statement! They want to co-ordinate the efforts of various Indian associations and other Indian bodies, to try to provide better education for Indian children in Malaynadu and for their higher studies in India. Our estate children don't even have the opportunity to reach secondary level of education. They are only concerned for their own children. They want to negotiate for better shipping facilities between Madras coast port and Malaynadu and to attend to the grievances of the deck and other class passengers while we are only shipped like cargo on the decks. They have also mentioned in passing to fight for better wages and working conditions for Indian labour on estates and elsewhere. But we are not listed among their priorities.

"The planters and the government treat their goals and objectives with disdain. How many of them have ever stepped into an estate? They are more concerned with liaising with the Indian National Congress as though the INC can solve our problems from across the sea. It is the same *velekaran* government that rules both India and Malaynadu and it calls the shots. Nehru is a great leader who calls himself a socialist. He has a large following in India and he is very inspiring but when he came to Malaynadu he did not speak so strongly. He appeared to have merely read out a statement prepared for him by the CIAM. He said that the Indian workers should get wages equal to those of the Chinese and stop the evil of toddy drinking. He wants us to form labour unions, fine, but who is going to come and explain to our simple minded rubber tappers what a union is?

"Look, ngada, at the Chinese workers here at the mine. There are people from outside talking to them about unions and working class struggle. Some say they are from the Communist Party. Maybe we can learn something from them. Learn the methods they use to stir the workers.

"The estate workers need local leaders. We, Ramasamy and I hope to stir the estate workers like what the Chinese are doing here. Some of you might like to join us. If you don't want to get involved, that's alright. Remember we are the same people from the same motherland of India trying to find a better life here. Please keep our plan a secret. If the authorities get to know about it everything will be gone, even our employment here."

One of them said, "Look, whatever you do, do it outside of here. Don't get us involved and ruin our life here. We don't want any trouble."

"We cannot not get involved," said another. "As workers in this mine we have to stand with the Chinese workers who also expect trouble from the authorities. We don't go to their meetings because they speak Chinese. Some of them have spoken to me explaining their plans to do something very big to demand higher wages. They expect us to stand together with them as workers."

"What is your name, brother?" asked Desa.

"My name is Krishnan," he said.

"Ah, my younger brother's name is also Krishnan. Krishnan, why don't you find out more on how they conduct their meetings? Ask your friend to translate what the leaders are saying. We would like to prepare a strong message for our people also. I am sure some of you come from the different estates around here and may have contacts with the people there."

"I used to work in Hartford estate," said one.

Another, "I'm from Worster estate."

There were others from other neighbouring estates. Desa

planned to use these men to make contact with the estate workers to communicate with them. As the days went by he and Arokia learnt more and more of what the Chinese were planning and got some names of people with leadership qualities in the estates.

Both Desa and Arokia met Doraisamy in the timber and discovered that conditions were deteriorating steadily. The manager wants them to work longer hours with less pay. Some of the workers who were too tired to work, added water to their collection of latex. They were caught with the help of Antoine and whipped by no other than *kangany* Perumal. Desa got Doraisamy to arrange days for meetings where he and Arokia would give talks to small groups encouraging them to keep up their efforts to resist quietly. His plan was to lift their morale with examples of the great Tamil heroes in the glorious days of the Tamil kings. As an example he told them stories of the adventures of the Pandian and Chola kings.

"We have come here now as slaves of the *velekaran* to slog for a living; but let us not forget that the Chola raja Rajendra sent a naval expedition to Southeast Asia and overpowered the Malay maritime empire of Sri Vijaya. Chola raja Virarajendra overpowered Ceylon."

He was telling them that a Tamil hero would proudly take the arrow in his chest and not in his back, meaning that a Tamilian would never retreat in battle. He used examples like these to develop their self-esteem to stand up with dignity for their rights.

***

Desa got feedback from other coal mine workers who had made contact with other estate groups. He got the locals there to arrange small group meetings and he would go with Arokia and give them talks. From following Desa on many occasions Arokia had learned the techniques of delivering talks so now when there were two meeting on the same night Arkokia would take on a meeting by himself. They continued to conscientizse the workers on their rights. More and more estates were involved and they developed a method of communication through dispatch riders on bicycles to convey messages. They were planning for a coordinated strike action in tandem with what was developing at the coal mine.

One day the Chinese friend of Krishnan came to meet Desa. Word had got around that the Indians too were planning to go on strike and that the initiative was being taken by Desa and Arokia. This Chinese friend said that the leader who was coming to address them would like to meet them. A meeting was arranged. This individual was a member of the Malayan Communist Party by the name of Ah Kow.

This man explained, using the medium of the Malay language which was the spoken market language known sufficiently by most to communicate basic ideas, the working method of the Communist Party. Their objective was to set up workers' committees at workplaces, whether factories or estates. Their policy was to unite all workers and peasants on the basis of class and not ethnicity using self-determining perspectives, community programmes and guerrilla tactics.

For Desa this was a new approach that widened his own perspective beyond the Tamil community. The Communists were thinking of the country of Malaya which was ethnically and racially divided. Desa's sphere of influence was limited to the estate communities so the bigger picture of cementing class unity, cutting across ethnic divisions was beyond his scope. But he could already see that estate workers were not only Tamils, there were also Telugus and others whose native tongue was not Tamil. He began to understand the broader picture of class struggle that cuts across not only ethnicity and language but also caste boundaries and that the enemy was the class of the *kiranies* and *kanganies*, even though they were of the same ethnic origins, working with the white capitalists.

Desa and Arokia began explaining the principles of class struggle using examples from India where people from the north and south speaking different languages were working together and among the workers, different castes of Indians were also working together not only for better wages and working conditions but also for independence. Nationalism was bringing all the Indians together. He was hoping to widen their vision of the workers' struggle.

"When rubber prices go down the bosses will protect their profit margins and the first thing they will attack is the workers' wages. We have to organize and defend our wages and living conditions.

"Ghandiji was telling the people not to merely agitate for better living wages but also to be part of a mass political action, a national movement. He boosted the power of the peasants and artisans. To unify the movement he used a symbol, the hand spun, hand woven cotton cloth of *khadi*. He urged everyone to boycott British textiles and wear the *khadi*. We also need a symbol and why don't we all start wearing the Ghandi *topi*?" he urged.

They not only started to wear the Ghandi *topi*, the Gandhi cap, white in colour, pointed in front and back with a wide band made of khadi, they even began to fly the tricolour of the Indian national flag.

With these symbols Desa could see the blossoming of their self-esteem which was the fundamental ingredient, the yeast that would make them rise. He also realized that this was going to be a long struggle. He told them, "You nga are not mere tools in the hands of the capitalists. You nga are human beings with dignity. You nga don't have to remove your slippers or get off your bicycle when the *velekaran* passes by. You nga wear your Ghandi *topi* and stand fast."

For weeks now they were meeting workers in all the neighbouring estates and establishing better communication links through the bicycle dispatch riders.

Desa met the leaders of the different estate committees he had established. His strategy was to get the workers to go on strike in stages.

He said, "In your own committees you discuss this plan. Give notice to the management that if your wages were not increased, nobody will work on Sundays. You don't have to assemble and picket. Just stay away. If you group together you will become a target."

In Dolby on the muster before the Sunday they were given a pep talk and warned against stopping work. The management had got wind of some murmurings. But the workers went ahead with stoppage. The *kanganies* and the *kiranies* were frantically trying to round them up for work. There was no work. After a few weeks they stopped work on Saturdays and Sundays. The management couldn't really rally them to work but on working days their tasks were increased to tap more trees, working longer hours. There was no concession to pay increase. Instead those who exhibited signs of leadership were called up and warned. They continued with their work stoppages and some of the committee members were arrested and detained.

***

Meanwhile in India Kuppu visited Janeki and found her restless and depressed. He was keeping his promise to look after the welfare of Janeki in Desa's absence. The only way to help was to provide the only thing within his means. He brought a bag of rice.

"Have you heard any news from Desa?" asked Kuppu.

"Yes, he has sent home some money, but he is not working in the estate. He is working in a coal mine with Chinese workers. He says things are very difficult for the Indian estate workers compared to the Chinese workers who are very active and even militant. They are better paid than the Indian workers. He and Arokia are working quite successfully in organising them, but he says that it is a long struggle which means he is not going to come back soon."

"I took part in one of the demonstrations in Keeranur wearing the *khadi*. The peasants were protesting against the *jamindars* on high rents for land and also calling for independence from the *velekaran*. Please write and tell Desa that I asked about him and Arokia and if you give me his address, I will send a letter to him also."

"He said not to address him as Desa. Both of them have changed their names. Desa is Subramaniam and Arokia is Ramasamy."

"You don't worry about Desa, he is a good leader and he knows how to survive."

"Kuppu, I want to go and join him in Malaynadu."

"It is only six months since he has been away. Give him time to settle down. You have still got your training to finish."

"I don't know; can you help me to make a decision, ma?"

"You are more educated than I am; how can I help you to make a decision?"

"Everybody talks about *Swaraj, Swaraj*, but nothing is really changing here."

"Yes, I know, let me think about it. You take care, Janeki, and write me if you need anything."

"Thank you, you are a good friend."

***

Finally the Indian Government, hearing of the deterioration of the plantation workers' situation in Malaya, took heed of the CIAM's recommendation to halt Indian emigration and imposed it in June 1938. Now the planters began to realize that they could no longer arbitrarily arrest, detain, banish and deport the workers because they could not be readily replaced like before.

On the other hand London was complaining of low output resulting in loss of profit. The rumours of war increased the demand for rubber. Estate workers were made to work overtime to increase the level of production. Soon rubber companies in London were reaping a profit of 250 per cent.

Shortage of labour gave the workers an advantage to make their demands stronger. Eventually, wages for the Indian male rubber tappers were restored to 50 cents and females 40 cents to the 1928 level. This was indeed a victory for the struggle. However, this was not the case in all the estates. In one particular estate wages were raised to 55 cents and 45 cents. It was short-lived. It lasted only four months because the London-based plantation companies exercised a veto on wage fixing. It dropped again and went on like this until the following year.

Desa had written home and sent more money saying that conditions were improving.

***

Janeki immediately wrote to Kuppu asking him to come.

Janeki was restless; she wanted to go to Malaya and join Desa. She and Kuppu discussed the possibility of returning to Malaya, for now he too had decided to go to Malaya, since things were apparently looking better there. The ban was still in force so it was not possible to go.

"You give me some time," said Kuppu, "I will find a way because I know of people who have managed to go around the ban. In India all these ways are always possible, nga."

***

Rumblings of war were in the air. Way back in 1931 the Japanese had invaded Manchuria and in 1937 the second Sino-Japanese war began. The rumblings of war were being re- echoed in Europe where the war efforts required large supplies of iron and rubber. The demand for rubber suddenly skyrocketed. Estate managers in Malaya were pressured by London to increase production. The Indian estate workers complained of the high cost of living while provision shops, with rumours of war, hoarded goods and increased prices. They asked for cost of living allowances. Instead of cash they were paid in rice.

With an increase of 20 per cent in cost of living Desa urged the workers to demand COLA (cost of living allowances). Labour was short because of the ban and demand for rubber was acute. To increase output the estate management had no option but to increase wages. The workers' wages went up to 75 cents at one stage.

The unrelenting organisation to boost the self-esteem of workers to continue the strikes and demands by Desa and Arokia paid off in good dividends for the workers. They were able to send home decent sums of money.

***

Kuppu got back to Janeki with a plan. Although the emigration ban was imposed it was not being strictly implemented. There were loopholes and greasing the palm of the immigration officials was a done thing. Kuppu managed to get passage for both of them. They got all other papers done in the last week of July and boarded the Rajula in August. Little did they know that they were making the last voyage of the Rajula from Madras to Singapore for many years to come.

The Indian Government enforced the strict implementation of

the ban only at the end of August while for five months they were not serious about it. It was not that they acceded to the request of the CIAM but circumstances became imminent.

Already in March of 1938 Adolph Hitler of nazi Germany ordered his troops to enter Austria and was pushing to grab Czechoslovakia. It appeared that war was inevitable in Europe and the great powers of Europe began to mobilise their forces. Britain needed her ships and the Rajula was requisitioned in September 1938 and became a troop ship. It only came back to the Asian waters after the war in 1946. Kuppu and Janeki barely managed to slip through.

Chapter 14

Betrayal, Betrayal, Betrayal, Betrayal

Having learnt from the Chinese on how they organized their workers, Desa and Arokia also tried to set up secret committees. In Dolby estate the committee meetings were becoming noticeable and Antoine took a curious interest in what was happening. Although uninvited he sneaked into one of the meetings and was surprised when he recognized Desa whom they were addressing as Subramaniam. He immediately carried the news to *kangany* Perumal who then sent spies to the meetings. After he had gathered enough information, he submitted to the manager. A plan was hatched to nab Desa and the whole committee.

Desa got wind of this and together with Akokia disappeared into the coal mine and stayed away for a while. The committee members in the estate were also lying low and not organizing anything big yet. The workers continued working six days a week while trade union representatives encouraged them to keep up their efforts.

Desa and Arokia got more involved in the strike actions at the coal mine. The Chinese were making high demands urged on by the Malayan Communist Party. Its aim was not just to improve the workers' living conditions but also to undermine the British colonial rule and destroy the capitalist system. This systematic underground activity was slow but effective. When the management was preoccupied with sending home big consignments of rubber they did not notice the clandestine activities. When things were relatively calm Desa and Arokia surfaced and found time to go back to the estate.

Desa was in for an almighty shock.

Desa was building up the momentum among the workers for a

big show down when the unexpected happened.

He found out that Janeki and Kuppu had come to Malaya and were in the estate, not in Dolby but in Worster estate. Before he approached them he had already been briefed that the couple had arrived as husband and wife. Desa was enraged. He and Arokia made their way to Worster. They located Kuppu and Desa confronted him.

"How dare you came back here and bring Janeki with you without informing me at all?" He grabbed him and pushed him down. As Kuppu was getting up Desa landed on him a series of punches. Kuppu was down again and bleeding, shocked and unprepared for such a reaction from Desa. Arokia pulled Desa away.

"I asked you, as my best friend to look after Janeki and you have done this treacherous thing to me. You betrayed me." Desa slapped Kuppu across the face and bristling with anger he walked away not wanting to even see Janeki. Arokia stayed back to talk to Kuppu.

"It is no use talking only to me. Let us go to Janeki and talk this out together," said Kuppu. When they met Janeki who was quartered with the other women in the *coolie* line, she was happy to see Akokia.

"Arokia, where is Desa?" she asked and at the same time noticed Kuppu's bleeding nose. "Kuppu, what happened to you?" She immediately opened her travel bag and took out a clean cloth and pressed it against his nose, saying, "Just hold this, nga. She rushed out and got some water and began nursing him gently."

Arokia watched this tender loving care.

"Both of you have got a lot of explaining to do."

"Let's not talk here, let's go outside," said Kuppu.

The three of them walked out into the timber to the latex collecting depot. The day's work was over and the place was empty. They sat down in the shed.

"Desa got mad because we heard that both of you have come here as husband and wife. Now, is that true?" asked Arokia.

"Let me explain," said Janeki. "I am the one who wanted to come and be with Desa."

"Why didn't you let Desa know?"

"Wait, listen, nga. I asked Kuppu's help. The government had stopped emigration but Kuppu had some important contacts. Even then I, as a single woman, could not leave. I could only leave either as a prostitute or as wife with husband. Kuppu was also willing to come to Malaynadu. They would only grant us papers if we travelled as husband and wife. We had to bribe people to prepare the papers."

"The reason we couldn't inform Desa was that we had to get all these things done in a hurry. The Rajula was leaving Madras for the last time. If we missed it we would never have come," said Kuppu in a nasal voice.

"Desa does not even want to see you again," said Arokia to Janeki.

"I can understand his anger, but he never gave me a chance to explain," said Kuppu.

"He has to know the truth. You will have to be the middleman, Arokia," pleaded Janeki.

Chapter 15

In Tandem with Chinese Workers

Desa went back to the mine and found the mine workers were also building up for a big showdown. He stood with them but realized that the Indian workers in the plantations should also coordinate and act in tandem. He discussed this with Ah Kow and the other Chinese leaders and they agreed that this massive strike should be a coordinated one.

Desa could not bring himself to go back to Worster. He was torn between his anger against Kuppu and Janeki on the one hand and the urgency of moving the workers to strike on the other. He forced himself to put his private life aside and went to Hartford estate to direct operations from there. He got the bicycle dispatch riders to go in all directions to convey the message to go on strike in three days.

But tragedy struck before that. The British police had informers everywhere and they got wind of the planned strike in the coal mine. They moved in with 250 military police and 200 Malay troops. Even as the workers dispersed they opened fire. Four Chinese workers were killed and several wounded. More than a hundred Chinese workers were arrested and taken away. Having received this news Arokia stayed away from the coal mine.

Desa called off the strike action by the Indian workers. The impact was lost. They would have to wait for another time. The spies were also in the estates. They had to lie low for a while. Desa went into hiding and Arokia could not locate him.

***

The workers had no choice but to work or starve. Desa's task was to keep their spirits up. When he came out of hiding and returned to the mine Akokia pulled him aside and demanded to talk with him. Desa had cooled down somewhat but still deeply hurt. Arokia explained in detail what actually happened and how Janeki and Kuppu had planned the voyage to Penang. It took Desa three days before he could accept the story. Arokia arranged for a meeting outside the estate, for neither Desa nor Arokia could walk in and out of the estate freely; they would have been caught for trespassing. They met in a coffee shop in town. Desa wanted to know how they travelled.

"The steamer was fully booked out, so I was told. I had to give under-table money to get one third class cabin passenger ticket for Janeki and I was a deck passenger. The Rajula was not going to travel for a long time. If we had missed it we wouldn't be here," said Kuppu.

"The last time you wrote you said that things were getting better, so I wanted to come to be with you," said Janeki.

"In our *vur*, they are clamouring for independence and there are demonstrations and strikes also but no change is in sight," said Kuppu.

The ice began to melt and after some hours and several cups of coffee there was reconciliation. Desa apologised and held Janeki's hands and thanked Kuppu for all his help. Both Desa and Arokia explained to them what they had been doing with the Indian workers and how they had been collaborating with the Chinese workers.

Kuppu and Janeki had found employment in Worster estate. Kuppu's reputation might have been known but they were desperate for workers now and took him in without questions. Desa, however, had become notorious. As leader, instigator and trouble maker with a criminal record he had a higher profile. Kuppu had been away longer and less noticed. Arokia played a secondary role. Desa was a wanted man; his picture on a wanted poster was on rubber trees in different estates with a cash reward of fifty dollars which was no mean sum. Informers and betrayers were ubiquitous. The meetings he went to were clandestine. He had to be extremely careful. Now he only met the leaders of committees. They knew of Desa's employment at the coal mine and his whereabouts.

This being the case living together with Janeki became a problem. In the estate there was no privacy. If he were found in the estate compound he could be held for trespassing. She couldn't live in the *kongsi* with other men at the mine. They agreed upon a solution.

***

Near the estate in Kampong Kuang Desa found a Malay small-holder who lived in a kampong house surrounded by his rubber trees. Desa negotiated with Abbas, the small-holder, to rent a tiny atap hut at the back of his house for a minimum sum. He could slip in and out on his bicycle unnoticed. Arokia remained at the mine while Janeki and Kuppu continued to work in Worster estate. They agreed that Kuppu and Janeki would keep up the appearance of husband and wife. The police could easily get at Desa through Janeki if it were known that she was his wife, and she herself could be put in a dangerous situation and blackmailed. Kuppu agreed to secretly bring Janeki to meet Desa in the hut on the pretext of going out as husband and wife. Kuppu would drop her off and spend time in the kampong eating stalls and fetch her back to the estate in the evening. This arrangement worked quite well.

There was nothing much in the hut except for a mat and a cardboard box in which Desa kept his meagre belongings. She would bring some cooked food and they would eat together. Desa and Janeki were hungry for each other, making love without end.

After work at the mine Desa would sit by the oil lamp in the hut writing epistles for the workers and his messages would be carried in scrolls hidden in the metal cylinder of the bicycle into which the seat was inserted. He kept inspiring the workers to remain steadfast and carry on as though they had docilely submitted to the new regulations but to be prepared for action at a short notice. He also had time now to update his journal with more details.

***

On 1 September 1939 Germany invaded Poland. Two days later Britain and France declared war on Germany. The colonies of these major powers were also dragged into the war. With wars being waged in the east and west, America entered the war scenario. A world war was unleashed.

Before the war reached the shores of Malaya, the pressure was on for the workers to produce more and more for the war effort. The workers also took advantage of this pressure to make more demands.

Chapter 16

Team Work

Abbas' hut became the operation centre for Desa and his team.

Desa, Arokia, Kuppu and Janeki had plenty of time to sit and plan their strategies for the coming months in the well-concealed Abbas' hut. Working as a team they mapped out all the estates in the surrounding areas within their reach and scheduled meetings and talks to form estate committees following the pattern of the Chinese initiatives. Within their reach was only a small fraction of the 3.3 million acres of rubber estates supplying 40 per cent of the world's rubber requirements.

"London wants the rubber, the rubber companies want to maximise their profits and the government uses its laws and enforcement agencies to enable these things to happen. They are all the same people, they rule India and they rule Malaynadu. We are the powerless slaves," said Desa.

"True, but without us there will be no rubber," said Janeki.

"When you talk about us do you mean us Indian workers or all workers?" asked Arokia.

"I meant us Indians," said Janeki.

Arokia made a comparison, "You know, the Chinese workers have recently got an increase of five cents, making a total of 70 cents per day while we Indians are still receiving only 50 cents."

"This is because we are not united as the Chinese are. That is why we have to get our people out of thinking like frogs in the well. By creating links with other estates we have to make them feel that we are indeed a powerful workforce," said Desa.

Although the demand for rubber was increasing in pace with the war efforts, the greed for higher profits was also increasing so the management tried to maintain high yield at low cost. The UPAM, brought the wages back to 60 cents for men and 55 cents for women. The cost of living had gone up by 30 per cent by now and they were back on subsistence level. The strikes continued, involving more than 2,000 Indian workers.

Under the guidance and inspiration of Desa and his team the workers were becoming bolder. They gave notice that they would work only three days of the week. "Why do we have to slog when we get no extra pay" was their common outcry. When they began cutting down on work the management retaliated by cutting off the water supply to the *coolie* lines.

In Dolby estate at a meeting of the committee one night Desa was told by a member,

"We were visited by a writer from Kuala Lumpur. His name is Nathan." .

"R. H. Nathan, he writes a labour column for the *Tamil Kody*. I have read his writing. He has been promoting active social reform. What did he have to say?" asked Desa.

"He said they were forming unions of plantation workers and asked us to sign up as members. He also told us that if we were union members he could help us financially from a union fund that they are collecting."

"That's a good idea and we will be better organised in our struggle. You all should join the union even though unions are illegal right now," encouraged Desa.

Desa managed to rouse the people to action.

"We are being overworked while the company is making huge profits. We must aim to get paid as much as the Chinese workers are paid. Now is the time to strike because they need our labour and must value it. We will send messages to all the estates around to go on strike for short periods and demand higher wages."

They managed to successfully carry out several strikes.

The workers, further encouraged by this new turn of events, continued to maintain their three-day week. The management was beginning to feel the pinch. The workers' pay was drastically cut and workload increased and their rice ration decreased. Difficult though it was they were carrying on the strike actions with constant pep talks from Desa. This form of resistance went on for months. They persevered despite long working hours which even the women had to endure with the help of children who stopped going to school. There was an increase in malnutrition due to rice ration cuts and the rate of infant mortality was high. Desa and Arokia stood shoulder to shoulder with the Chinese workers on strike at the coal mine and at nights he would meet the estate committees.

Within the two years the Indian government had effectively tightened the flow of Indians to Malaya, so there was no more unlimited supply of cheap labour. There was a shortfall of 7,500 labourers according to UPAM which declared that the main cause of unrest was agitation by propaganda and intimidation fostering discontent and inciting labour to disobedience. It was obviously referring to the activities of the Communist Party and the initiatives of the four people in the hut. The Punjab regiment was now permanently stationed in Malaya. The push for rubber production was intense. Rubber became an essential service. The workers were urged to be patriotic. Patriotic to whom? Not to India or Malaya but to mother England. England's war effort was being supported by Malayan rubber and it was not enough. The workers were asked to make a monetary contribution to the war effort called the Patriotic Fund and encouraged to offer voluntary unpaid labour calling it *santhosha vellai* (happy work). The real situation was that women were made to work long hours and the infant mortality rate was high. Since strikes were still continuing the workers were ordered to give 15 days' notice for strike action which meant time for the authorities to take preventive action. The government could use powers under local emergency regulations to prevent unauthorised strikes and to break such strikes.

Rubber production did increase by 37 per cent resulting in 331,589 pounds of rubber. Rubber price also increased to 38.56 dollars per capita output. Although the workers' wages did increase a little it was not commensurate with the cost of living which had doubled. The management had grudgingly granted only a 5 cent COLA.

The Chinese were so aggressive that they pushed for an increase of wages from 60 cents to one dollar twenty cents. The Indians were still clamouring for 75 and 65 cents.

Desa, Arokia, Kuppu and Janeki, as a team, worked to rouse the workers. Janeki took it upon herself to encourage the women to come out of their shells and stand with the men. As a team they studied and analysed the situation in all the neighbouring estates and travelled to them to hold clandestine meetings. With all the information gathered they drew up a list of demands. They were:

1. Both Indian and Chinese plantation workers should receive equal pay;

2. Men and women should receive equal pay with 30 per cent COLA;

3. Those *kiranies*, their names listed, who have abused the workers should be punished and dismissed;

4. Estate schools should be revived with proper facilities, with sufficient teachers and books;

5. All estate staff from the white man down should stop sexual harassment of female workers;

6. Paid maternity leave for a minimum of ten days made compulsory;

7. Crèches to be hygienically maintained and adequately staffed;

8. Medical facilities with proper and sufficient medicine to be provided and free transport to hospital when necessary;

9. Free access into the estates given to relatives and friends of workers who were not to be punished as trespassers;

10. Freedom of assembly and speech for workers in estates;

11. The rule requiring workers to dismount from bicycles when passing European and Asian managers or *kiranies* be abolished;

12. Working hours reduced from 12 hours to 9 with overtime;

13. Workers to have the right to present petitions without being punished;

14. Freedom to organize trade unions of plantation workers.

One other demand to prohibit toddy shops within estates was later removed. The problem was not the toddy but the abuse of it and the consequent family problems. This was a problem of the workers to be dealt with by the workers and not that of the estate, so it was considered.

These demands were circulated to all the estates. The bicycle dispatch riders, some of whom were mere boys, were accosted and arrested and their bicycles confiscated. Workers from all the estates reacted to this harassment and started protesting and demonstrating. The Chinese too had regrouped and started their protests. It became a coordinated effort.

The management, having got the message of the demands reacted by calling in the police and making arrests. Over 20,000 workers, armed with sticks and *parangs*, were becoming violent. Desa and his team did not call for violence but the protests escalated on their own steam. Some European managers and Indian conductors were assaulted.

Desa and his team split into different estates urging them not to hurt people but it was alright to destroy property. They went wild wrecking machinery in the rubber processing plants and damaging the most precious trees.

The managements called in the volunteer reserve forces and armoured car units. It was a repeat of the first strike action but only bigger and wider. The Punjabi police were back on the scene opening fire. Some workers in different estates were killed and many wounded. The mobile field ambulance took them away. Hundreds were arrested under local Emergency Regulations, which had been hastily declared. The jails were filling up. The Chinese workers too lost many lives and sustained more casualties. There was order to banish these undesirables but they could not be deported because no ships were sailing.

The estate managements were in a state of panic. The UPAM sent telegrams to London but London was too preoccupied with the war. The British forces in Malaya too could spare no personnel to the plantations. The threat of the Japanese was imminent.

Chapter 17

War

On 8 December 1941 the Japanese invaded Malaya. They moved in from southern Siam into Kedah province by land and attacked Kota Baru by sea. Ironically the first defenders of Malaya were the Indians from the 8th Indian Infantry Brigade of the Indian 9th Infantry Division. The Japanese advanced south into the peninsula. The British forces began to retreat.

The Japanese forces moved systematically through the plantations on bicycles. If they were resisted by the planters they killed the planters. Leaving a small contingent of soldiers at the estates, the main body took whatever food supplies were available from the ration store and from the workers' homes and pushed its way down south. The Japanese kept coming like ants out of an anthill. They knew where they were going because they had detailed topographical maps. This invasion was well planned in advance secretly with the help of a fifth column.

The Europeans also began to move in their cars. The planters and estate managers, although very reluctant to leave, packed up and moved. The one main road in the west of Malaya was clogged with south-bound traffic. Some, however, preferred to arm themselves and stay on. Those who left made sure that the rubber processing machinery was all destroyed, at least those that had been spared destruction by the riotous striking workers.

***

In Dolby, Humphreys ordered the entrance to the estate to be barricaded and retreated to his bungalow up the hill with his short gun and ammunition. He insisted that work should carry on as usual. Little did he know that the Japanese were not merely moving on the main road, there were brigades on bicycles moving along the laterite roads through plantations.

It was late at night. Desa and Arokia had left the mine, met up with Kuppu and were holding a meeting with an estate committee. Janeki was with the women in Woster estate. Perumal and his henchmen were waiting to move in on the committee. Little did they or anybody else realize that the Japanese had surrounded the estate. The Japanese troops moved in and rounded up all the workers from the lines and a group of them moved up to the bungalow where there was a small gun battle. The manager and assistant with the household surrendered. The people were taken by surprise while Perumal and his pose, intending to surprise the working committee, were themselves taken by surprise. The committee members tried to run into the timber but the whole estate was surrounded. They too were captured at gunpoint.

Chapter 18

Death Railway

The next morning trucks arrived and all the able-bodied men were loaded and taken away. Only the women, children and old people were left behind. Desa got separated from Janeki. Perumal, the *kiranies* and even the two *velekaran* were apparently not spared. A small troop of soldiers stayed behind. The women were scared for their lives while the estate settlement was practically deserted. Desa was desperately worried for Janeki.

They were all transported to Sungei Siput and loaded onto trains packed to capacity. Soon they were joined by the coal freight train from the mine loaded with Chinese workers. They had no idea where they were being taken but they were headed north because the train went through that infamous Taiping as Desa recalled.

The coaches were overcrowded and along the way more and more men were forced into· the carriages so much so that many of the men climbed onto the roof of the train. The steam engine chugged along for eternity until they reached Padang Besar in Perlis. After a short break during which dried biscuits were handed out, the long northward journey began.

The Japanese forces had captured both Siam and Burma and were planning to move into India. Their forces stationed in Burma needed supplies and reinforcement and the only way to transport them was by sea through the Straits of Malacca and the Andaman Sea. These waters were teeming with Allied submarines and they were vulnerable to attack. The alternative route from Bangkok to Rangoon was by land and the terrain was covered in thick tropical jungle of hills and valleys crisscrossed by treacherous rivers. A road would take too long to build so they decided on constructing a railway despite the obstacles.

The empire had to move on. Material and labour were needed. For materials they dismantled the branch railway lines in Malaya and used the people they conquered as forced labour. Desa and his train-full of people, Indians, Chinese and Malays together with the Allied prisoners of war were the work force. The train headed to Padang Besar and then crossed the border into Siam. When they reached a small station called Ban Pong, instead of turning right to Bangkok the train turned left and dropped off the men at different sections of the railway track that were being constructed. Desa, Arokia and Kuppu ended up in Kanchanapuri, also known as Kanburi, where the construction work was well under way. This was known as the dreaded "death railway" stretching 258 miles.

***

Among the men who were not transported out were the Asian *kiranies* and *kanganies*. They were the ones who really knew how to run the plantation industry and the Japanese spared them for that very reason. The *kiranies* and the *kanganies* swiftly shifted their loyalties to the Japanese bosses and to curry the favour of their new masters, they became very cruel and abusive towards the workers. The black Europeans became black Japanese.

The Japanese made good use of them. First they got them to round up the able-bodied men under the pretext of organising a special task force. They were loaded onto lorries accompanied by military personnel carriers. They were post haste sent to Burma. Next they got the *kiranies* and the *kanganies* to jump start the rubber works.

Some of the equipment were already destroyed by the earlier rioting workers and whatever remained had been ordered destroyed by the manager.

The Japanese had portable welding equipment which they carted with them on their advance push down the Peninsula in order to fix their broken bicycles. Their move was well prepared and meticulously planned except for insufficient food supplies. They got the *kiranies* and *kanganies* to martial the remaining workforce and gather all the necessary components to get the rubber production going again. The men and women gathered the broken pieces together. The coagulating trays were mended, the wheels of the sheet rubber rollers were welded, the rollers repositioned and greased to get them moving. The smoke houses were intact except to get the poles fixed to hang the sheet rubber. The women were ordered to go and collect wood for the fire.

Within a couple of weeks, the *kiranies* called for muster and allocated tasks for tapping to the remaining men, women and even children. The Japanese officer gave them a pep talk.

"We want you to work in the estate and increase the production of rubber for a good cause. Japan needs the rubber for its war effort and with a strong Japanese army we will defeat the British and win freedom for your motherland India." He was appealing for a new-found loyalty.

There was no talk of wages. They had to work and find their own food. The families thanked their gods that their lives were spared but it was not pleasant.

After involuntary work the women and Janeki remained behind closed doors afraid to show themselves. Whatever food they had had been taken by the troops. They had no choice but to go out and forage for food from what was left of their own vegetable gardens. The older men went out first and later the older women. The younger women began to dress shabbily with untidy hair just to look dirty, ugly and older so as not to attract the Japanese troops. The Japanese were able to see through them but they had strict orders from their commander to leave them alone, at least for now because they needed their cooperation. This order had come directly from Major Fujiwara who had plans for the Indians. Their intention was to jumpstart the rubber production. Japan needed the raw material.

No jobs, no shops, no provisions, no medicines not only in the plantations but throughout the country. International trade had broken down with no transportation of goods and food. Padi fields were bombed. There was neither planting nor harvesting. Whatever was available of the staple food of rice was requisitioned for the troops.

Janeki and the women began to turn the soil and plant tapioca and other vegetables and looked after the disabled. Young children with no schools to attend were made to work collecting rubber and looking after chicken. The older ones became goatherds. Eggs were kept for hatching and the only two cows in the estate provided milk. This and goat's milk were shared by all. They settled into a routine while time dragged on.

With this new-found authority the *kiranies* and *kanganies* started acting like the *dorais*. The *kangany* in Worster estate was one Palanivellu. One day he sent word to Janeki through a boy that he wanted her to report to him at the office. When she met him he said, "Janeki, you are not very good at tapping rubber. You are slow and you injure the trees. You can do weeding around the trees. After work you can come to my house and do some cleaning for which I will pay you some money."

Janeki had no option to say "yes" or "no" to working in the field but she could refuse to work in his house. She also knew that he would make life hell for her if she refused. So she said, "Yes."

Palanivellu lived in the staff quarters in a single unit by itself. She started work the following day. She had to sweep the floor, wash the cooking utensils and also his clothes. Janeki picked up the coconut broom, a bundle of long sticks, the shaved off backbone of coconut palm leaves. She tapped the holding end of the broom on the floor to make it compact and started to sweep the floor. Dirt and dust flew everywhere, the floor was filthy. The dried remnants of curry were stuck to the earthen pot. She gathered the pot, plates, ladles and cups and went outside to the standing tap. Rolling up her sari above her knees and squatting on the floor she soaked the pot and began washing the other utensils. Performing such a menial task she was thinking, "*I am a trained nurse, what am I doing here working like a servant?*" She did not notice Palanivellu standing behind her. He cleared his throat and startled her. She almost dropped the earthen pot and broke it. She was not sure how long he was standing watching her. She stood up and straightened her sari embarrassed and angry.

"Carry on; you are doing a good job. Don't forget to wash the clothes and hang them up on the line outside." He walked away. Janeki was not comfortable.

***

From dawn to dust work on the railway tracks never stopped. When a worker sat down to rest a while he was whipped. The days were hot and nights cold with the high pitched whine of mosquitoes singing in the ears. The only meals were a thin soup made from dried fish and bamboo shoots and an evening meal of broken rice broth and dried fish. They sat on bamboos and sleeper logs and ate in poor light not looking too closely at the food which contained weevils and maggots and other unidentified foreign objects. They had to eat to live because no one had an appetite. They were breathing in the overwhelming stench rising from the mass graves only feet away. Bodies were half buried with decomposing limbs sticking out swarming with flies which also descended on their food. From illness and ill treatment men were dropping dead. Cholera, malaria, and diarrhoea were rampant.

They lost count of days and nights and weeks and months.

Chapter 19

Indian National Army

Major Fujiwara's plan was to win over the Indian troops of the British army who had surrendered as the British were withdrawing. His other objective was to gain the support of the local Indian civilians most of whom were employed in the plantations. The British forces were routed in Jitra, in the province of Kedah and Mohan Singh, a captain of the British regiment, surrendered to the Japanese. Major Fujiwara met Captain Mohan Singh and got him to entice the captured or surrendered Indian soldiers to form a battalion and an army to march with the Japanese forces to liberate India. This novel concept immediately cottoned onto the Indian psyche. Captain Mohan Singh was able to muster 16,300 Indian prisoners-of-war as freedom fighters for India and the Indian National Army (INA) was formed. Major Fujiwara had a bigger vision of appealing to the whole Diaspora of Indians in South East Asia to form a league called the Indian Independence League and he got Rash Behari Bose, an Indian revolutionary, who had escaped to Japan from the British in India, nominated as the chairman of the Indian Independence League. It immediately aroused the nationalistic sentiments of the Indians. The CIAM who had been playing politics with the British regime saw greener pastures on the other side and not only joined the Indian Independence League but also took up leadership roles in it encouraging all the Indians to enlist in the INA.

The CIAM members were already canvassing the country for volunteers to join the INA. They moved into the estates, some of them, perhaps for the first time, and enticed most of the able-bodied men who escaped the first round up for the Death Railway.

Chapter 20

Sexual Harassment

Janeki worked for Palanivellu for a week. All the time she was conscious that he was watching her furtively. One day she asked him, "What happened to my husband Kuppusamy?"

"Oh, he has gone to work for the *japankaran* (Japanese man – used collectively). They are building a railway line in Burma."

"In Burma? So far away? When will he come back?"

"Nobody can be sure. He may never come back."

"I know he will come back."

"You can keep hoping, but you might as well get used to the idea that you may never see him again. You are lucky, you are comfortable here."

"We are not comfortable here. The workers are hungry and the children are sick. When are we going to get paid for the work we are doing?"

"Why do you want money? There's nothing much available now to buy with money."

"You said you will pay me when I work here for you."

"Money is no use, but I can give you some rice if you are obedient."

"What do you mean, obedient, I have been doing all the things you have asked me to do."

Palanivellu was taken aback, no worker, much less a woman, would dare speak like this to a *kangany*.

"You watch your mouth di."

Little did he realise that she was far more educated than he. He had the advantage over her and he knew it. He took hold of the broom and offered it to her, at the same time closing the door. He turned around and grabbed her from behind. She tried to hit him with the broom but he quickly snatched it away from her. He tried to grope and she screamed. He slapped her across the face and she screamed even more loudly. He tried to put his hand over her mouth when there was a loud bang on the door. She screamed again. He began, "Who...," when the door was kicked open with a heavy boot. Palanivellu immediately let go of Janeki when he saw the Japanese officer who demanded, "What are you doing?"

"Sir, she was refusing to work," began Palanivellu.

The Japanese officer who happened to be walking outside the quarters heard the screaming and moved in instantly assessing the situation. Without saying another word he went up to Palanivellu and slapped him left and right. Palanivellu was immediately on his knees. The officer turned to Janeki. "You go back now," he ordered.

Janeki adjusted her sari, the upper part of which had been pulled down. The buttons on her bodice were ripped off. Quickly she made her way back to the lines.

Janeki related the episode to the other women and they were not surprised by what the *kangany* had done but very surprised by the conduct of the Japanese officer. All the Japanese were not bad and there were decent ones among them.

In the absence of the men many of the young women had fallen victim to Palanivellu and other *kiranies* not only here but also in the other estates. Many of the women had accepted this as their fate, their karma.

Janeki was quietly working on the women not to give in to the demands of the *kiranies* and *kanganies*. She got them to carry small packets of chilli powder and to use them if they were molested. The women tried not to work or move about alone but always in twos or threes even when they were gardening or looking after the goats and chicken. They also lived together in cubicles finding strength in numbers. The estates suffered from the lack of manpower because orders from higher up were to spare the men for the army. More and more of the men-folk were recruited for the INA. Janeki also realised that she could not stay in this estate much longer because Palanivellu would look for an opportunity to punish her for what had happened.

✳✳✳

The loyalist and patriotic chords were plucked in the hearts and minds of the Indians. They were all fired with nationalism and the men were ever willing to join the INA rather than live and work in the plantation under starvation and without pay. The rallying force behind this euphoria was the Supreme Commander of the INA, Netaji Subbas Chandra Bose, an impressive and charismatic leader who had travelled through Germany and Tokyo and garnered the support of the Axis forces with a grandiose idea of infiltrating India with overseas Indians trained in espionage as the Fifth Column to prepare the groundwork for the invasion to liberate India. He had taken over command from Rash Behari Bose. In Singapore he declared himself Head of State, Prime Minister of the Provisional Government of Free India, calling it *Azad Hind and the outcry of victory was Azad Hind Zindabad* and *Chalo Delhi,* march to Delhi.

The news of this spread like wild fire up the peninsula from Singapore.

Chapter 21

Pushing the Railway

Meanwhile the pressure was on to complete the railway to Rangoon as quickly as possible. Army discipline within the Japanese forces was breaking down under the stress. Even some of the Japanese soldiers who appeared to be insubordinate were put to work on the railway as punishment. There was even exchange of gunfire among them. It only made Desa and his friends realise how desperate the situation had become. The order was that nothing should come in the way of pushing the railway line to its completion. As the men were dying more men of all Asian nationalities and Europeans were continuously arriving. From dawn to dusk work was in progress; even the meals were taken in shifts. Nights were the only time for rest because of blackout not to attract the bombers. The tired men slept immediately as soon as they lay down wherever they could find a place inside the tents or out in the open.

***

The war was being fiercely fought on different fronts while life in the estate was dully trundling along. The workers in the estate shared one small radio and used to gather around it to listen to music and hear the news in Tamil. Chandra Bosh's speech was being broadcast which began with a rendition of the inspiring *Bande Mataram* (I salute my mother) that immediately caught the attention of the listeners. It was a tune they were all familiar with. It was a patriotic song, on par with the national anthem, set to the tune of *Raga Durga* in the style of a marching song. *Raga* is a melodic mode and *Durga* is a raga in Hindustani classical music.

The workers found a new vista opening up and left the estate in droves to enlist in the INA. Anything was better than the grind in the estate.

Chandra Bosh was an imposing figure, a remarkable orator and a shrewd operator. He appealed to the women in what women of today would call feminist language. Over the radio came his booming voice:

"There's a whole section of our population you've completely ignored. How can you have a revolutionary army, how can you have a revolutionary movement, how can you think of independence for our country without involving women? We must give women the opportunity to join the army, undergo training and fight for the country. I know that lots of educated and progressive families have gone away from here and now we have only women from the working class, rubber tappers and people like that, hardly educated, afraid even to go to the bazaar alone. No. But this is the substance from which our country is made; these are the women who will take part in the movement. After all, in our independence movement women have always been involved; they haven't been given their due recognition, but they have come forward in the thousands, so we will have no difficulty. I know that women in our country are suffering from very grave social and economic disabilities, but to overcome them freedom is an absolute essential, but even after freedom, women will have to fight for their rights and their proper place in our society, because men won't give it to them that easily, they've had their own way all these centuries, using foreign invasions and things like that as an excuse, so it's so ingrained in them. So this will be an opportunity for women to fight for their own rights."

It was an impressive speech and women everywhere became infatuated with the man. When the recruiting officer came to the estate many women signed up including Janeki. She found herself separated from Desa again so soon after being reunited with him. Rumours had it that they had been taken to Burma for work and it might take a very very long time if they came back at all. Janeki had not really acquired the skill of tapping rubber and was not comfortable with the *kiranies* even more so than with the Japanese men around. This was an opportunity for her to get away and why not fight for India.

The representatives from the CIAM who came to the estates to recruit men came again this time with women who talked about a women's regiment and encouraged the women to enlist in this women's arm of the INA. Janeki together with a number of women in the estate joined the INA.

***

The European bosses of Malaya were emaciated, gaunt, half-naked, skeleton-like figures with open sores covered with flies or open wounds crawling with maggots. It became obvious that a European was no different from an ordinary mortal and a physically weaker one at that. One of them could barely stand up. A Japanese soldier came up to him, slapped him across the face and hit him with the butt of his riffle. He collapsed. Desa thought he recognized him although he was not so sure. Yes. It was Humphreys. Desa's first thought was, "Serves the bastard right." On second thoughts he felt sorry for him; the Japanese had no right to treat any human being like that. When everyone was busy, Desa lifted him up to a sitting position and gave him some water to drink. "You, Nedasa, what are you doing here?" was all he said.

Desa was sure that Perumal and Antoine were on the train but he never saw them in the camp. They might have been taken to another location.

At night Desa would think about Janeki. *What would she be doing in the estate? Was she captured by the Japanese? If she was, Kadavule, she would have been brutally abused. Why did she ever think of coming to Malaynadu? Maybe, I should have stayed with her in India and not have been so thick headed to come here. We cannot turn the clock back! We've hardly begun to have a life together. Will I ever get to see her again? This seems to be a dead end. There must be a way out...*

Some Europeans, six of them, attempted to escape. Lost in the jungle with no survival skills; they were caught and brought back. They were publicly whipped. They were dragged out. One of them, supposedly the leader, was a tall Australian. He was ordered to dig a hole, a deep hole.

"You white bastard, get down into the hole and stand straight. The rest of you fill up the hole."

Nobody moved. The short, fat sergeant cracked his whip biting their backs. They reluctantly filled the hole. The Australian was buried up to his neck.

The sergeant barked at him, "You escape into the jungle and do you think you will find food? We feed you here. Feed him," he ordered a soldier who brought a bowl of rice and tried to make him eat it. Buried up to his neck the escapee could hardly bend his head with both hands in the earth let alone breathe. He was made a spectacle and a warning to the others against escaping.

"You see, we give him food and he doesn't want to eat."

The sergeant stepped forward and kicked the Australian in the head.

"Bury him!"

He was buried alive. He then made the others dig their own graves and shot them dead.

Desa and Kuppu were holding on conserving their energy whenever they could but Arokia was not taking it well. He succumbed to malaria, and then he developed a bout of diarrhoea. Even with high fever he was made to work. Those who did not work were not given food. Desa working beside him would douse him with water to cool him down.

Those who died on the job were thrown into a large hole as big as a room and covered in dirt. Arokia was staring at them wondering if that was also going to be his fate when he noticed something.

"Desa, Kuppu come here ngada. Look," he pointed at a body, "I saw his fingers move. He is alive."

Desa, Kuppu and a few others jumped into the hole stepping over corpses and started frantically digging with their bare hands and pulled out the half buried body. They brought him up. He was still breathing but very faintly. They threw water on his face and cleared his nostrils. One of the men had half a tin of condensed milk. They gave him the milk diluted in water. He revived, but barely conscious.

"What's your name," asked Desa.

"Marimuthu."

"Where are you from?

"Sungai Boaya estate, Selangor."

"Let him rest," said Kuppu.

Chapter 22

Death in Siam

Arokia was deteriorating, burning with malarial fever.

One morning Arokia did not wake up. Desa was devastated and so was Kuppu. Before they could throw the body into the mass grave Desa and Kuppu dug a grave for him and buried him and erected a simple wooden cross and carved on it, his name and Orattanadu, his hometown. Desa cried for two whole days.

"Arokia came back with me hoping to earn and send back good money," said Desa. "How will we ever get back now? If we do, what will we tell Arokia's family?

"Why do all our ventures end up as failures?"

"It is karma, da," said Kuppu.

"It is karma only if we have no control over what happens to us."

"Exactly, we have no control over the situation here."

"May be it is time for us to take control, da."

"What do you mean?"

"There must be a way out."

"Oh, yes? Look what happened to the *velekaran* who tried to escape."

"I promised Janeki and my family that I will be home in two years. Janeki and you decided to come to me instead. This war has overturned all that I planned. Every night I worry about Janeki. I do not trust the Japanese. Our marriage seems to start and stop, start and stop. If I do not take control I will never see her again at all."

"This is hell on earth, da. We have been here more than a year and many of those who came with us are already dead. At the rate men are dying, there will be no more workers to construct the railway even though more and more men are being brought in every week. The men are too weak even to attempt an escape."

"It is death either here or in the jungle. I don't want to die here. I must plan to escape somehow."

They heard that Netaji Subbas Chandra Bose, a famous Indian leader, was coming through to Siam by train. They were all excited to see him, but were encamped behind barbed wires and none of them could get out except for work. The Japanese authorities really did not want Chandra Bose to see the state of these men.

A small group of them decided to at least get a glimpse of him. The night before he was due to arrive they sneaked out through the barbed wire fence and crossed the river taking a long detour to arrive at the railway tracks. There they hid and waited to catch a glimpse of him passing by. At last the train came. It moved slowly packed with people and his supporters. The Indian flag and the Japanese flag were flying on each side of the coach and he was standing out in front waving at the people.

"He looks so fair like an angel sent from heaven," commented one of them.

They later made their way back to the camp without the guards knowing. This little episode gave Desa the idea that breaking out of the camp was not all that difficult.

He told Kuppu, "We can plan an escape so long as we take strict precautions against being captured."

Chapter 23

Escape

"The train that brings in men goes back empty..."

When Desa discussed the possibility of escape with Kuppu he was at first sceptical but began to see that staying was no option. They began saving up some of the dried fish. They couldn't very well get around with their *veshtis*. Desa saw a leg sticking out from the mass grave. He dug around the corpse and dragged off the trousers crawling with maggots and washed it in the river. The only clothes they could get were those of dead men. They hid them until they were ready to make their move. The Japanese sentries were all around the camp but they too were tired and sleepy.

"We go in two different directions and meet up under that tall tree. If one of us is shot the other will keep going. If one is caught he is as good as dead and we will die rather than betray each other. Kuppu, now is the time, da."

It was a dark moonless night. The camp was asleep. Desa and Kuppu crawled out from different points into the long grass and kept moving slowly stopping now and then to see if they had been noticed. They met up at the given place as planned. Behind the tree they changed into their "new" clothes. They lay still listening until they were certain they were not noticed then moved again until they reached the railway track with the parked wagons. They were flat bed open wagons camouflaged with heavy-leafed tree branches. There were no lights; a blackout was maintained every night for fear of air raids. Desa stealthily climbed into one of the wagons and lay flat at the bottom covered by the leaves while Kuppu did the same in another wagon. Very early in the morning the train began to move.

Desa had no idea in which direction it was moving. Actually it was moving towards Bangkok to collect more material for the railway. As it shunted to a halt Desa slid out of the wagon and tapped on Kuppu's wagon. They saw the name Ban Pong and hid in the jungle. Men appeared from nowhere and began removing the camouflage and loading the wagons with tracks and sleepers. Desa decided to retrace his steps on the railway line followed some distance away by Kuppu to be less conspicuous. Kuppu spotted a bicycle, but it was a total wreck. He salvaged a piece of broken mudguard and pulled out the tube from the flat tyre. Kuppu had a mind for practical things and was good with his hands. They came to a split of tracks and followed the line that went south and kept walking for days. Hardly anybody had ever escaped the death railway and survived and they were surprised how easy it really was.

***

The women who had enlisted to join the INA were taken by buses arranged by courtesy of CIAM to the Sungei Siput railway station. The train took them to Singapore. From the railway station they were transported to the Waterloo street camp.

Janeki found that there was a new regiment for women named after a famous twenty year old Indian heroine who fought in India's first War of Independence against the British in 1857. She was the Rani of Jhansi who rode a horse wielding her sword in open battle, the Indian Joan of Arc. She died fighting in the battle of Gwalior. Janeki was now a soldier in the Rani of Jhansi Regiment formally inaugurated by Netaji Subhas Chandra Bose who assumed the position of Commander-in-chief of the INA. The Indian Independence League (IIL) had quickly grown spreading into 40 branches with a membership of 120,000 (August 1942). The INA had 16,300 men. By 1943 the IIL membership grew to 350,000 and that of the INA to 100,000.

The women's regiment with its own training camp launched a crash course training programme both physical and psychological. Their nationalistic spirit was boosted by the raising of the Indian flag and the singing of the Indian national anthem, the *Bande Mataram*, and other nationalistic songs while marching, and infused with historical and political lectures on India. The patriotic song *Bande Mataram* was particularly inspiring written by Bankimchandra in Bengal expressing devotion to the Motherland. In 1870 the British rulers in India were trying hard to enforce their anthem, *God Save the Queen* on the Indians. In 1876 Queen Victoria used the additional title of Empress of India. The British administration, in fact, banned the *Bande Mataram*. It only became more popular after it was sung by the celebrated poet Rabindranath Tagore himself.

Physical combat training involved assault manoeuvres, bayonet and obstacle training with .303 rifles, range practice and machine gun training. Some 50 women had to undergo nurses' training. Janeki volunteered for she already had nursing skills. She was put in charge of the nurses with the rank of Corporal.

***

Desa and Kuppu walked for days and nights, sometimes walking during the day and resting at night and at other times walking during the night and resting during the day. They lost count of days. The railway line was their guide. While resting one day Kuppu worked on his scrap material. With a piece of stone he sharpened the rough edge of the bicycle mudguard piece into a knife. He cut strips of rubber from the bicycle tube. Cutting the Y branches from a tree, he fashioned two catapults. They successfully hunted birds and squirrels.

They replenished their water when it rained. Kuppu, the practical handyman, folded large yam leaves into a cone and collected rain water. They saw monkeys eating fruit hanging in clusters on the branches of low trees. They too ate as much as they could collecting the fruits fallen on the ground and taking some with them bundled in their *thalaipa* cloth. Later they found out that it was called *langsat*. Whenever they heard the train coming they would hide in the jungle. More workers were being ferried to the death railway.

At nights they were terrified at the sounds of of wild animals real or imagined.

"Kuppu, remember our first flight into the jungle? I heard the tiger so clearly."

"So did I but I didn't care anymore. I was prepared to die then."

"Poor Sokalingam, how could a single man put up a fight against a tiger? I hope he died quickly."

"We were lucky and that was a good experience; I kept the fire going all night."

They dared not light a fire now because they could hear aeroplanes overhead. Each night they found a hiding place among outcrops of limestone; by days, among shady trees but always close to the railway line. In the open space they could be easily spotted by animals so they kept a sharp lookout all the time. The animals themselves seemed to avoid the railway lines because of constant traffic. They could actually feel the vibrations on the track before they heard the train approaching.

They lost count of how many days they walked or was it weeks. They came across huge cakes of what looked like soft mud. Stirring it with a stick they concluded that they were indeed dung, elephant dung. Seeing the damaged fauna and flora they saw the path taken by a herd of elephants that had crossed the railway line.

They approached a town named Chumphon which appeared to be a military base with camouflaged buildings. They steered clear of this place. The town they later came to was Ranong. In all those towns they passed through there were hardly any men around except for Japanese soldiers. They had all been transported to the railway construction site.

One day when they were totally exhausted walking on the track they were approached by some aboriginals. They were *orang asli* with knives and blowpipes. Kuppu was scared and he just sat down. He remembered the trackers who hunted them down with Roberts. But these looked different. These *orang asli* knew that they were escapees from the Japanese. They had seen others who had run away from the Japanese. They gave them water and took them to their home which was beside a small canal. They were fed sago, tapioca roots, and wild boar meat. They managed to communicate in broken Malay. They were very hospitable and also interested in the Indians and about India. Desa and Kuppu stayed with them for some time learning that they belonged to a group known as the Negrito and Kensiu was their tribe. Their language was a mixture of Khmer and Malay. They were short, below five feet in height with dark skin, almost like the Indians, but with woolly hair. They took their visitors with them to the hills to hunt wild boar with blow piles. Communication was more a sign language than articulation although simple Malay words were used.

Desa and Kuppu learnt a lot about the jungle and what plants and fruits were edible. After spending more than a month with them and having regained their strength and with more survival skills, they decided to move on.

Chapter 24

Rani Regiment to Battlefront

Months went past very quickly and a contingent of the Rani regiment was ordered to move to the battle front at the Indo-Burma frontier. The men of the INA were already engaged in war together with the Japanese Army which had commenced its push into Indian territory.

Janeki and the women were well fed and fit for battle. They were issued with their combat kit with rifle, rations, spare uniform and first aid necessities. They, of course, added their own personal wares.

"Wow, I can't believe, di, that we are really soldiers going to war," said Sarojini one of Janeki's companions.

"We have indeed transformed, di, from being estate *coolies* harassed and oppressed living from hand to mouth into hardened soldiers," added Parvathi.

"Yes," said Janeki, "it is definitely better than estate life but we do not know what we are going into or how many of us will come back alive."

"If we die, we die for Mother India, di," said Sarojini.

The women were put on the train headed for Siam. Their destination was Rangoon, Burma. There were also INA and Japanese soldiers on the train. The women could not make out if the Japanese were friend or foe.

***

The *orang asli* led Desa and Kuppu through a jungle path crossing a canal and a stream, shorter than the railway track to the outskirts of a large town. There was no need for them to go into town except to find food. The *orang asli* brought them to a vegetable garden. They knew the gardener and often came for a supply of fresh vegetables. The Siamese gardener was an old man who supplied vegetables to the town market. The *orang asli* spoke to the gardener about Desa and Kuppu and they left. Desa and Kuppu thanked them profusely for their help and hospitality. The old gardener, whose name was Chai, welcomed Desa and Kuppu into his small house.

"You are welcome here but you must not show yourself. There are people watching. This is my wife." She joined the palms of her hands and bowed to them.

"This is my daughter-in-law and my two grandchildren." She also greeted them in the same way. Desa and Kuppu were so impressed with their gentle culture which was so similar to the Indian culture of *namaste*, a non-contact greeting or salutation, literally "a bow to you." They were offered some tea and banana cakes.

"The Japanese are very bad. They came here and took my two sons away. We found out that they were sent to build a railway."

"We too were there and very badly treated," said Desa sparing the details so as not to upset the parents and the wife of one of his sons.

"We escaped," said Kuppu.

"Yes I know, the *orang asli* have explained."

The vegetable garden was located some distance away from the town hidden in the fringe of the jungle. Having taken his sons the Japanese did not bother him very much. When he took his vegetables to the town market he had to give a portion of it to the Japanese for free and sell the rest.

"What is the name of the town?" asked Kuppu.

"Surat Thani," said Chai. He was tired and getting old.

"If you can help me to do some work in the garden you can stay here, but I cannot pay you any money."

Both Desa and Kuppu immediately agreed. Food and shelter were more than what they could bargain for. "I will explain to you how to do the gardening. You must be very careful and keep a look out. If you see anybody approaching run into the jungle and hide. If we spot anybody suspicious my grandson will run to you and warn you."

"Yes, we understand, you tell us what to do."

They worked and stayed with the gardener and his family. They became skilful vegetable gardeners.

They were given some space in the tool shed with mats to sleep on. They ate meals with the family and made sure to hide their mats away and not show any evidence of their presence. They were happy working away with food to eat and a place to sleep. Weeks went by.

One day the grandson came running, making signs for them to go into the jungle and hide. One single Japanese soldier came to the garden. He searched the place and demanded a bundle of vegetables.

Desa and Kuppu were hiding and listening. The soldier entered the house. After some conversation there was a commotion in the house. They heard screaming.

Desa said, "We have to help them, the soldier does not know about us and it's two against one."

"He probably has a gun."

"I'll go for the gun and you will go for him and together we will overpower him."

"Are you sure we can do that?"

"We must help."

The soldier had knocked the old man down. Found some ropes and tied up him and the wife. He ordered the children to get out. The children ran to Desa and Kuppu. Kuppu told the children to stay there and keep quiet.

Desa and Kuppu, the latter holding a hoe in his hand, sneaked back quietly and were able to see what was happening through the window. The Japanese was taking his own sweet time. He slapped the daughter-in-law across the face, held his gun to her face and told her to shut up or he would kill her. The old man began to protest loudly, perhaps loud enough for Desa and Kuppu to hear. The soldier punched him in the mouth and his wife began to cry. Feeling sure that nobody else was around the Japanese placed his gun on the floor and started to unbuckle his pants. The door was closed but had no lock. He began ripping the daughter-in-law's clothes off and was on top of her when both Desa and Kuppu rushed in. Desa went for the gun and even before he could grab it Kuppu crashed the hoe on the Japanese's head. The soldier, caught totally by surprise, looked at Kuppu, twitched and fell on top of the girl, blood gushing from his head.

Desa moved him and helped the girl up. The Japanese was dead. They all stared at the dead soldier. They had to get rid of him. The old man brought some gunny sacks and with everyone giving a hand they put the body in and tied the bag. The children came running back to their mother who embraced them and started instructing them to keep this a secret. Kuppu was shivering. He couldn't believe what he had done. Desa held him tight and said, "Let's do it." They went into the jungle beyond the garden and dug a grave.

It was already evening and they couldn't delay. All four of them loaded the body on to a wheelbarrow, took it out and buried it and camouflaged it with dried branches and leaves.

That night the old man and the family especially the daughter-in-law thanked both of them. The old man said, "It is no longer safe for you to remain here. They will surely come looking for the missing soldier. We will tell them we never saw any soldier. Before daylight you both should be gone."

"Yes, you are right," said Desa.

They packed some food for them, dried meat and salted vegetables and uncooked rice. Desa and Kuppu bid their farewell and as they were leaving Chai stopped Desa and handed him the gun.

"You take this with you. We don't want it here. It may be useful to you in the jungle."

"If we are caught with it..." began Kuppu

"We are not going into town. I'll take the risk." They slipped into the jungle and were soon back on the railway line.

They were back on their routine plodding along the railway looking for birds and squirrels not knowing how long or how far they had to travel before they reach Malaya.

Chapter 25

Like Ships Passing in the Night

They heard a train coming. They hid in the jungle fringe behind trees and watched. They saw a train loaded with Indians moving north. They did not look like prisoners or plantation workers because they were in military uniform. They were Indian soldiers and in some of the wagons they thought they saw Indian women soldiers. They couldn't believe their eyes. They had never seen Indian women soldiers in Malaya.

"Where are they coming from? Indians going to war? And against whom?" Desa wondered.

"They are not wearing the uniform of the *velakaran* soldiers. I have never seen such an army, not even in India."

They were puzzled but it had nothing to do with them, so they continued their own march.

***

Janeki sitting in the train and looking out the window saw only the green jungle flying past. She was wondering where Desa could be. She had no idea that a railway line was being constructed from Bangkok to Rangoon and already completed. She had not heard of the Death Railway. There was no news about it. All she knew was that Desa, Kuppu and Arokia were taken to Siam to work on the railway. *Will I ever get a chance to see him?* She wondered as the train chugged along. They had passed each other like ships in the night.

Janeki's train was forced to stop along the Death Railway line and the troops were allowed to get out and stretch their legs and what she saw made her shiver. Men like resurrected corpses were working along the line. From their attire she gathered they were plantation workers. She strained her eyes to see anyone who looked like Desa or Kuppu or Arokia. They all looked almost alike, gaunt, emaciated, starving and looking sick. She went up and down the line staring at the faces of all the men. There was no sight of her loved one. She saw many Europeans, also in the same desperate state. It dawned on her that the Japanese were responsible for this and there she was going to fight the Indians alongside the Japanese. She was in a state of confusion.

***

One night Desa and Kuppu were sheltering in a shallow cave at the foot of a limestone hill. In the clear sky the moon was bright. Kuppu heard something move in the bush. They waited quietly. It moved again and grunted. It was a wild boar. When it showed itself again Desa pointed the gun at it and fired and kept firing until he emptied the gun. Except for one all his shots missed the wild boar. The one shot, however, killed it. The rest of the night was spent cutting it up with the sharpened bicycle mudguard. The skin was so tough that the piece of metal kept twisting and breaking. Shielded by the limestone hill they braved lighting a fire. It was morning by the time they got the meat cooked. It was a feast and they spent the rest of the day at the limestone hill. Seeing that the gun was useless without bullets Desa threw it into the bush. It came in handy at the right time. They enjoyed the wild boar listening to the birds sing and the bats flying in and out of the cave.

***

The railway construction that commenced from two ends, Bangkok and Rangoon in June 1942, finally made the connection at the Three Pagodas Pass on 17 October 1943. Janeki's train travelled the full length of the Death Railway joining it from the south at Ban Pong and moving into Kanchanapuri where Desa and his friends had laboured. It went over the bridge near the confluence of the two rivers, the Mae Klong and the Kwai Noi. Going slowly through the precarious Hell Fire Pass it went over several wooden bridges skirting the Kwai Noi River until it crossed the Burmese border at the Drei Pagoden Pass or the Three Pagodas Pass. Then crossing the Atarano River the onward journey brought them to Moulmein and on to Rangoon. All along the way there were still men working. Janeki strained her eyes looking for Desa all the way. When the regiment reached Rangoon in April 1944 battles were already under way at the India-Burma border. At Rangoon they were placed in Kamayut, a camp where they immediately recommenced their training. All they did was train and march and make a grand display of their training. That was what they were, a show piece to impress the Burmese and Japanese top brass. Their parades were witnessed by the Burmese president Ba Maw and the Chief of Staff Aung San who were suitably impressed.

There was also another propagandist motive which, in all probability, was at the back of Chandra Bose's mind. On entering India the women of the Rani of Jhansi Regiment would form the vanguard of the army. The Indian soldiers of the British army in India on seeing their own girls falling one by one would be so shocked that they would drop their arms in mutiny leading to the collapse of the British power in India. If that was his motive it was indeed a sinister one planned to betray the women. The women would have gone ahead and done as ordered because they were so infatuated with Bose. They would have done anything for him. However, this did not happen.

The Indian forces under British Command in Bengal were told that the Indian National Army was a puppet army of the Japanese made up of traitors. For them the Rani Regiment of women was all part of the INA.

***

Desa and Kuppu kept plodding on until they came to a town they recognized as Padang Besar. They were in Malaya, not knowing that they had crossed the Siamese border. However, there was no sign of any border saying Siam or Malaya. The shops seemed to display words in the Siamese language.

Here they found a lot of Malays but they were hesitant to approach them because they were not sure if they could trust them. The Japanese generally treated the Malays better than the Indians or the Chinese. They were most brutal to the Chinese. Why were these men staying behind? They could be informers, for all they knew. They kept themselves close to the buildings so as not to be seen openly. Sighting some Indian women they approached them at nightfall. Nights were always dark because of the blackout. They found out from them what had been happening.

One woman said, "The *japankaran* have come to liberate us from the *velekaran* and so we and the *japankaran* are going to march to India and drive out the *velekaran* there and bring independence to India. The Indian soldiers under the *velekaran* retreated in defeat. Now they have deserted the *velekaran* and joined the new army that has been set up to fight for the independence of India called the Indian National Army which will join forces with the *japankaran* to free India. 30,000 Indian soldiers had joined up and even Indian women who were far more docile than the men had joined the army forming a women's regiment called The Rani of Jhansi. *Chalo Delhi!* They are going to march to Delhi."

The Indians were very upbeat about this. Desa was becoming more than a little confused. The women had guessed that Desa and Kuppu were escapees but they kept that to themselves and did not ask them any questions. Seeing that they were hungry the Indian women gave them some food. Desa and Kuppu thanked them and quietly slipped away. They spent the night in the kampong sitting under a tree, discussing the situation.

"The Indian leaders in India have been campaigning for independence for a long time. The *velekaran* are bad. They treated the Indians badly, shot them dead mercilessly and yet the Indian armed forces had not rebelled against the British command there. If the Indians in the Indian National Army made up of the Diaspora Indians marched against India, the Indian soldiers will be fighting and killing our own fellow Indians under the *velekaran*'s command. This does not make sense at all unless all the armed forces in India deserted."

"I don't think anything like that would happen. Ghandi is not advocating armed rebellion but non-violence. The concept of an Indian Nationalist Army is a contradiction to what is going on in India."

"The people said that the Indian soldiers outside India were going to fight alongside the *japankaran*. This is both disturbing and confusing. After what we have experienced at the Death Railway how can we ever think of teaming up with the *japankaran*? How can we ever trust the *japankaran*?"

"Even though the British are bastards the *japankaran* are bigger bastards. Their brand of inhuman cruelty and brutality far surpasses that of the *velekaran*. They are so bent on expanding the Japanese empire that nothing and nobody will stand in their way."

"The cruelty of the *japankaran* is open for everyone to see but the *velekaran* does it behind prison walls."

"We cannot trust the *japankaran*."

Moving further south into Kedah and Perak, Desa found the same enthusiasm for the Indian National Army and this newfound energy had somehow boosted the self-image of the Indian which he had been trying very hard to achieve.

Now Desa understood how the Indians were all fired up and looked upon the Japanese as their saviour. He was very disturbed by this.

"Something is badly wrong and misguided. The Indian National Army has no ships or fighter planes or heavy artillery to confront India and expect the *japankaran* to provide all these. If they can treat the Indians the way they have done on the Death Railway they will surely not liberate India out of love for the Indians. The INA is only an infantry force and will likely end up as cannon fodder. I cannot imagine how India can be liberated; if at all, India will end up captive to Japan and that would be an unimaginable tragedy."

As they made their way south, they stopped in Kuala Kangsar. Again there were more Malays around than Chinese or Indians. These people really believed that the arrival of the Japanese army to fight the British was the beginning of freedom and independence for Malaya just as the Indians believed and hoped for the independence of India. When they saw the movement of the Japanese troops they stood by the roadside and gave them the thumbs-up sign just as they gave the south bound fleeing British the thumbs-down sign. Only the Chinese were sceptical.

The Chinese were keeping very much to themselves. Desa and Kuppu went to a coffee shop looking for some work even to wash plates. There was no job available.

They sat down outside the coffee shop.

Chapter 26

The Battle of Imphal

The battle front line to penetrate India from Burma was in the state of Manipur in north-east India. The aim of the Japanese forces was to destroy the Allied forces at Imphal and push into India. Lieutenant-General Renya Mutaguchi planned to capture Imphal by advancing to the Brahmaputra River valley and cut off the Allied lines. Having successfully pushed through Burma, Malaya and Singapore with relative ease, Mutaguchi considered the British and Indian troops as inferior. The Americans had now joined the British. Imphal was well garrisoned by infantry divisions and parachute and tank brigades. Lieutenant-General Genzo Tanagita, Major-General Tsunoru Yamamoto, Lieutenant-General Masafumi Yamauchi led their different infantry divisions while Lieutenant Colonel Nobuo Ueda led the 14th Tank Regiment and Lieutenant Colonel Kazuo Mitsui led the 3rd Heavy Artillery Regiment. Together they accounted for a formidable force. Imphal was surrounded by steep hills thick with jungle and the Japanese thought that the British would not be able to use their tanks in such a terrain and therefore left their anti-tank weapons behind.

The Indian National Army played an insignificant role. The Japanese originally intended using them only for reconnaissance and propaganda and most probably never took the Rani of Jhansi Regiment seriously. However, Chandra Bose insisted on deploying the INA. Its 1st Guerrilla Regiment covered the left flank while its 2nd Guerrilla Regiment was attached to the Yamamoto Force. The others were used as scouts and pathfinders.

The Japanese made progress but later among the Japanese generals there was disagreement. The Allied air forces with both British and American transport aircraft established air superiority over Burma. They flew in men, equipment and supplies into Imphal and parachuted ammunition, rations and drinking water to outlying units.

The weakness of the Japanese was that they were short of supplies. The soldiers were reaching starvation level. By the end of May 1944 the Commander of the Japanese 31st Division ordered a retreat in the face of the counter-offensive by the British.

The tide changed and the Japanese lost Imphal suffering a massive defeat. The Japanese were being pushed back with heavy casualties. The Rani of Jhansi Regiment was ordered to retreat back to Bangkok. By June they were already on the move. They were never at the front line and their only contribution was being a show piece of women who could march as well as men. Because of the high casualty rate the nurses section of the Rani regiment was asked to stay behind and attend to the wounded. Janeki stayed behind with the nurses while the rest of the regiment retreated. They were ordered to discard their Rani of Jhansi Regiment uniform and wear nurses uniform or civilian clothes. They managed to get nurses' uniforms from the nurses in the military hospital and the Burmese *longyi*. A *longyi* is a sheet of cloth sewn into a cylindrical shape like a *sarong*. It is worn around the waist, running to the feet and held in place by folding the fabric over without a knot. The only give away was the language otherwise they looked no different from the Burmese. Janeki was kept very busy everyday while weeks and months passed by.

Chapter 27

MPAJA

Sitting in front of the coffee shop, Desa and Kuppu met Ah Kow who recognized Desa.

He said, "You are so thin, I almost did not recognize you. Where have you been?"

Desa explained his dreadful experience and introduced Kuppu adding that Arokia who also worked at the mine had died from illness and bad treatment by the Japanese.

"In the estates and villages the situation is getting very bad. Those who are left behind are made to do forced labour," said Ah Kow.

"Is the rubber tapping still going on in the estates?" asked Desa.

"In most estates the processing machines have been destroyed, but in some estates they are restarting work. Otherwise the tappers are forced to do all kinds of work without pay. The biggest crisis is food. There is shortage of rice. You cannot even buy it anymore. They have just introduced Japanese money, so all the dollars are useless. The shopkeepers cannot estimate the value of the new money. You have to get a work pass and a work badge before you can work. If you work they give you ration cards and tickets for food. People have to queue up for a long time and the food often runs out."

"What about the coal mine?"

"The buildings there were hit by bombs and destroyed but now the Japanese are reopening the mine because they need the coal to run the trains. There too they use forced labour. The Japanese will soon start up the rubber plantations because they also want rubber for their war effort. We are continuing to reach out to workers, trying to form unions and we need people. We now have the Malayan Peoples' Anti Japanese Army, the MPAJA, and are asking the workers to join. Seeing the way the Japanese are treating the people especially the Chinese and the women they are having second opinions about the Japanese. This army is our popular front, the front of the Communist Party of Malaya, CPM. We need a lot more Indians joining us. Would you like to join the party and help the workers?"

"Could you tell more about this army, the Malayan Peoples' Anti Japanese Army?"

Ah Kow explained, "You have not been in touch with what has happened since the Japanese invaded Malaya on 8 December 1941. The CPM offered the British military cooperation. The British immediately made a friendly gesture by releasing all left-wing political prisoners. They had to act very fast, so they trained our members in guerrilla warfare and sabotage work in Singapore at what they call the 101st Special Training School. This happened while the Japanese were still advancing from the north of Malaya. They managed to hastily train about 165 of our men just before the Japs reached Singapore. They, although not well equipped, were sent behind the Japanese lines to conduct armed resistance against the occupying Japanese army. This guerrilla force was the beginning of the MPAJA."

Many of those who first joined were Chinese, both men and women, so the Japanese have been very cruel to the Chinese. While our members were hiding in Batu Caves in Kuala Lumpur the Japanese attacked on secret information and killed 100 CPM members. In spite of that we have been increasing in numbers. Today Indians and Malays are also our members. What about you two?"

Desa thought for a while.

"We need to think and discuss this further. Can you give us some time?"

"OK, I've got a meeting in the coffee shop. I will come out again in four hours' time. Meet me here."

Desa and Kuppu discussed.

"The Indians will be asked to work again in the estates. Having taken away most of the men to the Burma Death Railway, they will rope in all the local people to work in the estates especially the Indians who are the ones who know the work," said Desa.

"There are no ships carrying passengers. There are no more immigrants from India. Our men and women will be in demand," responded Kuppu.

"Knowing the *japankaran*, their exploitation will be far worse than that of the *velekaran* for the workers. Right now our people are head over heels in love with Chandra Bose and look up to the *japankaran*. Their self-esteem has been boosted but I fear they are heading in the wrong direction."

"I think you and I know something about the *japankaran* that they don't. They are much more fragmented now than before. Conditions are extremely bad and through unions they might be able to make some demands."

"The MPAJA might not be a bad idea. It could wake them up to face reality."

"Ah Kow wants us to reach out to the Indian workers and the MPAJA might serve as a vehicle for us to do that."

"Yes, but Kuppu, I must first find Janeki."

"We can get employment in the estate. The new people wouldn't know who we are. We should think more carefully before joining Ah Kow's party."

"If we get employed in the estate we will be under the *japankaran*'s forced labour. I have had enough of the *japankaran*. I do not want to work under them."

"Let's ask Ah Kow to give us some time to get back to him."

When Ah Kow reappeared they dialogued with him. He was immediately sceptical that they would come back to him.

"OK, I can't force you but we need people like you, we need leaders. Every other Thursday I have a meeting with a committee here in the coffee shop. You can meet me here, but nobody must know."

Chapter 28

Rani Regiment Retreat

The British army of the 14th Regiment, led by General William Slim who pushed back the Japanese, took over the hospital at Monywa, northwest of Mandalay on the eastern bank of the River Chindwin, and retained the nursing corps. Already accepted as a nurse, Janeki was then sent to another hospital in Maymyo, a beautiful scenic hill town located in the Shan Highland east of Mandalay with a climate conducive to good health at the height of 3510 feet. There were casualties from both sides. The INA personnel and the Japanese casualties were prisoners of war. The rest of the Rani Regiment that left were attacked and fired upon by the Burmese resistance forces and were also hit by the Allied bombs. They lost a few women. They died without even being on the front line. The survivors of the Rani women made it to Bangkok and later back to Malaya where the Rani of Jhansi Regiment disbanded. Janeki remained in Burma.

Janeki was kept so busy that she had no time to think of Desa, but whenever she was off duty, day or night, she thought about him and worried about him. She heard more horror stories about the Death Railway and the thousands who had died.

Janeki found a close friend in Lucy, a Burmese from Rangoon. They both shared their personal stories.

"Lucy, I don't see much point in working here. I am not considered a prisoner of war and I am not obliged to stay. I want to get away and look for Desa."

"Me too; I want to get back to my family in Rangoon."

Janeki has been thinking:

People say that hundreds of workers from Malaynadu have died

*while constructing the railway. Coming up to Rangoon there was no
sign of him and his friends. Desa could well be dead. If that is the case
my life is at a dead end. Being so close to India I could cross the border
and go home. But I am not sure if Desa is dead. He could still be alive
on the railway.*

*I will make an effort to find him. If I can work my way back along
the railway line I could still look for him. I will search every railway
sleeper along the way. Even if he has gone back to Malaynadu I will
continue to search for him. It is already two months and I am wasting
my time here and there are other nurses who can do my work.*

On 7 June, Janeki consulted Lucy on making her way back to
Malaya.

"Janeki, I heard that a number of bridges along that railway have
been bombed. There are no trains running."

"I will walk then."

"It is not safe."

"I don't care; I must go."

"We can make our way down to Rangoon together and you can
decide what to do from there."

"Agreed, but we will just have to disappear without telling
anybody."

"There's one bus that comes up to Maymyo twice a week from
Mandalay. I can get a friend to book tickets for us. It is better for us
not to take the bus from here, we can be spotted. We have to walk
down to the village and catch the bus there dressed like village girls
in *longyi and eingyi* with hats." *Eingyi* is a form-fitting waist length
blouse with a mandarin collar.

They carried out their plan and reached Mandalay and from
there the going got tough. The retreating Japanese forces were still
putting up a resistance and the British army had derailed trains and
blew up the railway lines. They had to find other means of transport
although it was not safe to travel - sometimes in lorries or bullock
carts to reach Rangoon. Rangoon was a war zone. Even after the
Allied paratroopers had landed in the mouth of the Irrawaddy River
and moved into Rangoon to cut off the escape route for the Japanese,
fierce fighting was still going on. The Japanese army refused to

surrender even when they were wounded, sick and starving. It was a disgrace to the empire to surrender. Many preferred to heroically commit suicide. The badly wounded were given a lethal injection or a grenade to do with it what they wanted. There were double suicides where two close friends would embrace each other holding a grenade between them. Janeki heard these stories related to her. She stayed with Lucy's family for a few days making more enquiries about the railway to Bangkok. The people had so many terrible stories to tell about it that they called it the Death Railway.

Janeki and Lucy spoke to some of the survivors who had returned to Burma. There were several white men too who came to Rangoon and were hospitalised. She learned of the ill treatment, starvation and death. Some she discovered went to Bangkok and others south to Malaya. Many more were still there hanging around the small towns with nowhere to go. They had been abandoned by the Japanese. Janeki had saved up most of her army allowances and the extra she received as a nurse in the hospital. Lucy's family also gave her some money. She took only what was necessary. Travelling by bus, lorry, bullock cart or boat, she made her way down in search of Desa.

* * *

Desa and Kuppu set out in search of Janeki. Reaching Worster estate their enquiries drew a blank. In Dolby estate nobody knew of Janeki for she had not worked there. They found out, however, that *kangany* Perumal was now the conductor and the new *kangany* was their old mate Antoine. These two buddies were the eyes and noses of the Japanese bosses. Desa and Kuppu stayed clear for they did not want a confrontation right now. Even at Hartford estate no one had any clear idea of Janeki.

They also learnt from the workers what had happened in many of the estates. The Japanese, when they moved into the estate had rounded up the *kiranies* and got them to coax and coerce the able-bodied men to go with the Japanese to work on the Burma railway. The *kiranies* often singled out the newly married men and sent them out. After they had gone they forced their wives to become their mistresses. Desa was mad on hearing this and wondered if any *kirany* or even Perumal had done the same with Janeki. He would kill them.

Desa consulted Kuppu, "It will be difficult for us to visit all the estates by ourselves. Ah Kow and his party have funds and a way of moving around efficiently. Perhaps, being with them might give us more access to the estates. What think you da?"

"We have no jobs and no money; joining them will take care of our basic needs. Yes, I think we should."

They went for the rendezvous on Thursday at the coffee shop.

Chapter 29

Joining the MPAJA/CPM

"Ah Kow, how can we join your party? We can help organize workers to form unions," said Desa.

"I'm afraid unions have been outlawed. Right now our objective is fighting the Japanese. While the Indians have the INA, fighting with the Japanese, we have the MPAJA, fighting with the British against the Japanese. The closest we have come to unions is the civilian arm of the Communist party, the Malayan Peoples' Anti-Japanese Union, MPAJU. Perhaps you can help in this area."

What an about turn of loyalties, thought Desa. "If it came to a confrontation, will I have to fight the Indians too?" asked Desa.

"The Indian National Army comes under its own command and its target is India. The Japanese are our enemy, not the Indians. You will also have to undergo some training. Come into the coffee shop."

Ah Kow told the man in the kitchen to fix Desa and Kuppu a meal and coffee. Before he went to the back room for a meeting he said, "Desa, you wait here for me."

When it was almost dark he came out with three other men and a woman and asked Desa and Kuppu to follow him. They walked along the back lane in a single file through some vegetable gardens to the huts of the gardeners. Partly hidden behind some kampong houses they entered what looked like another ordinary kampong house. This was where they operated from. They slept the night there. Early in the morning before sunlight they had some bread and coffee. Desa and Kuppu were given rubber shoes and shirts to wear.

They began tracking into the jungle. Ah Kow and another Chinese man walked in front followed by another man and

Desa. Behind Desa were Kuppu and the woman and another man brought up the rear. Kuppu watching the woman thought, *What is such a young and beautiful woman doing fighting in the jungle.* In the late afternoon they reached a limestone cave. The entrance was concealed behind a grove of trees and plants. Without disturbing the camouflage they snaked their way through them into the cave. They lit their oil lamps and walked one and a half hours before the cave opened up into a large enclave. It was a huge well walled by sheer vertical limestone cliffs opening way up high to the blue sky. There were bamboo huts with thatched *nipah* roofs which were living quarters and a larger one for meetings. The centre was a training ground. After a meal of rice and egg with soup, Desa and Kuppu were shown a place in one of the huts where they could sleep.

In the morning after a breakfast of porridge for everybody they were asked to sign some papers then assembled in the training ground. There were young men and women, more like boys and girls, all Chinese except for two young Indian lads. They sang the *Internationale* and the commander started them off with physical exercises followed by military hand to hand combat exercises. This was followed by drill and marching with wooden rifles. In the afternoon, after a lunch of chicken soup and rice everyone had a short siesta. The troop was marched to the far end of the enclave into the mouth of another cave. This cave descended underground. The passage was lit with oil lamps until it opened out into a large yard. This was the rifle range.

Here they were trained to use the rifle and other small arms and the handling of explosives. This intensive training went on for one month interspersed with lectures on the communist ideology much of which was lost to Desa and Kuppu because they were delivered in Mandarin. At the end of the training they were divided into small groups and sent on different missions. Desa's group was assigned to collect arms and ammunition.

As the British forces were retreating in a hurry they had abandoned most of their weapons and ammunition. These were hidden in strategic spots in the jungle, others were just left behind - much of which were taken by the INA. There were still plenty more around which the MPAJA grabbed. There was looting going on everywhere and small arms and ammunition too were looted. The task of Desa's group was to search and retrieve these looted weapons which meant going house to house. Often the people denied having them. When threatened they surrendered them. They were told in no uncertain terms that these weapons would be used to fight the Japanese. To the non-Chinese Desa had to explain, "If the *japankaran* catch you with the weapons they will not just take them from you. They will shoot you first. If you have weapons the *Kempeitai* will surely find out, do you want them to come to your house?" *Kempeitai* is the Military Police Corp, the military police arm of the Imperial Japanese Army from 1881 to 1945.

They readily handed over whatever guns and ammunition they had looted. The very mention of the *Kempeitai* sent shudders through them. The *Kempeitai* were the Japanese military police known for their naked brutality. They would kick, slap, punch, arrest, detain and torture even without any provocation, simply to demonstrate their power and control. They were dreaded and feared by all. Each day Desa's group took back a sizable assortment of small arms and ammunition before the *Kempeitai* could move in.

Desa also discovered that the plantations were practically dislocated. Workers were forced to do other work. Some of the plantations were being jump started where the infrastructure was sufficiently intact.

The workers were already down to below subsistence level. Rice dwindled to a stop and they had to depend on tapioca. Such being the case the esteemed INA itself began to harass the workers. Their representatives came and insisted, on the command of Chandra Bose, that they make monetary contributions towards the army. The workers were down and out and victimised. Many deaths resulted from malnutrition especially among the children. The people began to have second thoughts about the Japanese as liberators.

Desa despaired. It was an impossible situation to even contemplate starting any unions. He, however, began to win some support from the people for the MPAJA which was the only force resisting the Japanese and suspicious of the INA.

The different groups were sent on strike missions. Desa and Kuppu were on different missions. They were now called mobile squads with the objective of identifying the enemy and those giving assistance to the enemy and eliminating them. They also had CPM sympathisers who would send information. Desa's squad received information that three *Kempeitai* officers were in a coffee shop dressed in civilian clothes. One was recognized by his looks and they also had pistol handles sticking out of their pockets carelessly concealed. The shop keeper had daughters upstairs and they were asking for them speaking with Japanese accents. They were obviously not on official duty. When Desa and his unit arrived one of the *Kempeitai* was roughing up the shopkeeper. Desa intervened to stop the aggressor who pulled out his gun. Desa's squad immediately opened fire. There was an exchange of fire. The three *Kempeitai* were dead, one of them shot by Desa. One of Desa's squad was wounded. The unit leader told the people in the shop to quickly bury the bodies and clean up all evidence. They took the weapons of the *Kempeitai* and slipped into the jungle. This was the first time Desa had killed a man.

Back in the camp other mobile squads too brought back casualties and sometimes cadres were lost. They had a problem dealing with casualties because they had no medicine or medical facilities and no doctor.

Learning to live in the jungle was a struggle because of shortage of food and illnesses like fever, dysentery and beri-beri. Medical attention was a necessity especially when many casualties were arriving.

Desa's squad was sent on another mission, this time to secure medical help and supplies. They were sent to the small town of Gopeng.

Gopeng was 12 miles south of Ipoh with a dispensary that also had beds for treating emergency cases. It had a good supply of medicine and the only medical facility for the whole region. Desa's squad surrounded the dispensary hiding in the deep monsoon drain outside. They waited until the last patient had left and moved in.

"Yes, how can I help you," said the dresser.

Desa immediately recognized him. It was Devasagayam Pillay from Dolby estate. He was very surprised to see Desa. The unit leader said, "We are from the MPAJA and we need you to come with us. We have many casualties and we cannot always bring them here to you. We need you and your medicine to attend to our casualties at our base in the jungle."

"I am sorry. I am a family man with five small children. I cannot leave them. You can bring your casualties even at night and I will attend to them. I cannot go with you."

One young member of the squad drew his gun and placed it on the forehead of Devasagayam.

"You come with us or you die." He said.

Desa stepped in and pushed him aside. "He is the only medical man in this whole region. You kill him, then what?"

He turned to Desa who also drew his gun and pushed it against the young man's chest.

The unit leader stepped in. "This kind of indiscipline is not tolerated in the CPM. Put your guns down," he commanded.

Devasagayam said, "I will not turn your casualties away. You can take all the medicine if you want but I will not leave my family. I will even supply you medicine when you need it."

They saw that he was determined and also saw in him an ally who would help them in an emergency. The leader ordered the unit to take all the available medicine in the dispensary, then he turned to Devasagayam, "We will send you one of our members, a woman, and you must train her how to administer emergency aid and explain all the medicine to her and how to use them. If anyone checks on you, you say she is a patient. We will come to you now and then. If the *Kempeitai* finds out we will kill you before they do."

They collected all the medicine in the dispensary and vanished. Devasagayam was grateful to Desa. His house was just opposite the dispensary and he was looking forward to going home early because it was Christmas Eve. Devasagayam was a Christian. He walked home devastated. He said nothing to his family but his wife knew something was wrong. How was he going to explain this to the Japanese? The next day, Christmas Day, he went to the dispensary and smashed the lock and hung it back on the door, then went to the police station and made a report that the dispensary was broken into and all the medicine were gone.

Later in the day the *Kempeitai* arrived and questioned him. He stuck to his story. They brought a crime investigator who studied the break-in. That night they came back and arrested Devasagayam. He was accused of collaborating with the communists. The dispensary doors were ten feet tall and heavy. They decided that if there was a break-in there would have been marks on the door but there were none. A broken lock was merely hanging on the latch loop. Devasagayam knew the game was up. They tortured him for information about the communists but he stuck to his story that what he saw was what he found in the morning. He was imprisoned in Kampar, a further 12 miles south of Gopeng. Desa later visited him in prison on the pretext of being a relative.

Chapter 30

Janeki Moves South

By July Janeki reached the town of Thanbyuzayat, the name meant "a white iron resting hut." It lies at the foothills that separate Burma from Siam. She approached some men who looked like Indians but they were Burmese. They knew nothing about Indians coming here from Malaya to work on the railway. The only workers here were the Burmese and the white prisoners of war brought from the Rangoon jail. There were plenty of graves with no markings on them. There was a large hospital camp with wounded and sick patients. Janeki spent some time there talking to the nurses and the patients. Their stories of suffering and ill treatment were fresh. The Japanese took some of the white prisoners of war on the train to Bangkok. She learned nothing about the men she was looking for.

***

Desa and Kuppu met up with Ah Kow. They tried to get a clarification on their position and role as members of the MPAJA which was not identical with the Communist Party of Malaya and therefore they were strictly not party members.

"You both have been initiated as party members but you are also MPAJA. Soon you will be asked to recruit members for the MPAJU. Right now, we have an agreement with Force 136; they are the British commandos who have made contact with us. In return for arms, money, training, and supplies the MPAJA will cooperate and accept the British Army's orders during the war with Japan. So you will have to carry out these orders. OK, since you are Indians your task will be to eliminate those who collaborate with the Japanese and get recruits from the Indians to join the MPAJA and the MPAJU."

They were assigned to another mobile squad for this task. It was called the "Traitor Killing Squad." It was in retaliation to the Japanese's espionage squad whose task was to spot MPAJA members, who would be tortured and killed when caught.

The unit moved into estates usually after muster time when all the workers were in the timber and the Japanese bosses had retired to the bungalows. They surrounded the office building where the *kiranies*, conductors and *kanganies* were working, moved in, shot them and burnt the office building and disappeared before the Japanese could come down. They had done this to a number of estates before they came to Dolby. This time Perumal and Antoine were among those eliminated. Antoine was already shot by Kuppu and Desa shot Perumal. In their dying moment both Antoine and Perumal fixed their eyes with an incomprehensible stare at Desa and Kuppu. Their one-time close friend had turned traitor. As for Perumal, he got what was coming to him.

This second echelon of authority, the "black Japanese" were not only collaborators but lackeys of the Japanese who bullied, cheated and thrashed their own people.

That night Desa could not sleep. He could not believe that he had become so hardened. When he first arrived in Malaya and started work in the rubber plantation he was like the liquid rubber, the milk white latex flowing innocently, freely and smoothly into the earthen receptacle. Before long if not collected it will harden into a lump. When the liquid latex undergoes a chemical process by the addition of sulfur under high pressure and temperature it becomes vulcanized. The process is generally irreversible. Hard vulcanized rubber is like ebonite and it is named after Vulcan the Roman god of fire. Desa realized that he had indeed become hard hearted. He was part of the squad that killed his one-time close friend Antoine. And he also felt no remorse in killing Perumal, the man who recruited him and cheated him and oppressed the workers. "*Desa, the vulcanized rubber!*" He heard himself saying.

***

Janeki made her way down braving enormous risks but she always found Burmese families to approach. She had picked up a fair command of the language. She did not want to miss any of the stops be they labour camps or villages or small towns. She went through places named Kendau, Wagale, and Thetkaw to Alepauk covering 11 miles. She went through the same process of questioning and searching. In Alepauk she had to take shelter with the Burmese families because of aerial bombing. The Allied air force was systematically destroying the Death Railway. She heard that further down many of the bridges were being bombed. She refused to stay long in any of the towns where there was scant information on what she wanted. She continued down through Kun Kuit Kway to Tanyin. Travelling with the villagers in a bullock cart she reached Beke Taung making about 24 miles. In all these places she scrutinised every grave she could find for names and clues of Desa and his mates. Everywhere she drew a blank.

***

The Indian estate workers did not suspect that Desa and Kuppu were among those MPAJA members who eliminated their *kiranies*. They thought that they were Chinese from the Communist Party. Desa and Kuppu also kept it a secret. The workers were spared the "black Japanese" oppression.

The MPAJA went round the estates in civies arranging secret meetings without the knowledge of the Japanese bosses who were preoccupied with their new-found luxury. But after what happened to their lackeys they became more cautious and deployed sentries. In spite of that they had grenades thrown into their bungalows.

Desa spoke, "You were all under the impression that the *japankaran* had come to free us from the oppression of the *velekaran*. Neither the *velekaran* nor the yellow *japankaran* are our friends. Their only interest in us is to use us to make themselves rich. You have no idea what the *japankaran* are really like when they have set their mind on building their world empire. Kuppu and I were among the hundreds of our brothers who were sent to the Burma railway. They treated us worse than working animals. We drank dirty water, got sick, worked and died. Many of the men who went from this estate will never come back. Arokianathan who worked in Dolby estate was with us. Although he got very sick he was made to work until he died. If any of them do come back it would be a miracle. You women prepare yourselves to be widows and your children orphans. You don't like to hear this but this is the truth. Even here and now if we don't fight the *japankaran* we will have no future. Under forced labour we are already suffering so much and, to make things worse, the conductors, the *kiranies* and the *kanganies* have become the black *japankaran* and continue to cheat and bully the workers. They are selfish bastards.

"You were all so enthusiastic about the INA. Many of your men and women joined them and have gone to Burma to fight to bring independence to India. The *japankaran* don't love us, so do you think that they are going to make India free? They only want to fight their enemy the British and take over India. And what is our INA doing? They are fighting our own brothers and sisters of India, fighting and killing ourselves when it is not even our war.

"Now Chandra Bose wants your money to support the INA. At first he asked you to contribute voluntarily and now he is forcing you to pay and using the *Kempeitai*, to threaten you to pay. Do you still want to make sacrifices for Mother India when the INA with the Japanese are killing Indians on the Indian frontier?

"The Chinese here are the ones who have been most harshly treated by the *japankaran* who overran China and are now fighting in Burma. They have taken over this country. Just like you had the Indian National Army, the Chinese have built up another army, a people's army called the Malayan Peoples' Anti Japanese Army – The MPAJA. Kuppu and I have joined this army. Since the only future for us is to resist the *japankaran* I invite you also, men and women, to join this MPAJA. Surprisingly, the *velekaran* is also supporting the MPAJA, again not because they love us, but because the *japankaran* are their enemy and they need all the support they can get.

"I call you to think beyond the MPAJA. Look on it as a stepping stone to revive the workers' unions. It is through the unions that we can demand the rights of workers, whoever the bosses might be."

"We have been deceived and betrayed from all sides, how much can we trust the MPAJA?" asked one of them.

"It is for us to make it work. As I said, join it now and we can start building the bases for the unions. Right now the unions are outlawed. We must be united to reclaim our right to form unions. *Makal Sakthi*! If we are united we will have the strength. There is a rumour that the *japankaran* are losing the war in Burma which means that our INA too will not see its aim fulfilled. Kuppu will take down the names of those who want to join the MPAJA."

For many of the workers this speech was an eye-opener. The call for nationalism and the independence of India by Chandra Bose had indeed boosted their self-image and they were prepared to be more assertive now. Desa saw this as a good platform to work on.

∗∗∗

Janeki moved on through Tanbaya, a camp marked Kilo.55 camp, Mezali, Melioe, reaching Kilo.100 camp near the border. At all these places she learned nothing new. She crossed the border to the crucial point when the tracks which began from Moulmein and Ban Pong met, a place called the "Three Pagodas Pass." Here Janeki found out for the first time that there were Indian workers but nobody was sure where they came from.

She conversed in Burmese with one of the men who had worked here.

"The Indians were the front workers on the line from the south who came and joined us here. Many of them died when they arrived here and many more died on the way here. There are graves of those who died here."

A lot of the graves had names painted on wooden crosses. There were European names and she was told they were English names, Dutch names and French names. There were other Burmese and Siamese names and only a few Indian names. Then there were also several graves with no names. She was also shown mass graves, huge mounds with any number of bodies in them. When Janeki saw them she almost despaired.

"Oh, Desa where are you?" She sat down and cried.

Chapter 31

Search for Janeki

At each estate they visited after his address to the workers, Desa would hold a conversation with the women.

"How have the women been treated here? How many of them had become mistresses of the *kiranies*?" He would ask. At Sogomana estate in the course of a conversation like this he was confronted by two women. They were different. They stood straight and held themselves with dignity.

They objected to his criticism of the INA and particularly of Chandra Bose of whom they had a very high opinion. He found out that they were soldiers of the Rani of Jhansi Regiment. This was the first time he had confronted the regiment and it was the women's section of the INA. These women had just returned from Burma.

Both Desa and Kuppu had the same thought at the same time. *Could Janeki have joined the Rani of Jhansi Regiment?*

Desa asked the women many questions about the regiment and how they managed to get back. Many women like them from the estates had joined up.

Desa and Kuppu as members of the MPAJA and the CPM could only see these women as representing the enemy.

"Are you still with the Rani of Jhansi Regiment?" asked Desa.

"We are soldiers of the Rani Regiment of the INA. We are prepared to fight the *velekaran* for the freedom of India."

"Many of you joined the INA because you were so enamoured of Chandra Bose. Do you know that other women here at first voluntarily gave their jewels and savings to support his campaign in Burma? Later the India Independence League officials were forcing the men to join the Army and the *Kempeitai* were pressuring the people to pay when it had no money for food? Now, people do not trust the *japankaran* and we have another army, the Malayan Peoples' Anti Japanese Army. Many of the men who have deserted the INA have joined the MPAJA.

"If you insist on being a member of the Rani regiment your lives could be in danger. You would be considered collaborators of the *japankaran*. On the other hand, you can join the MPAJA or if you choose not to you better keep quiet and not speak about your Rani Regiment. Tell us what happened in Burma?"

One of them said, "We were winning at first at the front line and were waiting to enter India when the fighting changed. We lost the battle of Imphal and we were ordered to retreat."

"How did you get back?" asked Kuppu.

"By train; we came back in different batches."

"Do you know of a woman by the name of Janeki?" asked Desa.

"Oh, do you know Janeki?" asked one of the women.

"Yes, was she with you?"

"Yes, she was a great leader."

Desa's inside surged with hope and excitement.

"Janeki Bai was our second Lieutenant," said the other woman.

"Janeki Bai...?" Desa was deflated. "What did she look like?"

"She is thin and very tall. She comes from Ipoh."

"The Janeki we know of is the daughter of Kaliaperumal," said Kuppu.

"Do you know of anyone else by the name of Janeki?"

"She could have been in a different section, we are not sure."

"Do you know of any woman from Woster estate who joined?"

"There were at least one or more from all the estates around here."

Desa thanked them for the information and warned them to be discreet and to be careful with whom they talk to. He left.

"Kuppu, let's go back to Woster estate and find out. She was known there as your wife."

They immediately dropped everything and headed for Woster estate. They had friends and collaborators through whom they sneaked in and spoke to the women there. They made contact with one of the women soldiers, Jeya, who had returned from Burma. They found out that Janeki had indeed joined the Rani of Jhansi Regiment.

Jeya further filled in on the details of their life at the front.

"During our training Janeki had joined the Nurses' Corps and became the leader of the group. When we were asked to retreat the Nurses' Corps was asked to stay back to attend to the war casualties. That is all I know. The rest of us were broken up into batches and we made our way back. Some of us died on the way back."

Desa gave them the same advice that he had given to those other women and thanked them for the information.

From the men they found out that many of the INA soldiers had deserted. The retreat was disastrous. They and those of the railway workers who were still alive and strong enough made their way back. From them they learned that the Death Railway had been bombed by the Allied Air Force. Others were still trickling back if they could get on the south-bound trains from Siam.

Desa and Kuppu were discussing the situation.

"If the men are deserters we can persuade them to join us but if they plan to regroup the INA they are enemy to be eliminated," said Kuppu.

"If Janeki insists on being in the army she too will be considered a collaborator," said Desa.

"We have to find her before the others do."

"There are two things that she could have done. Being so close to the border she could have decided to return to India; or else, she might have gone to the Death Railway looking for us."

"She could still be at the nursing hospital or she could be on her way back any time now."

"Kuppu, it is no longer your problem. I must go to Burma to find her."

"How would you travel? It is war time and there are no boats. The Death Railway is bombed."

"Whatever, I have to go and find her. You carry on with the work here and tell Ah Kow that we have split and are working in the different estates recruiting men for the MPAJA."

"Desa, think carefully. Janeki would know by now that we were taken to the railway construction. She would rather go looking for you than try and go back to India. With the war front at the border crossing it would not be easy."

"It would be too dangerous for her to make that journey at this time."

"Don't forget, she is a combat fighter and do you think the hazards will stop her?"

"If she were making her way down and I make my way up we could easily miss each other just like we missed her when she went in that train."

"I think the only way she could travel south is by train."

"O.K., Kuppu you stay on and recruit members for the MPAJA. The people are no longer interested in the INA and food for the stomach is more important to them now than independence for India. There is no way you can contact me and if you are going to work in Woster, I will write to you, if there is postal service. Good bye and take of yourself. There are informers and enemies everywhere."

"Here da, you take this; it is not much but I can earn some more. Your money will run out soon."

Chapter 32

Desa Moves North

Desa accepted the Japanese banana notes and got some of his things together. Desa and Kuppu parted company. It was the 2 August. He made his way to the Sungei Siput railway station where he found the schedule of every south bound train even though the trains were not running according to schedule. He opened a cardboard box, flattened it out and, using a piece of charcoal, he wrote in big letters "JANEKI." As the train pulled in he stood on the platform and held the sign up so no passenger could miss it. There was only one train scheduled for the day. He caught the next north-bound train, just hopped in with no ticket. Since the next south-bound train was not due until sometime late the next day he decided to skip some of the smaller stations. He passed Salak Utara station and got off at Kuala Kangsar station.

There was no danger of passenger trains crossing each other because there was only a single track although there might be goods trains. At the Kuala Kangsar station Desa was not taking any chances, even when a goods train went past he held up his cardboard sign. He parked himself on the platform bench and wrote in his exercise book. He wrote whenever he had an opportunity.

***

Janeki did not give up hope. The railway was destroyed and she made her way by boat because the railway was skirting the Kwai Noi River. She stopped at the townships or camps of Nieke, Taimonta, Kon Koita, Krian Krai, Tamajo and Takanum. She stayed wherever she could and was very economical with her money. She had been on the move for more than a month, lost weight and was feeling desperately low. In these Siamese towns the scenario was the same. Some Indian workers were there but they were still recovering from the ordeal of exhaustion. Some of them did come from Malaya, from Kedah and Perlis so they knew nobody from the other states. These were the ones who arrived early and formed the vanguard of construction workers. To travel on she had to take different boats. She was sitting on the boat staring at the water wondering why she had decided to leave India. There were some men on the boat eyeing her. One of them had been drinking and got fresh with her. He tried to make conversation but she remained incommunicative. She was on guard. He came over to her and grabbed her. She made a swift move bringing her knee up to his groin and landed a punch on his stomach, pulled his weight towards her, sidestepped and pushed him overboard. This took everybody by surprise because no one knew that she was a trained combat fighter. She got off the boat at every camp because she did not want to miss any of the camps in her search and got back on any boat that came along. She was determined to find Desa. So she went through Kinsayok, Hintok, and Malayan Hamlet where she searched frantically. From there she had to walk to the next camp, the Konyu R Camp. She was wondering if the whole thing was a futile effort. Konyu, Tampie, Tonchan Spring camp, Tarsau, Wun Yi to Wampo. They were not really towns but camps and fairly close to each other. There were many smaller camps on the way, some abandoned. Many times she had to negotiate the broken bridges. These wooden bridges were constructed on trestles supporting the lines. They were precariously built against the hill slopes with the cliff on one side and valley on the other. Since the bridges were bombed she had to climb down the broken trestles overhanging deep valleys and up again to reach the other side. Here again her training came in handy. There was no other way, for the jungle was too thick to penetrate, apart from the river, which in some parts were far away. There were Siamese people tracking to their villages and she joined them. In their villages she got food and shelter and stayed with them to regain her stamina to continue. All along she saw graves and graves, and at every grave she would spend time looking for names and places. She passed a place called "Hellfire Pass" before she came to Wampo.

Chapter 33

Kuppu Carries On

Kuppu, in the meantime, found that he could not make headway in organizing union activities because unions were banned. The working capacity of the people was badly damaged, the economy stagnated, inflation shot up and the people's lives were under severe strain. Rice and food of any kind were of paramount urgency. Without documents of some kind like work pass, work badge, arm-band, ration card, tickets for food, there was no access to food. Even to listen to the radio, one had to obtain a pass. Usually the radio was confiscated rather than a pass issued. People had to listen to news secretly. The use of English was banned and Japanese was taught in town schools. In the estates, schools were hardly functioning. On top of all this was the vigilant presence of the feared Japanese, the *Kempeitai*, who made no secret of their brutality. The people became quiet and submissive, cowed by fear.

The MPAJA offered some hope of resistance and retaliation. It was successful in skirmishes to disable some of the Japanese control and able to acquire some cachets of food. The young men in the estates and even some women began to look up to the MPAJA. Kuppu focused on the MPAJA recruitment. Ah Kow was now a member of the CPM politbureau. Through the central executive committee of the state of Perak, Kuppu was recommended to lead the party cell in his district. He organized sabotage and ambushes against the Japanese, raiding several police stations and capturing small arms. The MPAJA rapidly increased in numbers with eight regiments. It became a formidable army. While Kuppu belonged to the central and northern Malaya regiment, Desa was moving into the area of the Kedah-Perlis regiment.

***

From Wampo, Janeki had to take the boat to Wan Lung and then to Chung Kai and Tamarkan where the Kwai Noi and the Mae Klong rivers meet. Still there was no sign whatever of Desa or Kuppu or Arokia. She went on land to Kanburi also known as Kanchanapuri. It was the 31st of July. This was a big camp mostly destroyed with huge mounds of mass graves and clusters of individual graves. As usual she scrutinized all the graves, some had rocks, and others, crosses. After spending a whole day, she found no trace of the dear ones she was searching for. At least she was hopeful that they were not among the individual burials. She dreaded the thought that they could be in mass graves. There were a number of construction workers lingering on in this camp. There were Chinese, Siamese, Cauasians and Indians. She spoke to the Indians.

For the first time she was on to something. She found two men who came from the state of Perak in Malaya at an eating stall selling very simple meals of noodles. They were called Rayer and Kesevan.

"Why, nga, are you all still here? Why haven't you gone back?" she asked.

"We missed the last train that was carrying the prisoners of war to Bangkok. All of us here have been very sick and recovering and many with bad wounds in the leg which are not healing. There was a hospital here which has been bombed and no doctors and no medicine. We wait until we are strong enough to move," said Rayer.

"Do you know of any men from Perak who were here?"

"Yes, there were many men from Perak; from the towns and from the estates. We were hardly given any time to get to know one other. We were not allowed to talk to others. It was work, work, and work until many of us dropped dead on the railway track. We just carried their bodies and dumped them in the big hole. Who are you looking for?" asked Rayer.

"There were three men who were taken from Dolby and Woster estates near Sungei Siput. They were Nadesan, Kuppusamy and Arokianathan."

"Other than those who died, some of them tried to escape. They were caught, brought back and punished for all of us to see and then shot dead. We don't know of anyone who might have escaped and survived the jungle. Since not all were caught some could have escaped if they were not killed by tigers or other wild animals. It was difficult to keep count," said Kesevan.

"*Aiyoo, Kadavule!*"

"*Ammah*, did you come all the way here to look for them?" asked Rayer.

"No, I have come from Burma looking for them. Could they have gone up towards Burma?"

"Those who were the first to come here could have moved up with the line. We came in different train loads," said Rayer.

"Please try to think. These three men would have been together, if they were here. One of them is an educated person who could read and write."

"Oh, yes. There was one who would always write on a notebook or any paper he could find. I think I remember, yes, there were three of them and one of them died," said Kesevan.

"*Aiyoo, Muruga!*" said Janeki. Murugan is a popular youthful Hindu deity.

"His friends would not have him thrown into the big hole. You go and look at the individual graves," said Ryan."

"I did, and couldn't find any name."

"Where did you look? There are more graves on the other side of the hospital."

Janeki immediately went looking. After negotiating a maze of graves she found one with a cross and the name *Arokianathan – Orattanadu* written in black paint. She was grief stricken but relieved that it was not Desa. She went around scrutinising all the other graves. Some had no names. She went back to the two men.

"Yes, I found the grave of one of them, Arokianathan from Orattanadu. What could have happened to the other two?"

"They could have gone back with those who deserted the Indian National Army. We don't understand, what is this Indian National Army?" asked Rayer.

"It was an army made up of Indians from outside India and led by Subbas Chandra Bose. The idea was to fight with the *japankaran* to free India from the *velekaran*."

"Fight with the *japankaran*!" exclaimed Kesevan.

"It is the *japankaran* who have forced us to work and die here by the thousands. The *japankaran* are our enemy!" said Rayer with anger.

Janeki did not tell them that she was a soldier in the Rani of Jhansi Regiment, part of the INA. The great contradiction began to dawn on her.

How could we have been fighting with the japankaran who have been so cruel to the Indians? They have used us to fight their war. The velekaran, on the other hand are also using us to fight their war. On the warfront Indians are fighting and killing Indians. We have been the frontline pawns on their chessboard. We have been used and caught between the clash of empires. We looked up to Chandra Bose with so much hope and expectation. Surely, he must have known what the japankaran were doing here constructing the railway on the blood, sweat and lives of Indians. He made no protest. He allowed the sacrifice of lives here for the glory of liberating India. I remember what he told us in one of his speeches that "the enemy of my enemy is my friend." He played us out. What a price to pay! Now the japankaran have lost the fight in Burma and India is still under the velekaran.

"I am a nurse, let us go to the bombed hospital and see what we can find."

With the two men hobbling along she went to the ruins and rummaged through the dispensary. She found some gauze and bandages, antiseptic solutions in gentian violet, mercurochrome and potassium permanganate, penicillin and needles and a quarter bottle of saline. The other bottles were all broken. She also found a thermometer, a stethoscope, scissors, tweezers and splints. She collected these items and laid them out on a piece of plank. Other men also came around to help. They set up a table and helped to clean the items. She spent two days and a night there attending to the wounds of these men. With their help she managed to clean and apply antiseptic solutions and injected penicillin into some of them. With the little she found she did the best she could to set them on the road to recovery.

"I have to leave now. If the men I'm looking for have escaped and survived or are on their way back I'm going to follow the track."

"If you are lucky you can catch a boat at the river down below that could take you to Tamnan," said Kesevan.

She thanked them and they thanked her and she left.

***

The South East Asia Command (SEAC) of the Allied forces had its headquarters in Colombo, Ceylon and it was in liaison with the CPM. The agreement was that paratroopers, ammunition and food supplies would be air-dropped into the jungle. Kuppu was part of the team assigned to collect the food and ammunition. They were in contact by radio and were to standby for the airdrops by Force 136. They retrieved the goods which included bundles of counterfeit banana notes and stashed them away in strategic locations in the jungle not far from the main road and railway line. They were placed in readiness to strike the Japanese who transported their supplies from Singapore.

In one of these occasions among the paratroopers Kuppu noticed a familiar face. It was none other than Roberts who ordered the shooting by the Punjabis that killed six of his mates. Roberts, on the other hand, did not recognize Kuppu at all. What an irony, they are on the same side now. Kuppu tried to keep a straight face and not show his animosity and anger.

It was during one of these missions that Kuppu got to know a female comrade by the name of Chin Leng, a young girl from Ipoh.

***

Desa slept on the platform at the Kuala Kangsar station and waited for the train to arrive. The next day, 3rd August, he went through the same ritual of holding up the sign. There was no response to his sign. He got on the north-bound train and decided to keep going for it was pointless stopping at every station when only one train would come the next day. The train stopped at Padang Rengas and at Bukit Perapit. He decided to stay on the train. Again he travelled without buying a ticket. He knew as a bus conductor that without a ticket all that could happen to him was to be told to get off at the next station. So he proceeded on through Taiping, loathing stopping over there. Just as he feared he spotted the conductor coming along. In these turbulent times the conductor was used to seeing many passengers without tickets. He ordered Desa to get off at the next station. He had no choice but to get off at the small station of Kamunting. He had the whole day to kill. He managed to get out of the station and walked down the road. There were rubber trees on one side and a padi field on the other. He made it to the house of a padi planter. He was surprised to find an Indian padi planter because most were Malay. His name was Murthy. They exchanged stories and he and his wife were hospitable enough to offer him a meal.

***

Kuppu would often retire to the jungle hideout for strategic planning and more training. Many young Chinese women too were attracted to the CPM. In the camp Kuppu became friendly with Chin Leng. She was Chinese educated. They would meet and talk in Malay but they had to be careful. Such a cross racial relationship would more than raise eyebrows.

"You don't recognize me, do you?" asked Chin Leng.

Kuppu tried to remember; the face was familiar but he could not remember talking to any Chinese girls.

"Do you remember the time when Ah Kow brought you and your friend to our hideout?"

"Ah, yes, now I remember. You were one of the group. I was really surprised to find a girl among the party members."

They developed a clandestine relationship. They would try to be on the same squad on raid missions. This was very rare because Kuppu was assigned usually to Indian areas with other Indian comrades. There were certain rules a couple had to follow in case of a relationship. The intended partner had to be a committed member, not sympathetic to any Japanese cause and definitely not a "Kuomintang sympathizer." Moreover, the couple had to report their circumstance to the Party for approval. Until the approval was granted they were not to see each other. At first, the Party was against a mixed-race partnership. Then they realised that they were fighting a class struggle that cuts across ethnic strata. After weeks, they were given the green light but marriage was still a long way off because the situation in the country was still unstable and critical for survival.

They began seeing each other at every opportunity they could get.

***

Desa made his way back to the railway station from the padi planter's house. As he approached the station he noticed some activities. There were Japanese soldiers about. He immediately flung his sling bag into the rubber trees and kept on walking. He heard a motorcycle coming from behind. The motorcycle with a side car was followed by a jeep with soldiers. One of the soldiers got off the jeep and pushed him forward. They were the *Kempeitai*. They were looking for members of the MPAJA or communist sympathizers or British loyalists. They ushered everyone into the station and searched them. It was indeed quick thinking on the part of Desa to have ditched his bag. In the bag he had his membership cards of both the MPAJA and the MCP along with his service pistol. Of course, his journal contained enough incriminating material to have him shot on the spot. They questioned them and those whom they considered suspicious they loaded onto the truck and took them away to the police station. Desa was among them. Throughout the night they were all interrogated. It was already early the next morning, 4th August, before Desa was called in. "Where did you get those shoes from?" was the first question the officer asked. These rubber shoes were supplied by the MCP and that was what made him a suspect.

"I bought them in a second-hand shop," lied Desa.

"Where?"

"In Sungai Siput."

"What were you doing there?"

"I work there in Dolby estate."

"And what are you doing here?"

"I am on my way to Alor Star for my niece's wedding."

"Then why are you not on the train?"

"I had to get off here to meet a cousin to borrow some money."

"Who is this cousin?"

"He is a padi planter who lives quite near the station."

"What is his name?"

"His name is Murthy."

"Do you have your work pass?"

"Yes, but I left it behind because I am going back there to work."

"Do you know about the MPAJA?"

"I have heard of it."

"Are you a member of the MPAJA?"

"No."

"Did anybody ask you to join the MPAJA?"

"No. But I have given my name to join the INA."

"Alright, you may go."

So relieved now, Desa had to walk from the village of Kamunting all the way back to the railway station. He was walking fast afraid that he might miss the south-bound train. He wanted to get to the station first even before looking for his hidden bag because he was afraid that the train might not stop at this small station. He looked around for some cardboard and rummaging through the rubbish dump he found a cardboard box. He walked along the railway line and picked small bits of charcoal that had spewed out of the funnel of the train engine. With these he managed to scribble the name Janeki on the cardboard. He got on to the platform and waited.

"Has the train from Bagan Serai come yet?" He asked a railway worker.

"It will be another hour before it comes," he said.

"What were the *japankaran* soldiers doing here yesterday?"

"They were looking for members of the MPAJA," he whispered the last word. There was a shooting in the town where some *japankaran* sympathizers were killed by the MPAJA. So the *japankaran* police, the *Kempeitai*, (whispered) were searching for them thinking that some of them might catch the train and get away."

They were actually looking for local people who were members of the MPAJA and since Desa was from the south they did not pay much attention to him.

Desa sat down and waited. He remembered the remains of a fire near the rubbish dump. He went back there, dug into it and found a piece of burnt wood with charcoal. Using it he darkened the capital letters on the cardboard. Back on the platform he waited for the train. At last it came. He went through the same ritual. After a brief stop the train moved on. There was no Janeki. Frustrated, he sat on the bench and waited for a while before getting up and out of the station to look for his bag. It was already late in the afternoon. He decided to wait until it was evening before retracing his steps to find his bag to allay any suspicion. The rubber trees all looked so identical that he was not quite sure where he dumped his bag. He went from one tree to another using his hands and legs to search in the undergrowth. It was starting to get dark and he couldn't find it. He decided to go back to Murthy's house.

"What, *aiyiah*, I thought you had gone."

"Yes, on the way to the station I was caught by the *japankaran* police and rounded up together with those at the station."

"Yes, I heard there was a shooting in town."

"They took all of us to the police station and questioned us. If you will forgive me, *aiyiah*, they asked me what I was doing here and I told them that I came to see you to borrow some money from you."

"*Aiyoo*! Why did you mention my name to them?"

"Actually they were not interested in me because I am not from here. They let me go. There is no reason for them to look for you but if they do come and ask you, you just tell them that I am your cousin and you gave me some money and that I am on my way to Alor Star for my niece's wedding. That is what I told them. Otherwise you can just tell them that you do not know me at all. I am sorry to drag you into this."

"I know it is late but it is better for you to go and not stay here."

"You are right. I just came to tell you what happened. Thank you and goodbye."

Desa left Murthy's house and made his way back to the railway station.

Chapter 34

Chin Leng

One day Kuppu asked Chin Leng why she had joined the CPM.

She said, "The Japanese have a selective policy to treat the Chinese badly because they hold a grudge against us for supporting the Chinese government during the first and second Sino-Japanese wars.

"My mother was from China and she always spoke very highly of the Chinese government and made no secret of her animosity of the Japanese. Little did we realize that there were spies all around us.

"They hate us. The *Kempeitai* will find the slightest reason to be brutal to us. They treat the Chinese women very badly. Do you notice, they treat the Malays differently? I went to the Anglo Chinese School in Ipoh and every morning we were made to sing the *Kimigayo*, the Japanese national anthem, to show our loyalty to the Japanese Emperor. Then they ordered all English and Chinese schools to be closed down. One day, I remember it well. It was the first day after the school was closed. The *Kempeitai* raided our house. We had a secret compartment in the house and my mother quickly pushed me inside and locked it, telling me not to make a sound. There was a slit in the door and I could see what was happening. The soldiers went straight for my mum, pulled her by the hair and knocked her to the ground. They began kicking her and then one of them buried his bayonet into her stomach. I was so scared and helpless. I couldn't get out and if I had shouted I would have ended up like my mother. They dragged her out and left her in the sand. I could hear her groaning. When the soldiers left I began shouting and banging the door. When the coast was clear, some of the neighbours came and brought my mother inside the house. They also let me out. I held my mother in my arms when she died. My father and brother were not in at the time. They came home when news of the tragedy reached them.

"I read a leaflet of the Communist Party calling for women's equal rights to inheritance, equal wages and crèches in the workplace, for an end to polygamy, prostitution, the keeping of "slave-girls" and feudalism. I decided to avenge my mother's murder. You see, how many Chinese girls have joined the CPM and the MPAJA? Students, mistresses and *dulang* washers have joined up." A *dulang* is a large shallow wooden pan. *Dulang* washing is the panning for tin ore.

Kuppu admired her courage and conviction and valued her friendship. He then explained to her the strike action in the estate and the punishment and the hardship he faced at the death railway in Burma. They were like-minded in opposing the Japanese.

***

Janeki made her way down to the river. At the rickety jetty she waited for a boat. There was no boat. She was welcomed to spend the night at a fisherman's hut. The next day, 2 August, she hitched a ride in a sampan to Tamnan. Again she had to climb up a pathway to the top where she found the camp. It was deserted except for a few stray dogs and the dead. She spent most of the day looking at all the graves. She was determined not to leave a single stone unturned. She found no signs. She made her way down to the river and waited for another boat. A small boat came along. It was quite a long stretch to the jetty near Ban Pong. She had to negotiate with the boatman for ten rupees. She gave him five 1 rupee notes and one 5 rupee note. These were the notes issued by the Japanese government during its invasion and occupation of Burma picturing the famous Temple in Pagan similar to the banana notes in Malaya. The Siamese boatman accepted the money and took her to Ban Pong which is beside the river Mae Klong. Here Janeki again went through the camp with a fine-toothed comb looking for clues to find Desa or Kuppu. The hospital building down a valley was completely razed to the ground by the bombing. Having ended her search she made her way to the railway station which was a mere bamboo hut with an atap roof. There was no train that day or the following day. She walked into the village and bought some food with her Burmese money. She spent the two nights at the station with a few people who were also waiting for the train from Bangkok. There was only one train a week on Wednesdays. Janeki barely had enough Burmese Rupees which were readily accepted. Perhaps it was considered worth a little more than the banana notes. She paid for a ticket to Padang Besar. There was no point in stopping at the stations along the way because if Desa and Kuppu had made their way back they would had had months' head start. She decided to make her way back to Malaya. At least she would be on the train even if it took three days or more. She was on the train on the 4th of August.

***

The only place where Desa could spend the night was at the station and the only item he had with him was the cardboard with the love-lettered word. He had already lost two nights and was still in Kamunting. He slept on the platform. Just as daylight was breaking through in the morning of 5th August, he got up and quickly went back on the road looking for his bag. He wanted to find it before the rubber tappers found it. Again using his hands and feet searching between the trees, he found his bag. Luckily it had not rained during the night. His money and exercise book were dry. All the contents were still there. He wandered if he should discard his pistol. His *thalaipa* was still in the bag and he buried the gun inside it. He raced back to the station. The south-bound train was late coming, the schedules were not regular. He waited anxiously as always before the train arrived. He waved his cardboard but Janeki was not on this train either.

It was his good fortune that the timing was such that the south-bound train came before the north-bound train. He boarded the next north-bound train again without a ticket taking another chance. After passing Pondok Tanjung, Bukit Merah and Bagan Serai, bad luck or karma, he was spotted again by the conductor and asked to get off the train. He got off in Parit Buntar. It meant another night on the platform.

***

Kuppu and his squad were poised to attack the goods train from Singapore carrying supplies for the Japanese troops. They managed to derail the train. There was an exchange of fire with the Japanese soldiers on the train. They did the damage and managed to escape into the jungle but Chin Leng was wounded. They carried her right into the camp. She was delirious and they had no doctor. Kuppu wished that Devasagayam Pillay was around. He searched and found that he was released from prison. Kuppu found him working in Ipoh District Hospital. Kuppu met him in his house and pleaded with him to come and help his wounded friend.

"Look at these hands." Devasagaym stretched out his hands, palms down showing his fingers. His nails were badly discoloured. "They drove slits of bamboo under my fingernails. They wanted me to reveal the hideout of the communists. If I had known I would probably have told them because I could not bear the pain. They eventually believed me that I had no knowledge of it."

"I am so sorry to hear that."

"If I go with you now and get caught I cannot promise that I can keep the secret."

"I understand."

"How bad is she?"

"She was hit on the side above her hip. The bullet is still inside and she is not healing."

"I have a friend in Chemor; I'll give you his address. You bring her tonight and I will meet you there."

***

Janeki was on the train moving south on 4 August. The first stop was at a small town called Ratchaburi. All along the way she was looking out of the window as she used to in the bus trying not to catch the eye of Desa, the bus conductor. She sighed. This time she was looking at the jungle with different shades of green sweeping across like brush strokes of a painter. Beyond the green was the black interior of the tropical jungle.

How could Desa and Kuppu ever cut through that jungle? Could they have stayed in the caves of those white and black limestone hills? How could they cross those deep valleys with muddy meandering rivers or climb over the hills? If they had followed the railway line, it would have taken them a very long time ... Please, Muruga, let them be safe.

She fell asleep and woke up when the train stopped at Chunphon. She got out of the train and stretched her legs. She was very tired so she got back into the train and slept through the night. 5 August.

The train had stopped at every small station and sometimes for a longer time at other stations. After what seemed like many hours the train stopped again at Surat Thani. It waited long and there were hawkers on the platform. Hunger forced her to get out. Counting her money she bought two sticks of fish balls on skewers and some peanuts. She carried her own bottle of water. She was not sure how long more she had to travel. The waiting became longer than usual and the passengers were grumbling and asking questions. These people were used to bombings along the railway line and from their gestures she gathered that they were speculating that the train had stopped due to a bombing somewhere on the line. In any case, there was apparently a hitch somewhere. The train did not move for the rest of the day and night. She, with the rest of the people, were stuck at Surat Thani. People got out of the train and sat or stretched out on the platform. At about eight in the morning of the 6 August, the station master was shouting down the platform for the passengers to get back on the train. It was after nine o'clock when the train hissed to a start. No one was told of the cause of the delay.

The scenery, although beautiful, made her drowsy and she fell asleep.

Chapter 35

Samy

The next morning at the Parit Buntar station, Desa walked down the railway line and found a faucet attached to a piece of pipe sticking out of the ground. He eased himself on the grass and washed his face, refilled his bottle and returned to the platform to await the south-bound train. It came chugging along with black smoke and hissed to a halt. Again Desa paraded up and down the platform holding up his calling sign which was shouting the name of JANEKI louder than the sound of the train. Nobody responded. Desa wondered if he was doing the right thing, but what else could he do? He wanted to get to Burma quickly and yet he did not want to miss the chance of meeting her if she were on the way back. He knew that the trains could not possibly pass each other in motion because there was only one track. If they did cross it would be at a big station with at least two platforms. He just had to take one day at a time.

It was 6 August and he did not want to have any more unnecessary delays, so Desa bought a ticket to Bukit Mertajam - a big station. The train passed through Nebong Tebal, Simpang Empat before reaching Bukit Mertajam. He alighted here and waited. This station had two platforms so he crossed over to the other side jumping down onto the rails and climbing up the other side because the underpass was blocked. He used the station toilet, the smell from which was like walking into a brick wall, to freshen up. It was dark by the time the south-bound train arrived. He stood under the light and held up his JANEKI sign. Many people alighted from the train. Many looked at him and walked by. He found a hawker selling *pisang goreng* (banana fritters). He bought four pieces and some peanuts from a *kachang puteh* (pea nuts) man. He sat down and continued to write. It was going to be another night on the platform.

He was so engrossed with his journal that he did not notice the man seated on the same bench.

"What are you writing?" he asked.

"Oh, just what happens each day."

"Are you from a newspaper?"

"No. I'm waiting to meet someone from the north."

"But the train has just come and gone."

"I know; she might be on the next train. I am waiting for my wife."

"I see, but the next train will not come until about this time tomorrow night."

"Then I'll just keep going up north to meet the train."

"You are not very familiar with the train movements, are you?"

"Well, not long ago I came down by train from the north and the train stopped at every station."

"Now the trains are more irregular. The train that just came down has gone to Prai station which is a junction where the passengers going south will have to change trains. Later tonight the same train will go up north and reach Padang Besar early tomorrow morning. The same train will then leave Padang Besar and come back here tomorrow night. Only this year the trains are beginning to run more or less regularly. Many parts of the railway line were damaged by the war. Even this station was bombed. I was here when it happened. I remember it clearly, it was on 17 Decembr 1941 and the bomb fell right in the middle of the station. The underpass was destroyed and has never been reconstructed. Long after the *japankaran* pushed the *velekaran* out there were no trains running at all. We were lucky to see a train once or twice a month and now although they are more frequent, their arrival and departure times are usually late. By the way where are you from?"

"I work in a plantation in Perak. After I meet my wife we will go back there."

"My name is Ponnusamy, everybody just calls me Samy. I run a sundry shop in Kulim, not far from here and I also drive a lorry for an American company, at least it was an American company. I came to pick up some bags of rice from Siam and the men are loading the lorry right now."

Samy was curious about the wife that Desa was talking about. A wife travelling alone from Siam was very unusual. He did not want to probe. Desa introduced himself.

"I am Nadesan Pillay from Triuchy. My wife and I got separated during the war and I heard she is coming from Perlis. I want to make sure I do not miss her because she does not know I am looking for her."

"You have a better chance of seeing her if you wait here rather than move up. The train coming down usually stops at every small station though sometimes it does not stop at some stations."

"Then I will wait here."

"But you have tonight and all day tomorrow to wait. Why don't you come with me to my house for the night? I will be coming again tomorrow night to the station to pick up more rice and I will bring you back."

"That is very kind of you, *aiyiah*, but I prefer to wait." Desa hardly knew the person and he was cautious and definitely did not want to risk missing the train.

"I will bring you back in good time before the train arrives. Besides, you look as though you could do with a bath and a good meal and a rest."

Desa considered this. Moreover, it would be nice to shave off his bead and be more presentable when he meets Janeki.

"I don't want to impose on you ..."

"Look, if we Indians don't help each other we are doomed in this country."

When he said that, it stirred an interest in Desa for this man. He accepted the invitation and soon they were in the lorry driving away from the station. The two workers were comfortably reclining on the rice bags while Desa was offered the front seat with the driver.

***

Devasagayam often met his friend, Pakiasamy. They would both go to the toddy shop in Chemor for a drink on the weekend. "*Machanh*, I need you to do me a favour," said Devasagayam.

On 5 August at 9.00 p.m., Kuppu convinced a Chinese taxi driver to drive them to Pakiasamy's house which was off the main road. The taxi managed to negotiate the narrow path to the house. They carried Chin Leng inside. Devasagayam was waiting with his medical kit. His fingers had healed and he was always good with his hands.

He gave her chloroform and deftly opened the wound and removed the bullet, stitched up the wound and dressed it up. It all took place very quickly even though the taxi driver was anxious and impatient.

"Kuppu, Chin Leng will still need the wound to be treated and she needs more medicine. I am a marked person but I know of someone who can help with some medicine but you must be discreet because she too is a marked person. Her name is Sybil Kathigasu. She and her husband run a small clinic in Papan which is not far from Ipoh. I am not sure if she is still there or captured by the Japanese. She will definitely help you if she is still there."

When Chin Leng came to, Kuppu took her back, but as an expression of his gratitude to Devesagayam, he gave him a parcel of canned food and a bottle of whisky.

***

Janeki woke up when the train stopped, this time at a town called Hat Yai. Janeki desperately needed a wash. The water in the train toilet had run dry. The train, however, did not stop for long. The driver was trying to make up for lost time. She used the precious water in her bottle to wet her face.

Suddenly, she was aware that she had reached the town of Pekan Siam. The station sat on the border with a long platform stretching across the border. The north end of the platform was in Siam and the south end was Padang Besar in Malaya. She alighted and made enquiries about the train into Malaya.

The next train for Prai in Malaya would leave at 9.00 o'clock the next morning. Janeki freshened up in the toilet and found a vacant bench on the platform.

She spent the night there wondering what awaits her in Malaya, especially in the estate.

Chapter 36

Belfast Estate, Kulim, Kedah

6 August 1945

The road from Bukit Mertajam to Kulim, slightly over 10 miles, was narrow, winding and dark but there was not much traffic on the road. Samy managed his lorry load of rice even with only one headlight working. From the town of Kulim they had to go another 10 miles to his estate. It was very dark when they left the tar road and entered the estate.

The sign, barely visible in the single headlight read Belfast Estate MAP.

"This is a very big estate of over ten thousand acres divided into four sectors. Each sector has its own assistant manager. We are in the main division. It was well run by the American company that owned it but now the *japankaran* are not really bothered to maintain it properly. They got the *kiranies* to manage it with a skeleton staff and the remaining workers. The estate was known as the Malayan-American Plantations Limited (MAP) owned by the United States Rubber Company. They used the rubber from here to produce rubber shoes in America.

The shoes you are wearing probably came from our rubber trees here," said Samy.

When they reached the estate office building they had to wait for the Japanese officer to come and inspect the rice bags. While waiting Samy told Desa, "You act just like the other workers and do what they do."

Samy handed the document, equal to a bill of lading, given to him by the station master which he had countersigned. The officer looked at it, taking no notice of Desa and ordered the *kirany* to count the bags. When he was satisfied, he gave the keys to the newly fortified old smoke house to a *japankaran* soldier, who opened it and ordered the rice to be unloaded and packed inside. Desa threw his weight behind the bags and discovered that he was not nearly strong enough under its weight. Only after it was done and locked up were they allowed to go.

Desa followed Samy to his small sundry shop. Attached to the rear of it was Samy's house.

"Naga, I have brought a friend, Desa, to stay the night with us. Serve the meal for the both of us and prepare a bedding," Samy told his wife whose name was Nagammah.

She bowed her head and left without saying a word. If she had anything to say it would be said in private.

Samy showed Desa the bathroom which was outside, walled by zinc sheets with an open sky. A cement trough contained water. Desa closed the zinc door with an iron clasp that hooked into a ring. He had brought his bag with him into the bathroom. He was not going to let anybody look into its contents. He hung it on a nail and stripped, hanging his clothes on another nail. He took out his *thalaipa* and spread it over his bag. Finding a small bucket he scooped the water from the trough and poured it over his head. He took a deep breath sucking the air into his mouth and blowing it out. The water was cold but very refreshing. On the horizontal wooden beam he found a small bar of *Sunlight* soap which he used to wash his hair and bushy beard. It has been days since he had a bath or a shower. Using the *thalaipa* as a towel he dried himself and dressed. He came out looking and feeling and smelling like a new man.

While he was bathing Nagammah confronted her husband.

"Who is the man? How can you bring a stranger into the house? We have two grown-up daughters. Where will he sleep?"

"Don't worry, Naga, he is waiting to meet his wife at the railway station and he will be gone tomorrow. He can sleep in the shop."

"What will the *japankaran* say if they found out?"

"They already saw him just like another worker."

"You make sure he doesn't take our things and run away at night."

"OK, I'll make sure. Here he comes now. Bring out the food."

They sat on the floor with banana leaves spread before them. She served the rice and dhal curry with fried fish and lady's fingers.

"I have not had a good and proper meal for many days; and rice, I thought I'll never see rice again. Thank you so much," said Desa.

"Please eat well nga," said Naga without looking at Desa.

Having washed down the meal with *moru* they went to sit outside the shop. Samy offered Desa betel leaves and both of them started munching away.

"You know the *velekaran* managers just dropped everything and drove off in their cars before the *japankaran* arrived. Many of the workers too ran away from the estate. They kept the *kiranies* and the *kanganies* and they took away most of the able-bodied men in their trucks," said Samy.

"They did the same thing in nearly all the big estates," added Desa.

"We came to know that they were sent to build a railway line in Burma."

"Yes, that is true." Desa was still assessing Samy and was cautious about revealing too much about himself.

"Then the people from the Indian associations came and recruited the other men to join the INA. I never joined them. There are not many workers left here now."

"Are they still working on the rubber?"

"Yes, but very slowly."

"How are the *japankaran* behaving?"

"There are only three of them here. They don't have many men to spare. They don't interfere too much with us. But when the troops arrived the first thing they did was to ransack my shop. They took everything. I also thought of leaving the estate but finding a job or a house to stay was almost out of the question. I have two daughters come of age here. Later the *japankaran* officers realized that I had connections outside the estate to procure provisions. So they used me to go and buy food and other basic necessities. They even helped me to restock the shop which they felt was necessary."

"You are very fortunate."

"Yes, but the bloody *kiranies* insist on taking provisions on credit and don't pay."

"Very typical of them!"

"The *japankaran* are now using this estate mainly as a food depot. They get the rice which has become a very rare commodity, sent from Siam and stock it here. Every now and again we see military trucks coming and taking the rice to different parts of the country to supply their troops. The people hardly get any rice now."

"I had almost forgotten the taste of rice until tonight. The meal was a feast."

"They ration out the rice here. Nadesan, tell me about yourself. You look more like a *kirany* than a *coolie*."

"Oh, please, don't compare me to a *kirany*. I am a worker and *kiranies* don't care for the workers. In our estate they were the lackeys of the *velekaran*. And now they are bullying the workers showing the *japankaran* how well they can control us."

"They have also been abusing the women and I am extra careful because of my daughters."

"We have tried going on strike but the *velekaran* was very powerful, he used the Panjabi soldiers to shoot and kill us."

"We, Indians, in this country need to be organized and united. I think the time has come to do this now. The *japankaran* occupation has been an awakening for the Indians. The *velekaran* gods have fallen to the ground. India is calling for independence and our people have responded to the call to join the INA with great enthusiasm."

"Look, *aiyiah* Samy, I do not place much confidence in the INA which is a tool in the hands of the *japankaran*. Do you think the *japankaran* are really interested in us or in our welfare? Do you know how they treated the Indians on the Burma railway? Thousand of Indians from the estates have been worked to death there only to provide a supply line for their troops. The Indians have woken up, yes, but to an illusion. It is all *mayam* (an illusion)."

"I too believe that we have to start with our younger people and make them see the reality of our situation."

"Why are you asking, nga! We have been used by one power after another and even by our own countrymen. We can only rely on ourselves as workers."

"Perhaps, we should start with our boys and girls who have no proper schools to attend. Nadesan, it is getting late. We can talk some more in the morning. Do you mind sleeping on the floor in the shop?"

"*Aiyiah* Samy, I am grateful to have a place and you have given me a full stomach, what more nga can I ask?"

"Alright, Nadesan, sleep well."

Would Janeki be on the train tomorrow? If not, I will continue my journey north and right into Burma to the military hospital. She was not among those who died on the way back, so she must still be there. If I cannot find her there she may have gone back to India.

His thoughts drifted to India.

I wonder how Ammah and Anghi are coping selling vadai. Kamala should have finished school and working, if not married, and Krish playing cricket in school....

He fell asleep.

***

Janeki was stirring on the bench as daylight of 7 August broke.

At Padang Besar station office, for she could not find an immigration counter, Janeki presented her papers from India with the entry date at Penang and her tin ticket as proof of employment in Worster estate. She was allowed to reenter with no questions asked and the man at the station was not even interested in her papers. It was only later that she learnt that the northern states of Perlis, Kedah, Kelantan and Terengganu belonged to Siam. The Japanese had allowed Siam to re-annexe them. Actually, until the beginning of the twentieth Century, these states were part of Siam. She also found out that only one train went south to Prai Junction where she would have to change trains to go further south. She bought a ticket with Burmese money to Prai and changed the rest of her money to the Malayan banana notes.

Some carriages were being shunted and joined to the train already in the station. Janeki freshened up at the toilet and was still in her Burmese clothes. She had no other. By eight o'clock passengers were allowed to board the train. She picked a nice window seat on the left. By nine the station master blew his whistle and waved the green flag; the train hissed to a start. It picked up speed and soon she was swaying with the rhythm of the movement. She remembered the train song she used to sing as a child that went *Chikabuku, chikabuku, chikabuku...*

I am reentering Malaynadu with a very slim chance of meeting Desa or Kuppu. Perhaps I will go back to the estate and meet up with the rest of the Rani of Jhansi Regiment women. If I cannot be rejoined with Desa I have no reason to remain in Malaynadu. If I can then find a way back to India I could join our people to fight for the independence of India.

Her thought carried her across the sea to India.

I wonder how Ammah and Appa are getting on and Subra and Susila and my two dear little sisters, Pushpa and Natchathiram. Susi must be preparing their breakfast and sending them off to school. My fellow students would have graduated as nurses and I don't know where I am or what I have become and what awaits me.....

She fell asleep. She woke up for a while when the train stopped at a small station named Bukit Ketri and went back to sleep.

***

Desa woke up with the sound of the bell and the cocks crowing. The estate was waking up. Although few in numbers they were going through the daily routine. He went to wash up but found the bathroom occupied. While waiting he studied the items on sale in the shop. They were very basic and ordinary items like pepper, salt, curry power, onions, garlic, ginger, dried tamarind, dried chili and dried fish and a big bunch of green bananas with some combs turning yellow and ripe papayas. Solid cheroots, unlike his *nipah* sticks, caught his eyes and he decided to buy some later. He made his way to the latrine. There was a row of six attached toilets three steps raised from the ground and each with a wooden door. Inside there were two cement slabs and between them a deep hole containing a rubber bucket at the bottom. At this time of the morning the smell was rather strong. As he came out he saw Samy's daughters coming out of the bathroom and quickly diving into the house. They were indeed beautiful girls and their parents had good reason to worry. He managed to wash himself.

Samy had already opened the shop.

"Were you able to sleep last night?" he asked Desa.

"O yes nga, I slept very well."

"Come let's have breakfast." The wife came into the shop and laid the banana leaves. She served *thosai* (a fermented pancake or crepe made from rice batter) and coconut chutney with black coffee. This was luxury beyond measure during the Japanese occupation. Samy did not make much from the shop but he was paid for driving the lorry. He also maintained the estate lorry.

"We don't have *thosai* every morning. It is tapioca most of the time."

"It is special because of me, isn't it? Thank you very much."

"We were talking about the young people and the children here. The school building is still standing but we have no teacher. You can teach, can't you?"

"I know what you must be thinking, but I have to find my wife first."

"Forgive me for asking. How come she is coming from the north and travelling alone?"

"Let me ask you a question, *aiyiah*. Why did you not join the INA?"

"I was thinking about it but, like you, I also wondered how we can liberate India from the outside. I also do not trust the *japankaran* although some of the officers are OK. Besides I have my two daughters to think of."

"You are right. My wife, her name is Janeki ..."

"Yes, I know."

"How do you know her name?"

"There it is staring at me from the top of your bag."

"Of course. Now Janeki had joined the women's wing of the INA. Chandra Bose has opened a women's regiment called the Rani of Jhansi Regiment and she was sent to Burma to fight alongside the Japanese to free India. It seems that the *velekaran* has pushed back the *japankaran* from the Indian border. The INA retreated and the women were sent back. Janeki is a nurse and she was held back to look after the casualties in a military hospital in Burma. I don't know if she is still there or if she had decided to come back and the only way back now is by train. That is why I am going north to find her and I will keep going right into Burma until I find her."

"Now I understand."

"I don't want to miss the train from the north today. I have been looking at this piece of cardboard. Can I have it?" It was leaning against the bananas.

"Why, yes. Ah, I know what you want it for. I saw you holding that sign at the station. I also have some black paint and you can write her name in nice big bold letters."

Desa set to work on his billboard while Samy attended to the shop. Desa was happy with his work. "Janeki" was screaming at him.

"*Aiyiah* Samy, is there a barber in the estate? I want to have a haircut and a shave."

"Yes, I will send word and he will come here. Don't go near the office; the *kirany* might spot you and start asking questions."

So Desa sat inside the shop and started writing his journal while waiting for the barber to arrive.

The barber eventually came along and all he had with him were a pair of scissors and a comb. He appeared to be in his sixties. He took a wooden stool from the shop and asked Desa to follow him. Desa sat under the spreading rain tree in full yellow bloom and the barber started combing his hair. As he started cutting, Desa's hair dropped in tufts on the ground and created a pattern of black spots on the yellow carpet of rain flower, lit up by the bright rays of sunlight piercing through the tree.

"*Aiyiah*, what *vur*?" asked Desa.

The barber said, "Thanjavur."

"Your name?"

"Rengasamy"

"You?"

"My name is Nadesan. I work in an estate in Perak. I'm just visiting."

"Any news from India?"

"There are many problems there and Nehru and Ghandiji are urging the people to cry out for independence from the *velekaranraj.*"

"Here, at least under the *velekaranraj* we had enough food to eat; now under the *japanraj* we are starving."

"Things will change for the better, I am sure. We too will have *Swaraj* sometime in the future; but we have to make it happen. *Aiyiah*, Rengasamy can you give me a shave ma?"

"Yes, yes." He unfurled his *veshti* and drew out a razor – a "cut-throat." "You hold this," he said then went to the shop and fetched a tumbler of water. He undid his belt and secured the *veshti*. Looping his belt on a tree branch he took the razor and began flicking the blade up and down on the inside of his belt. He was sharpening the razor.

He carefully left it on a stone and lifted Desa's chin. He used his scissors to trim the bushy beard as short as possible, wet his face and set to work with the razor. It was indeed a clean job and Desa felt his face almost as smooth as a baby's bottom.

Desa paid him fifty cents.

"Thank you very much, *aiyiah*. I cut the hair of the *japankaran* and the *kiranies* and they don't pay me a cent."

Desa remembered seeing a small piece of mirror in the bathroom and immediately made his way there to look at himself.

Ah, here is the old Desa. I am sure Janeki cannot miss me.

***

Janeki

7 August, 11.30 a.m.

Janeki was wide awake when the train approached Arau station. It was only a small shed on the platform and the other side was scattered with coconut palms. The train stopped long enough for some coconuts to be loaded along with some Siamese goods unloaded, probably rice.

The scenery from then on was much the same, coconut palms and rubber trees with railway sleepers piled up along the track. The train stopped again at another small station, the Tunjang railway station.

***

Desa

7 August, 11.30 a.m.

Desa went to the back of the house and examined the vegetable garden where Nagammah was working.

"You have lovely brinjals and lady's finger."

Nagammah did not look at him and took a while to respond. "How long have you been married?"

"Oh, almost eight years."

"How many children do you have?"

"We have no children, not yet."

"What are you waiting for?"

Desa took it as a rhetorical question. It began to dawn on him just how many years have elapsed and they have hardly lived a decent married life. He slowly walked away.

At the shop Desa noticed that Samy had laid out newspapers for sale. He was surprised to see such a variety of them because the Japanese had stopped the publication of all the pre-war newspapers.

"We only display the Tamil, Malay and Malayalam papers here. The *Perak Shimbun* is a Malay paper published in Ipoh. They are all *japankaran* propaganda," said Samy.

Desa looking through the papers, "I notice the *japankaran* have allowed so many Tamil newspapers to be published by the Indian Independence League."

"Yes we have the *Sutandira India*, the *Sutandirotayam*, the *Yuvabharatham*; and one in Malayalam, the *Sutandira Bharatham*. They all speak about the liberation of India by the *japankaran* and Chandra Bose's struggle for Indian independence."

"You also have two papers by the youth section of the Indian Independence League, the *Bala Bharatham* and *Punaswaraj*."

"Yes, they all carry the same message and even lessons in the *japankaran* language."

"I'm sure there is no news of the Burma railway..."

"Oh yes, there is. They boast of the great achievement of having completed the line connecting Bangkok and Rangoon in a record time."

"Ah, if only the people knew the truth of how it was built and at what cost!"

***

The next stop was Alor Setar, a big station and the train stopped here for a long time. There were many people getting on and off the train. One woman got into the train carrying a bundle of fruit. Janeki had never seen this kind of fruit before and she asked her about it.

"This is *buah kundang*," said the woman. There was a mixture of ripe and unripe fruits the size of plums, green or yellow in colour.

"Can you eat them?" asked Janeki.

"Yes, would you like to try some?" She took a ripe fruit from the bundle and wiped it on the cloth that formed the bundle. "You can even eat the skin."

Janeki took a bite. It was sweet and juicy like a ripe mango.

"Oh, lovely," said Janeki cupping her hand under her mouth to catch the dripping juice.

"You can also eat the green ones," said the woman who picked one and wiping it cut it into two halves with a knife. The flesh was white with a single bright purple coloured seed. She gave it to Janeki to taste.

Janeki took a bite and almost screamed; the tingling sour taste went straight to the top of her head. Sharp though it was Janeki sucked the juice and found it stimulatingly nice.

"Sorry, we normally dip the green ones in a bit of salt before we eat them."

"Did you buy these fruits?"

"No, I found them under the tree and in the drain. Look, there are many of these trees around the station and it is the fruit season now. It is called the *setar* tree. The fruit is also called the *buah setar*. The dry drain where the fruit collect is called the *alur*."

"O, really. *Alur* is also the Tamil word for drain."

"Yes, ah. I make a lot of things with this fruit. The green ones we eat with salt or dry them and pickle them. Sometimes we make *rojak* (a fruit salad) or *sambal balachan* (a sweet and sour sauce made with prawn paste). The ripe fruit, we either eat them as they are or I make *halwa* (an extremely sweet, semi-solid jam)."

"I am sure they will all be very nice and tasty."

"Here, take some of the ripe ones." She gave Janeki two fistfulls of the buah kundang. "I bet you do not know that the town of Alor Setar is named after this fruit tree, the tree that grows along the drain – *alur setar*.

"Thank you for the fruit and I have learned something today," said Janeki.

Janeki did not realize that the train had reached another station, the Junun railway station, a small one shed station.

The train moved on to Gurun railway station, also a small station with not many trees.

After that the vista opened out to padi fields.

✦✦✦

"When are we going to the station?" Desa asked Samy in the shop.

"We have plenty of time. After lunch, we will have a rest and then we will go. Don't worry, I will get you there before the train arrives."

"*Aiyiah*, Samy, how much do you sell these cheroot?"

"These are locally made. I used to sell the *Pathy mark* cheroots from India, but we don't get them anymore. These are five for ten cents."

"I will take ten," said Desa and fishing out twenty cents from his bag.

"No, *thamby*, you save your money. No need to pay."

"No, no, *aiyiah*. You are trying to do a business and every cent counts. I have money to pay." He left the money on the table.

Lunch was tapioca curry with *ikan bilis* (anchovies). Desa was restless throughout siesta time and anxious to get to the station. Before long they were on the lorry with two workers leaving the estate.

"There is something very historical I'd like to show you. It is on the road to the station," said Samy. On the Kulim road, they stopped at the St. Anne's Catholic Church named after the grandmother of Jesus. "This is a very old church that goes back for more than half a century. More ancient than the church is a rock beside the church."

Samy parked the lorry at the entrance of the church and they walked to the rock.

"These inscriptions on the rock date back before the time of Jesus Christ. The stone is known as *Cherok Tekun* and the writings, as you can see, are similar to Tamil. Can you make anything of them?"

"I have seen similar writings in India. They go back to the *Sangam* period." A *Sangam* was an assembly in the classical period in the history of Tamil literature in South India.

"This is strong evidence of Indian culture here known as Kadaram. I am told that it carries a message that a war was fought here by a certain king called Rama and how he defeated his enemies."

"Very interesting, let me copy some of this writing." Desa took his journal and scribbled down the letters on the rock. "I don't know when I will get another chance to come this way again."

They continued their way to the Bukit Mertajam railway station.

***

When the train pulled into the Sungei Patani station Janeki noticed a commotion on the platform. People were talking and gesticulating, throwing up their arms in the air. She could not quite make out what was going on, evidently something unusual had happened.

On leaving Sungei Patani the train cut through wide padi fields. The irrigation bunds were being reconstructed while some patches were being ploughed by the muscles of the buffalo. In other patches the bright green padi leaves were shooting out of the water beds. Other areas were brown with ripe padi. Of course, the landscape was torn up here and there with craters created by the bombs.

Chapter 37

Reunited

7th August 1945

Samy parked his lorry at the loading bay where the platform ended in a ramp.

While Samy went to the station to verify documents, Desa went on to the platform with his calling cardboard and bag. He positioned himself at the north end of the platform so as to catch the attention of all the passengers as the train entered the station.

As he sat on the bench Samy came to him waving his arms.

"Nadesa, Nadesa, news has come through the radio that Japan has been bombed. It is considered to be the biggest bomb ever made by the Americans. A whole town has been destroyed."

"*Aiyooh, Kadavle!*"

"The American President Harry Truman announced that yesterday morning the bomb was dropped on the city of Hiroshima. This bomb was supposed to be 2,000 times more powerful than the largest bomb ever used."

"A whole city of people died? How true a man this Truman can be, killing innocent people like that?"

"Well, this might stop the *japankaran*."

"I wonder." Desa was more interested in seeing Janeki.

"Samy, what time is the train supposed to arrive?"

"Between six and six-thirty they say, often late but never early."

Desa sat down on the bench for a while then got up and walked up and down the platform. The big clock with Roman numerals showed six–twenty. More people had gathered on the platform. At six-thirty five the train blew its whistle announcing its arrival. Desa got ready with his sign.

Desa held up the sign high as the carriages passed.

Janeki looking out of the window caught sight of her name wondering why anybody would be holding up her name. The sign was partly blocking Desa's face. She moved down to the next window and then recognized him. Something surged within her but the carriage was moving away from him down the platform. She hurried towards the exit and kept focused on him until the train stopped. Jumping out of the train even before it came to a complete stop, she made her way towards him.

When the train stopped, Desa lowered the sign and wondered if it was another frustration until he saw a woman dressed in the Burmese outfit of the *longyi and eingyi* walking towards him. Desa had only known Janeki dressed in a sari. He stood staring at her. She looked different. Then, ah, yes! It was her. On recognition he started running towards her. She too began running. Two lost souls from two ends of the Bukit Mertajam station platform were rushing towards each other until they threw themselves into the arms of each other.

"Janeki!"

"*Athanh!*"

They did something never done in public. They embraced without a care in the world.

An old Indian lady on the platform shook her head in disapproval, "A spoilt generation, behaving like shameless dogs in public!"

Neither of them knew how long they held on to each other until Samy was standing beside them.

"At last your dream has come true, Nadesa."

They were lost for words. The train began to move. Janeki's meagre belongings were still on the train but she did not care.

"Janeki, *kannu*, you have brought the world back to me."

"*Athanh*, I knew deep inside me that you were not dead."

"Janeki, this is *Aiyiah* Samy. He has been very kind and hospitable to me."

"Why don't the both of you sit down on the bench and talk while I see to the loading of the rice onto the lorry," said Samy and left them alone.

Janeki held Desa's hand and let her head drop on his shoulder. They remained silent for a while, too much to say, unable to utter a single word.

"I knew they had taken you to the Burma Railway," said Janeki.

"Did you join the INA?"

"Yes, the women's wing, the Rani of Jhansi Regiment."

"Kuppu and I escaped but we lost Arokia."

"I know."

"You know?"

"Yes, I went down the railway line looking everywhere for you and I saw Arokia's grave. Whether you were dead or alive, I could not tell; but I kept going, believing you were alive."

"On the way down we were hiding when we saw a train load of women soldiers going up, but I never could have guessed that you were on that train."

"We passed each other? *Kadavule!*"

"Janeki, you must not make it known to everybody that you were a soldier in the INA because the people who oppose the *japankaran* will target those who are sympathetic with the *japankaran*. It is dangerous and you could get killed."

"I really believed that the *japankaran* will help us to get rid of the *velekaran* in India as they did here in Malaynadu. But after I made my way through the Burma railway and heard the stories told about the treatment of the workers and saw the mass graves, I began to doubt the sincerity of the *japankaran*. But now they are losing the battle in Burma and are being pushed down from the Indian border."

"News reached here today that Japan has been bombed, and that the whole city of Hiroshima is destroyed. They say that it was the biggest bomb ever dropped and it was done by the Americans. The people are saying that the *japankaran* might now surrender."

"Ah, that explains the commotion I saw at the station in Sungei Patani. The people must have been talking about the bomb. I don't believe that the *japankaran* will surrender. The *japankaran* will never surrender. I have seen and heard that the retreating *japankaran* army in Burma have dug in and preferred to commit suicide rather than surrender."

"The *japankaran* might spare you for having been in the INA, but there is also another army called the Malayan Peoples' Anti Japanese Army and they will kill you. We shall talk more about this later. We must plan what to do now."

"Is it safe to go back to our estate? The *kiranies* have treated the workers badly especially the women." She made sure not to mention the episode with the *kirany*.

"We need a place to stay tonight. Let us discuss it with Samy; he is a good man. Are you alright? You have lost so much weight."

"Let us put our lives back together again, *Athanh*."

"Yes, *kannu*."

Samy approached them, "What are your plans?"

"We are not sure but we need a place to stay for the night."

"Yes. Why don't you come back to the estate with me? There are many empty cubicles because of the shortage of workers. I will arrange for you to stay in one of the cubicles tonight and tomorrow you can make plans."

"We do not want to impose on you after you have been so kind to me. Perhaps, we can buy some food in Kulim town?"

"Look, I cannot stop my lorry anywhere with the load of rice. It is too dangerous. We will go straight back to the estate. Janeki needs to freshen up and we will leave you together. Tomorrow we will discuss what to do. Not now, alright?"

Desa and Janeki looked at each other and nodded.

On reaching the estate Samy took both of them into his house and told his wife to look after them before the Japanese officer came to inspect the load.

"Ah, you've found your wife."

"Her name is Janeki." Desa told Nagammah.

"Come *ammah* Janeki, come inside. Where are your things? I will prepare some food."

"Please forgive me. I don't have anything and I would like to have a wash."

"*Aiyio!* What happened to you, were you robbed or something?"

"It's a long story, *ammah*."

"Leela, bring a *thundu*, *ammah*." *Ammah* literally means "mother" and is a common endearing word used to address women, both older and younger. Leela was the older of the two daughters. The younger one was Anakili. As soon as Leela saw Janeki, she said, "*Akka*, come with me." She took her to a room inside. "You need more than a *thundu*. Do you tie a sari?"

"Yes, and I haven't tied one for a long time."

"Here, you take this. One of my saris. It is very ordinary."

"That's alright. I also need underclothes. I have not changed in many days. I will buy some new ones for you."

Janeki had an arm full of clothes.

"Come I will show you the bathroom." She led the way.

Desa sat in the shop with his bag and looked at the newspapers. There was, of course, no mention at all about the bombing.

Samy returned after the bags of rice were all accounted for.

"I have asked one of the workers to clean up a vacant cubicle for you to stay tonight. But let us have something to eat before that. Naga," he called, "Food ready ah?"

"Coming," she said.

"I don't know how to repay you for your kindness," said Desa.

"I was just thinking, in these times you cannot be sure of anything. This estate is short of workers. The only pay you will get is food by coupons and a small token of money, but you will have a place to stay. Think about it. We also have a school with no teacher. The *japankaran* are not really interested in rubber here; they want to maintain this place as a rice depot. It is only the *kiranies* who are pushing the workers. If you are not in a hurry to get back to your estate in Perak, you can stay and work here for some time. You discuss it with Janeki and tomorrow we will talk more about it. What do you say?"

"Janeki and I will have to plan our future and we will discuss this. Thank you."

Janeki appeared clean and fresh in a sari and they all sat down to eat. Nagammah somehow managed to cook rice with chicken curry and brinjal.

They all watched the way Janeki was eating, relishing every mouthful. After the meal, they all, Samy, Nagammah, Leela, and Anakili, accompanying Desa and Janeki, made their way to the cubicle. They brought a mat and some sheets. The two girls were excited and did all they could to make Janeki and Desa comfortable.

When they had left Desa and Janeki sat down side by side and held each other close.

"How did you find such nice people?"

"Indians, by nature, are hospitable, aren't they? It was just by accident that I happened to sit next to Samy in the railway station. We started talking and he invited me over."

"The girls gave me this sari and inner clothes. I want to buy some clothes back for them. I have some Malayan money but not much. How much money do you have?"

"Not much either, but let's talk about that later."

He blew out the oil lamp and drew her closer to him and they both rolled over on the mat. The intensity with which they made love left both of them completely exhausted, but they could not sleep. They sat up and kept talking through the night in the dark. Janeki related all that happened to her except the part when the *kirany* took advantage of her. Desa also related his experiences holding back his involvement with the CPM and the MPAJA. In the early hours of the morning they made love again and slept through dawn.

8 August 1945

It was mid-morning when Desa got up. Janeki was not beside him. He almost panicked. Looking out the window he saw her hanging out her old clothes to dry together with Desa's *thalaipa* and spare *veshti* and *juppa*. Immediately looking at his bag, Desa saw that the pistol was still in it with his journal. He would have to explain to her now. He did. He told her the whole story and bound her to secrecy. Samy appeared at the door and knocked.

"Ah, did you sleep well?"

"Yes, indeed, we slept very well."

"I have already spoken to the senior *kirany* about you. Come, we will go and register at the office." Samy had already decided for them to stay in the estate.

Desa turned to Janeki, "Remember we are just two ordinary workers from another estate." They went to the office.

"Come, come. Samy says you want to work in this estate. Have you worked in a rubber plantation before?" asked Kanchiparampil, the *kirany* seated behind a table in the office.

"Yes, we have worked in different estates in Perak," said Desa.

"Samy says that he has found a cubicle for you. That's OK. We cannot pay you a salary but only a token for small expenses and coupons for basic food rations. You have to grow your own vegetables. We will supply you with tapping knives and sharpening stones used by others. You have to look around for buckets and utensils left behind by other workers. We cannot provide you with anything else. If you agree, you sign this paper."

Desa and Janeki looked at each other and signed the paper without saying a word.

"Tomorrow morning you report for muster at 5.00 o'clock."

The Japanese bosses did not put in an appearance at all. They were evidently shocked by the news. Both Desa and Janeki bowed their heads and walked out while Samy remained with the *kirany* and chatted for a while.

As they were approaching the shop, the two girls, Leela and Anakili met them. They had already collected an assortment of utensils and accompanied them to the cubicle to help set up house. They were really excited and happy to be of help. They even brought some breakfast. Desa went about collecting wood and then began sharpening the tools of the trade while the women were busy scrubbing the utensils clean. Desa surveyed the grounds and started digging a plot for planting vegetables. He collected tapioca plants from the other abandoned gardens, cut them up and stuck the cuttings into the soil. He was already an experienced vegetable gardener.

They had to depend on Samy for lunch and dinner because they would only be issued with food coupons the next day after they had started work.

9 August 1945

The following morning at muster the Japanese bosses were also absent. The *kiranies* handled the tasks. Janeki went with the women and Desa went with the men. The workers were talking about the Hiroshima bombing wondering what would happen next. They had learnt from the returning INA soldiers or deserters that the Japanese were losing the war in the north in Burma and rumours had it that the British were planning to come back.

Desa and Janeki got their food coupons and received their rations and cooked their own meal for the first time.

The next day news was abuzz that a second bomb was dropped in Japan on the town of Nagasaki, also a big bomb called an atom bomb. In the estate they were told to carry on as usual.

"This sounds serious and I suspect that the *japankaran* might surrender," said Desa but Janeki was adamant that the *japankaran* will never surrender. The estate routine went on as usual and Desa and Janeki fitted in with it.

In the days that followed there was a constant movement of military trucks carting away the rice from the estate evidently to supply the troops. Soon there were only a few bags of rice left in the smokehouse. All kinds of rumours were flying about. Chiang Kai Shek's army from China was coming to occupy Malaya. The British were going to land on 20 August 1945 to reoccupy Malaya. The Japanese police warned the people not to spread rumours and that rumourmongers shall be punished.

One evening Desa and Janeki went into Kulim town to buy some clothes. With the money they had they could buy practically nothing. The rumours of a change of government sent the value of the Japanese banana currency plummeting to an all-time low.

"*Ammah*," said the shopkeeper to Janeki, "On Saturday, chicken that used to be 20 cents a Kati was 150 *japankaran* dollars on the black market. Today it is 1000 dollars a kati."

The Japanese Military Yen, commonly known as the Banana notes were over printed by the Japanese Imperial Army administration without the basis of any reserves and when hit by inflation they were not worth the paper they were printed on.

The food rationing cards were worth more. Their combined reserve of dollars had almost no purchase value. So they went back without buying anything. Samy had already become aware of their good intention of repaying him. He told them not to worry.

Chapter 38

Japanese Surrender

On 15 August 1945, Desa picked up the *Syonan Shimbun*, an English language Japanese newspaper that ordered everyone to keep quiet and await official instructions from the government.

Samy called Desa into the shop and showed him the hidden short wave radio.

"I was just listening to the All-India broadcasting network. It is all about Japan and the bomb.They are talking about Japan, Listen: "In Japan, Emperor Hirohito was contemplating seeking peace but it was resisted by those who could not stomach the humiliation of surrender. President Truman was losing patience that the Japanese were non-committal in spite of catastrophic devastation by two atomic bombs. So he sent more than one thousand bombers, the B-29s, to pulverise Japan. On 14 August 1945, yesterday, Emperor Hirohito unconditionally surrendered and Truman declared that the war was over."

Samy who had all this time addressed Desa as Nadesan now called him "Desa" after hearing Janeki call him by that name. "Desa, when Janeki met you at the station she said something unusual."

"What did she say?"

"She said, "I knew you were not dead," I was wondering why she would say that?"

"Ah, you see she was making her way back through the *japankaran* Burma railway, now being called the Death Railway. When we were separated she had found out that I, along with my friends, had been taken to construct the railway. It was one hell of an experience. One of my friends died and the other friend and I escaped. If we had stayed we would surely have died. She kept on believing that I was alive.

"Do you know how many people died building that infamous railway? There were 180,000 Asian labourers and half of them died. That is 90,000 Asians, the biggest number of those were Indians. There were 60,000 Allied prisoners of war, British, Australian, Dutch, American and Canadian. Of them 16,000 died. The whole railway line is one big cemetery. The Europeans often made sure to identify their dead and bury them individually. Most of the Asians ended up nameless in mass graves. "

"Yeah, you said you were on that train yourself coming south. I see."

"There is one other thing I want to ask you. Do you know anybody here who may be a member of the MPAJA?"

"Don't speak too loudly, yes I know a number of them who just come and go."

"Is it possible for me to meet up with any of them?"

"Why do you want to meet them? You know it is very risky."

"I am one of them, and I want to make contact."

"Do you know what you are saying? If they find out you are not the only one who will lose your life."

"I know, I have told you because I trust you. You are not supposed to know that. You don't know that. Can you just arrange a meeting quietly?"

"Desa, let me think about it. I cannot risk my family."

"I understand. If you do feel uncomfortable and threatened, then Jankei and I will leave. I too do not want to bring trouble to you and your family. You've been too good to me."

***

Kuppu had just returned to camp after a raid on a Malay police force as a reprisal against its collaboration with the Japanese only to hear the news that the Japanese had surrendered.

"The Japanese are already moving their garrisons from the countryside. There is a vacuum in the authority. We have to move in quickly and take charge. Move out now and grab all the Japanese arms you lay eyes on. We have to do that before the British return," said Ah Kow.

They went out and collected huge caches of arms of all sorts, both Japanese and British, and took them to the interior of the jungle to their hideouts and concealed them.

With freshly pressed uniforms and boots, and three stars on their caps representing the three races in Malaya, and with new guns air dropped by the British, the MPAJA marched out of the jungle with the beat of drums into the streets of Sungei Siput. Crowds lined the streets, especially the Chinese, cheering and greeting them as heroes. They took control of the police stations.

They immediately went about recruiting more members on the spot, raising funds and collecting food.

***

That night Samy, Desa and Janeki had a long discussion.

"Now that the war is over and if things are going to change, what is going to become of our working class people?" Samy was wondering.

"The many things that happened in the last three years and eight months have given our people a vision beyond the estates."

"The only Indian political organisation we can see is the CIAM."

"But the leaders of CIAM will not represent our people. The CIAM is dominated by the Malayalees who do not even speak Tamil. They are like the *kiranies* who have no real interest in our welfare. Others, like the chettiars and business people keep to themselves. The English speaking civil servants don't even want to know that we exist in the plantations."

"Our workers have never had any political awareness. Their only interest appears to be in religion and enough pay to make a living or frequenting the toddy shop. The group that spoke about religious reform and uplifting the Tamil society and culture through education was the Athi Dravida Sangam that was active about ten years ago."

"What were they trying to do?" asked Janeki.

"Their aim was to change the lifestyle of the working classes, to give them a sense of dignity and self-esteem, so that instead of living like beggars, they would earn the respect of their fellow Indians and the other races in this country."

"I remember I was still in school in India when Naicker in Madras was talking about Dravidian Nationalism and Tamil Reform."

"Although the Athi Dravida Sangam was highlighting the social evils of our people they emphasised the need for education."

"Why don't we start doing something about this?" proposed Janeki.

"Yes," said Samy. "We have many children in the estate who accompany their parents into the timber to help collect the latex when they should be in the school room learning to read and write."

"Janeki and I saw the school building. There is very little left. We can fix the broken furniture and the blackboard and get it functioning again but there are no books."

"Why don't we first get the approval of the management and some help from them?" suggested Janeki.

"The *japankaran* appear to have lost interest in the estate. Perhaps we can approach Kanchiparampil, the senior *kirany*," said Samy. "He is quite a reasonable man and not like the other Malayalee *kiranies*." They did that the next day.

Samy and Desa went to see him.

"*Aiyiah*, Kanchi, we have a request to make. Since the war began our school has not been used and our children have had no chance of any education. We would like to get the school working again and start lessons for our children," said Samy.

"It sounds like a good idea, but we have no teachers."

"Our new employee, Desa here, has had some education and can teach, at least the basics of reading and writing."

"What education have you had?" The *kirany* asked Desa.

"I studied up to the ninth standard in Tiruchy."

Kanchi made no comment. He realized that his own level of education was slightly lower than that.

"You know, the *japankaran* want the *japankaran* language to be taught in all our schools and that is being done in the towns. We have no one who knows the *japankaran* language in the estate and that is one of the reasons we have not restarted the school."

"We do not have to make it an official school. The *japankaran dorais* seem to have lost interest in the estate. Besides, you know that the war is over. Can't you give the approval?" asked Samy.

Desa said, "We can repair the chairs and desks and clean up the classrooms, but we need some help from you to get slates, notebooks, pencils, erasers and chalk."

"I believe in education and it is good for our children. I will discuss this with the other *kiranies* and let you know. We cannot pay any teacher; it has to be voluntary. In the meantime you can get the schoolrooms ready. Even though the war is over, nothing has changed here."

Samy and Desa did not expect a positive response. They were not expecting any pay because the money was almost useless anyway.

"The *kirany* also realizes that the *japankaran* have lost interest in the estate and probably, foreseeing the return of the *velekaran*, the British or the Americans, a functioning school will make a good impression," said Samy.

"You might be right there."

Leela and Anakili had rounded up a number of older children and together with Desa and Janeki they got working in the classrooms in the late afternoons after their daily tasks in the estate. Soon other men came with tools and started fixing the broken chairs and desks. It wasn't a proper school building with doors and windows. It was really a covered shed divided into compartments. The women swept and washed the floor. It all created a new spirit and enthusiasm.

Kanchiparampil discussed the school project with his *kiranies* and through contact with suppliers of educational materials he was able to get a decent supply of wood-framed slates, slate styli, exercise books, pencils, erasers, and chalk. He even got some grammar books and short stories in Tamil. The school soon got under way with regular classes. The children were divided into two classes only, Janeki taking the twelve-and-above children while Desa the younger ones. The children too were very keen to learn.

A week later Samy brought Kanchiparampil to the school

accompanied by the *japankaran* manager. This was the first time Desa and Janeki set eyes on the *japankaran dorai* of the estate. He appeared friendly, surprisingly. They seemed to be very pleased with the school and the *japankaran dorai* told them to get whatever was necessary and the estate would pay. He made no mention of the *japankaran* language being taught. Samy and Kanchi were taken aback by the sudden change in the *japankaran* but Desa, however, was reserved and aloof. Noticing this Samy cornered Desa and asked him if his behavuiour was because of the Death Railway experience. Desa said nothing. When they were alone Samy told Desa, "I have arranged a meeting with the local MPAJA representative in three days time. I will fill you in on the details later."

As arranged, Desa met two Chinese and an Indian, members of the MPAJA. One of the Chinese, Shin Foo, was a CPM member. The Indian was Mr. Mohandas, who was responsible for organizing the peoples' committees and labour unions. Desa was brought up to speed on all that had been happening since the bombing in Japan. The latest news was a communiqué from the politburo. The Party has been instructed to support Russia, China, Britain and America for world security. The Party was to establish a democratic government in Malaya and the electorate was to be drawn from all races. Freedom of speech, publications and societies were to be permitted. The MPAJA is to acquire a legal status with the abolition of the Japanese political structure. The members of the MPAJA were to be treated well and compensation made to families of those who died in the Allied cause. It called for the reform of the country's educational and social conditions, to develop industry and commerce to assist the poor, to increase wages to a standard minimum and impose an eight-hour working day. Traitors, corrupt officials, hoarders and profiteers were to be punished and prices stabilised. As a result of this mandate, the MPAJA had already come out in the open and begun to initiate peoples' committees in the towns. Desa was quite exhilarated by this new development which practically discounted any militancy on the part of the CPM, especially if it were to be legalised.

"Is it possible to trace a friend of mine who is an active MPAJA member in Perak?" Desa asked them."

"Yes, give me his name and membership number and we can find him," said Shin Foo.

"His name is Kuppusamy and he works in the Sungei Siput area, was an employee in Dolby estate; but I do not have his membership number."

"We will try to trace him and get back to you. Can you help in the Kulim town's formation of the people's committee?" asked Mohandas.

"I will do what I can but I will be more useful in the estates to form something similar there," said Desa. They left willing to meet again in a week's time.

***

After the War, the Communist Party of Malaya's aim was to acquire a political platform as the people's democratic movement, seek independence from British rule and establish a Malayan People's Government.

In one of their regular meetings, Ah Kow gave a briefing.

"We are in a position to take hold of the country and establish an independent Malayan republic. Taking this opportunity the politburo has come up with eight principles of a representative government. They are freedom of speech, assembly and association. Free education is to be provided in the Chinese, Malay and Tamil languages. There must be provision for work for everyone. Prices of essential goods are to be controlled. We are to create a national army in which the MPAJA will play a major part. Many of the former INA members are joining us and taking an active part in the general labour unions. The opportunity is with us at the moment. But for some reason the central politburo is not giving us the order to move yet."

This gave all the members a boost of hope in the CPM and the MPAJA.

***

Back in the estate Desa was hopeful about the regime change and related to Samy what he had learnt from his comrades. The next morning there was confusion at the muster. The Japanese were very angry and shouted at the workers. Samy cornered Desa and told him what had happened. The smoke house was raided last night and all the remaining rice was gone.

Samy became very suspicious of Desa.

"They say it was done by the MPAJA. Only yesterday you met them. Did you give them a tip off? If you did and they find out, you are finished."

"*Aiyiah*, Samy, I did not even tell them where I am. I place my hand on my head and swear by God I never said anything about the rice. You must remember these men are trained to look for food. They must have been watching this place for some time and noticing the military movements. They could have ambushed them, but thought it might be easier to raid the store. I am sorry it happened. I am meeting them again and I could ask them about it."

"No, just don't say anything. I don't want any trouble. You are a newcomer and you could be a suspect. You better hide your journal and everything in case they search you."

"*Aiyiah*, all this rice is for the Japanese army, so what is the harm if our people take some of them?"

"The rice is important because they pay me in kind with a bag of rice now and then for carting it for them. That is why we can still eat some rice."

"I think things are going to change and such things will not happen anymore."

"I hope you are right." Samy was not one hundred percent sure of Desa now, but he decided to give him the benefit of the doubt.

Desa met the MPAJA comrades a week later and brought back very different kind of news. They began to reassess the situation.

"There is conflicting news coming from the CPM and the MPAJA. Seeing that the *velekaran* are going to return they want us to continue fighting them for the independence of Malaynadu. The *velekaran* intend to disband the MPAJA who are now almost in control of every town. The *japankaran*, on the other hand, seeing their predicament, do not want to be taken as prisoners of war and many of them committed suicide rather than surrender. Others want to join forces with the CPM to fight the *velekaran*. Loyalties are changing like the monsoon wind. Today you are on one side and used by Team A and tomorrow on another side, again used by Team B. It is the Indians who are like the ball being tossed around," reflected Desa.

One night when Desa and Janeki were in the cubicle having their meal they could not help hearing the commotion of their neighbours. They had received some payment and the men had returned from the toddy shop. The wife was nagging at her husband, the pitch in her voice rising; the man shouting back at her. The shouting and screaming were soon followed by the thud and din of objects being thrown about, crashing and breaking; young children crying...

"This is what happens when the men go drinking toddy," said Janeki.

Desa did not respond immediately; then reflected, "Ours is a great culture gone wrong. We have no self-esteem, no self-discipline, and no ambition to become better people. We've always lived in subservience and unable to break out of it. We work like mules and it's understandable if the men want to have a drink."

"But the women also work hard but they don't drink and shout," Janeki defended the women.

"But some do and also shout. I am sure both of them next door had something to drink," asserted Desa. This could have developed into a gender-based argument but they decided not to push it. Janeki said, "Perhaps we could do something to educate them."

***

Ah Kow told them, "We have liberated and occupied many towns and villages and in Ipoh our 5th Independent Regiment of the MPAJA has rescued one of our faithful supporters, Sybil Kartigesu."

Kuppu looked at Chin Leng and they remembered the name mentioned by Devasagayam. Hesitancy on the part of the CPM leadership was worrying.

In the camp there were some mixed feelings among the members on the new communiqué. While the formation of people's committees was setting the stage to bring about a revolutionary change in Malaya by uniting the working classes, the new position appeared to be very pro-British; this was a step back into colonialism. The message from the CPM leadership appeared to be conflicting. The basic goal of the CPM was self-determination for Malaya and that would not be achieved with the return of British rule. They were in a dilemma.

Ah Kow brought different news. He said, "Many of the Japanese are not willing to surrender despite their Emperor's unconditional surrender. Some have already committed suicide and there are others who have approached us. They want to negotiate with us and join us to fight the British."

"The Japanese were killing us and we were killing them. We even killed all those who collaborated with them. Now you expect us to fight alongside with them? How can we trust them? I will never join the Japanese. I would rather fight them," said Chin Leng with emotion in her voice.

"They are now a spent force. The British are going to return with a full force. In our MPAJA guerrilla army we have 9,900 fully armed personnel with about 45,000 reservists and political, intelligence and logistics operatives. We also have arms and ammunition stashed away. If we do not resist the British we will never achieve our objective of independence for Malaya."

Kuppu had this to say, "I have suffered under the Japanese in the Death Railway, if they want to fight with us they must submit to our control and our political will. Without this condition we should not consider collaboration."

All agreed.

∗∗∗

Samy had news for them on 12 September 1945.

"I just heard on the All India radio this morning. There was a formal surrender of the *japankaran* to the *velekaran* in Singapore. They have immediately established a military administration.

The *velekaran* will soon be moving back to take control of the plantations. The workers will be able to get back to regular work."

"A lot of things have happened during the war. The coconut has been broken. We have been exposed to new struggles like the Indian nationalism through the INA, the Communist struggle in forming peoples' committees and labour unions. We have also seen how we have been used by both sides fighting their wars and ending up fighting and killing our own people. This has to be a lesson for all of us," said Desa.

"Our people need to start thinking for themselves along the lines of our culture, our Dravidian roots and social reform," said Samy.

"Yes, we discussed that earlier and we have to be prepared for the coming changes."

Janeki who was listening to them said, "We should start with the young people. Now we have got the school going and there are the older youth who have missed school but need some kind of formation. They are the ones who are going to face the changes head on."

"Apart from outside oppression we are also fighting among ourselves, quarrelling in the family, children crying when the parents fight," said Desa

"And the older children are reacting and rising up against their parents and so on," added Janeki.

"Ours is a great culture that has gone wrong somewhere," reflected Desa.

"It is still a great culture and if we are to follow the lines of our cultural roots we need to set right many things that have gone wrong," said Samy.

"Perhaps some training in discipline in the right direction might help. If we have to undertake any action there has to be basic unity among ourselves," said Desa.

"Both of you have helped to set up the school. Both of you are also trained in discipline." Samy was leading somewhere.

Desa and Janeki exchanged glances.

"I have been thinking for some time of starting a youth group or a kind of young people's force. I am not very young myself and I need people like you to help in doing this."

"If we want to do something for the young people we must get their help also. Why don't we call Leela and Anakili to join us in the discussion? They were so helpful and enthusiastic in starting the school," said Janeki.

"But they are girls. Perhaps some of the younger men..." began Samy when Janeki interrupted him, "Do you plan to have only boys in this youth group? I think girls should also be recruited on an equal basis."

Desa and Samy exchanged glances.

★★★

The first thing that the British did after formalising the surrender was to set up the British Military Administration (BMA). The CPM and the MPAJA were already in control of the towns and the British were not at ease with that. But even before they could talk terms with the CPM, their immediate concern was to disarm and remove the Japanese troops and confine them in the same prisons from which the British POWs were being liberated.

The main concern of the MPAJA was the shortage of food especially rice and that was also a challenge for the new administration which was also being pressurised from London to get the plantations operational. Among the civilian POWs in the Changi prison in Singapore, there were planters and they were quickly dispatched to manage the estates.

Chapter 39

Return of the British

Kuppu's group, still somewhat confused about its position and loyalty, received news that the British reoccupying troops had landed. The Royal Marine Commandos had disembarked from two warships in Penang and raised the Union Flag.

The feeling among the members was one of suspicion of the British. Ah Kow was saying. "The British have been our war-time allies but before that they were out to destroy us and I fear, now that they are returning to power, they will resume their repressive measures against us. They have used us and we too have used them to achieve different goals. We may have developed some friendships but we are ideologically opposed to each other."

"Do you really think that the remaining Japanese will join us and fight the British?" asked one comrade.

Another said, "They will do that only because they are too ashamed to surrender."

"We have orders from the top to disband our forces. I fear this is going to cause a split in the party," said Ah Kow.

Kuppu voiced his concerned opinion, "Remember, right now, we have the largest active armed forces in the country and a split will destroy our strength. I have a feeling that instructions from the top are not consistent with our goals."

"Kuppu, you should not question orders from the top. Be careful what you say in future," cautioned Ah Kow.

***

Desa, Janeki and Samy were talking to a group of young teenagers in the schoolroom asking them what they would like to do for a start. One of the boys said, "We need a football. We will cut the grass on the field and start playing football."

"I think that is a good start," said Jankei, "*Aiyiah* Samy, can you get them a football?"

While Samy was about to answer a man came to them and said, "A military truck has come to the estate and they are taking the *japankaran* away and also a *velekaran* has come over and he is talking with the *kiranies*."

Samy left them and went to find out and later shared with them the new development.

"The *velekaran* is the new estate manager. He is an Irishman with a funny name of Connolly.

"What name?" asked one of the youth, "*Komali?*" They all burst into laughter. *Komali* means a joker or jester.

"He wants to call the muster tomorrow morning and wants to address everybody. For now let us not say anything about our youth group," said Samy.

***

Ah Kow and his central Perak group met regularly to discuss the predicament of the party and the MPAJA. He said, "Now that they have established the British Military Administration, they are attempting to dismantle the MPAJA but not really succeeding. Seeing that they do not have direct control of the MPAJA they are pressurising the CPM to disband the MPAJA. They have also shut down the newspapers that were publishing left- wing propaganda. Because right at this moment we appear to be without a leader and directives seem to come from the Central Military Command, the CPM is caving in and wants the MPAJA to disband.

"What happened to our leader?" asked a comrade.

"There have been no directives from him for some time; only general statements from the politburo."

***

At 5.00 a.m. when the workforce had assembled outside the office the junior *kirany* called them to order.

"Things have changed in the estate. The *japankaran* bosses have gone away and the *velekaran* have once again taken over the estate. Look smart because the new *dorai* is coming to talk to you."

Word had already got around about the name of the new boss.

They waited and shortly the *velekaran dorai* appeared followed by Kanchiparampil, the senior *kirany*. Kanchi spoke to them.

"Your new *peria dorai* is Mr. Connolly. He..." There were giggles in the audience. "He is not new to rubber estates. He was a planter before the war. Please greet him in the usual manner."

"*Vanakam, Aiyiah Dorai.*" They all said holding their palms together at the forehead and bowing their heads.

"*Vanakam*, my name is Mr. Connolly and..." again there were giggles. "What's so funny?" He looked at them. There was silence. He continued, "I am your new manager. The war is now over and the Japanese have gone and now there is a new beginning in the estate. We are going to run the estate in proper order. I am sure you all know what that means. I notice a lot of undergrowth and all that has to be cleaned and cleared out. The factory also has to be cleaned out and the machines put back in good working order. A mechanic will see to that. We will spend this whole week doing just that and we will start tapping next week. You will be paid from today onwards ... accordingly (he did not spell that out because payments for cleaning and tapping are on a different scale) and provided with rations. I have appointed Mr. Kanchiparampil as the temporary assistant manager. I want you all to reregister your names in the office. We will also be employing new workers. He will see to it that everything is done properly. Get to work, then." He disappeared with five *coolies* to help get his own bungalow in order.

"How to work for a *Komali*?" said one as they dispersed laughing.

Chapter 40

Thondar Padai

Everybody was quite happy with this new change of events and hopeful for better times ahead. The cogs of the estate began to move with the *kiranies* supervising. Desa and Janeki also threw themselves in with enthusiasm. Everything fell into the old routine. The school and the crèche also got a new impetus from the management with money for repairs.

Desa, Samy and Janeki discussed how to motivate this group of young people whom they had recently called together. Now with the new change they too were looking to be employed.

Samy said, "These young people have lived through the war; seen and experienced the *japankaran* atrocities and suffered. They also have childhood memories of estate life under the *velekaran*. They have seen both the good and the bad happenings. Many of the new workers joining us would be ex-INA members or ex-MPAJA members and they will have different experiences to share. We have to give our young people a clear identity of themselves."

In the evenings Desa and Janeki got the youth together for talks and cultural education. They met in the school building.

Desa began, "While the younger ones are attending school most of you, I notice, have registered as tappers. Good, you are young working people now. One thing you must remember is that you are workers and not slaves. Your work is not free service, you cannot be forced to work and the wages should be enough for you to live a decent life.

"We are Indians and although some of us are Telugus most of us are Tamils and your parents were all from south India.

"We come from an ancient civilisation that goes back many many centuries. The Chola kings of Tamilaham, more than 2,300 years ago, were from one of the longest ruling Tamil dynasties in southern India. We were warriors and seafaring traders who went as far as China. The heartland of the Chola kings was the fertile valley of the Kaveri River. Janeki and I come from that place, from the town of Tiruchirapalli and many others have come from the neighbouring districts of Thiruvarur, Nagapattinam, Ariyalur, Perambalur, Pudukkotai, Thanjavur, Karaikal, Kumbakonam and other districts. Under Rajaraja Chola the first and his son Rajendra Chola the first, the dynasty became a military, economic and cultural power in South Asia and South-east Asia. His reign extended from Ceylon across the Ganges to Bengal.

"There was a powerful ancient Malay empire based in Sumatra known as the Srivijaya Empire which controlled Sumatra, Java and Malaynadu. By winning a naval war against Srivijaya, Rajendra Chola conquered Kedah and occupied it – this state of Kedah which was known in Tamil as Kadaram. Since Rajendra Chola I conquered Kadaram he was known as the Kadaram *Kondon*, the conqueror of Kadaram. Kadaram was the name of Old Kedah. *Aiyiah* Samy showed me a rock not far from here with ancient writings carved on it. See here," Desa showed them the page in his journal, "I copied those letters. Only an expert can read them. *Aiyiah* Samy tells me it is about an Indian king who destroyed his enemies in a war here in Kadaram.

"The Chola kings built great temples which also had great wealth. These temples were not only places of worship but also business centres. They built temples of Dravidian design like the Sivan temples along the Kaveri River. The largest and tallest temple of the time was the Sivan temple of Thanjavur, the Brahadeeswara temple depicting sculptures of Siva in various forms. They also built temples for Lord Vishnu. The Sri Maha Mariamman temple here in the estate is a magnificent structure which would have followed the rich tradition of the Cholas.

"From engravings we know that there was a high level of excellence in religion, art and literature in the society. The Chola kings are mentioned in the Sangam literature which formed the golden age of Tamil civilisation. The Sangam goes back way beyond the Cholas when Tamil poets and authors met in the ancient academy from time to time to share knowledge. Through the Sangam literature we can understand the history of the Tamil people.

"This is why education is so important to us. Janeki and I will teach you how to read and write so you too can learn about the world and events. The book is a window that opens the world to you.

"We can also understand why we had lost all that greatness of the past and reduced to being treated like slaves today and why we had to come to this land to earn a living. If we can keep in mind that we were a great people of dignity and learning we will have the will to rise up once again and live with dignity. Let us talk more and more among ourselves about our life here and decide what we should do. *Aiyiah* Samy has given us all the support we need and wants us to become a force to be reckoned with."

One young man stood up and asked, "What should we do to change things for the better?"

"First you should look around and see what are the things that have gone wrong, are no good and bad for us."

They became very much aware of themselves as Desa's talk had boosted their self-esteem and they began to look at their current situation and how they could bring about social reform.

"We don't want to be just a society. We want to fight for the rights of the workers. We need a name. So we should call ourselves a force," said Karuppan.

"Young People's Force?" suggested someone.

"What if the older people, the adults also want to join us?"

"O.K., your main aim is to improve our living conditions."

"What do you mean by that?"

"We want to bring justice in God's name and in service to the people. We will fight for justice if we have to."

"An Army in service of Justice, *Thondar Padai*," suggested Supaiah.

"We had the Indian National Army, the Jhansi Rani Regiment, The Malayan People's Anti-Japanese Army and now we have *Thondar Padai*, I like that," said Samy who has been quietly listening all the while.

They found a new identity and a renewed purpose in life.

They met periodically and discussed local issues while the estate functions were gaining momentum. Provisions were supplied even though on a meagre scale. They were all waiting anxiously at month's end to get paid.

By the end of October 1945, the British had declared the Japanese banana note to be of no value. This the people had already realized and whatever savings they had were worthless. They were paid in new currency. They were given an assortment of notes. They all had the head of King George VI and different coat of arms. The one dollar note was green in colour, the fifty cents, purple and orange, the twenty-five cents green and orange, the twenty cents brown and orange, the ten cents blue and pink, and the five cents red and green. There were also a half and one cent coins, square shaped bronze coins.

They were, however, told that all pre-war Malayan and Straits Settlement currency notes and coins would still be legal tender, that is, valid. The war would have seen the end of that money but for the fact that some old women would have concealed them thinking that all monies were the same. So there was a mad scramble to search all nooks and crannies for concealed money.

When they added up all the loose change of their wages, the men received twelve dollars and forty cents while the women received nine dollars and eighty cents. They worked that out and found it to be extremely low and unequal.

Desa questioned the *kirany* who said, "I don't know, ask the manager." Desa approached Kanchi, the new assistant manager. He explained, "For the first six days spent cleaning up you were paid forty cents a day and the women thirty cents. The rest of the days, which amounted to twenty days, you were paid fifty cents and that is the standard pay for now while the women get forty cents. All this depends on the rubber price."

Chapter 41

Loyalties Collide

Kupu and his squad had just returned from collecting rice and other food supplies that were hoarded by some Chinese businessmen.

Ah Kow had news for them. "The British want to take control from us and they want the MPAJA to disband asking us to surrender our arms; all our arms whether they were the ones air dropped by the British or the ones we have taken from the Japanese. They have promised to pay 300 dollars for a rifle and more for machine guns and sten guns. There is no firm directive from our Buro, so you think about it and we will decide without too much delay."

They talked through the night. Later into the night Kuppu and Chin Leng held their private discussion.

"I do not know how to decide," said Chin Leng. "The British are against communism and if I were to be a true communist, the British capitalists are my enemies. I hate the Japanese for what they had done to my mother and I cannot work with them. The Japanese took over Chinese businesses and closed down Chinese schools and rumour has it that both in Singapore and Malaya the Japanese have killed 40,000 Chinese. I can never work alongside the Japanese, ever."

Kuppu's feelings were not all that different, "The British shot and killed us and the Japanese tortured us to death in the Death Railway."

***

Many of the men were happy just to see the money and rushed off to the toddy shop while Desa, Janeki and Samy began to question the dealings of the new regime. They were gathered in Samy's house at the back of his shop.

"This is disappointing! We are not even getting what we were paid before the war. We were getting sixty and fifty-five cents then. After our strike action we even reached seventy five cents. There is no cost of living allowance even though we were demanding for it then," said Desa.

"I don't even know how to gauge the value of the new money to price my goods," said Samy.

"How then are we going to workout a cost of living allowance?" asked Janeki.

"Food is still scarce. No new provisions are coming in although I am told that soon they will become available. Initially the prices will be high. In three days time, it will be *Thivali* and the people will want to celebrate," added Samy.

"The temple committee has not been all that active apart from the usual poojas on Fridays; the inside of the temple looks awful," observed Desa.

"Why don't we get them to light up the temple and we can get the youth group to do some cleaning up and they can also get the lamps going," suggested Janeki.

"My worry is that I won't have enough provisions in the shop. Whatever I have they will take them on credit anyway," lamented Samy.

"Well, we will just have to make do with a modest celebration," declared Desa.

The next day the *bhai* and the Bombay man came along with their saris and bangles and broaches, vermillion and scented oils. Desa noticed that the *kangany* was also with them with his note book. After some haggling and bargaining the women sought financial credit from the *kangany* who dutifully noted the details in his book. The *bhai* and the Bombay man would directly debit the account with the *kangany* while the women would be in debt to the *kangany* with interest. Janeki and Desa took note of this bad practice to later alert the youth group to take account of this in their social reform action.

Samy went to the temple, met the temple *poosari* (temple priest) a pot-bellied middle-aged man, bare bodied with a rather dirty *veshti* and an equally dirty *poonool* across his chest.

"*Poosari* Pakirisamy, the estate people want to celebrate *Thiwali* but the temple has been neglected for a long time and it needs to be cleaned up for the celebration."

"I know, I'm alone and I have no helpers. We don't have a temple committee anymore."

"Yes, maybe, we should form a new temple committee. But *Thiwali* is only three days away and I will try and get some helpers to clean the temple. I can supply you with incense and you will have to prepare the *vibuthy* and *kungumum*. Please look smart, yourself." *Vibuthy* is ashes collected from burnt cow dung.

The following day, after work, the boys were busy cutting the grass on the field. Samy had already procured for them a new football. Desa and Janeki approached them, "With just the sickle and scythe it will take you quite a while to cut all the grass," said Desa.

"We'll do it," came the answer. They were so enthusiastic in preparing the field that it was a shame to stop them, yet Janeki put it to them that the day after tomorrow was *Thiwali*.

"We want to celebrate *Thiwali* but the temple is very dirty. Do you think you all can help to wash the walls and the floor?"

They stopped and looked at her. She quickly added, "I'll get the girls to sweep up all the rubbish and dirt and you can do the washing."

One of the boys said, "*Akka*, we will do as much cutting as we can and tonight we will wash the temple."

"Good," she said marveling at the energy of the youth. She then met the girls.

Thivali

"Since we are all in the mood for celebrating *Thiwali* the boys have agreed to wash the temple. Can you help by sweeping up all the rubbish and dirt?"

"Sure, Janeki *Akka*, we can do that," said Leela.

"But first we need to prepare the *mun theebam*." *Mun theebam* is a clay lamp.

"We can make them. Angammah *athai* (aunty) knows all about it and she can teach us to make them. They are very easy to make. We have to find clay first."

"We only have one day, can they dry by tomorrow evening?"

"Sure, if it doesn't rain. We'll go and look for clay." Leela took a few girls with her. The rest found Angammah and began talking. Other older women also joined in.

Angammah said, "Besides the *theebam* we also need to draw *kolams* but the temple is so dirty." A *kolam* is an ornamental figure drawn on the floor.

"Don't worry, the temple will be nice and clean by tonight. The girls are going to sweep and the boys wash."

"Now for the *kolam* we need some rice. Could we get some from *Aiyiah* Samy's shop?" asked one of the girls.

"If we are not going to make very big *kolams*, we don't need much; one or two *chupaks* will be enough. We have to soak it, pound it into flour and mix it with water," said Angammah.

The girls came carrying half a latex bucket of clay. They all got around Angammah who was going to demonstrate how to make clay *theebams*.

"First pick all the grass, twigs and stones out of the clay. Divide the clay into four lots and do what I am doing with one of the lots. Spread it on the cement floor. By adding a little water at a time we knead the clay like this."

Following Angammah, the others were also kneading the clay until it came to a malleable consistency.

"Let us make little balls that fit into our fist, let us all do it. Hold the ball of clay in the palm of your left hand; use the right thumb to make a depression in the middle of it. Don't make it right through but spread the depression all around until it becomes a bowl, trim the edges evenly and with the thumb and middle finger sharpen one spot and depress it with the forefinger. Now wet the palm of your hand very slightly and remove the bowl and put it on the ground. You have a *theebam* that will be hard when it is dried. Can anyone get me some old cloth?"

She tore the cloth into a strip, twisted it and rolled it into a rope.

"Cut them into three inches long. This is the wick. It will be nice if we can soak the wicks in ghee, but we will have to do with cooking oil. We should have enough clay *theebams* to fill the entrance of the temple. If *Aiyiah* Samy can spare us the rice we can start working on the *kolam* paste."

Samy was again the rallying person. He managed to get a goat from somewhere and got the men to slaughter it and distribute the meat to the families. They were already in the *Thivali* mood.

The temple was a solid stone structure with a narrow rectangular entrance with steps leading to it. Inside was dark and filthy. In the niche, the statue of Mariamman sat holding a trident in one hand and a bowl in the other but she was dirty and dusty. Leela and Anakili washed the goddess and dried her failing colours. On the side, leaning against the wall of the shrine stood a fading framed picture of the Goddess Letchumi which was cleaned and reinstalled by Janeki.

As the sun went down the girls using lanterns had swept the temple floor clean and dusted the cobwebs on the wall and ceiling. The boys had cut almost half the field and came to the temple with buckets. Their bare bodies were dripping with sweat. Very swiftly they flooded the floor and washed it clean splashing water on the walls and scrubbing them. A fruitful day's work efficiently accomplished over and above their daily task in the estate.

Rows and rows of *theebams* were drying in the sun the next day. Angammah and the other women had pounded the rice, and sieved the flour the night before. They only had to add the water and mix the flour for the *kolam* paste.

The *poosari* had hung a string of new mango leaves smeared with *santhanam* and dotted with *kungkumum pottu* across the entrance of the temple as a crowd gathered around Angammah at the temple gate. She started in the temple *pooja* centre, then the floor, the entrance and the steps. She started with a medium sized *kolam* by making sixteen *pullies* (dots), a matrix of dots, forming a grid, then dipping her thumb and two fingers into the paste, starting at the bottom left corner, she deftly traced a clean white line running like a snake curving and looping each *pulli* symmetrically but with a definite pattern and ending up by joining the starting point. It was a geometrically perfect pictorial art form. She went on crafting more complicated patterns finishing with a huge lotus flower.

"Every girl in India is expected to know how to do this." She told them.

They had requested the manager to grant them a holiday for *Thiwali* on 4 November 1945. He grudgingly granted it.

The mother rubs gingelly oil on the heads of the children. After the oil bath they put on new clothes, pay respects to their parents, asking forgiveness for having been naughty before they sit for breakfast. By mid-day all the children had taken their oil bath while most of the adults had theirs before sunrise.

As the sun was setting the estate folk gathered at the temple. The *mun theebams* were arranged on either side of the Goddess Mariamman, and around the framed picture of Goddess Letchumi, as well as at the entrance, and on both ends of the steps and down the path leading to the temple. Goddess Letchumi embodies beauty, grace and charm with promises of good luck. Inside, the *poosari* clad in a clean *veshti* and *poo nooul* recited verses in Sanskrit, did the *arathi* and distributed *vibuthi*. Desa and Samy were remarking how well this day had turned out.

Everything was fine except for a group of men nearby talking loudly, even shouting at one other, using fowl words. All afternoon they had been in the toddy shop and were quite drunk. This had marred an otherwise beautiful day of celebration. Desa realized that Janeki was not around. He looked for her among the women and the young people but she was not there. He went back to the cubicle and found her lying down.

"What is wrong, *kannu*? Is your body not well?"

"*Athanh*, I think I am pregnant."

"Oh, my God!" he sat down beside her and lifted her into his arms. "This is good news, a gift from Goddess Letchumi." He felt her stomach and she was in tears of joy.

"Is everything going well at the temple?" she asked.

"Yes, I was worried when I did not see you. *Aiyiah* Samy is very happy except for a group of drunken men."

Chapter 42

Leadership Crisis in CPM

Kuppu and Chin Leng were in a dilemma in confronting the new situation. At the meeting the following day things became clearer. Ah Kow called the meeting to order.

"Have you all been considering what you want to do? The situation has become very complicated. The British want to terminate the MPAJA and have offered to pay for the arms we surrender. Although many of us don't like that, we have been receiving instructions from the bureau to co-operate with the British. This instruction has come directly from our Secretary General Lai Te. This leader of ours, as you know or perhaps do not know, is a French-speaking Vietnamese. He worked in France, Russia, China and Indo-China and he came here as a representative of the Commitern and soon developed into a personality cult. We all respect him for his leadership and efficiency in organizing the CPM.

"During a recent meeting at the politburo, he said he had to leave urgently for Singapore and disappeared. After searching for him our leaders found out from a Vietnamese interpreter who worked for the All-India Radio, that Lai Te was indeed a double agent. He was operating for both the British and the Japanese. He has absconded with the party's funds to the tune of one million dollars, the money we had collected from the different states since the Japanese surrender and sent as our contribution to the Party Fund. He has betrayed us."

"Did nobody ever suspect him?" asked one comrade.

When the CPM was weak Lai Te joined the party as a representative of the Commitern and very efficiently organized and strengthened the party. Nobody questioned him. He was so clever that before the war and during the Japanese occupation and now after the war, he had been able to keep his double agent activity a secret. Some of our leaders did suspect but were too afraid to voice their opinion. He had been asking the different area groups to submit the specific locations of our secret arms dumps in the jungle. Our area leaders were careful and not ready to reveal the intelligence on our weapons caches. If we had obeyed him blindly we would have no weapons to carry on an armed struggle."

"What options do we have now?" asked Kuppu.

"There are three options. You can disband, surrender your arms and get paid. Two, you can infiltrate the trade unions and fight for justice for workers. The unions have already begun organizing in Singapore and branching into Malaya. Three, you can go into the jungle; take up the armed struggle in a guerrilla force. Think carefully before you decide."

***

At one of the meetings with the youth group, the youngsters brought this up.

"Desa, *Anna*, you told us to watch and see what is wrong. We think toddy drinking is bad and we should close the toddy shop," said Karuppan, a seventeen year old.

Desa tried to explain. "Toddy is a nice drink, I like it too. The problem is not toddy but the abuse of it. When we cannot control our drinking it starts to control us."

"You see, our men cannot control it, so we should control the toddy shop," came the response.

"When the men work hard starting early in the morning and become physically tired, it is understandable to have the desire for a drink."

"We can drink water, we can drink *moru*, why does it have to be toddy?" asked Suppiah, another young man.

"Drinking has ruined my family. Father comes home and argues with mother and beats her and even beats us," said Parvathi, a teenage girl.

"We should close down the toddy shop," shouted someone from the back and he was supported by others.

"When you grow older you too will want to drink. Don't you think you should train yourselves now on how to control your drink, so that you too will not end up like them?" asked Desa.

"We want to reform our society and toddy is bad and we should stop it," said Karuppan.

"Would you like to take it to the management?" asked Desa.

"The management is the one who allowed it. Even the manager orders his drink and gets it sent to his bungalow. Do you think he will stop it?"

The young people were saddened that the *Thivali* celebration was spoiled by the drunken few and had also experienced the evils of family disruption. They were dead set on putting an end to toddy drinking.

Desa had a discussion with Samy.

"The young people are very much against toddy drinking. I think we should educate them on how to control toddy drinking."

"Yes, that is something that should be done. But that would be a long process of education. It is you yourself who said that our great culture had gone wrong because of drinking. Toddy drinking, that is, uncontrolled drinking, does indeed disrupt the family, doing untold damage to the morale of our people. The *velekaran* allows it to be run after the fashion of a British pub. The *velekaran* in his country have many other attractions but our estate people have nothing else. It merely dulls their mind and after being pushed around by the *kiranies* and *kanganies* all day they find relief and false courage in toddy. They take it out on their wives and children. Having beaten the wife he forces himself upon her and practically rapes her before falling asleep in a drunken stupor. This suits the management because it numbs the mind away from protests and helps to procreate a local labour force. If the young people are angry about this, I understand them."

"I see your point, but the energy of the young force has to be disciplined."

"Yes, you and Janeki are the best people to train them."

"*Aiyiah* Samy, I have good news. Janeki is pregnant, not because she wants to increase the labour force for the *velekaran*."

"That's wonderful Desa, take good care of her."

It was the mid-month early pay day and there was another same scenario at the toddy shop. This time Karuppan, Supaiah and others from the youth group acted on their own.

They challenged the drunken men who tried to put up a fight. They were easily outnumbered and overpowered by the young boys. They dragged three of the men and tied them up to the rubber trees. They were shouting and swearing but the young men would not let anyone go near them. Only when they dosed off and began snoring did they untie them. They wanted to teach them a lesson.

At the next meeting Desa told them that they were rather harsh on the toddy drinkers.

"Yes," said Karuppan, "now they will be more careful when they drink. We also want to put an end to this."

"How do you plan to do that?" asked Desa.

"Anyone who gets drunk and disturbs the family or others, we will continue to punish them. We want to save our community from this curse. We will start by taking a pledge to abstain from toddy ourselves."

The young people wanted to be better organized and more structured. So they held an election. Karuppan was elected president and Supaiah the vice president. With Janeki's subtle suggestions, Leela was elected secretary and Anakili the treasurer.

"What kind of activities do you want?"

"We have formed a football team and want to challenge the teams from the other divisions and estates."

"Can you write all this down, Leela?" asked Janeki. "That is the job of a secretary to keep records of everything. If the boys want to play football, what do the girls want to do?"

"We want to start a chicken farm, so that we can supply eggs," said Suganthy, an older girl.

"We need money," said someone.

"Let's collect money then," said another voice.

Karuppan said, "Let's collect a fee from every member."

"How much?" another voice.

"I suggest one day's pay," said Suppiah.

"Now the treasurer will have something to do," said Desa.

"Then you will have to register your name as a member. Remember it is voluntary," said Janeki.

"Once you have registered, then you must pay every month," said Anakili.

"What happens if someone fails to pay?" asked someone named Gopal.

"In order to take care of all this you have to draw up some rules for your group," said Janeki.

"Can you help us to draw up the rules?" asked Karuppan.

"Yes, we can, but you must determine what your goals are."

They all had a buss session and slowly their aims became clear. They were listed down.

1. Improve our living conditions (main general goal).

2. Increase in wages and cost of living allowance.

3. Equal pay for men and women.

4. Estate dresser and proper medical care.

5. Close down toddy shop.

6. Take a personal pledge to abstain from alcohol.

7. Full-time teachers for the school and proper books.

8. Stop *kiranies* or anybody from molesting our women.

9. Maternity leave with pay.

10. Permission for workers to mount bicycles in front of European managers and Asian staff.

11. Freedom to form this group.

"That is already quite a lot for a start, but these are demands like those of a labour union. These are not rules for your society," said Desa.

Chapter 43

Workers' Agitation

Samy said, "There is a lot of labour unrest in Singapore encouraged by the communists. More than 200,000 workers had stopped work and the government used the troops against them. Many workers were killed while others arrested and deported. Labour unions have also been formed in Johore and they are also spreading into Malaynadu. Since different kinds of workers in the railway and in hospitals were involved they were called General Labour Unions (GLU). The reason for the strikes was that real wages were below the pre-war level because the cost of living had gone up four times. As more and more of these GLUs have begun to appear they have now formed the Pan Malayan General Labour Union (PMGLU). However, in the estate we are seeing Indian Labour Unions and many ex-INA people are joining them. Some of them have approached me and are interested in the *Thondar Padai* and would like to work together."

The *Thondar Padai* was fast gaining momentum. They asked Desa and Janeki to give them combat training. They found a clearing on the edge of the estate and used the place for drills. They marched up and down using sticks as rifles. With the money collected the men got themselves uniforms of kaki shirts and short pants and the women wore long pants. Donning Gandhi caps, they marched bare-footed. They became a militia ready for action.

They had organized inter-estate football games and got to know the youngsters of the neighbouring estates and shared with them the workings of the *Thondar Padai*. Soon other *Thondar Padais* were also formed in the other estates.

The *Thondar Padai,* having started as a youth group whose main target was the toddy shop, through football tournaments within the four divisions of Belfast estate spread to inter estate football matches. These football players became *Thondar Padais.* It became a network that spread beyond the state of Kedah tackling larger and more fundamental issues affecting Indian estate workers in the area of economic welfare and joint actions with trade unions.

They still kept a vigilant eye on toddy drinking.

One day, the *Thondar Padai* decided to picket the toddy shop in Bukit Raja estate. The other *Thondar Padais* joined forces to picket the toddy shop. They prevented the men from entering the toddy shop. There was a young European assistant estate manager there. He had called the police. This time the policemen were all Malays who were recruited and trained by the Japanese. The British retained them. In the presence of the police, the young assistant manager presuming that no one would ever dare to challenge him, walked up into the toddy shop and came out with a glass of toddy and began sipping it in front of everybody.

The police stood by and the crowd was also watching the defiance. The *Thondars* were furious. Karuppan walked up to the European and knocked the glass off his hand. The police moved in and there was a fight. The police shielded the European and the fight was between the *Thondars* and the toddy drinkers with the police intervening. Many of the toddy drinkers were beaten up and so were the *Thondars* including Desa and Samy. The police arrested Karuppan, Desa, Samy, three of the Bukit Raja *Thondars* and three toddy drinkers, nine in all. The case was brought to court and dragged on for months.

This did not deter the *Thondar Padai,* indeed it made them more determined to fight.

***

The wages stayed the same; the cost of living remained high. Even though the situation was somewhat better than what they had experienced during the Japanese occupation, they expected much better after the war. The workers too were not going to be as subservient as before. Desa and Janeki got the *Thondars* to do a study like what they did in Dolby estate. They got the youngsters to probe into the details of the list of grouses they had drawn up earlier and come up with a list of demands. This they did and Samy got the representative from the Indian Labour Union to meet them.

This is *Aiyiah* Mohandas, from the Indian Labour Union," introduced Samy.

Mohandas addressed the *Thondars*.

"*Aiyiah* Samy is the leader of the Indian Labour Union in South Kedah. I also know *Aiyiah* Desa who is like an older brother to you. I have heard a lot about the *Thondar Padai* and the good work you are doing. Our Labour Unions are also getting bigger and stronger. In order to have greater demanding power we are trying to join the different unions into a Pan Malayan General Labour Union (PMGLU). Whenever or wherever there is a strike, other unions can be called in to support you. *Aiyiah* Samy has the contacts. If you need any financial help you can also approach me."

"We are planning to hold a strike here and we hope you can support us," said Karuppan.

"Let me have a look at your demands and inform me in advance the date of your action." They all thanked him.

Desa pulled Mohandas aside and asked him if they had located Kuppu.

"Yes we know where he is. His group is now deciding what to do; whether to work with the unions or go into the jungle and continue the armed struggle. I will soon arrange a meeting when he is surer of his position. What have you decided to do?"

"I am not all that well known as a member of MPAJA or the CPM. I shall remain under cover and I have decided to keep my gun. I will cooperate with the unions but I want to concentrate on building up the *Thondar Padai*."

"Good. We will keep in touch."

Janeki, because of her condition, was staying away from the active combat training and helping the girls with their chicken farm and fine-tuning the demands for the strike.

They narrowed down their original eleven points to the following eight demands:

1. Equal pay with Chinese estate workers.

2. Equal pay for men and women for the same work.

3. Confinement leave of two months with full pay

4. Provision of clean drinking water.

5. Removal of trespass restrictions.

6. Full-time school teachers.

7. Dresser and dispensary

8. Closure of toddy shop.

When presented to the management, they were summarily rejected and the *Thondars* decided to go on strike. They fixed the first Sunday of September for the strike and informed the *Thondars* of the neighbouring estate and Mr. Mohandas. The women also got ready because there was sure to be a force of resistance. They were prepared with sticks, chilli powder and pots of boiling water to be used in self defence. They all assembled in front of the estate office. The manager immediately called the police who ordered them to disperse in fifteen minutes. The strikers stood their ground. The Malay sergeant ordered the police to move in with their lathi and they clashed. When some of the policemen got hurt, they opened fire. The strikers began to run. One of the four shot dead was Karuppen the leader of the *Thondar Padai*. Sixty-six men including Desa and Samy were arrested and eleven women including a 15 year-old girl and the eight-month pregnant Janeki.

In the days that followed nobody went to work. They refused to work until their members were released. The manager negotiated with the police and got the men and women released. Rubber was in demand and labour was in short supply so the manager agreed to increase wages by 20 per cent. This was due to the fact that post-war reconstruction of the world economy was crying out for more supplies of rubber and also of tin. The Chinese strikers in the tin mines also got their demands met for this reason. Although the workers paid a heavy price in the loss of lives, they won a partial victory.

✳✳✳

With loyalties pulling in different directions they were left with three options. Many MPAJA fighters surrendered their weapons and, on 1 December 1946, the MPAJA was officially disbanded. But not so in reality because they continued as the MPAJA Old Comrades Association and these members were on recall at a moment's notice to support a secret army.

Kuppu and Chin Leng were still undecided on what to do.

"The labour unions are becoming strong now and the party is giving its full backing to them. Labour is now in high demand with an increase in the bargaining power for both the Indian and Chinese workers. The workers are ready to strike because there is no improvement in food, clothing and housing after the war. People are undernourished and sick and the British are only giving them pre-war wages. I would like to join the unions in their struggle," said Kuppu.

Chin Leng was somewhat hesitant.

"I would rather go into the jungle and fight with the party."

Before she could elaborate they were interrupted by a member.

"Kuppu there is a message for you," said the member handing him a letter. Kuppu read the letter and his face registered immediate surprise and joy.

"What is it, Kuppu?" asked Chin Leng.

"It is a letter from a union leader who is also MPAJA in Kedah. He says that my close friend, Desa, is there and asking to meet me. If I go to Kulim he will arrange a meeting place for us. Chin Leng, I would like you to come along."

Chin Leng remained silent.

"I will get permission from Ah Kow. You know Desa is also MPAJA and we used to work together here. He went in search of his wife. I do not know if he found her."

Chapter 44

Baby Boy

Janeki was in labour. She was attended to by a couple of old women. Desa and everybody else were ordered to stay out.

These old women, Munniammah and Kanniammah, were the accepted midwives who had assisted with the birth of several babies in the estate. Munniammah went inside the cubicle where Janeki was lying down and immediately began to close the door and the windows while Kanniammah started a fire to boil water. While the water was boiling she took some oils and entered the cubicle making sure to close the door. Desa was anxious not knowing what was going on inside.

"Get up, *ammah*," said Munniammah to Janeki and the two women helped Janeki to stand up against the wall.

"Raise your arms up," said Kanniammah removing her sari and lifting her petticoat over her head. Munniammah began applying gingelly oil on Janeki's swollen belly and started massaging with an upward and downward motion. This was to set the baby into a proper position and to lessen the pain and stimulate contractions. Kanniammah came out with a copper bowl of gingelly oil, removed the water from the fire and placed the bowl on the fire to warm the oil. She placed her hand over the oil to feel the heat. The smell of the hot gingelly oil reminded Desa of hot crispy oil - *thosai*. When she thought it was warm enough she took it back inside, again making sure to shut the door before Desa could get a peek in. There was silence.

After the massage the women got Janeki to squat over the hot oil. Munniamah then applied some hot oil on the vulva outlet to avoid tearing and facilitate delivery.

Samy joined Desa outside. They waited for what seemed an eternity to Desa. The *Thondar Padai* members who were returning from the timber also began to gather around in expectation. Samy asked one of the *Thondar* boys to fetch some coffee. Two hours had past and nothing happened. While some of the women waited, most of the men went about their daily chores. It was another hour before Desa heard the deep breathing and groans of Janeki. He got up and walked towards the door and listened closely. The labour had begun. The door opened and Kanniammah came out and carried the hot water inside. After a while there was silence again and Desa began to panic. Samy got him to come back and sit down on the step. Then again they heard the painful shouting from Janeki, this time louder. Again it stopped and again there was silence. Then the baby cried. Desa was ready to knock down the door when it opened a little. Kanniammah stuck her head out and said, "Everything has come good. You have a baby boy and the mother is also alright. But you cannot come in yet."

Desa was visibly relieved and his face brightened up. This was a red-letter day in his journal.

After the baby and mother were cleaned up Desa and Samy were allowed in. Desa first looked at Janeki. She looked pale but she smiled. Then he saw the baby, eyes closed and sleeping. He was only allowed to look and not touch. He held Janeki's hand. The baby began to stir and cry. Jankei sat up and the baby was placed in her arms but she was not allowed to breast feed the baby yet. The hungry baby was fed with drops of goat milk.

"It will be two or three days before you can give your breast to the baby," said Munniammah and left.

"Congratulations, Janeki, you have a lovely son," said Samy. Before he could even finish the sentence the door opened and Leela and Anakili burst in and got excited over the baby and mother. They were joined by Nagammah, their mother, who brought some light food for Janeki.

"Eat, *ammah*, you have to be strong, and drink plenty of milk," she told Janeki. There was great rejoicing.

"Anakili, *kuti*, go to Angammah's house and get a bottle of milk," said Samy. *Kuti* is a small animal, also used for a small girl.

"Stop calling me *kuti*, I'm a big girl now," protested Anakili.

"OK, run along, Anakili, *amadi*," replied Samy.

The next day the baby was crying loudly. Kanniammah came and gave the baby some more goat milk. After she left the baby began to cry again.

"Forget about their instruction," said Desa, "the baby is hungry." He lifted the baby and gave him to Janeki to breast feed. The baby began sucking furiously.

Since the postal service was operational again both Janeki and Desa wrote to their parents telling them of the good news and enclosed some money.

"What shall we name him?" asked Janeki.

"I was thinking of calling him Rajen," said Desa.

"I like Rasaiah," said Janeki.

"Alright, he shall be N. Rasaiah Pillay."

While Janeki was in confinement she was excused from attending court on the case of the strike. The case was eventually dropped because the manager agreed to grant a couple of their demands, including the provision of one full-time teacher and two part-time teachers for the school. These teachers will cover all the four divisions of the estate.

***

The *Thondar Padai* too was very much involved in its own strikes and in sympathy strikes. Older men, many ex-INA members, joined the *Thondar Padai*. They increased their subscriptions and became better equipped.

There was a month old strike going on in Selambau estate and the *Thondars* joined them in sympathy. It all started when Amalor, a woman who had been working in the estate for 25 years found her four goats missing. She went to the estate office to report the loss.

"*Aiyiah, sinna dorai*," said Amalor addressing Fernandez, an assistant manager there, "my four goats on which my whole family depends are lost. Somebody took them. Can you please investigate?"

"Amalor, *ammah*, we are not the police. You must report this to the police so that they can investigate."

"Can you ask the *peria dorai* to help? He knows the police."

"I will talk to him. In the meantime you go and do your work."

Fernandez took his time and when he had to see his boss about a number of things he brought up this matter.

"Mr. O'Leary, Sir, one of the women workers has lost her four goats and wants an investigation to find out who stole them."

"Why can't they learn to look after their own things? I cannot be bothered with this and I don't want the police coming here and disrupting our work. You just get rid of her." Fernandez told his *kangany* to tell her she is no longer needed in the estate. The *kangany* who is the petty boss told her off for disturbing the manager. "Did you go and search for your goats?" he asked her.

"Yes, we did, we searched everywhere but we cannot find them. Some people must have driven them out of the estate, or may even have slaughtered them."

"I'm afraid we cannot help you. If you go looking for your goats outside of the estate, don't come back."

"Why am I being chased away because I lost my goats, do you know where they are?"

"Are you accusing me of robbing your goats? You dare to argue with me!"

The *kangany* assaulted her and ordered her to leave the estate. Bala, a factory hand at the estate, was ordered to load Amalor's belongings on a cart and take them out of the estate. Bala, a member of the *Thondar Padai*, refused to do so. The *Thondars* would no longer be pushed around and be subservient. The others, seeing this as an act of injustice, called for a strike joined by other *Thondars* including Desa and Samy. The strike went on for days until the police were called in.

O'Leary called Duncan the officer-in-charge of the police department, the OCPD.

"Duncan, this is O'Leary from Selambau."

"Hello, how are things over there? I heard the workers are striking."

"Yes, that is why I am calling. This has been going on for a couple of weeks just because a silly old woman refused to obey orders. Production has come to a standstill. Can you send some policemen to put the fear of God into them?"

"Sure, that should not be a problem. While I prepare to send them could you please prepare a police report of insubordination or whatever, just for the record?"

"Yes, I'll do that."

The police arrived in several trucks armed with rifles, batons, lathis and bayonets. There was a shouting match between the workers and the Malay policemen culminating in a police attack. Soon after the outbreak of war, the Sikh policemen were disarmed in Kulim. The Malay policemen had been trained now to strictly obey orders. The police went on a rampage chasing the workers, breaking down doors, smashing pots and pans, and destroying the fireplaces. Those who were caught were brutalised. Bala was badly hurt and died of head injuries. The women were not spared. 25 women suffered from swollen arms and legs and head and body injuries. No one received medical attention. The management couldn't care less if they lived or died. The management and the police had acted in concert.

"All Amalor wanted was some help to find her goats and they turned it into such an unjust attack. The manager and the police chief are very close friends. They may even know something about the goats that we don't know. The goats are worth very good money and for Amalor, they are her livelihood," said Desa.

This incident made the *Thondar Padai* very angry. They decided to become militant and fight back if anything like this ever happened again. They began to arm themselves with stones and sticks and *parangs*. One of their members has been killed. They put their tools down and refused to work until there was justice. Weeks went by and nothing was done. One night they waylaid the *kangany*, took him into the timber and beat him to death. This was justice done as far as the *Thondars* were concerned.

Desa, Janeki and Samy were not pleased with their action but they understood their sense of retribution.

***

Mohandas sent word to Desa to meet him at the Kulim old town coffee shop. Desa went the same afternoon and met him hoping he had some news of Kuppu.

"Greetings Mohandas *aiyiah*, what news?" said Desa.

"I have received word from Kuppu and he is willing to come and see you."

"That is good news, how is he?"

"He is with the CPM and is the cell leader in Sungei Siput. Like you, he has not surrendered his MPAJA membership. It is not wise to meet in the town. I have a friend, also a member, in Kampong Tunku Putera, just a mile from here. We could meet there. You tell me a date and I will send word."

"That will be great. My wife and I would like to meet him and also, perhaps, my baby son. We are also in the middle of organizing another strike. The Sunday following two weeks from now should suit us."

"It is best not to let other people know about this meeting. Even though most people here will not know him, the British Special Branch has spies all over the place."

***

The management with the consent of the UPAM enforced more restrictions. Desa and Samy travelled to other estates and spoke to the *Thondar Padai* branches.

In his address to them Desa said,

"The managers in the estates are imposing more and more restrictions. If we violate those restrictions we will be punished for breaking the law. We have to come up with more demands to counter the restrictions. If the demands are not granted and we go ahead and violate those restrictions, then we put the onus on them, saying that we went against the restrictions because they failed to meet our demands. Let us draw up new demands and present them in all the estates at the same time."

They began to draw up a new set of demands. Janeki was busy

with the baby. She asked Nagammah, Samy's wife to take care of the baby rather than leave him in the crèche which was still not up to standard. She found time to continue training the *Thondars*. She trained them on how to use the club as a defense weapon.

One night when Desa was writing his journal he heard a commotion outside the *coolie* line. A tapper by the name of Ganapathy was being beaten up by a group of *Thondars*. He managed to stop them from killing the poor fellow. Ganapathy was a great advocate of toddy drinking but that was not the reason for being bashed up. He was a snitch. They caught him passing messages to the *kirany* on the demands they were drawing up. He had been spying for the management, reporting back to the *kirany* what the *Thondars* were up to. They let him off with a warning, "If we catch you again we will kill you."

They went ahead anyway in drawing up the demands. Desa and Samy sat with them and went through the demands. They were:

1. Increase our pay to achieve equal pay with the Chinese estate workers.

2. Equal pay for women with immediate effect.

3. We demand some war bonus like what the European staff and government servants are given.

4. Minimum of one month's notice for eviction from labour lines.

5. Maternity leave for two months with full pay.

6. Certified sick leave without pay cut.

7. Removal of trespass restrictions. Make access roads public.

8. Transport should be provided for bringing in the latex from a distance exceeding half a mile.

9. Proper living quarters with kitchen, bathroom and latrine, and potable water.

The reason for the demand against the trespass restriction was because the management had imposed a law to keep off "agitators" and "undesirable" outsiders, thus preventing the *Thondars* from other estates joining forces during a strike action. This also made it difficult for Desa and Samy travelling to the estates to hold meetings and give talks.

As was expected, their demands were rebuffed and the *Thondars* went on strike. They refused to work until at least some of their demands were met. The management was also adamant and refused to budge. To the surprise of the *Thondars* lorry loads of Japanese prisoners of war were brought to the estate as replacement workers. This kindled their anger because these same men who had oppressed them during the war were now replacing them. The *Thondars* could not confront them because they were protected by the police. Soon the management found that these Japanese were doing more harm to the trees than tapping rubber and were withdrawn.

The estate workers had no idea that the Japanese POWs were still in the country.

They later discovered that 20,000 Japanese POWs were returned to Japan the following year.

Chapter 45

Politics

Desa and Samy sat in front of the shop, as they often did, chewing betel leaves or smoking *surutu* (cheroot). This time they were talking about the glad tiding of the new born baby among other matters.

"We are going to name our son Rasaiah. He is born on this soil and I am wondering what country he will belong to," said Desa.

"If he is going to grow up here then this is his country; my daughters too are born here," said Samy.

"But we are not considered citizens of this country."

Janeki came along, "Rasaiah is sleeping now. Sounds like a serious discussion going on. Can I join you?"

"Certainly, *ammah*, pull up another stool," said Samy.

"Janeki and I have also been discussing this matter," said Desa.

Desa had asked Samy to acquire other newspapers besides the ones he had for sale and had been following political developments.

"The political horizon of the country is fast changing. The country now belongs to the *velekaran* and if not for the bombing of Horoshima and Nagasaki it would have belonged to the *japankaran*. I dread to think which devil is worse. The primary concern of the *velekaran* is rubber and they don't care much for us as long as we deliver it while for the *japankaran* it was the expansion of their empire and nothing could stand in the way of that. I still maintain that the cruelty of the *japankaran* was far worse."

Janeki, who did not experience much of the *velekaran* rule, interrupted, "Not all the *japankaran* are cruel."

Desa, shocked by her intervention, asked her, "Why do you say that? Is it because your Rani regiment was trained by the *japankaran* and you worked with the *japankaran*?"

"Well, I worked closely with some of the *japankaran* doctors and they were decent men. But that is not the real reason."

"What, then, is the real reason?"

She hesitated because she did not want to bring up the incident with Palanivellu, the Malayalee *kirany*, in the estate when she was rescued by the Japanese officer. She would rather tell Desa in private.

As if on cue, Mohandas appeared and joined them.

"Come, Mohandas, pull up a stool. Help yourself to some *vetrilei-paku*. We are just talking politics," said Samy. *Vetrilei-paku* is betel leaves and areca nuts.

Desa, sensing Janeki's hesitancy, dropped the subject.

"As I was saying, all along, we Indians have been the marginalized race, oppressed from all sides, sandwiched between the *velekaran* and the *japankaran*. The *velekaran* are back again and, all along, they have never really involved the Indians or the Chinese in the administration of the country. They also left the Malays to their traditional peasant lifestyle, except for the ruling class. The Malays, claiming the right to the soil, now want the country all for themselves."

"We are wondering whether we belong to this country or not and what future there is for us and our children," said Samy.

"Well, it is quite well known that the *velekaran* have established the Malayan Union where Chinese and Indians would qualify for citizenship," said Mohandas.

"Yes," said Samy, "but some Malays are not happy with that. They are saying that we are here as workers to build their house and, as mere masons, we do not own their house. What kind of masons were we! We cleared the jungles, built the roads and railways, and planted the rubber trees not for the Malays but for the British. So this is the way we constructed the home for the Malays, is it?"

"*Aiyiah* Samy, this is Malaynadu and the Malays consider it their country and we and the Chinese came here to work and then go back to India and China. We are not political but they are."

"As far as I know, this Malay nationalism actually began in 1938 with the *Kaum Muda*, a youth group that is in many ways similar to the *Thondars*.

"Actually I was inspired by them to start the *Thondar Padai*. They were working to improve the Malay youth in sports, education, agriculture and health. They were looking, primarily, for independence from the *velekaran* imperialism. Just before the *japankaran* moved in, one hundred of their members were arrested for collaboration and detained by the *velekaran*."

"What happened then?" asked Janeki.

Mohandas filled in the picture. "After these members were released they actually approached the *japankaran* authorities to negotiate for Malayan independence. The *japankaran* simply disbanded them. They went underground and cooperated with the CPM and the MPAJA. They did not give up their struggle. When the *velekaran* returned they regrouped and formed three strong leftist groups. The main one was the Malay Nationalist Party together with the Awakened Youth Organization known as API and the Cohort of Awakened Women known as AWAS. All these happened only a year ago."

Desa opened the pages of the Straits Times.

"Now a new political party has been formed by a group of Malay loyalists and civil servants called UMNO, the United Malays National Organization."

"Alright, so much for the Malays fighting for their rights. We Indians have been in this country, not counting the early Chola conquests, for more than a hundred years as workers. What political representation do we have?" asked Janeki

"Why are you asking, nga!" said Samy, "we've never bothered much about politics. We are involved with the unions and that's about it. All we had were the Indian Associations and they were in the towns. They joined together and formed the CIAM, the Central Indian Association of Malaya, and their main interest was in getting council positions for themselves in the government. Many of those leaders never knew the real conditions in the plantations.

In the beginning they were not political. Only now, three months ago, a political party has been formed for the Indians. You know more about it Mohandas, tell us."

Without the four of them realizing it, suddenly Supaiah and a few *Thondars* were squatting on the ground around them listening with interest.

"This lawyer, Thivy, who graduated from England, was very much influenced by Subbas Chandra Bose. Of course, he joined the INA and went to Burma to fight the *velekaran* with the *japankaran*. Janeki, you may have come across him. After the war he became an anti-colonial activist and was imprisoned by the *velekaran* in Changi, Singapore. Now he has been released. He, you might say, is the first Indian to step into politics. In August this year he founded the Malayan Indian Congress (MIC). You notice the name? It is the Indian Congress named after the Indian National Congress. The aim of the MIC is to fight for the independence of India, not Malaynadu. It is a political party in Malaynadu with its interest in India. Again it is a party that has begun without consulting us, the plantation workers. Our politics was not sufficiently grounded here. Let's wait and see if they will take up the cause of the estate workers," said Desa.

"It looks like the Malays have become politically conscious, very much more so than the Indians and the Chinese," began Mohandas. "The *velekaran*, in order to consolidate colonial rule, proposed the idea of a Malayan Union last year and established it in April this year. UMNO is strongly opposed to the Malayan Union because it gave equal rights to people for citizenship and managed to get the rulers of the Malay states to concede all their powers except in religious matters."

Desa jumped in, "Even before the Malayan Union came into force, UMNO members organized rallies and marched to protest the formation of the Malayan Union. The newspapers have carried the pictures, let me show you." Desa pulled out some old copies of the *Straits Times*. "Look, Malay men with white cloth wrapped around their songkoks and Malay women holding placards declaring, "Malaya belongs to the Malays. We do not want the other races to be given the rights and privileges of the Malays."

Mohandas continued, "Now the *velekaran* are having second thoughts about the Malayan Union, not because of pressure from UMNO or MNP."

"Why are the *velekaran* changing their mind now?" asked Janeki.

"The *velekaran* were rather hasty in proposing the Malayan Union. Now they realized that giving citizenship to the Chinese and Indian *coolies* meant giving them voting rights. They knew that the CPM has great influence over them and that could mean an electoral majority for the CPM. That was their fear."

"That makes sense," said Samy.

Mohandas had more inside information, "Now the *velekaran* are having secret talks with the Malay elite about replacing the Malayan Union with a "Federation of Malaya" consisting of the nine Malay States with Penang and Malacca but excluding Singapore. Many of the non-Malays, especially the Chinese, are not happy because the federation excludes Singapore."

"This is the latest news we have," said Desa pulling out the current copy of the Straits Times. "The non-Malays have got together to form a joint action group. The Federation of Trade Unions, the ex-comrades of the MPAJA, women's groups and youth groups and even the MIC have all banded together to form the All Malayan Council of Joint Action (A.M.C.J.A.) headed by a prominent Chinese businessman by the name of Tan Cheng Lock. This only happened yesterday."

"How is it that we Indians in the estates are not made aware of all these movements?" asked Janeki.

"The initiators of these groups are mainly the English-speaking white-collar workers in the cities and they seldom consult the workers in the plantations or the mines. But it is the CPM that connects the two and keeps voicing the needs of the rural workers.

We will soon get to know more because all this is happening very fast now. I know because I am involved in some of these groups," said Mohandas.

"So many things are happening all at once and this is creating confusion among the people. Mohandas *aiyiah*, why don't you come one day and give our *Thondars* a talk on these new political developments?" asked Janeki.

"Please come, *aiyiah*, I will gather all the *Thondars* from all the divisions," said Supaiah.

"Certainly, I will be happy to do that."

Chapter 46

Reunion

Kuppu persuaded Chin Leng to accompany him and got permission from Ah Kow. They had to travel as workers and not betray their membership under any circumstance to anybody except the CPM branch in Kulim. They both took the train to Bukit Mertajam. From there they took a bus to Kulim. They were met by a comrade in Kulim and made their own way to Kampong Tunku Putera.

Mohandas had sent word that Kuppu was coming and to meet him at the old town coffee shop in Kulim. Desa and Janeki told Samy that they would like to take their baby out to town and buy some toys. They took the bus to town and accompanied Mohandas to Kampong Tunku Putera.

They met in a kampong house surrounded by fruit trees - mango, rambutan, mangosteen, banana, papaya and durian trees - and occupied by a Malay family. It was a rather large house that stood on stout wooden stilts. The only cement construction was the steps leading up to the house. The rest of the house was wooden. The steps led to an open foyer with an entrance to rooms inside. The windows had four doors, the bottom half was barricaded with carved wooden railings allowing maximum air flow. The floor plan was a cross with the main body and each wing supporting a pointed thatched roof. The beams above the windows holding the roof were decorated by handcrafted woodwork. It was indeed a beautiful kampong house. A Malay man in sarong welcomed Mohandas and ushered all of them in. Kuppu, Chin Leng and another comrade were already in a room inside.

Mohandas introduced them to Haji Syed Kamaruddin who

warmly welcomed them. Kuppu immediately embraced Desa in a big hug and politely greeted Janeki.

"I had no idea that you had finally met each other," he said.

"Thanks to Mohandas *aiyiah* we were able to trace you," said Desa.

"You people have a lot to talk about, so take your time," said Mohandas nodding to the other comrade. They left. Mohandas was holding a conversation with Haji Kamaruddin in the foyer.

"This is my comrade and very close friend, Chin Leng," introduced Kuppu.

Desa joined hands and greeted her. She did not quite know how to make the greeting, so she bowed her head. Janeki also bowed her head for she was holding the baby.

"This is our son Rasaiah," said Janeki offering him. Kuppu carried the baby.

"He looks like his mother ... and his father." Having kissed the baby he handed him to Chin Leng who, rather awkwardly, took him in her arms. "You both look very well."

"You look rather thin. How are things with you?" asked Desa.

"I did not go back to the estate. I am with the CPM and quietly still with the MPAJA. We are at a critical stage of deciding what to do. The changeover after the war has happened very fast."

Kuppu explained the turnover of events and the real dilemma they are in at the moment. Desa and Janeki explained their different experiences until they met.

"I met a very good person by the name of Samy and we are with him at Belfast estate. The unions are really up and moving now and we have organized a youth group. It is called the *Thondar Padai*, whose objective is to fight for justice and uplift the living conditions of our people. We are carrying out strikes in the estates in Kedah. We are experiencing a Malayan Spring. Why don't you join us?"

"Strikes are also happening all over the country, Desa. We do strongly support the unions by backing them with personnel and finance, but the CPM's struggle is bigger than just the unions. With the help of the *velekaran*, the CPM is now a legal political party and the MPAJA has gone underground. We have established cells in all the towns and I am the cell leader of Sungei Siput. The *velekaran* have betrayed us and we want to get rid of the *velekaran* altogether and they are our common enemy.

"The Labour government in England appears to be weak. Britain is not getting very much support from the other European countries. In all its colonies the native forces are rising up. India is restless; the local uprisings there are making it difficult for them to control India. They are going to end *velekaran* rule in India. The intention of the CPM is also to bring an end to *velekaran* rule in Malaynadu and gain independence with full equality for all races. We continue to do what you and I were doing but this time we attack *velekaran* sympathisers instead of *japankaran* sympathisers and the *velekaran* planters. The *velekaran* have declared that any demonstrations would be suppressed and their leaders arrested. We also have to take counter measures and sometimes use violence to achieve our political revolution.

I hope you understand that Chin Leng and I want to be together."

"Kuppu, the CPM has given you a very good grounding in politics and I couldn't agree with you more."

The baby began to cry. Janeki excused herself and went to the adjoining room to feed Rasaiah.

Chin Leng shared her experience with the Japanese. They talked until it was late evening.

"By the way, Desa, we were sent to collect supplies that were air dropped in the jungle. Many *velekaran* also parachuted into the jungle and guess what? One of them was Roberts, the bastard who ordered the Sikhs to shoot us. Desa, we have unfinished business."

The host Malay family would not let them go before they shared the evening meal with them. The meal was delicious *prawn sambal* and *petai* with *nasi lemak*, a favorite dish in Malay cuisine. Prawn cooked in *sambal*, a hot spicy sauce. *Petai* looks like broad beans, green in colour. It grows in long pods on tall trees and is gathered directly from the forest. *Nasi lemak* literally means 'fatty rice' in Malay. Rice (*nasi*) is soaked in coconut cream and steamed.

They learnt that their host Haji Kamaruddin was also a comrade. He was also a member of the Malay Nationalist Party which was formally the Kesatuan Melayu Muda (KMM). Although it was racist and radical in the beginning, now it is working towards a unified Malaya through multi-cultural cooperation. One thing common to both the MNP and the CPM was opposition to colonialism.

Desa and Kuppu wished each other well and promised to meet again when the situation became more stable. They parted company separately.

Chapter 47

Political Struggle

Desa had been keeping abreast with events through the newspaper. He shared the news with Samy.

"On the political scene another group is forming, spearheaded by the Malay Nationalist Party (MNP). They have brought together the Malay women group and Malay youth group in a coalition called the Centre of People's Power or Pusat Tenaga Rakyat (Putera)."

This is what we would call *makal sakthi*. Since the *velekaran* government was dealing exclusively with UMNO, Putera, headed by MNP representing a wider range of opinions and not as radical as it was in the beginning, distanced itself from UNMO. The *velekaran* proposed the federation through clandestine consultation with UMNO. Putera decided to join A.M.C.J.A.. The Putera/A.M.C.J.A. coalition is jointly presided over by Dr. Burhanuddin Al-Helmy and Tan Cheng Lock. This new multi-racial coalition wants to have bargaining power regarding the future of Malaynadu. Its aim is to fight for an independent united Malaynadu, with equal citizenship for all, with a People's Constitution and elected parliament. If they succeed we have hope for equal political rights in Malaynadu. It is growing fast. It remains to be seen whom the British will listen to in the end."

The ordinary trespassing law was being used to keep union organizers from addressing the workers on plantations. Janeki had arranged a meeting of the *Thondars* and others in the estate for a talk by Mohandas. Since he was representing the Unions he disclosed that the Pan Malayan General Labour Union (PMGLU) had now been renamed the Pan Malayan Federation of Trade

Unions (PMFTU). In the midst of his talk a large police force came into Belfast estate. They barged in, went straight for Mohandas and arrested him for trespassing. Mohandas was representing the PMFTU.

When the workers closed ranks around Mohandas to protect him the police opened fire, killing one worker and wounding five. They handcuffed Mohandas and took him away. The management and the police were taking harsh measures against the workers. But this only made the *Thondars* more determined to fight back. They began arming themselves with whatever weapons they could find or fabricate. They were very angry young people.

24 April 1947

The *Thondar Padai* held a meeting. Supaiah who was now the leader addressed the members on their intention of celebrating Labour Day on the first of May. "I will ask Desa *anna* to explain to us the meaning of Labour Day."

"Labour Day is the day when we call upon workers of the world to unite," said Desa. "The first International Workers Day was celebrated in America in 1886 when the workers and the police clashed. Many workers and policemen were killed. We too have suffered a lot at the hands of the police but our celebration should be orderly and peaceful. Whenever the police confront us we should tell them that they too are workers and workers have rights. Labour Day in this country is not a holiday. Hopefully, in the future, it will become a holiday.

I remember in India, Workers Day is celebrated at the beach opposite the High Court in Chennai Patinam. It was first celebrated there in 1923 on the first of May by the Labour Kisan Party of Hindustan. They were calling for non-violence, an 8-hour working day and independence for India. In our peaceful celebration we should call for justice for workers. In India they raise the Indian flag. We should also do the same but raise three flags – the Indian flag, the British flag and the Kedah state flag. This is to show that we are not against the government but want justice for workers."

"Thank you, *anna*, for telling us what May Day is all about," said

Supaiah. "We should invite all our *Thondar Padai* branches and the labour unions to come and join us here. We can raise the flags, do a parade by marching and have food and drinks. Do you agree?"

They all said yes and the women were ready to prepare the food.

The government had made it very difficult for the unions to be registered, but as a matter of courtesy, the Kulim Rubber Workers Union, together with the Kulim Indian Labour Union, sent a joint letter to the manager of Belfast estate informing him that a meeting would be held at the Home Division to discuss matters regarding the May Day celebrations.

They did not receive an acknowledgement but went ahead and called the meeting and fixed the celebration to begin at 3.00 p.m. by which time most workers be back from the timber. Invitations were sent.

The young *Thondars* from all the divisions and other neighbouring estates came and union members also began arriving. They all gathered in front of the temple. There were more than 400 workers, Indians and Chinese, including women and children.

Samy welcomed the people and explained the purpose of the celebration. They raised the three flags together and sang the *Bande Mataram*. Just as they began the parade, trucks of police personnel pulled up. Without warning a young British police officer waved his pistol at the crowd and ordered them to disperse. The people were taken by surprise but refused to disperse. The marching *Thondars* stood together. The officer pointed his pistol at the crowd and opened fire. There was total confusion. The police also used their rifles and fired live bullets at the crowd. People fled, some fell dead, others were wounded. Two of the dead were Chinese workers. This was a totally uncalled for provocation by the police. The estate manager who had been notified, instead of responding had planned the police assault on unarmed workers, women and children. This was a devastating blow for the *Thondars* and unionists.

***

After Kuppu and Chin Leng had returned to Sungei Siput, Ah Kow addressed the group. He said, "We've been successful in some of our demands. Strikes have been intensifying in Singapore among the dock and wharf workers and industrial workers and also the plantation workers. The Singapore General Labour Union (SGLU) has a membership of 200,000. We have also followed by encouraging our unions to go on strike throughout the country. The police are raiding the left-wing groups and arresting workers and detaining them without trial. Troops and police are called in to break the strikes. Now we have the task to move out with our hit squads. While the unions are on strike, we have to strike the enforcement agencies and the planters who are working hand-in-glove with them. We too will have to use violence and intimidation. Your squads have been assigned, so be prepared to move."

The decision was already made for Kuppu and Chin Leng. They were militant members of the CPM. Having been without a leader for a while because the central bureau had kept Lai Te's betrayal a secret lest it caused instability in the party, the new leader was the veteran MPAJA guerrilla leader Chin Peng. Sungei Siput was no longer safe for the members, so they had to move into the interior of the jungle. The MPAJA against the Japanese now became the MPABA against the British.

***

Desa put the newspaper down and began playing with Rasaiah. Janeki joined them.

"Our Rasaiah is one year old today," "*Amm, Amm, Ammah*," responded Rasaiah.

"Ah! Yes, my *anghia paiyangh* (daddy's boy) is one year old today!" said Desa carrying Rasaiah and cuddling him.

"You and I too should spend more time with him," said Janeki.

"Yes, he is growing well. What kind of a future is there for him?" wondered Desa.

"Perhaps, we should not get so involved. The *Thondars* are quite capable of carrying on by themselves.

"Yes, but I'm afraid they may become too violent. We have to restrain them. Just as we brought Rasaiah into the world, we too had a hand in bringing the *Thondars* to birth. They still need direction.

The struggle must go on. If we don't, there cannot be a bright future for Rasaiah. If we stop protesting there will be more oppression."

"I didn't say stop protesting but for you and me not to get too involved. Rasaiah may be left with one parent or none at all. We have to be very careful because the authorities are tightening up their laws on freedom and are authorising the police to use violence."

"Kuppu appears to be fully involved with the CPM and they too are using violence. It is not the Gandhian way. Nehru was a socialist and I remember what he said. He was talking about a democratic socialism through peaceful means in a political struggle. The CPM, on the other hand, resorts to violent means of political revolution."

"Right now I don't know if the Gandhian way or Nehru's socialism will succeed in this country."

Leela came running into the room. "*Appa* asked you both to come quickly."

"What, *ammah*, what has happened?"

"Just come."

Samy related to Desa and Janeki in front of his whole family what he heard on the radio.

"At the stroke of midnight our mother India became independent. Jawaharlal Nehru in his speech proclaimed India's independence from the British Raj. Nehru is the first prime minister. There are official ceremonies taking place today in New Delhi. I think we should also have a celebration in the estate. I shall talk to Kanchi and call a meeting and get the *Thondars* to organize."

Word was sent around and the people gathered after work in front of the Temple.

After announcing the good news Samy said, "It is barely three and a half months since the tragedy of Labour Day. Our celebration on that day was abruptly brought to an end with death and bloodshed. We are just getting over that tragedy, but we shall have another celebration today. This is a great day for India and for the struggles of Mahathma Gandhi. Rivers of blood were shed in India and thousands of Indians gave their lives for freedom. We must never forget that. Let us wear the Gandhi *topi* and light the *theebam*. I will supply the sweets from my shop. Each family should prepare something and bring them to the temple. We will offer *pooja* in thanksgiving and pray for the future peace and prosperity for our mother India."

"Janeki, Rasaiah's birthday is India's independence day. It is a good omen for his future," said Desa.

Things got underway with jubilation. Children were running gleefully and women were dressed in festive saris with flowers in their hair. The *Thondars* brought crackers and fireworks. One wondered where they got them from or whether they themselves made them. It was a gala evening and Mr. Connolly stood watching it all from his window up the hill.

"Perhaps, someday we will celebrate the independence of Malaynadu too," said Desa.

***

Kuppu was in a squad made up of three Indians and two Chinese. They were sent to Bromsgrove estate near Chemor where the workers were on strike. Water to the *coolie* line had been cut off for days. They were not supplied with rations. Kuppu sent word to the strikers to stay clear of the estate office and the manager's bungalow. That night, well armed, the squad moved stealthily into the estate. The two Chinese focused on the office while the three Indians made their way up to the bungalow. The Chinese threw grenades into the office. At the explosions, the *kiranies*, considered "running dogs", rushed out and the Chinese members opened fire on them. About the same time, the manager opened his door to take a look and was fired upon. The *kiranies* and the white manager were killed. The squad melted into the trees and was gone. Other squads were being sent to tin mines, government buildings, police stations and railways to kill as well as to destroy property. The aim was to cripple the economy. They would quickly retreat into the jungle.

The British forces with Ghurkhas intensified jungle warfare. Both the CPM and the British were familiar with each other's style for they had fought together against the Japanese. Both were being tested by the formidable dense vegetation of the equatorial Malayan jungle, infested with mosquitoes and leaches, to say nothing of other wild animals. The British fell back on the experience gained by Force 136 led by Colonel Spencer Chapman against the Japanese. The British could not penetrate the jungle terrain with heavy military machinery but they were experienced in air mobility in the dropping of supplies and paratroopers. The CPM also knew how they operated. In the clashes there were casualties on both sides but by far more CPM members lost their lives because the British were using *orang asli* trackers, Ghurkhas and Malay soldiers.

***

At a gathering of the *Thondars,* Samy brought fresh news.

"While there is political struggle on one side, the workers struggle is also intensifying. There is rapid expansion of the PMFTU throughout Malaynadu. It has a membership of over 250,000 now. Strikes are becoming more frequent everywhere, both in urban centres and in plantations. Often the Indians and the Chinese go on strike together. The CPM is very much involved in motivating the strikers. There is an average of 27 strikes a week. We have been asked by the union to go on a special strike on 20 October.

"What is the reason for this strike?" asked Supaiah.

"It is a protest against the proposed constitution of the Malayan Federation which rejected the proposals drawn up in the People's Constitution. It is a hartal, a one day total strike, like the ones they have in India. It is a political maneuvre. Starting at six in the morning everything throughout Malaynadu and Singapore will shut down in estates and mines, tin mines and coal mines, factories, shipyards and railways. Shopkeepers, like me, will close shop; farmers and fishermen and even housewives will stay home. This is going to be a united action. We have received communication from the A.M.C.J.A."

The hartal was a resounding success. Banning trade unions made no difference to the *Thondars* or the strikers. They became militant; many *Thondars* lost their lives. The situation in the estates was getting from bad to worse.

Desa joined Samy outside his shop in the evening.

"Have you heard any news about Mohandas?" asked Desa.

"He has been taken to Sungei Patani police lock-up and probably

344   Love & Struggle beyond the Rubber Estates

handed over to the Special Branch," said Samy.

"Things are becoming very risky and dangerous. When the *japankaran* lost the war and were leaving we gave them the thumbs down sign and the thumbs up sign to the incoming *velekaran*. The "new beginning" spoken of by the estate manager, the *komali*, and the new hope for a better life have all been a shadow play. We are once again stuck with colonial oppression," said Desa.

"I also believed that," said Samy. "We are losing many good young men among the *Thondars* but they are fired up to fight for justice. Rubber production has also dropped and the planters are worried. The government, as usual, is on the side of the planters and the police are becoming aggressive."

"In the so-called 'new beginning' we were actually producing a good yield of rubber. It was our rubber that helped Britain to recover after the war. I read in one of the papers that Purcell, a former civil servant in Malaynadu was saying that, 'without Malaya, the sterling system as we know it could not exist.' That is what they cared about and not the social and economic reforms that are so badly needed here now. Wages are once again inadequate. We are undernourished, families are in bad health, housing needs are neglected and we can no longer afford to buy new clothes. Our demands are ignored. The *Thondars* are sacrificing a lot for justice."

"Now that the rubber price has once again dipped by 20%, they have immediately cut wages by 20%. The UPAM is behind all this. Can we negotiate with the UPAM?"

"The PMFTU has got all the estate workers' unions to form the Pan-Malayan Rubber Workers' Council (PMRWC) to negotiate with the UPAM. But they don't want to negotiate while the strikes are continuing."

Chapter 48

Emergency

Ah Kow brought his group up to speed on what had happened.

"Agreeing with the Malay elite, the British government put aside the Malayan Union. Disregarding the proposals of the A.M.C.J.A embodied in the People's Constitution, and in spite of the Hartal, it has gone ahead and signed the Federation of Malaya Agreement in Kuala Lumpur on 21 January 1948. Singapore is a separate colony while Penang and Malacca remain British territory. A wide range of authority is bestowed on the rulers of the Federated States.

"The Pan Malayan Rubber Workers' Council and the Pan Malayan Council of Government Workers (PMCGW) had applied for registration. In February, their registration was denied. Now on the 13 June, the PMFTU and the state FTUs were notified that their registration were rejected and they have been outlawed.

"We got information that the High Commissioner is preparing an Emergency Regulation Bill together with a Sedition Bill and a Printing Presses Bill.

"We have not heard much from our leader Chin Peng but we have been given the green light to eliminate the strike breakers. Our killer squads will have to move out again. Remember you have to be very careful and not get caught. If you don't return we will shift camp."

***

Desa was reading the newspaper. The Straits Times was playing up the communist threat saying that all violent actions during the strikes and demonstrations are instigated by the communists with support from Moscow. They were also tightening up the laws and arresting people under the Sedition Act which was conveniently applied to any form of rebellion. He conveyed the news to Janeki.

"You remember when our *Thondars* joined the last strike, 14 workers in that estate were dismissed. So Vanivellu, secretary of the Kedah Federation of Rubber Workers' Union wrote a letter to the employer asking him to reinstate the 14 workers, or else, the remaining workers might leave the job. Well, he has been arrested and sentenced to 18 months hard labour. Now the police have arrested the FTU leader in Perak, R.G. Balan, together with four other unionists. They are trying to frighten us off."

Janeki laid out the evening meal which was rice and *dahl* curry with brinjal from their garden. Rasaiah was playing with some rubber seeds. They sat down to eat what was not a very substantial meal. In between mouthfuls Janeki also fed Rasaiah. They finished with bananas.

Jeneki said, "In those days when we went on a strike we did get some results. Now we are losing lives and our leaders are being arrested."

"You are right. They are now attacking our strikers using provocateurs who are hired gangsters. Now the government has introduced three new amendments to the Trade Union Ordinance to control labour activity. They are tightening up the laws alright.

"*Athanh*, work in the estate has become very sporadic. Pay is very irregular and low. All we talk about now is strikes and demonstrations and killings. Is there a future for us in this country? We are now a family and we have Rasaiah to think about. I think we should go back to India. I have managed to save up some money."

"I understand what you are trying to say. India is independent but the wounds have not healed especially the wounds caused by the separation of India and Pakistan. Poverty will not be eradicated overnight. Even as it is, we will keep the option open."

∗∗∗

Kuppu and Chin Leng were again in two different squads. The squads were sent to two different estates not far from Sungei Siput.

It was 8.30 in the morning of 16 June 1948. Kuppu with two Chinese comrades parked their bicycles behind rubber trees. The workers were in the timber, the *kiranies* were having breakfast. The three comrades walked up to the manager's bungalow and knocked on his door.

"Come," said the manager.

"*Tabek Tuan* (Greetings, my Lord)" they saluted him. The dog barked. He stood up. They shot him point blank. They also shot the dog to keep it quiet. They slipped away into the timber and rode off in their bicycles before any alarms could be raised.

About the same time, Chin Leng's squad had entered another estate whose layout they had already surveyed earlier. There were 12 comrades in the squad. They surrounded the office soon after the manager and his assistant, both Europeans, entered it. Four comrades went in with pointed pistols and tommy guns.

One grabbed the manager and the other the assistant.

"We are not after you, so you stay put and don't move." One of them told the *kiranies*. They tied the two Europeans to their chairs. The fourth comrade ordered one of the *kiranies*,

"You, open the safe and give me all the money."

Two of the others who were surrounding the office went to the store and collected tins of kerosene. Joined by another two, the four of them headed for the smokehouse stacked with bails of rubber marked RSS (Ribbed Smoked Sheet) fob (freight on board) ready for shipment at the port of Penang. They splashed the kerosene and set the rubber ablaze.

In the office they riddled the manager and his assistant with their tommy guns.

"Don't move! The office is surrounded," they told the staff. As the rubber grabbed the flame shooting black smoke into the sky the squad slipped away.

Even before the killer squads regrouped in the jungle hideout, the shit hit the fan. On the same day, at an emergency meeting, Sir Edward Gent, the British High Commissioner to Malaya declared a state of Emergency in Malaya. The Communist Party of Malaya was banned.

A concerted attack was launched against all communist party premises. The office of the communist daily, the *Min Shang Pau* (Voice of the People) - a Chinese language paper - was raided and sealed. Its editor had already been arrested earlier for sedition. Police reinforcements were sent to all the UPAM estates in Perak. All European estate managers were given police escorts.

The managers, too, were in a state of panic. Some wanted to pack up and leave while others armed themselves and were preparing to send their wives and children back to England. As a first step, they sent them to the Station Hotel in Ipoh. They were issued licenses to carry small arms. One could see these Europeans in towns walking around wearing gun belts like cowboys. Many of them could be seen in Ipoh at the Whiteaway Laidlaw & Co., Ltd, a shopping store for whites.

Kuppu got wind that a nation-wide coordinated swoop was being planned. He immediately sat down and wrote a letter to Desa. He dispatched it through the CPM courier.

Chapter 49

Crack Down

Desa was reading the *Jananayagam*, the Tamil paper subsidised by the CPM. It carried the news of what happened in the estates near Sungei Siput when one of the *Thondars* came to him and said Samy wanted to see him. Samy gave Desa a letter that had come to him posted in Kulim.

"Who can this be? I don't think I know anybody in Kulim," said Desa.

He opened the letter.

Dear Desa, Janeki and Rasaiah,

I hope you are all safe and well. I am in the middle of a battle. I am afraid that the government, through the Special Branch, is going to crack down on all the leaders of the MPAJA and the CPM and the labour unions. They have already marked people. I want to warn you to go into hiding immediately or at least put Janeki and the child in some safe place. I would suggest Kamaruddin. He is still in communication with the CPM secretly and outwardly with the MNP. I think he may be safe, but find out first. Don't undertake any activity now and warn also the leaders of the Thondar Padai.

I love you my brother and sister. I don't know when we will meet again. Good luck to you. All for the victory of justice!

Kuppusamy

17. June 1948

Desa handed Kuppu's letter to Samy for him to read. Samy immediately went inside beckoning Desa to follow. He turned on the radio. It was Friday, 18th June 1948. Radio Singapore announced that the High Commissioner Sir Edward Gent had declared a state of emergency.

"The Emergency Regulation Ordinance (ERO), 1948, has been passed which allows the Chief Secretary to detain, by order, any person for a period not exceeding one year. It also gives the British High Commissioner the right to make any regulations he considers desirable in the public interest. All leave for police personnel is cancelled and the special units of the military police have been put on high alert."

Desa said, "Police are granted greater powers of arrest and detention. This is tantamount to declaring war on the communists. With such emergency regulations, the government can do almost anything it wants."

"We have to decide and act immediately. Let's talk it over with our families."

Samy called his family together.

Desa showed Kuppu's letter to Janeki and they immediately decided to go to Kamaruddin's house.

"Let me go and meet Kamaruddin first and talk with him and his family. In the meantime you pack all the necessary things to take."

Samy said the same thing to his wife and daughters to get ready while he visited his cousin in Gurun.

"Could uncle Rama also take Janeki *akka* and Rasaiah?" asked Leela. "It is better to be with someone we know than to blindly trust a stranger."

"OK, this is what we will do," said Desa. "While Samy visits Rama, I will go and see Kamaruddin."

"No, nga," objected Janeki. "We cannot afford to delay. I suggest we all go to Rama's house first. If it is too inconvenient for Rama to put us up then, *athanh*, you can go and see Kamaruddin."

"Tomorrow morning we will leave. We will take the train up north. But, Desa and I have already discussed this; we both will come back to the estate. We have to prepare the *Thondars* because they are very vulnerable," said Samy.

"Can't they look after themselves?" asked Nagammah.

"They are hot-headed young fellows. They may just decide to stand up and fight them. This time if they do that, it will be suicide. The government is going to use all its might to crack down on us. We have to work out strategies with the *Thondars*," said Samy.

Early next day they put their plan into action. Samy packed two bags of rice and condiments and added some sweets for Rama's children. Samy drove his truck and they left without telling anybody. They boarded the train in Bukit Mertajam. It did not take long to reach Gurun.

"You all wait in the station while Desa and I go and meet Rama," said Samy. On the way Samy told Desa, "I am Ponnusamy and he is Ramasamy, that's how we were named."

They found the house. Rama was not in but his eldest daughter spotted them.

"*Ammah, Periappa* is here," she called to her mother. *Periappa* literally means "big father" to denote an uncle on the father's side who is the older brother of the father.

"What nga? Come nga, come nga, come in nga," said the mother looking rather surprised because they very seldom saw him. "The houseman has gone to work but today is Saturday and he will be back in a short while, let me mix drinks," she said.

"Let that be, nga," said Samy. "We have very important things to talk about. There is trouble. This is Desa *aiyiah*, a close friend."

"*Vanakam, aiyiah*," said the mother whose name is Parvathi.

"Actually, our families are also here. They are waiting in the railway station. We came to discuss with you if they could stay with you for a while," said Samy.

"What is there to discuss? Bring them at once." Then turning to her daughter whose full name is Thilagavathi, she said, "Thilaga, you go to the station and bring them over."

"Can we go and meet Ramasamy at his workplace?" asked Desa.

"No, we had better not. He is a government servant working with the PWD and I don't think he should be seen with us. We will wait for him."

Soon Thilaga brought the whole gang. There was quite a stir with everyone greeting each other and introducing Janeki. They all fussed over Rasaiah.

"Where is Vijay?" asked Anakili. Vijay, short for Vijayakumar, was Thilaga's younger brother.

"He has gone to play football. He will take his own sweet time coming home," said Thilaga.

Just then Ramasamy walked in.

"What's all this noise? Ah! *Anna*, when did you come? Are you well?"

"I am well. This is Desa, a close friend."

"Welcome, your full name?" "Nadesan, Nadesan Pillay."

"Rama, have you heard what's been happening?"

"Yes, they have declared emergency in the country and we have all been issued warnings."

"What kind of warnings?"

"We are not to take part in trade union activities and ordered to report anyone suspected of being a communist."

"Rama, you know I am involved in the Kedah Trade Union and they could come after me and Desa is involved with the *Thondar Padai*. We have brought our families to stay with you, but we both will not show our faces here. If you think it is too much of a risk for you and your family let me know now and we will go away."

"I think it is alright for the women and children to stay as long as they don't talk much with the neighbours. The only problem is this government quarters is rather small.

Thilaga who has been listening said, "We can all squeeze in while you and Vijay can sleep out here."

"Are you sure, *ammah*?" asked Desa. "With Janeki and Rasaiah there are two extra people. I could find another place for them."

"Don't, Desa, *mama* (uncle). We will be alright and *ammah* will not object. It is nice to have people in the house," she said.

"*Anna*, what will you do?" asked Rama.

"We are going back to the estate and prepare ourselves for whatever happens."

"Isn't it better for you to hide?" asked Rama.

"We are responsible for the *Thondar Padai* and we have to be with those young people."

Samy spoke to his family and kissed his wife and daughters goodbye. Desa spoke to Janeki, "Remain indoors as much as possible. Here, keep my journal hidden in a safe place and don't show it to anybody. Take care of yourself and Rasaiah." He hugged her and kissed Rasaiah goodbye.

Samy and Desa took the south bound train to Bukit Mertajam.

It was night when they reached the estate. They called an emergency meeting of the *Thondars*.

"You all know that emergency has been declared. That simply means that the government has given itself the power to do whatever it wants. It has banned the *Thondar Padai*. That does not mean that the government is going to leave us alone. It will hunt down the members. We must therefore destroy all evidence of the *Thondar Padai* and our membership in it. Collect all the books and registers, bills and membership lists and everything else that even vaguely refers to the *Thondar Padai*. Burn them all. Whatever weapons you have, hide them away in the jungle. Just carry on as ordinary workers and deny having been members of the *Thondar Padai*.

Desa went to the jungle and found a spot under a tree to bury his CPM and MPAJA membership cards and his pistol. Samy destroyed all evidence of the Kedah Trade Union in the shop.

The next day was Sunday and they continued searching for any slight evidence that might remain. Nothing happened that day.

Early Monday morning, at 2.00 a.m., some of the *Thondars* knocked on Desa's door.

"*Anna, Anna*, Desa *anna*! Wake up and come quickly."

"He opened the door, "What has happened?"

"Quickly get your things, we must run. They have come. They are at the office building breaking the door open."

"Where is *aiyiah* Samy?"

"He is in the shop. We cannot go there now."

Desa quickly put on his pants and ran out with Supaiah and two of the *Thondars*. They ran into the timber and to the fringe and on to the jungle. Most of the other *Thondars* also did the same going in different directions. They hid in the jungle the whole day. Monday night two *Thondars* sneaked back to scout around. They returned with news that the raiding troops had all gone. They quietly returned to the *coolie* lines. They discovered that the police were interested only in the CPM and MPAJA members, and trade union leaders. They had arrested Samy and taken him away.

Desa told them to lay low. The manager's bungalow was being guarded by armed policemen. Desa wanted to go to Gurun to inform Samy's family of what had happened.

First he went to see Haji Syed Kamaruddin in Kampong Tunku Putera.

"Ah, *Inche* Desa, are you well? Come, come, lah, enter."

Desa took off his slippers and washed his feet with a scoop of water from the earthen jar next to the steps and went upstairs. They sat on the floor and talked. His wife brought some tea and *kuay* (cake).

"The government has cracked down on all opposition," began Desa.

"I know," said Kamaruddin.

"Our leader Samy has been arrested and the *Thondar Padai* banned. Earlier on, Mohandas was arrested. We are on the run."

"Our Putera has also been broken up and our party together with the youth and women groups were also banned."

"We took our families; Samy's and mine to his brother's house in Gurun. They are safe there and I am going there now to give them the bad news. Without Samy I feel awkward to leave my family there."

"I remember your wife and the baby. Are they well?"

"Yes, I would like to ask you if it is alright to bring my wife and baby here to stay with you for a short time. Actually, Kuppu, whom we came to see here, recommended you to us."

"Do you think they are looking for you in particular?"

"I am not sure. I have been keeping a low profile."

"If they are really looking for you, you are safe nowhere. We are a little out of the town and it is relatively safe here. Sometimes, at night, some members of the CPM meet here. If you stay inside, there should not be a problem. The people in the kampong have respect for me."

"I will not stay here; only my wife and baby. I want to make arrangements to go back to India."

Chapter 50

Escape Route

"Have you decided not to remain in Malaya? You see, under the new federal law if you acknowledged Malaya as your permanent home giving it your undivided loyalty you can be given citizenship. You have to choose India or Malaya. In the MNP all along we have advocated a multi-racial independence, creating a One Malaya. We are against dual citizenships. What have you decided?" asked Haji Kamaruddin.

"You see, my son was born here and he should be a natural citizen. I would like to take him to India and show him to our parents. When things have become more stable here, we will come back."

"How long have you lived in Malaya?" "I came in 1936."

"Do you have any documents to show that?"

"I have my employment papers and work ticket."

"It is important that you keep them because if you go back to India now it may not be easy to come back to Malaya and claim citizenship."

"Do you know of anyone in Penang who can help me find passage to India?"

"Yes, I may have some people I know in Penang."

"Haji Kamaruddin, if you say yes, I will bring my wife and son here and then go to Penang and book tickets."

"Yes, you can bring them here."

"Thank you, Haji. Haji, I do not know anybody in Kulim or in Sungai Patani. Is there any way you can find out what has happened to Samy?"

"I will ask around," he said.

Desa left the kampong but before he went to Gurun he made his way back to the estate and quietly crept in. He met Supaiah and got an update.

"After they took *aiyiah* Samy away they did not bother us anymore. We think that the manager must have told the police to leave us alone so that he could get some work out of us. We have started our normal routine. Everything is quiet."

"Did you find out where they took *aiyiah* Samy?"

"No, nobody seems to know."

"Where are his family and your family?"

"Somewhere safe. Better you don't know."

They talked also with some of the other *Thondars* and Desa slept in his own cubicle that night. Early next morning when everyone was at the muster he slipped away.

Desa left for Gurun feeling sad and troubled on how to break the news of Samy's arrest to his family. Thilaga met him at the door.

"Where is *periappa*?" she asked.

"I have bad news, *ammah*."

He described to them everything that happened in the estate.

"*Aiyoo, Kadavule*," said Nagammah and began to cry. Thilaga and Janeki tried to console her. Leela and Anakili also began to cry.

"I have asked a friend to find out where they have taken *aiyiah* Samy. As soon as I find out I will let you know. You all have been very good in taking care of Janeki and Rasaiah. We do not want to be a burden on you. I have found a place for Janeki and Rasaiah. I will take them away now and I will come back to you when I get some news.

"Janeki, we will have to leave now. Get your things."

She handed Rasaiah to Desa and went in to get their things. Janeki hugged Leela and Anakili and said goodbye to everyone. They left.

"Have you got my journal?" asked Desa.

"Yes. Where are we going?"

"We are going to Haji Kamaruddin's house in Kampong Tunku Putera."

On the way he explained to her his plan of going back to India. Haji Kamaruddin and his wife welcomed Janeki and Rasaiah.

"They have taken your friend Samy to Sungei Patani. Under the Emergency Order they can hold him without charge for any length of time. He is not allowed visitors for now.

You tell his family to go to the Sungei Patani Police Station and ask for visitation rights. They must not take no for an answer and keep pestering the police. They should also talk to people and if possible to the press saying that Samy has not committed any crime and they are not allowing the family members to visit. They don't like publicity and may allow the family to visit," said Kamaruddin.

"Thank you for your help," said Desa.

"I also have a contact for you in Penang," said Kamaruddin giving Desa a slip of paper with a name and address. "Go to him and ask about the ship."

"Thank you again. I will go straightaway." "Janeki, stay invisible; I will be back soon." He kissed Rasaiah and left.

Before making his way to Penang he went back to Gurun. The train was not running so he took the bus. Having conveyed the message to Samy's family, he took the bus straight to Prai.

Crossing over to Penang island on the ferry he stared at the water which once again reminded him of the driftwood. Again he wondered about the future, not only for himself but for his family. From the friend of Kamaruddin, Desa found out that the Rajula was running again. During the war she had been recommissioned as a troop ship; after the war she was sent to England to be refitted and now she was back plying between Penang and Madras. The friend told Desa where to go to make a booking. Desa spent the night in a cheap hotel and immediately fell asleep exhausted. He booked the passage the following morning. SS Rajula was in port and would be sailing in two days. He made his way to Kampong Tunku Putera. He spent the night there with a feast of local fruits from Kamaruddin's orchard.

Next day they bade farewell. Kamaruddin's wife gave Janeki a lovely Malay *sarong and kebaya*, a *sarong* is a large sheet of fabric wrapped around the waist and worn by men and women; A *kebaya* is a figure-hugging embroidered blouse.

"Haji Kamaruddin, thank you for your kind hospitality. We will return to Malaya."

Haji Kamaruddin took Rasaiah into his arms, carried him high and looked into his eyes. "He has your eyes, Desa and his mother's good looks."

"Thank you, Haji, you are very kind." responded Desa.

"Desa, Janeki, your stay in Malaya has been very difficult. You have struggled through many obstacles and have given the Indians here a new hope. You must come back. We are facing new struggles now, not only the Malays or the Indians but all the people in Malaya who have struggled for a better living. We must work together. Rasaiah, here, will be one among the new future generation of Malayans in whom we place our hope.

"May Allah go with you dear friends."

They shook hands and departed.

In Penang they did a little shopping for the members of their families so as not to return empty handed. Desa boarded the Rajula for the fourth time. After settling in the second class cabin, they took Rasaiah onto the deck.

Desa reminisced on his many voyages on the ship as Malaya slipped away.

"Janeki, Kuppu is still fighting the battle for Malaynadu. He said, "We have unfinished business."

Father, mother and baby Rasaiah sailed into the setting sun.

not The End

Glossary of Terms

aiyiah – sir

aiyo, Kadavule – Oh, God

aiyoo, Muruga – Oh, Murugan, the popular youthful Hindu deity

akka – older sister

ammah – literally meaning mother, is a common endearing word used to address women, both older and younger.

ammahdi – Same as *ammah*, but a more loving way of addressing, especially a girl who is not yet a mother.

anghi – an endearing form for dad

anghiapaiyangh – daddy's boy

anna – elder brother

appa – means father, but also used to address the son.

arathi – a worshipful rite

athai – aunty

athanh – son of father's sister, a cousin or brother-in-law. Also used as a love expression for a husband.

BandeMataram – I salute my mother

banian –A cotton vest or undershirt

bhai – a friendly way of addressing a Sikh

Chalo Delhi – A battle–cry, 'March on to Delhi'

chupak – one quarter *gantang* or one cup

coolie – labourer

cumbly – usually a sheet of woollen cloth but because of the hot weather they were given cotton sheets.

dulang – a large shallow wooden pan. Dulang washing is the panning for tin ore.

eingyi – a form–fitting waist length blouse with a mandarin collar

Gandhi topi – the Gandhi cap, white in colour, pointed in front and back with a wide band made of khadi

gantang – 2.5 kg or 4 cups

halwa – an extremely sweet semi–solid jam.

hill country – Malaya was called Malay *Nadu*. Malay means hill and *nadu* country.

ikan bilis – anchovies

itli – a steamed rice bun

jalthi – move it

japankaran – Japanese man – used collectively

juppa –upper garment

kachang puteh –pea nuts

kajal – a form of homemade eye makeup

kangany – an overseer of the workers who also acts as a recruiter of workers for the plantations

kanna – literally eye; like the apple of my eye

kannu – or *kanna*, eye; like the apple of my eye

katumaram – trees tied together (*katamaran*)

kempeitai – Military Police Corp, the military police arm of the Imperial Japanese Army from 1881 to 1945.

khadi - a coarse homespun cotton cloth

kirany – a clerk

kolam –an ornamental figure drawn on the floor

komali – a joker or a jester

kongsi – a clan–hall, a place where the Chinese live together

kuay – cake

kungumum – saffron powder or red turmeric powder

kuti – small girl, also for small animals.

ladu, muruku, Mysore pak, halva – different kinds of sweetmeat

longyi – a sheet of cloth sewn into a cylindrical shape like a sarong. It is worn around the waist, running to the feet and held in place by folding the fabric over without a knot.

machanh – literally brother-in-law, but used to address a close friend, among men.

makalsakthi – power of the people

MAKAL SAKTHI VALGA – LONG LIVE PEOPLE POWER

Malaynadu – Malaya was called Malaynadu by the Indians. It meant hill country (Malay – hill; nadu – country)

mama – uncle

mapillay – bridegroom

mayam – an illusion

mithai – sweet

mixture – an assortment of nuts and muruku prepared with spice. Often pronounced as 'micher'.

moru – buttermilk, a diluted form of yogurt

muntheebam – clay lamps

namaste – a non–contact greeting or salutation, literally 'bow to you'

one *chupak* – one quarter *gantang* or 1 cup

one *gantang* – approximately 2.5 kg or 4 cups

one *katty* – one and a third pound

orang asli – literally people of origin, the aborigines.

parang – a Malay heavy sheath–knife

periaappa – literally big father – the uncle on the father's side; the older brother of the father.

periadorai – big boss, usually the planter or manager

pisang goreng –banana fritters

ponn – bride

pooja – Hindu religious rites

poonool – the sacred thread

poosari – Temple priest

pottu – dot in the centre of the forehead

prawn sambal and *petai* with *nasi lemak* – Prawn cooked in *sambal*, a hot spicy sauce. *Petai* looks like broad beans, green in colour. It grows in long pods on tall trees and is gathered directly from the forest. *Nasi lemak* literally means 'fatty rice' in Malay. Rice (*nasi*) is soaked in coconut cream and steamed.

pullies – dots

puri – a dough of flour flattened and deep fried in ghee.

Raga Durga – Raga is a melodic mode and Durga is a raga in Hindustani classical music

rasam – a soup made from tamarind and pepper, Anglicized as 'molugu tawny' literally meaning pepper water in Tamil.

rojak – a fruit salad

rotan – rattan, a jungle vine

sambal balacan – a sweet and sour sauce made with prawn paste

sambar – curry made with dhal (lentils)

sangam – an assembly, refers to the classical period in the history of Tamil literature in South India.

santhanam – sandal wood paste

sarong and kebaya – sarong is a large sheet of fabric wrapped around the waist and worn by men and women; a kebaya is a figure–hugging embroidered blouse

se stengah – a whisky and soda, served over ice. The term derives from the Malay word for 'a half'.

sinnadorai – small boss

Sivalingam – symbol of the male creative energy associated with Lord Siva

Sivarathri – The night of Lord Siva, a Hindu festival

sudukadu – the burning field

swaraj – self-rule or independence

tabek tuan – Greetings, My Lord

Telugu – language spoken in the South Indian State of Andhra Pradesh

thalaipa – a head cloth or turban; a long seamless piece of cloth

thali – wedding pendant

thamby – literally younger brother, means lad. It is also an endearing way of calling one's first-born son.

Taiping – Great Peace, is made up of two Chinese characters (*tai* – 'great') and (*ping* – 'peace')

thesam – in Tamil means country (also adapted in Malay as Desa). In Tamil it also has another meaning which is light or brilliance.

Thivali – or Deepavalli – festival of lights

thosai – a fermented pancake or crepe made from rice batter

thundu – a small piece of towel

tilak – A small circular mark on the forehead

timber – the trees, the wooded part of the estate

tuan – boss in Malay

vadai – a fried cake made of black–gram flour

vanakam – greetings

velekaran – white man, used collectively

veshti – a long, unstitched cloth wound about the waist and reaching below the ankles, traditional Indian apparel for men.

vetrilei-paku – betel leaves and areca nuts

vibuthy – Ashes collected from burnt cow dung.

Yoni – symbol of the female creative energy associated with the goddess of Shakti

zamindari – a section of the landlords

Acronyms

A.M.C.J.A.	–	All Malayan Council of Joint Action
BMA	–	British Military Administration
CIAM	–	Central Indian Association of Malaya
COLA	–	Cost of Living Allowance
CPM	–	Communist Party of Malaya
ERO	–	Emergency Regulation Ordinance
GLU	–	General Labour Union
INA	–	Indian National Army
INC	–	Indian National Congress
KMM	–	Kesatuan Melayu Muda
MAP	–	Malayan-American Plantations Limited
MIC	–	Malayan Indian Congress
MNP	–	Malay Nationalist Party
MPABA	–	Malayan People's Anti-British Army
MPAJA	–	Malayan People's Anti-Japanese Army
MPAJU	–	Malayan People's Anti-Japanese Union
MSS	–	Malayan Security Service
OCPD	–	Officer in Charge Police Department
POW	–	Prisoner of War
PMFTU	–	Pan Malayan Federation of Trade Unions
PMGLU	–	Pan Malayan General Labour Union
PMRWC	–	PanMalayan Rubber Workers' Council
PMCGW	–	Pan Malayan Council of Government Workers
PWD	–	Public Works Department
Putera	–	PusatTenaga Rakyat
Putera/A.M.C.J.A.	–	the coalition of the two
RGA	–	Rubber Growers Association
SEAC	–	South East Asia Command
SGLU	–	Singapore General Labour Union
UMNO	–	United Malay National Organization
UPAM	–	United Planters' Association